Holiday Dream

ESSENCE BESTSELLING AUTHOR

GWYNNE FORSTER
CARMEN GREEN
FELICIA MASON

HARLEQUIN®
entertain, enrich, inspire™

HOLIDAY DREAM

ISBN-13: 978-0-373-53488-3

Copyright © 2012 by Harlequin Books S.A.

The publisher acknowledges the copyright holders of the individual works as follows:

CHRISTOPHER'S GIFTS
Copyright © 1996 by Gwendolyn Johnson Acsadi
First published by Kensington Publishing Corp. in 1996

WHISPER TO ME
Copyright © 1996 by Carmen Green
First published by Kensington Publishing Corp. in 1996

THE FIRST NOËL
Copyright © 1999 by Felicia Mason
First published by BET Publications, LLC in 1999

Recycling programs for this product may not exist in your area.

Printed in U.S.A.

CONTENTS

To my stepson, Peter Forster Acsadi,
the loveable boy who was the precious gift I received
when I married his widowed father, and who grew up
to be a wonderful and accomplished man whom my
husband and I love, admire and respect. He is always
there for us. No parents could want more from their son.

CHRISTOPHER'S GIFTS

Gwynne Forster

"You begin work Monday morning, and I leave home at seven-thirty. I don't go anywhere late, so please be on time." A shadow crossed his face in what she supposed he'd meant as a smile.

"Yes, ma'am."

Nadine Carpenter watched the unassuming, very dark, tall man of about thirty-five years, who strolled out of her office nonchalantly, but self-possessed, jingling his pocket change and obviously confident of his place in the scheme of things. Chauffeur? She had trouble seeing him in that role, but he had answered the ad, and she was desperate. His eyebrow had arched when she'd explained why she needed one. Several evenings recently, after leaving her Manhattan office and driving to her isolated home upstate in Accord, New York, muggers had threatened her when she opened her garage door. Either she hired a chauffeur for protection or gave up her lovely stone house and moved back to Manhattan, and she didn't see how she could do that. It was dark when she got home at eight o'clock and, with autumn approaching, it would soon be dark mornings when she left there. Wade Malloy had wondered about her; she could see that in his demeanor, relaxed though he had appeared, but he had taken the job. Still, she couldn't reconcile his ready acceptance of the employment terms and his occupation as chauffeur with his air of authority. But the employment agency had vouched for his references, so she wouldn't worry about his mixed signals and would just be grateful to have her problem solved.

She pulled her shoulder-length hair farther down over her left ear, patted it self-consciously and recalled that she'd done that repeatedly during the interview, a warning that she'd cared what he thought of her looks. She tried to get him out of her thoughts, but she found it hard to push aside the picture of him gliding out of her office with the posture of a man certain that whatever he left behind would be there if he ever decided to go back for it. Tremors of excitement flashed through her at the thought, and she cautioned herself not to let her tenderhearted nature soften her toward a man just because he might be down on his luck, as she supposed Wade probably was. She'd seen many chauffeurs, but not one of them wore the demeanor of Wade Malloy.

Her doorbell rang the next morning just as she reached the bottom of the stairs, briefcase in hand. She peeped through the viewer, saw Wade and opened the door.

"I didn't expect you to start until Monday, but I'm sure glad to see you this morning. I hate driving in a fog."

He opened his big umbrella, shielding her from the windy mist. "I figured on getting settled in this weekend, so why not? Today's on me. My stuff's in the trunk of my Thunderbird, so I hope you don't mind if I park it in your garage."

She didn't mind, she told him, conscious of his finger at her elbow as they walked to the two-car, stone garage. He stood at the back door of her Crown Victoria, his left hand resting on the handle. "Backseat or front?" She opened the front passenger's door, got in and closed it. They drove ten miles in silence, except for the tension of awareness that shouted loudly to them both.

She couldn't help being self-conscious about the rough texture of his pants touching her nylon-covered thighs and wondered if he sat with his legs spread wide apart intentionally or whether she had become paranoid. She groped for conversation to ease the tautness that simmered between them.

"The accommodations are simple, but I hope they're satisfactory."

"A one-room apartment over your garage is heaven compared to some of the places I've stayed." Her lashes flew upward, and she stared at him. However, he didn't elaborate further, and his tone said she might as well not ask. They reached her office on Park Avenue South fifteen minutes earlier than usual. He got out of the car and opened her door.

"The day is yours, Wade. Just be here at five." He nodded, and she turned to go.

"Hold on. Let me get this umbrella up. Wouldn't want you to get wet." She tensed at his firm grip on her arm.

"Thanks, but don't bother. It's only a few steps."

"I'll see you to that door." He did. Then, he tipped an imaginary hat and half smiled in a way that made her want to use him for a pin cushion, but she immediately chastened herself for being mean-spirited. She didn't see him, but she didn't doubt that he stood there until she got on the elevator.

Wade stuffed his son's letter in the inside pocket of his jacket and leaned against the hood of his boss's car, watching Nadine Carpenter as she approached. Tall, well built and about thirty, she was choice. But her sepia good looks, lithe strides and the gentle sway of her hips failed to entice him right then, though he appreciated beautiful women as much as the next man. He couldn't rid himself of the pain that his son's letter had caused, couldn't gloss over the meaning that it conveyed. Barely seven years old and already a genius at turning the knife.

"Dear Wade, my mother says I have to go stay with you, but I don't want to. Christopher." Wade stared at the childish scrawl and groaned. When would it end? He pasted a mask over his face as Nadine reached the car, he greeted her and then began the drive home. Well, he was staying there. What else could he call it?

"Ms. Carpenter," he began, hating that he had to ask, "I have to have my son with me for a while. I don't know for how long, hopefully indefinitely. Is that all right with you? If not, I can get a place somewhere."

"Of course he can stay with you, Wade. And please call me Nadine, otherwise I'll have to call you Mr. Malloy." He tried to cover his look of surprise.

"Where does he live now?" she asked.

"In Scarsdale with his mother. She's going on her honeymoon, and I get to keep him while she's getting a taste of true love." He hadn't meant to sound bitter, because that wasn't what he felt. He'd turned his life around so that he could gain custody of his son and teach the boy to love and respect him, and he wasn't looking a gift horse in the mouth. He felt her hand on his knee, glanced over at her and knew that she meant to console him and hadn't thought about the intimacy of it.

"Does he split his time between you and his mother?"

"My son hasn't lived with me since he was six months old, but I aim to change that now."

She glanced at him just as he ground his teeth and winced. He figured she ought to know that he felt more deeply about it than his words and casual tone suggested. "Scarsdale is a very upscale neighborhood," she began, obviously trying not to make him uncomfortable. "Do you think it's a good idea for you to bring him to that small room over the garage? He may make some invidious comparisons."

"It's all I've got right now."

Nadine didn't have much information about him, but she decided to take a chance. "You can have my second floor. It has two bedrooms, two baths, a sitting room and a back porch. I promised you room and board as part of the deal, because I'm not paying much. You don't have to bring your son to that garage apartment. I'll move my office to the basement," she explained before he could comment, "and I'll sleep in the guest room. It's a big house, Wade. I'll also have the living, dining and family rooms plus the kitchen and breakfast room."

Wade asked her why she'd bought such a big, almost-isolated house and learned about her practical side. The stone house was invincible to termites, fire and hurricanes, the property had big beautiful trees, and bordered Rondout Creek, which was a trout fisherman's dream, she told him. She also wanted to live in the country, and the place came at a price she could afford. He accepted her offer to let him have her second floor and told himself that he wouldn't think of the implications of living under the same roof as this delicate morsel. He resisted the urge to whistle. He had nearly slammed his foot on the accelerator when she offered him her second floor.

She leaned back in the bucket seat and sighed. When Wade sensed that she might be troubled and asked what the problem was, she questioned the wisdom of telling him.

"You can tell the help," he needled, gently. "That's been acceptable from time immemorial."

She looked over at him and couldn't resist a smile, because his face shone with a wicked grin. "I can't find my plans for that model home in the Rolling Hills Village. It's the best interior decorating job I ever had, and if I don't finish it by January tenth, the contract is void. I've looked everywhere. The owner has tentatively approved it, so I can't make changes unless I have that plan."

"Where did you last see it?"

"On my desk. I came back from lunch, and it wasn't there." Nadine told him that she was one of the firm's four decorators, the only woman. He nodded.

"Let me know if I can do anything to help." She smiled as she entered the house. It was a nice gesture.

Nadine didn't tell him that she might not find the plans nor that one of her colleagues might have destroyed or misplaced them in order to undermine her position with the firm. She moved her things down to the first floor guest room, picked up the phone and called Wade.

"Hamburgers, baked potatoes and salad will be ready in twenty minutes. Tomorrow you cook."

"You promised me board."

"I promised food—I didn't say in what state."

"Modern man eats his food cooked."

"Sure thing. And in case it escaped you, modern man also cooks."

"Okay. I cook tomorrow, but don't be surprised if you lose the next round."

Fast tongue for a chauffeur, she thought with some amusement and not a little surprise. "Don't worry. I have a housekeeper, but she's sick, so we'll take turns until she gets back."

"You bake a pretty good potato," Wade said, after putting the dishes in the dishwasher. "Good night." The wind swished in as he left by the back door, chilling her as she took in his slim, tight hips and easy gait. The door closed, and she sat down, suddenly melancholy. She had taught herself to be contented with her life. She had conquered the grief of losing her parents and had begun to pursue her dream of becoming a renowned interior decorator. But right then, there was an emptiness in her that she couldn't banish. It was almost like last Christmas when she'd been unable to face the holiday alone and, though she wasn't impulsive, had decided on the spur of the moment to go to Madrid. If she was lonely there, she had reasoned, it would be for a good reason. She knew she was considered a beautiful woman, but she was careful—no, she was religious—about not exposing her left ear, which had been marred by a burn in her childhood. Her mother had always said that the effect on her looks was mostly in her mind, but her mirror denied that, and her one venture into true intimacy with her college sweetheart had proved it. The boy had pulled her hair back while ardently kissing her face and had seemed surprised when he saw her ear. She cringed at the memory.

From then on, their tryst had deteriorated into the worst of disappointments. He'd said later that she had withdrawn, had turned away from him, but in her mind, it was he whose ardor had cooled. She hadn't had the courage to expose herself to the possibility of another such rejection.

I wonder who that turkey is, Wade asked himself as he stood at the curb waiting for Nadine, who approached the car accompanied by a man. His smile could only be described as feral, when the man stood back and let him open the door for Nadine and then waited for Wade to hold it for him.

Don't hold your breath, pal, he said to himself as he left the man standing there and got in the driver's seat. On the way to Accord, the man's obsequiousness with Nadine disgusted him. When he glanced in the rearview mirror and noticed the hand that tried to creep around her shoulder but failed when she moved away, he had to muzzle his temper and did the only thing he could do. He lectured himself. It wasn't his business who Nadine Carpenter spent her time with. Still, he reasoned, a woman like her deserved a better man than that one. He knew men, and this man was a gopher. He'd bet anything on it. He'd never been so glad as when Nadine directed him to let the man off at his house. He realized that he'd been perspiring and wondered what he'd have done if she had taken the man home with her. This job was not going to work out.

He turned into her driveway and, immediately, his finely honed sense of self-preservation—sharpened by years of work in hazardous areas of Latin America and sub-Saharan Africa—alerted him to danger. He flicked on the reflector lights and glimpsed two men dashing around the back of the house.

"Stay here and roll up your windows. If you hear a shot, get down between the seats." He raced to the back of the house, but the men had seen him and were running toward Rondout. Later, when he let her out of the car, he noticed that she didn't seem the least perturbed.

"You've got to install some flood lights around here, especially out back," he told her, holding his hand out for her door key. "I'd better look around, see if anybody's been in here." He satisfied himself that she was in no danger and investigated the grounds.

"Wouldn't you like some coffee?" She wanted to show him that she appreciated the protection he offered her.

"Thanks. It's my night to cook, so I'll just go put on something casual while you get the coffee."

"Be careful, Wade. Those men may still be out there." She hoped the anxiety in her voice didn't register with him. She'd been horrified when he'd gone after those men, not knowing whether they were armed. *I don't know Wade Malloy,* she reminded herself as she measured the beans, *but one thing is certain: he isn't afraid of much, and he isn't in awe of my status as his employer.*

The smell of garlicky, Italian meat sauce brought her to the kitchen just as he placed it along with spaghetti, French bread and a green salad on the kitchen table.

"Does it taste as good as it smells?"

"So I've been told, but don't get happy—you're going to eat it every other day until your housekeeper gets back, because it's the only thing I can cook." He seemed to derive great pleasure from that announcement, jingling his pocket change as he stirred the sauce. She'd noticed that he habitually played with his change, doing it rhythmically as if to some silent tune.

"That guy you dropped off tonight. What does he do?"

Nadine explained that the man was an interior decorator and her colleague.

"I should have known. When he wasn't pawing over you, he was picking your brain, and you let him do it." Aghast, her lower lip dropped, and she stared at him in a silent attempt to warn him against casual familiarity. He stared her down until she told him she hadn't realized it.

"Of course not, because he's clever. He kept telling you what a genius you are, and you continued to answer his questions about your work. Believe me, he got things out of you that I would never have told a competitor."

She focused on her plate. "Imagine. All that time, I thought you were paying attention to your driving. I realize that you're smart and that chauffeuring is probably the least of your talents, but I would appreciate it if you would exercise a little restraint and stop meddling in my affairs." His careless shrug indicated that her remark didn't rest heavily on him.

She savored the last of her spaghetti and meat sauce, drained her wineglass and pushed her chair back from the table. "Try it. It may distress you to keep your thoughts to yourself, but it won't kill you. Trust me." She spoke gently, but she meant it. It didn't make sense to get into an argument with her chauffeur. Weren't they supposed to be deferential?

He looked at her, winked and ginned. "You hired me for protection, didn't you?"

"Not that kind. Thanks for the dinner. You should bottle that sauce and sell it. You'd make a bundle."

His grin unsettled her. "Glad you like it. Look, if you were floundering around in deep water about to drown while I stood on shore, what would you expect me to do? Watch you? Or go in and get you?"

She folded her napkin and got up from the table. "You stacked that one in your favor." An unpleasant thought occurred to her and she asked him, "Are you saying that Rodney is a danger to me?"

He stopped smiling, and a frown creased his face. "In your cut-throat business, yes. He got as much information as possible about your work without telling you anything about his. What do you know about his work?"

She expelled a deep breath, impatient with the topic. "All right. I'll take heed, but you still have to stay out of my business." A smile played around his mouth, and she couldn't help staring at it. A luscious pout. She licked her lips, imagining the sweetness of his full bottom one as she sucked it into her mouth. Shudders raced through her and she regained presence of mind.

"Thanks again, Wade." His wordless stare sent hot darts to every one of her nerve endings. She had to get out of there before she did something she'd regret. But as she turned to leave the kitchen, she remembered that he had cleaned up the night before. "I nearly forgot—it's my night to clean."

He continued to stare, and no smile lit his face. "Go on, I'll do it," he said with a harsh rush of breath. "I'll do it," he repeated, when she didn't move.

"I'll help." They worked in silence, but the tension between them screamed for their attention. His pants brushed the side of her skirt, and both stopped as though electrified and stared at each other.

"Sorry," she murmured, but he didn't reply. His man's scent swirled around her, intoxicating her, luring her. His mouth twisted into a humorless half smile, and she felt moisture settling between her thighs. He caught her gaze and held it.

"Wade. Wade, I…"

"Go on, Nadine, I'll finish this." Unaccustomed to huskiness in his voice, Nadine gaped at him and would have objected, but his stance, his entire demeanor told her that if she stayed, something would have to give. She swallowed the saliva that accumulated in her throat when his eyes blazed, and she could see the man in him fighting to get to her. She turned and fled, realizing that in doing so, she had acknowledged their mutual attraction. She went to her room and tried to concentrate on the whereabouts of her Rolling Hills Village plans, but her thoughts remained on Wade Malloy.

The following afternoon, wondering about the inconsistencies in Wade as she stirred the coals beneath the grill she'd set up in the backyard, Nadine looked up from her task as Wade walked around the house with a young boy, obviously his son.

She smiled at Wade's introduction, though she marveled at the boy's stiffness and formal behavior with his father.

"I thought we'd cook out this evening. It's a bit chilly, but the fire will keep us warm. Would you like that?" she asked the boy. He looked steadily at her with Wade's light brown eyes, darkly handsome face and impudent air.

"It's immaterial to me."

She glanced at Wade who seemed as shocked as she. "How old are you, Christopher?" she asked, pointedly ignoring his remark.

"I've been seven for a few months now, and I am considered very smart."

"Clever, maybe, but not very smart," Wade interjected. "Smart children are respectful." Nadine turned away. She had not anticipated that the child would be antagonistic toward his father. She walked over to him.

"Christopher, I spent last Christmas alone in Spain. I figured that loneliness would be easier on me there than here." The boy cocked his head and looked at her.

"Why couldn't you stay here with your folks?"

She knelt to his level and looked directly into his eyes. "I didn't have any folks, Christopher. That's why I went away. I couldn't bear being here alone. I hope that when Christmas comes this year, I'll be able to count you as my friend. Then, at least I'll have you. What about it?"

"Okay. I guess," he said, obviously less sure of himself. She grasped his hand and went back to the grill.

"You may start right now by helping me grill these pork chops." She started toward the kitchen to get them, looked over her shoulder and saw that he followed her. She promised herself that she would soften him up, make him realize how lucky he was to have his parents.

Wade watched the two of them, and a smile spread over his face when his son jumped in front of Nadine and opened the screen door for her. Ellen might have raised him to be a stuffed shirt, but she'd taught him proper manners. He didn't know how he'd manage with the boy. Pain seared his chest when he recalled his son's refusal to go with him until his mother announced it was that or a babysitter. For years, he'd worked— sometimes in death-defying circumstances—to earn a living for himself and his family, but Ellen had wanted it all: good living *and* a man who was home every night. He couldn't be home with her, because his work took him all over the world, and she disliked the instability of constant travel. Yet he didn't blame her, because youth was a one-time thing, and she wanted her man with her while she was young enough to enjoy him. Well, that was refuse down the drain, he decided. If he was going to win his son's affection and respect, he needed a plan, and the boy was too much like him to come around easily. Wade walked over to the grill and added some coals. Nadine and Christopher approached and, to his amazement, the boy bubbled with talk and enthusiasm. Until he reached his father.

Nadine couldn't help noticing the sudden change in Christopher, who had withdrawn emotionally and become sullen. She asked him if he would go back to the kitchen for a roll of paper towels and, for a minute, was certain that he'd refuse. He left, and she looked at Wade, hurting with him.

"Give it time, Wade." She spoke softly, in a voice that soothed. "He'll come around. Try to find out why he behaves this way with you. Then you'll be able to deal with it. If I can help, just tell me."

He wouldn't have thought that a woman who went to work in Brooks Brothers–type suits, spread collar shirts, cuff links and bow ties would be so soft, feminine and understanding. He inclined his head toward the back door of the house where Christopher had disappeared.

"Thanks. I may need help before this is over. There's a reason for his attitude, Nadine. I worked away from home and, when he saw me, it was never to my good advantage. I've got a lot to make up for, and I haven't got much time."

"What about school? Those in this area are excellent. I've a friend who'll keep Christopher until we get home in the evening. She won't charge. I keep her children sometime."

Wade gave the turf a hard kick with the toe of his left shoe, as he fought to bridle his emotions. He couldn't remember the last time anybody cared how he fared. "Thanks." If he said more, he'd expose his raw insides. Christopher returned from his errand, humming, and Nadine asked him to sing something. The child demurred, and she turned to Wade.

"Do you sing, Wade?" The boy eyed his father as though something very important was at stake.

"Yeah. What do you want to hear? Classical, pop or jazz?"

"Classical," they replied in unison. He sang the "Toreador song" from *Carmen* in a deep velvet baritone while they gaped in awe.

"Wow," Christopher whispered, when he finished. "Wow." That evening, Nadine noticed that Christopher sang when he thought he was alone and made a mental note to inveigle father and son into singing together.

Getting the boy enrolled in school was less of a problem than she'd expected, but when she asked her friend Lorna to keep Christopher after school, the woman's reaction to news of the boy and his father surprised her.

"You sly devil, you. Who would have thought it? If you'd been wearing miniskirts and tight sweaters, it wouldn't have come as a surprise. But I'll say this for you, you sure can pick 'em. That man turns my head, and I'm a happily married woman. 'Course what you do is your business, honey, but I'd be careful if I were you."

One evening about three weeks later, they stopped at Lorna's house to get Christopher. Nadine didn't want to expose Wade to Lorna's brand of wisdom, so she suggested that he needn't go in, but he insisted that he wanted to thank the woman for her kindness. Lorna looked him up and down.

"I sure am glad to meet you, Wade. Your son is a wonderful boy, though he's going to have to learn that I don't bake hard-crust French bread. Besides, corn bread's got a lot more vitamins." Her glance at Nadine suggested that they shared a secret. "You two don't have to rush back here to get him every day, you know. Take a little time for yourselves."

Nadine noticed Wade's eyebrows shot up swiftly and his lips parted as though words might be forthcoming. Instead, he let the comment pass.

When they arrived home, Wade drove into the driveway and stopped in front of the garage door as usual. This time, he didn't get out but turned to Nadine and asked her in a voice devoid of inflection, "If we take time for ourselves, what will we do with it?" She shushed him, glad for Christopher's presence. The man didn't mind issuing a challenge to his employer, though he'd cloaked it in a demeanor of innocence. She didn't take offense at his directness; she'd learned that he said what he thought.

"Level with me, Wade. Are you testing my mettle, or your appeal? Which is it?"

He laughed. "I already know about the latter."

It was her evening to cook dinner, and she asked Christopher to help her. She didn't need his assistance, but she wanted to develop a spirit of camaraderie with him in the hope that he would extend that to his father. He hummed as he set the table. He turned a cup upside down, placed a saucer on it and sat a stemmed glass in that. She noticed that he searched through drawers and asked what he wanted.

"Something else to stack up here." They hadn't seen Wade lounging against the doorjamb. He walked over to the table, folded a napkin into the shape of a long-necked bird and stuck it into the glass.

"Gee whiz. Wade, can you show me how to do that?" Nadine gazed at Wade's face, the picture of love and joy, and her heart kicked over. His face glowed as though reflecting the morning sun and, when he glanced at her, she let him see the happiness that she felt. It wasn't hopeless. After dinner, she got a pad of multicolored drawing paper and gave it to Wade.

"Thanks, Nadine. You know, you'd look great wearing a halo, and I'd pin one on you myself, but mere man can't approach an angel." He winked and left her to ponder his enigmatic remark.

Two weeks passed, and they settled into an uneasy relationship, each well aware that at any time, the unexpected could push either of them over that fine line they'd drawn between them. Nadine knew it was dangerous to think of him as anything but her hired chauffeur. Yet, his problems drew her into his life. She watched him with Christopher, hoping that evenings of origami would have brought them closer together.

"You don't have to eat oatmeal," Wade told his son, "but you do have to eat the remainder of your breakfast. You have to—"

"I know what's good for me, because mother told me, and I'm not going to eat stuff like this. Our cook always made fresh biscuits or popovers every morning, and she poached my eggs."

"I'm not a cook, son, and we don't have one here, so you either eat what's in front of you, or stay hungry 'til you get your school lunch."

"I'll stay—"

Nadine interrupted him. "Christopher, you may enjoy hurting your father, but you are the one whose stomach will feel those terrible pains. When you asked him to show you how to make figures with that napkin, what did he do?"

The boy hung his head, glanced furtively at his father and muttered, "Sorry," before tackling his bacon, toast and scrambled eggs. Her glance at Wade found him distressed and unsmiling, and she couldn't help feeling his wound in her own heart.

When they stopped at Lorna's house to get Christopher that evening, the boy threw his book bag onto the backseat of the car, crawled in, closed the door and presented them with another scenario.

"You don't have to come in and get me, Wade. You can just blow the horn and I'll come out."

"Forget it, Christopher," Wade told him, a little testily, she thought. "I'm going in to get you every day, and that's that." She watched the cloud of sullenness settle over the boy's face.

"Christopher," she began, reluctant to reveal so much of herself. "My father wasn't well for most of my youth, most of my life, in fact. But those days when he was well enough to come to school for me were the only times when I didn't feel different from other children. I'd run to him, and he'd pick me up and swing me around. It was wonderful. You don't know how fortunate you are to have a strong, healthy father who loves you." She only sensed Wade's sharp glance at her, because she didn't look toward him, knowing intuitively that his face would reflect pain. Neither of them spoke until they arrived home.

"Get your shower and a change of clothes while I get dinner together, Christopher, and then I'll drive you back to Lorna's place. You'll stay there tonight, and I'll pick you up tomorrow around noon. Nadine and I have to go to a reception."

"Why didn't you just let me stay there while I was there?"

"One hour, son, so don't fool around," Wade told him, and she marveled at his patience.

Seeing him struggle to draw Christopher closer to him, watching his trials with the boy and eating with him at her table made it inevitable that she look upon him not as her chauffeur, but as a man. A handsome, virile and capable man.

She dressed for the firm's annual charity banquet—the main source of funds for its interior design scholarship fund—and scolded herself for thinking that Wade would be a much more elegant and genteel escort than Rodney Ames. She didn't have romantic inclinations about Rodney, but he willingly escorted her whenever she asked him, and a woman in her position needed to put in an appearance at important social functions. Besides, Rodney was such an obsequious stuffed shirt that she could count on him to put his best foot forward around people whose good will he valued. She slipped into a shimmering, avocado-green beaded evening dress, combed her hair in its usual style, added to her right ear a bunch of cascading zirconian stars and went into her living room to wait for Wade. He took her coat from the hall closet and held it for her.

"I hope the guy you put this on for is worth it," he mumbled, letting her see his irritation.

"I dressed for myself."

"Sure you did, just like you put on this man-trapping perfume for yourself." She attempted to move away, but he wrapped the coat snugly around her shoulders.

"Don't you ever keep your opinions to yourself?" she asked, furious with herself for having enjoyed the feel of his strong fingers on her shoulder.

"Do I ever? You'd be surprised."

She hated that her embarrassment was so obvious to him. "Come on." She started for the door, paused and turned.

"Shouldn't you call Christopher and see if he's all right? This is the first time he's stayed away from home all night. I know he's gotten used to Lorna, but..."

"He's okay. As long as Greta's around he'd stay over there indefinitely. That boy's gone head over heels about that little girl. Maybe he should have had a sister." His fiery gaze implied that it wasn't too late.

Nadine had to be joking, Wade decided, when she asked him to pick up her date and gave him the address.

"You mean you got all dolled up like this to go out with that guy who's only interested in picking your brain?"

"Wade, you're not my father, you're—"

"You don't have to remind me," he interrupted, "I know I'm your chauffeur. I'm also a man with sense, and you shouldn't waste your time on that guy. He's not worth it."

"You saw him once, so how do you know so much about him?"

"If you need proof that he's a wimp, I'll give it to you." He parked, went in the apartment building, rang the man's bell and waited for him. All the while he wondered at the anger that seemed slowly to build in him and that he tried unsuccessfully to shove aside.

To Wade's astonishment, Rodney Ames didn't even speak to him, but brushed past on his way to the car.

"Just a minute, pal." Wade detained him. "In case you didn't know it, the blueblooded Robber Barons may have been notoriously harsh in their business dealings, but they were famous for their graciousness to the hired help. But then, you don't pretend to be genteel, do you?" He walked past Rodney before the man could retaliate, got in the driver's seat and closed his door, leaving him to fumble with the back door until Nadine reached over and unlocked it.

Wade found a parking space behind the Plaza, let them out, got his high-beam flashlight from beneath the seat, opened his book to chapter eleven and settled back. Three hours later, he noticed the crowds leaving the hotel, turned off the light, put the book away and feigned sleep. The banging on his window alerted him to the couple's arrival, and he wondered how much alcohol Rodney had consumed. He got out of the car, opened the door for Nadine and assisted her in, but he let the hapless man look out for himself. Drunkenness disgusted him.

"Where to, Nadine?" His breath hung in his chest while he awaited her answer.

"Rodney's place, please."

The skin on his back seemed to creep up toward his neck, and he loosened his collar. What in the world had he gotten himself into?

"Rodney, would you please stop acting like an octopus," she whispered, hoping that Wade's gaze was glued to highway eighty-seven. His response was to show greater dexterity and imagination. She gave him a not too gentle shove.

"Come on, Nadine," he slurred, "I jus' wanna be friendly. What's a little friss between kins?"

"What's come over you? I want you to stop acting like a teenager." She'd moved as far away from him as the door would allow, but he took that as an invitation. "Mr. Ames," she said in her stiffest office manner, "get ahold of yourself. I'm your colleague, not your plaything."

"That's the problem, Nadine, honey. I don't want you to be my colleague. I want to play with you."

Wade eased up on the accelerator as he glanced for the nth time into the rearview mirror. He wiped the sweat from the side of his face and told himself that his concerns were in the front seat, not the back. Then she leaned against the door and had no further means of escaping the man's fawning and pawing, and he felt his blood heat up. He had learned with strenuous effort and practice to master his hot temper, but right then he felt it coiling its way to certain explosion. He hummed to himself, one of his old techniques for cooling his anger. But the man's hand went to her breast, and he skidded to the elbow of the road in a no-stopping area and brought the car to a halt. He got out, walked to the back door and opened it.

"That Jack Daniels or whatever you've been drinking has made you pretty courageous, buddy. You'd better sit up front with me."

"You're not my date. Go back and drive."

Wade laid a very heavy hand on the man's arm. He kept his voice low, cool and controlled, the voice with which he had managed hundreds of laborers in hot, insect- and snake-infested jungles and in scorching deserts. The voice that not even the most obdurate and mulish among them had dared to disobey.

"I said get up front. *Now!*"

"I'm not going to be ordered around by a chauffeur."

Wade grinned. "I'm not just her chauffeur, pal. As of now, I'm also her bodyguard. Get up front."

Nadine adjusted the straps of her dress and focused her gaze on the eerie shapes of trees and buildings as they whisked by. She didn't know whether she was more relieved or embarrassed. She did know that if she asked Wade to drive Rodney anywhere else, she'd lower herself in his eyes. Rodney had always been a harmless date, but this time, he'd overstepped the bounds of decency, and she would tell him about it when she next saw him. She felt sorry for Rodney, but she released a long sigh of relief when, without directive or discussion of it, Wade drove straight to the man's apartment building, parked and turned to him.

"This is your stop, buddy. Hop out." Nadine viewed it all as though she might have been watching a movie. Her disgust with Rodney's behavior wouldn't let her do anything to help him salvage his dignity and, when Wade reached over, locked the passenger door and drove off before the man could tell her good-night, she relaxed for the first time since she'd gotten in the car.

"I told you he was a wimp. No man would have let me get away with that without at least telling me where to get off."

"You know how to drive, Wade, but you're a lousy chauffeur. If you want to work for me, you'll have to improve your manners."

"Yes, ma'am." She bounced out of the car as soon as he stopped, opened the front door herself and called good night to him over her shoulder.

"Good morning, Nadine. I didn't know whose turn it was to make breakfast," he said, as though they'd parted on the best of terms the previous evening, "so I hightailed it down here as soon as I woke up." Nadine glanced at the kitchen clock. Nine-forty.

"How magnanimous of you!" She had a strange and compelling desire to box his ears, and she couldn't understand it, because she abhorred violence. Yet, her fingers itched for him. "I thought you promised to take Christopher shopping. He wants to buy Christmas gifts."

"Plenty of time for that. I'm going for him around twelve. What do you want for breakfast?"

"I already ate two bananas and drank coffee. The pot's half-full, if you want some." What was wrong with him, looking at her like that?

"Then I'll have the same. Want to come along with Christopher and me?"

"I'd love to shop with Christopher, but I've got to work on my designs today, and I'll have to reproduce those plans from memory. What are you staring at?"

He swallowed the coffee with a gulp as though he'd burned his esophagus. "That dress you had on last night didn't do a thing for you. You look just as good this morning with your face scrubbed clean and that white shirt hanging out over your pants." He didn't move, but she backed up. Heat simmered in his darkening eyes. His aura had suddenly changed, had begun to swirl around her. His cologne, the scent of autumn woods, wafted to her nostrils, and she lost her breath, mesmerized.

Wade watched her rub her palms against her hips, unconsciously sending him the message that they were sweaty, and then rim her lips with the tip of her pink tongue. He swallowed the saliva that pooled in his mouth.

"Get out of here, Nadine."

"You're ordering me out of my own kitchen? Of all the…" she stammered, thoroughly confused. "What gives you the right to—?"

He stopped her. "Listen to me, Nadine. Don't bother to be outraged. You know what I'm talking about. Just go!" She spread her legs, and he could see moisture around her lips and on her forehead. Shudders tore through him.

"And if I don't?"

He started toward her, and he didn't care if she saw the fiery determination and hotly aroused man that he knew blazed in his eyes. He walked around to face her when she turned her back.

"Why can't you face me now?" he tormented. "A second ago you were challenging me. Is it because I'm your chauffeur? Is that it? Your chauffeur is a man, Nadine. A man who knows that you didn't stay here in spite of my warning be-

cause you were standing on your right to do as you pleased in
your own house, though that's what you'd like me to believe.
You want to feel what you know will happen between us if
you stay here." He advanced toward her slowly, nearly breathless when he realized that she still didn't move. His fingers
grasped her shoulders.

"Either go, Nadine, or let me feel your arms around me."

"Wade…I…"

His low voice didn't attempt to seduce, nor did it plead. It
spoke of deep, compelling need and it reached her in her rawest,
most vulnerable chamber. That secret place where she stored
her longing to be needed, to have a man cherish and adore her,
to need her desperately.

"Wade…"

"I don't care if you send me packing tomorrow or the next
minute. Just hold me." He tipped her chin upward with his
index finger, saw the compliance that must have glowed in
her eyes and lowered his lips to her hungry mouth. She didn't
know when she opened her mouth to him, only that the power
and possessiveness of his strong tongue dancing in her mouth
made her want more of him, all of him. Her whimper brought
his arms tighter around her, and she melted against him, giving him kiss for kiss, caress for caress. The wind swished out
of her when he gently withdrew his tongue from her mouth and
kissed her eyes. She understood then what he needed, and she
held him to her. Secure in the cocoon of protective warmth in
which he'd cloaked her, she turned her face and touched his
lips with her own. As though sensing that she desired more
of him, he held her head for his forceful, passionate kiss. Her
whole body blazed with the unfamiliar jolt of his loving, and
she wanted it to last forever…until his full hand pressed her
left ear through her hair. Abruptly, she whirled away from him.

"Nadine, what is it? Why did you move away from me?
Have I hurt you?"

"No. I… Wade, we mustn't… I mean…"

"Shh. Don't say anything. I know who I am to you."

"Do you?" He turned away from her, picked up his empty coffee cup, put it in the dishwasher, looked up and flashed a smile. "No need to get bent out of shape. I can handle it."

She had to get out of there, something she should have done when he'd urged her to do just that. She put on a warm jacket, got a rake from the garage, and went to work on the blanket of leaves that covered the lawn. She raked until her arms ached, until she felt his hand gentle on her back.

"Let it alone, Nadine. Tomorrow's Sunday. I'll clean this up while you're at church. I'm sorry if I've upset you."

His arm lingered across her back in what she knew was an attempt to soothe her. She wanted to turn to him, to hold him and to let his strong arms hold her, but she did none of that. She smiled coolly and lied. "You haven't upset me, and everything is all right between us. I'm going in to get dressed. I have to go to my office this afternoon."

"Nadine, I try to tell the truth even when it hurts me. I don't believe you're not affected by what happened back there, though I'm sure you want to forget it. You're entitled to that, but please, tell it like it is."

"I think it best that we forget it." She hoped he wouldn't press her, because she didn't intend to tell him how she felt about their passionate exchange. She was already more vulnerable to him than she knew was good for her. *He's not an easy man,* she realized, when his gaze bored into her, scattering her nerves, while he stood mute before her. Scrambling for composure, she added, "I have to get to my New York office and do something about those missing plans. At least one man in my firm would shimmy around like a drunken sailor if I bungle this job, because he underbid me and still didn't get it." She couldn't fathom his demeanor. How could his posture be so loose while his face bore the tenseness of a man facing a jury's verdict?

"Then you have at least one suspect. What do you say we pick up Christopher, and I'll drive us all into town?" He must have detected her indecision, for he quickly added, "Then, if you should need help, I'll be there for you." She didn't misunderstand his phrasing. He hadn't simply said that he'd be there. He'd be there for her, and that implied something personal, a commitment to see her through whatever she faced. Unable to resist the kindness reflected in his eyes, she nodded assent.

Christopher explored Nadine's office while Wade leaned against the doorjamb watching her futile search for a roll of plans he knew she'd never see again. He wanted to say they should sit down and reconstruct them, but he wasn't ready to reveal himself. Instead, he said, "You may be wasting time, Nadine. If the contractor has already approved your plans, you don't have to worry about plagiarism, so why not borrow the contractor's copy and get to work? You did copyright them, didn't you?" Her look of surprise confirmed that he'd raised her curiosity about him, but he'd risked it because he wanted to help her. "Who's your contractor?" he asked while she was dealing with the surprise he'd given her. She hadn't copyrighted, she told him, because theft had never before been a problem. He looked at the contractor's card that she handed him and smiled inwardly; the man was one of his old acquaintances.

"How much do you remember?"

"Most of it. But I know I won't be able to reconstruct the fine points, those flashes of insight that wake me up at night." He could well appreciate that, because he'd gotten crucial inspiration that way more times than he could count.

"Well, why don't you get your stuff together, work in your office at home and you can pick my brain as much as you like." He couldn't stop the grin that spread over his face when her eyes widened and her bottom lip dropped. *I'd better stop this, before I dig a hole that I can't get out of,* he warned himself.

Nadine looked from Wade to Christopher as the boy tugged at his father's sleeve. "Come on, Wade," Christopher begged, "I want to see the Christmas decorations and the tree in Rockefeller Center."

"In a minute. The tree won't be up for a few weeks yet, but there's a lot we can do as soon as Nadine is ready."

Half an hour later, as they passed St. Patrick's Cathedral with its soaring spires and crossed over to Rockefeller Center, Christopher whooped with glee at the colorful flags of all nations, and Nadine wondered to what extent he'd been allowed the glory of childish expression. As Wade took his son's hand, pointed to the Cathedral, distinguished for him the towers, spires and steeples and explained their architectural and aesthetic significance, she realized that driving a car was probably the least of his abilities. She was going to confront him with his secrets, too, first chance she got, and make him tell all. Yet, an unfamiliar pain wound around her heart, pain for Wade in his struggle to win his child's affection and pain for the boy who had never grown to love his father. Neither parent seemed at fault, but the way they'd managed their affairs had hurt them all. She could see that the boy enjoyed his father's explanations about the cathedral, but she missed most of their conversation until she heard Wade promise to draw it for the boy when they got home. She stopped dead in her tracks. How could he draw that complicated building from memory?

Christopher skipped along trying to keep up with his father's long strides. "Are you going to take me ice skating, Wade? I can skate already. Mother paid a man to teach me."

"Sure thing." He must have known that she detected the resentment in his voice, because he shrugged as if to say, "So what?" The boy asked his father to let her join them. She smiled at his choice of words, but she noticed Wade's embarrassment.

"I'd love to join you if..." She looked at Wade. "Is it all right with you?" Her heart pitched in her chest when he smiled his gratitude for her thoughtfulness. She didn't need to be told that he hadn't explained their relationship to his son, and she'd tried to let him know that he had no reason to worry. What a mess. The wind blew her hair up over her head, and she quickly pulled it back in place and started walking. Children were too perceptive. She didn't want to hear what the boy was about to ask her, because she knew she had just raised his curiosity about her hair and the way she wore it.

They wandered through the miles of toys in F.A.O. Schwartz. "Look around, Christopher, and make your Christmas list. Things you want and things you'd like to give to someone else," Wade said. Nadine rolled her eyes upward in alarm, certain that they were about to spend hours there, but in less than half an hour, the boy had his list, though he didn't share it. She tried to banish the feeling of being alone, of being left out, of wanting to belong as Wade explained to Christopher the houses that lined route eighty-seven on the way home.

"Why don't we stop at the first decent restaurant and have dinner? If we wait 'til we get home, it'll be pretty late by the time we eat. What do you say, Nadine?"

She and Wade had never eaten out together and, if they did it now, it would be a social occasion, not part of their room-and-board agreement. She should say no, unless she was prepared to risk an escalation of their growing intimacy. And who'd pay for their meal? It was a cinch he wouldn't let her do it and devalue himself in his son's eyes.

"Well?"

"Can I have a coke, Wade?" Christopher asked with an urgency that only a child could attach to such a simple request. "Mother doesn't like for me to drink sodas, but sometimes she lets me."

"If we stop at a restaurant, you may have half of one. What about it, Nadine?" The hope that she saw in his eyes nearly brought tears from hers; he wanted to please his son. She tried to make light of it.

"It's your night to cook. At least tonight, I won't have to eat spaghetti and meatballs."

"Why don't you like Wade's spaghetti and meatballs, Nadine? They're the best I ever tasted."

"She likes it, son—she just doesn't want to eat it every other day." His tone changed perceptibly to a soothing basso.

"Of course, she can't say I didn't warn her." He drove off the highway at Ardona and found a neat little mom-and-pop restaurant whose owners willingly filled Christopher's order of one chicken leg, one hamburger and one hot dog. The boy chatted away, and she decided that the time had come to take a chance. If the idea didn't go over well, it would be too bad, because she felt strongly about it.

"Christopher," she began, somewhat tentatively, "none of the children I know call their father by his first name. I wince every time you do it. Your father deserves better from you. Much better."

"That's what my mother calls him," he replied, and she could see that her remark had dampened both their spirits. Wade didn't comment, and he didn't look at her, either, but she swore to herself that she wouldn't give up. Children should respect their parents.

The next morning, Sunday, Nadine drove herself to nine o'clock church service, hoping to avoid Lorna and her innuendos. But Lorna had apparently decided that the later service would be too crowded and had also gone to the earlier one.

"Honey, you're the talk of Accord. We were all at Alma's regular Saturday night bridge party—you really ought to go sometime—and Hugh Cliburn said he'd always wanted to get to know you better, but you didn't give him any encouragement. Hugh's a fine man, and *he's* single. He's also very stable and has a *professional* job." She emphasized the word. "Did you know he's been our postmaster for the last eighteen years? Everybody respects him. Why, he personally puts up the community Christmas tree every single solitary year." Nadine wondered how far she could stretch the definition of *friendship*.

"Lorna, Wade Malloy is not married. In fact, his ex-wife is on her honeymoon right now. And another thing. I am not having an affair with him, so stop pretending to be open-minded and modern, when you're really censuring me for letting him and his son stay in my house. They live on the second floor, and I live on the first. And if I wanted to sleep in his bed every night, Lorna, I'm past the age where I'd have to get permission from anyone other than Wade." She nearly giggled at the gaping mouth and wide eyes in Lorna's shocked face.

"Well, girl, you know I believe in live and let live. If he's got the music that makes you dance, far be it from me to interfere. I just don't want to see you make a mistake. He's a chauffeur, you know. *Your* chauffeur. And don't forget. Hugh is our highly respected postmaster." Nadine twirled her umbrella, suddenly wishing for a downpour that would offer an easy way out of that conversation. Lorna was a good soul with a big heart, but she'd had enough.

"I've got to hurry. It's my turn to cook. See you tomorrow evening." Laughter bubbled up inside her and finally spilled over. Lorna's mouth could have received a tennis ball with ease, and her eyes nearly popped.

"You mean he cooks, too? My Lord, where did you find him?" Nadine waved goodbye, got into her car and drove off. She already knew that Wade was good husband material, depending, of course, on what he was hiding.

At home, she found the kitchen clean and the house empty. Deciding that he'd taken Christopher somewhere, she changed into slacks, a cowl-neck sweater and a big bulky coat sweater and hiked out to the Rondout where she found them fishing.

"I want you to stop calling me by my first name, son. I'm your father, and I want you to acknowledge that every time you address me."

"How come you didn't say anything until Nadine mentioned it?"

"Because I'm planning to correct your bad habits one at a time. Now that you know you mustn't brag on yourself, we can start on this."

"Gee whiz, Wade, I dunno. That's all I ever called you." Christopher paused for a moment. "Wade, where am I going to stay when Mother gets back home? I don't like Casey, and I don't think he likes me."

"I'm going to try to keep you with me, son, and you start right now to practice calling me Dad."

As though he hadn't heard a word his father said, Christopher prattled on. "Mother isn't going to like that, but she's got Casey, so I guess… Gee, I don't know. Wade, why is Nadine always pulling at her hair and playing with her ear, huh? Look! I think I got a bite." She wished she had let them know she was there, but she couldn't resist listening for Wade's answer.

"No. You don't have a bite. Your hook's stuck in a weed. Why do you think Nadine plays with her ear? I've never noticed her doing it."

"Well, she does. All the time."

Nadine turned to walk away, stepped on a dry twig and, to her embarrassment, brought their attention to her.

As soon as he could do so inconspicuously, Wade curtailed the fishing expedition and took Christopher home. Nadine must have had a reason to listen to their conversation unobserved. He found her in her basement office trying to redraw the designs, her face so tightly drawn that he knew she wasn't capable of creative thinking. He lifted the telephone receiver after the first ring.

"Ms. Carpenter's home." He didn't like what he heard, handed her the receiver and stood in the doorway while she talked. He watched the shifting play of the dying sun rays in her thick black hair and wondered about Christopher's observation. Her hand went to her left ear, and he realized that he had seen her pat that ear any number of times. She crossed her legs, leaned back in her chair and desire stirred in him. He didn't mind that, he told himself; he'd get upset when being around such a woman—warm, sensual and surprisingly feminine—*didn't* send an occasional message to his groin.

"You've got some nerve," she told him after hanging up, but he shrugged it off.

"That's the same guy who showed so little regard for you night before last, wasn't it? I hope he called to apologize." He listened to her explanation that the man had been drinking and had never behaved that way before.

"Rodney is a highly respected interior designer," she continued, "and we've been professional associates for several years without his getting out of line. Well, not far out, anyway. He's harmless and, even if he weren't, you should have left the room while I talked."

"That guy bears watching, Nadine." He made up his mind to check on him, because he had a hunch that the man hadn't been that drunk, just pretending.

While Nadine was at work the next day, he did exactly that and learned that Rodney had recently signed a contract to design three suites in a newly renovated hotel. He asked for and got an appointment with the hotel's owner for roughly one week hence. That didn't mean the man was a thief, but he was at least a suspect in the theft of Nadine's place.

Several days later, Christopher brought a note from one of his teachers stating that he had been insubordinate in refusing to attend his swimming class. If he refused again, he'd be given a demerit that would automatically disqualify him from receiving any school honors. Nadine couldn't understand why he'd given the note to her rather than to his father. She soon understood the child's problem. Behind his braggadocio postures lay a deep-seated shame of an imperfection that he couldn't make himself share, not even with his father.

"No one's going to laugh at you because you have a large red blotch on your thigh," she told him when he confessed his reason for skipping the class. "Your classmates are only going to see what a good swimmer you are, so don't risk getting put out of school, honey." Those might have been her mother's words to her when she, too, had rebelled against going to swimming class, and she felt a little ashamed for asking the child to do what she had been unable to accomplish. Christopher bowed his head in an unaccustomed acknowledgement of defeat.

"You can talk like that, Nadine, because you're beautiful.

Wade said you are. So nobody's ever going to laugh at you. But if it was your leg, you'd be ashamed, too." Without his arrogance, she saw a hurt little boy and risked putting her arms around him. To her amazement, he rushed into them and wrapped his own arms tightly about her. She held him close, suddenly aware that she needed him more than he needed her.

"I don't want them to laugh at me, Nadine. I don't. And I'm not going to that class." Her fingers stroked his young back as she wondered how to help him.

That evening, Wade walked into her office, speaking as he did so. "What am I going to do, Nadine? I've spoken with Christopher's gym teacher and explained to her that he's an excellent swimmer and doesn't need swimming lessons, but she says he can't be excused from class."

"It isn't easy for him, Wade. Don't be fooled by his blustering. He's still very tender."

Wade's gaze perused her face in a way that suggested she might not be real. "He's becoming fond of you, Nadine."

"I'm just growing on him, Wade. Seems I have that effect on some people." She wished she'd swallowed those words. Wade's mesmeric, light brown eyes suddenly glowed as though they had become coals of fire. His hands dropped to his sides, and his fingers curled into fists as his hot gaze sent rivets of heat throughout her body.

"Wade…"

"It's not going away, Nadine. Not now. Maybe not ever. And certainly not until we do something about it one way or another." She didn't know how she'd gotten out of her desk chair, fled past him and up the stairs to her bedroom. She sat there trembling behind that closed door, wishing with all her soul that he'd break it down.

Wade sank into the recently vacated chair that still held the heat from her body. The floral scent that she always wore teased his nostrils and he rubbed the sweat off of his hands and onto his trousers. She didn't want to become involved, and he wouldn't pressure her; he'd never pressured any woman, never had to. But the more he saw of her, the more certain he was that he could drown in her. And love it. And the more certain he was that she had the strength to ignore her desire for him, to walk away and not look back. He got up and went to Christopher's room.

"Son, you have to go to your swimming class. Your mother never told me that spot bothered you so much, or I would have done something about it."

Christopher looked up, hopefully. "What could you do? You mean I don't have to have all those kids meddling with me?"

"Never mind the past, son. During the Christmas holidays, you're going to get a skin graft. When it heals, the spot will be gone."

"Really? The whole thing? It's almost as long as my thigh."

"Really. Now finish that story and get ready for bed."

Christopher didn't move, but kept his gazed fixed on his father. "You're really going to get my leg fixed?"

"Didn't I say I would? I've never lied to you, and I never will." Wade turned to go to his own room, but whirled around as Christopher began to sing the "Toreador song."

"I didn't know you knew that song."

"I didn't until I heard you sing it." The boy's smile warmed his heart, and he smiled in return. Then he quickly left; it wouldn't do for a boy to see his father's tears. Maybe they'd make it, after all.

Nadine watched Wade and Christopher as they said goodbye to Lorna and walked to the car where she awaited them. She had the impression that the boy was becoming more at ease with his father, less inclined to behavior that denied their relationship. He didn't resist or show reluctance when Wade took his hand, though she had yet to see the boy reach for his father's hand. Her heart ached for them both. How had Wade allowed such an enormous chasm to develop between himself and his only child? He didn't speak of it, and she hadn't had the opportunity or the courage to ask him. She tried not to judge him, because she knew she didn't have some crucial facts, and what she'd seen of his behavior with his son—gentleness, tenderness and patience, often suffering the child's hostility—reinforced her belief in Wade Malloy's goodness. Down on his luck, maybe, because he certainly hadn't made his living as a chauffeur. She unlocked the back door.

"How was school?"

"Not so good," Christopher mumbled. "I can't go back until I'm ready to go to my swimming class." She heard the unshed tears in his voice. "They're not going to let me be in the Christmas play, and I was supposed to sing 'O, Holy Night.'"

The grim expression on Wade's face elicited her compassion. He needed to bridge the gap between himself and his son, but he had to discipline him, too, and she knew that Christopher wouldn't take that well.

Her vision of it was borne out later that evening. Wade sat alone in his room trying to put himself in his son's place, to imagine what his own reaction would be to a stigma that was no fault of his own and of which he was ashamed. Still, he reasoned that, no matter the cause, he couldn't allow the boy to defy him and his teachers. As though shouldering the yoke of all the ages, he trudged over to Christopher's room. He was fighting for his child's affection, but children who loved their parents also obeyed them. He pushed open the door.

"I'm not going, Wade, so don't ask me to."

"I'm not asking you—I'm telling you. I can't let you skip school. I'd be breaking the law and ruining your future. You're a straight-A student, and that's a ticket to the best schools and prestigious jobs, and I can't allow you to ruin your chances."

"How do you know what happens?"

"Because I was an A student, top of my class, went to the best school and had the best jobs."

"So how come you don't have an office anywhere?"

"The judge gave your mother sole custody of you because my work took me all over the world. I was never in one place more than a few months, and he ruled that a child needed more stability than I could provide. Well, I have decided to fight for my rights as your father, and I gave up that work. For the past two years, I studied law. I've finished, and I'm preparing for the bar exams. After I take Nadine to work, I go to school and study. As a lawyer, I'll be able to fight for my rights, and I'll be settled in one place. I'm not giving you up, Christopher, so you can begin right now to obey me. I mean it." He hoped he hadn't come on too strong. The boy had seemed awed by his tale of adventure, but the famous Malloy temper had begun to boil at the mention of discipline.

"I don't care what you say. I'm not going. Mother never makes me do things like that."

"You're going to school."

"I won't. I'm never going back."

"Calm down, son, and come downstairs tomorrow morning ready for school." He turned out the light, closed the door softly and leaned against it. He'd tried to provide the best for his family, but his efforts had cost him his marriage, and it seemed that each time he made headway with Christopher, something happened to widen the chasm.

Nadine raced up the stairs. Christopher's screams had awakened her. She reached his door and paused when she heard the boy recounting his nightmare to his father.

"I dreamed you went away and left me, that you told Casey he could have me. I don't like Casey. You're not going to give me to him just because I won't take swimming, are you?" Wade sat on the side of the bed, trying without success to reassure him. She knew she should go back to her room, but she couldn't rid her mind of the desperation in Christopher's voice nor the pain in his father's eyes. She wanted to hold them both to her bosom, to comfort them and love them. She stood there, her arms folded beneath her bosom and tears streaking her cheeks.

She couldn't hear Wade's soft, whispered words to his son, but she realized after some time that the boy had fallen asleep.

Wade looked up and saw her.

"How long have you been standing there?" His hoarse, emotion-filled voice quivered slightly, as he slapped both hands on his steely thighs, rose and started to the door.

"Maybe twenty minutes. I know I should have left after I found you with him, but somehow I couldn't. What happened?"

He stopped within inches of her, and she could feel his magnetic energy churning and swirling around her, warming her, pulling her into its orbit. As though against their will, her eyes lifted to his face, to the raw anguish there, and she drew in her breath.

"He acted up with me earlier tonight, and his guilt about it gave him a nightmare."

She heard his words, but she knew his voice proclaimed a different thought and mood. He thrust out his hand to her, quickly withdrew it and curled it into a tight fist. His lips moved, but no words came. Finally he closed his eyes, squeezed them tighter and drew in a harsh breath.

"Nadine, why are you standing here? You know I need to bury myself in you. You know it, Nadine. Nadine…"

She couldn't walk away from him. Her hands went to his stubbly cheek, and she stroked him soothingly. "Yes, I know that, Wade. But can't you take what I offer without wanting more?"

He shook his head. "Not now. I—I need more. Much more," he said and stepped away from her, his palms thrust forward.

She watched him cross the hall to his room and knew that she'd never met a man who possessed greater dignity.

Christopher went to school the next morning, but when he wouldn't promise to attend his swimming class, he was made to spend the day in the principal's office. Wade looked down at the note without reading it.

"What does it say?" asked Christopher.

"It says I'm not supposed to come back to the school building until I agree to take swimming. And you have to go and see the principal."

After dinner that night, Nadine walked up the stairs not fearful but very nervous. Until the night before, she hadn't been up there since she'd given the space to Wade, and she didn't know how he'd react to another visit so soon. There was no door, so when she reached the top of the stairs, she knocked on the wall as hard as she could.

"Wade…"

"Yeah." He ducked his head out of Christopher's room. "You need me for something?"

"No. I want to talk with Christopher about his swimming class, if you don't mind."

"Sure. I appreciate anything you can do, because I haven't moved him an inch. He says he's not going, even if he's expelled."

"Could you leave us alone?" He nodded, walked out and closed the door behind him.

"I'm not doing it, Nadine, so don't ask me."

She sat on the edge of his bed and took his hand. "You said we were friends, Christopher, so I'm going to share with you a secret about myself that only one person other than my parents ever knew. Will you keep my secret?" He nodded. "You once told me that I didn't understand your problem, because I wasn't the one with the blotch. Suppose you had a spot that bad on your ear, right out in a place where everyone could see it all the time." He sat up in bed, and his stare told her that her words had touched him.

"That's why you wear your hair like that and you're always putting your hand on your ear?"

"Yes." She tried unsuccessfully to keep the tremors out of her voice.

"But you hide your eye, and Wade said you have pretty eyes. It can't be that bad."

Suddenly, she didn't think she could go through with it, and she rose to leave. He held her hand, restraining her.

"Don't go, Nadine. I didn't mean to say anything wrong. It's just you're so pretty. Let's see." She shook her head.

"I feel the same way about showing you my ear that you do about showing me your leg."

"Oh." He looked steadily at her for a moment. "I'm sorry." Realizing that she had only added to his insecurity, she gathered her courage and pulled her hair away from her left ear. He leaned around Nadine, braced his hand on her shoulder for support and looked at her left ear.

"Gee, Nadine, it's not so bad. And you look nice with your hair like that. I mean, you know, like normal."

"You promised not to tell."

His hand went to his heart. "On my honor. Not even Wade." Especially not Wade, she wanted to add, though she didn't.

"I showed you because I don't want you to be expelled from school, and I want to hear you sing in the school play. I'll bet your scar isn't any worse than mine."

She smiled inwardly. Christopher hadn't lied about being smart. The brief anger that flashed in his eyes, before his mouth curved into a smile let her know that he understood her game. Slowly, his leg came out from under the covers until she saw his knee and the large red, skinless scar above it. She didn't lie when she told him that it was little more than a blemish, that his classmates might look at it once or twice, but they'd soon forget it. "Just like my ear," she added.

"You think so?" She leaned over and kissed his cheek. He didn't move away, but spoke to her in words so soft that she barely heard them.

"Mother says it's not good to kiss boys, because it makes them into sissies."

She kissed him again.

"My kisses are different. Now, do we take you to school tomorrow or not?"

"I dunno. Gee, Nadine. Well…I guess. If you can show me your ear. Okay…I guess."

Fortunately, Wade had the good sense not to comment when Christopher came to the breakfast table the next morning dressed for school and carrying his book bag.

A few hours later, with Nadine at work and at a time when he should have been cramming for exams, Wade used his established credentials and got an interview with the manager of the hotel for which Rodney Ames had the interior decorating contract. He took the long elevator ride to the hotel's tower suite of offices unable to get his mind off of Christopher's cheerful journey to school. The boy hadn't offered one objection, and he couldn't help wondering what had transpired between him and Nadine the night before. He was grateful for whatever had happened, but he intended to find out. Less than five minutes after entering the manager's office, he knew he was looking at Nadine's drawings. The initials "NC" were unmistakable. He told the man of his suspicions and asked him to remain silent about it until he could provide proof.

"Why do you want to know?" He knew he'd expose himself and face her questions if he helped her find the lost plans, but he hadn't seen an alternative; if he didn't step in, she'd lose more than a set of plans.

"Trust me, Nadine," he cajoled softly. "I'm not stupid just because I drive you to and from work. You said McHenry's your contractor? I'm on to something, and I need to be sure of my facts."

She leaned back in her desk chair and looked out on Park Avenue South. "He's the one."

"Tom McHenry. He's head of McHenry and Deaver Associates." He nodded, and gave silent thanks for his good luck. He had known McHenry professionally for years.

Several days later, when the contractor identified the plans as the ones he'd approved for Nadine's project, Wade had to stifle the desire to shout, and had to cloak his face in a bland expression. But it wasn't easy to hide his joy. He and Nadine took the plans and left McHenry and the manager talking in the manager's office.

They entered the elevator, and he'd have expected anything except the way she chose to express her happiness; with face aglow and eyes shining, Nadine grabbed his shoulders and kissed him on the mouth. He knew that she meant it as a kiss of thanks, but the feel of her sweet lips on him—gentle as a wisp of spring breeze—telegraphed an urgent message to his sensual center, and he wanted more, needed more. He didn't think to check his aggressiveness, and his hands went to either side of her face, tight over her ears as he took over the kiss and changed it into a fiery sacrament to their mutual need. He vaguely sensed an uneasiness in her, but her submissiveness fueled the fire that she'd torched with her innocent kiss. His tongue rimmed her lips seeking entrance but, when she gasped at the feel of his virile power pressing against her belly, he pulled back. He had let himself forget that they were in a public elevator, and she'd been so attuned to him that she hadn't even noticed his hand pressing against her ear. The roughness beneath his left hand told him that ear was different from the right one. He kept that revelation to himself, careful to remove his hand gently, suspecting that it could be one source of her reticence and unease, the reason for her asymmetrical hairstyle. He meant to get to the bottom of it, if he could do that without hurting her.

He wasn't sure what he wanted from Nadine but having gotten past her businesswoman's exterior and glimpsed more than once her capacity for tenderness and caring, he had to admit that he needed more than physical release with her. Ellen was a good woman, but she wasn't a nurturer. She didn't envelop a man in a satisfied cocoon of sweetness and warmth as Nadine did. In all these years, he hadn't known he needed that. But he knew it now. And he knew it because Nadine gave it to him.

* * *

Nadine's company had closed for the Thanksgiving weekend, and she sat in her basement home office at work on her plans for Rolling Hills Village. Wade had taken Christopher into New York to buy Christmas gifts, and she had the morning to herself. She chewed the end of her pencil, and tried to figure out what she was going to do about Wade. She feared that what she'd thought was an old-fashioned crush on an extremely masculine, good-looking man was beginning to escalate into much more. A sense of uneasiness pervaded her, because she knew nothing about him other than what she'd seen since she met him. She didn't doubt that he was honorable, a decent man. But every person his age had a past, good or bad, and only a foolish woman would let herself fall for a man of whom she knew virtually nothing.

She poured more coffee from the thermos into the horrible green mug that Lorna had given her for a birthday present. She hated the thing, but it had grown on her. She leaned back in her chair, thought about the kiss in which Wade had nearly drowned her that day in the elevator and began to squirm, embarrassed by the moistness between her thighs. If only she were convinced that he would accept her blemishes along with the rest of her, that her scar wouldn't shock him, wouldn't make him turn from her, she'd walk…no, she'd *run* into his arms. *And if you knew more about him,* her common sense cautioned. Work was now impossible. She left the plans on her desk, went up to her room and changed into casual outdoor wear. At least she could rake the leaves.

Wade looked down at the three gifts Christopher had managed to buy during three hours of shopping in some of the largest stores in the world. Patience was a virtue, but the boy had an oversupply of it.

"We can go now, Wade. Mother likes the Mormon Tabernacle choir, so I hope she'll like the two CDs of that and the sweater. I know Granddaddy will love the fishing stuff. Can we shop some more next Saturday? If you don't want to, I can ask Nadine. I used up my allowance, though."

I'm not going to be jealous of Nadine and my son, Wade admonished himself, taking Christopher's hand. "We can shop next Saturday, but we're going to one of the shopping malls. And if you want something, son, you ask me. I'm responsible for you, not Nadine."

"I know, but she likes me and she doesn't mind."

Wade knew that, but he wanted his son to depend on him. While he'd been earning a living for them, the child had become so accustomed to going to his mother for everything that he didn't understand a father's role. He shook his head in dismay. How could he get the boy to address him as his father when the child didn't see him as one?

"Wade, do you think we can come back to Hunting World next week for just a little bit? I don't think I want to give Granddaddy any fishing stuff for Christmas. He can buy that himself."

"All right, son, but you're going to have to learn to make up your mind about things. And let's get a move on. It's getting cloudy, and I want to get back to Accord before the weather changes." He noticed that Christopher skipped along with him, instead of dragging behind as he'd usually done whenever they went anywhere. And the boy seemed to be holding his hand, rather than the other way around. Well, it was something. He locked their seat belts and started home, suddenly anxious to get there. A woman as high up on the corporate ladder as Nadine didn't dally with her chauffeur, he mused, but he consoled himself with the fact that he wasn't an ordinary chauffeur. If he decided that he had to have her, he'd get her if he had to unmask.

Nadine tied the black plastic bags of leaves and dragged them into the garage. She hardly recognized the place, because she hadn't entered it since Wade began driving for her. The tools had been cleaned and polished, a shelf containing clean

cloths, lubricants and cleaning agents had been installed and
the windows washed. Maybe he really was a chauffeur. She
smiled, thinking that there wasn't much chance of that; he took
control too readily, was too sure of himself and had too active
a mind to have been content with a job that demanded so little
of his mental acuity. She walked toward the back of the house
against the rising wind, her arms folded for added warmth,
and stopped beside the massive oak tree that had been an in-
ducement to buying the property. She fingered her mother's
wedding ring that always hung from an old gold chain around
her neck. *Get back to work,* she told herself, *time is running
out. Let him know you care and that you need him,* a niggling voice interjected. *He's my chauffeur,* an inbred instinct
to abide by society's proscriptions insisted. She threw up her
hands, admitting confusion, and went back in the house and
down to her office. A few minutes later, Christopher's joyous
announcement of his arrival put an end to her effort to accommodate her sponsor without sacrificing professional integrity.
She was happy for the child and a little ashamed at her envy
when he exclaimed excitedly about the gifts he'd found for
his mother. She needed a child of her own, but she knew better than to hope.

Wade was due to cook dinner, but Christopher loved cook-
outs, and she decided to prepare his favorite meal. She built a
fire in the stone oven and grill that nestled beneath a fireproof
tent a few yards from the back door. The tent made it possible to
use the grill in any type of weather, so she didn't worry about
the overcast skies. She prepared the meat and vegetables for
grilling and went back to her office to try and find a place in
the Rolling Hills house for an oversize Persian carpet. Sometime later, she looked at her watch; she'd better get the ribs
started. When she noticed the back door ajar, she knew a moment of fear, but it passed swiftly when she remembered that
she had Wade to protect her. Where was he? She hadn't seen
him since he and Christopher returned from shopping. She
wondered whether the thugs who had threatened her weeks

earlier had returned and geared herself for an unpleasant en-
counter. Cautiously, she stepped out on the screened porch in-
tending to look around without exposing herself.

She was at first charmed by what she saw and then her
adrenaline accelerated its flow as fear gripped her. There in
the open garden, Christopher knelt beside a very young fawn,
obviously lost from its mother and seemingly chilled by the
rapidly cooling temperatures, for it huddled close to the boy
and allowed him to stroke its body. She knew that the mother
had to be trailing the fawn's scent and couldn't be far away, and
she streaked out of the door, remembering the deadly power
of a deer's hooves. Immediately, she saw the big doe spring
from the thicket into the garden and head toward Christopher
and the fawn.

"Wade. *Wade!*" Her screams pierced the silence as she, too,
ran toward Christopher, though she didn't know how she would
help him, especially since he didn't see the big animal.

"Wade! Christopher, run! *Run!*"

She stopped short as a chunk of wood whizzed past her and
landed in front of the doe, disconcerting her. Seconds later,
Wade lifted Christopher into his arms and crushed his son to
him while doe and fawn disappeared into the thicket. Neither
the pungent smell of charring meat and vegetables engulfed in
the grill's smoke nor the gusts of wind that brought the odor to
her dry nostrils and smarted her eyes distracted her from the
scene before her. She stood riveted by the vision of a father's
face wet with tears of gratitude, his eyes closed in prayerful
humility while the son for whom he had desperately feared
patted him as though to comfort him.

"Don't scare me like that again, son. If that doe had at-
tacked you, if she'd hit you with those sharp hooves, I think I
might have died."

Nadine knew she had to control her trembling, that she
couldn't cry right then, because the moment belonged to Christopher and she couldn't detract from that by calling Wade's
attention to her. She thought her heart would bound out of

her chest when Christopher gripped his father's shoulders and clung to him. And though she felt left out, she pushed back the desire to go to them and ease herself into the circle of Wade's arms. She found the strength to walk casually over to them.

"I guess you realize how lucky you are to have a father like Wade, don't you, Christopher? He thinks fast. I ran over here with nothing in my hand, and I couldn't have done a thing to help." Still clutching Wade's shoulders, Christopher looked into his father's eyes.

"I didn't see her. Do you really think she would have hurt me?"

"As sure as the sun rises. When you go near a young animal, son, always be certain that you know where its mother is." He put Christopher down, but she noticed that he kept his arm protectively around the child.

"What on earth is that noise?" Christopher looked from Nadine to Wade before covering both ears. Nadine laughed heartily, glad for the opportunity to release her tension.

"Mr. DeVanzio is back from one of his tours, I see." At their inquiring look, she explained.

"He's an operatic tenor who's seen his best days. When he practices the scales, he always peters out by the time he gets to high C, and he can't make it. But he tries. Screeching, in fact. Caruso—that's his dog—always makes the note for him, and the whole neighborhood goes for cover." Wade's disbelieving, sparkling eyes warmed her heart. She realized that, out of that near disaster with the doe and fawn, he had a greater sense of closeness with his son and that he was happier than she'd known him to be. Because she rejoiced with him, she let her eyes mirror her heart.

Wade noticed Christopher's efficiency when the boy helped him clean up after dinner, but it pleased him so much that he didn't question it. He hummed his favorite tune. Christopher had volunteered to help with the dishes and had asked him if he was any good at geography, a subject for which the boy obviously didn't care much. If that weren't enough, he had seen Nadine shed tears of happiness for him while he'd held Christopher in his arms after their near tragedy. She couldn't have known that he hadn't held his son since the boy was six months old. All the times he had come home from working abroad, Ellen hadn't let him near the child, saying that he might be carrying a dreaded foreign disease to which the boy had no immunity. Christopher tugged at his hand.

"I have a geography exam tomorrow, Wade. I understand most of the stuff, but I can't figure out how water from the Nile river takes care of all of Egypt. It doesn't rain much. How come the river doesn't dry up? And how can the pyramids still be there after all this time and don't sink in the sand?" Wade raised an eyebrow, took the boy's hand and started up the stairs jingling his pocket change as they went.

"You don't want to know much, do you?" he said, pleased with the sharpness of his son's mind.

"We'll deal with those pyramids some other time, since you don't need that information for your test. Right now, you have to get to sleep." He tweaked the boy's nose, turned out the light and walked toward the door.

"Gee, Wade, you know more than my teacher. You sure know a lot. Thanks for helping me." Joy suffused him as he stood there in the dark. Maybe his fortunes were about to change. He had begun to gain his son's respect; now, he had to earn the boy's love and affection.

"No thanks needed, son. This is what fathers are for."

Wade made coffee and took two mugs of it down to the basement where he knew he'd find Nadine at work on her plans for Rolling Hills. Her absentminded nod of the head told him that she was deep in her work so, when the phone rang he answered it, grimaced and handed it to Nadine.

"I'm sorry, Rodney. It isn't a good idea. You got out of hand, and I don't allow men to paw over me." She hung up and Wade asked for her to agree to the date if Rodney called again. She demanded to know his reasoning.

"You need to let him show his hand. He may be in cahoots with someone. I'd be willing to bet that this isn't the first time he's been involved in the theft of an interior decorator's plans, even building plans. Don't forget that he had the contract *before* the plans were stolen."

When Rodney called again, she agreed to go out with him.

Her frown of displeasure didn't appear to carry any weight with Wade, who could barely suppress his smirk as he held her coat.

"At least you're not a siren tonight, though I don't expect that insensitive fellow to realize that you didn't dress especially for him."

She pulled away from him in a huff and put her left arm into the coat sleeve without his help, albeit awkwardly. "How could you live as long as you have without learning how to mind your own business?" She nearly laughed; her voice hadn't carried the outrage that she'd tried to put in it.

"The same way you learned to live as long as you have without ever revealing any of your own business."

She hoped he'd realize from her glare that he was out of line. *And speaking of secretive!* She whirled around, chin up in a stance of belligerence that she hadn't previously allowed him to see.

"I'm secretive? What about you? If you're a chauffeur, the world is flat and Louis Armstrong was a college professor."

"Let's go get your date. Why doesn't the guy pick you up sometime? Doesn't he know he's at a disadvantage the minute he gets into your car?"

That's the way I want him, she thought, but she didn't ease Wade's mind by verbalizing it.

To her relief, Rodney's behavior proved exemplary throughout dinner. But thoughts of Wade sitting alone somewhere waiting prevented her from enjoying the meal. Perhaps he wasn't alone, but was spending the time with a pretty young woman. Maybe... Rodney had spoken of nothing all evening but work as if he was fishing for information about her plans and his contract with the hotel. She sat up, more alert and now very suspicious. Wade was right; the man was a gopher. He may have taken her plans, but that was all. And he hadn't seen as much of those hotel suites as she had. Satisfied that she had all the relevant information he possessed and that she could safely relegate him to the past, she smiled indulgently.

"I'm ready to go."

On the way home, Roger's behavior deteriorated by the minute until she considered asking Wade to dump him right on the highway. But Wade must have sensed that she couldn't tolerate Rodney any longer for, without a word he pulled over and stopped, got out and walked around to her door.

"Will you sit in the front with me, Nadine?" Her answer was to extend her hand. He dropped the man off at his apartment and drove home without speaking to her. She didn't have to guess his thoughts, because his barely leashed anger radiated out to her. She tried instead to decipher her own feelings, to understand her deep regret that she'd gone out with Roger and to come to terms with the nonsensical feeling that, in doing so, she had somehow wronged Wade.

He drove into her garage, parked and walked around to her door, but she opened it before he reached her. She couldn't fathom his dark gaze, and she didn't welcome the hot darts that ricocheted through her while he held her arm until they reached her door.

"Stay here," he said when they entered the foyer and he started down the hall to search her rooms for possible intruders.

"Why should I?"

Without a word, he spun around like a man who had reached his limit and pulled her to him.

"Wa—"

He swallowed the rest of his name. She couldn't wait for his tongue and opened her mouth in a plea for it that ripped a groan from deep inside him. She pulled his head down to increase the pressure, as though to steep herself in the heat that had begun to erupt in her loins. His hands went to her buttocks, pulling her tight against him until his hard virile power nestled at the seat of her passion. Obviously frustrated, he lifted her until she fit him perfectly. Desire plowed through her and she sucked his tongue into her mouth and held it there, feasting on it, while his strong fingers stroked her back and her buttocks and his arousal quivered against her.

She heard her whimpers and knew that the sounds fueled his desire for her just as his groans led her to spread her thighs around his slim waist. He brought his hand from beneath her buttocks to the left side of her head, and she slid down from her perch in that faraway realm of sensation, back to reality and to herself.

Wade knew at once what had brought on the change in her and searched for some way out of his predicament. He had upset her when he caressed the side of her face, but he had also let their passion explode and get the better of them. Maybe he ought to be thankful for his innocent mistake, because if they consummated what they felt, she'd send him on his way in the morning. But he'd been almost out of control from the moment he saw Rodney Ames put his hands on her. He broke the kiss and drew a deep breath.

"I let it get out of hand, Nadine, but I don't think I'm sorry. At least I know that you want me as much as I want you. Just don't let me ever see Rodney Ames's or any other man's hands on your body."

She nodded as though barely aware that he still held her pressed close with his heat straining against hers. He carried her to the living room and sat down with her in his lap.

"You're sweet. No, don't move. I don't want to be separated from you right now. I… Nadine, do you realize what almost happened between us? Unless I leave here, honey, we can't avoid it. But it doesn't suit me to leave, and I don't want to. You know that I have to establish a permanent residence, but there's more now. My boy is settled. He's gotten used to the place and the school, and he's grown fond of you. I want him to see his father as a man on whom he can depend, not some guy who drags him around from place to place, breaking up his friendships, pulling him out of first one school and then the next. This is more important than I know how to tell you."

"I'm not asking you to leave, Wade, but you must know that I'm not comfortable with this relationship."

"Because you shouldn't consort with your chauffeur? Right."

She jumped up, not annoyed because he refused to see any agenda other than his own, but hurt because he either thought her a snob incapable of overlooking his status or didn't trust her with his truth. She had to keep her voice low and soft, because their passionate exchange was still so fresh and her emotions so raw that she couldn't manage a firm, assertive voice.

"I've come to believe that you are an intelligent, clever man, but right now you're behaving just the opposite. When you can tell me who you are and what you do for a living besides pretend to be a chauffeur, your lap may begin to look inviting. Right now, it...well, you figure it out. Good night." She couldn't suppress a smile when she looked back at him. "And thanks for burying Rodney."

Wade sat up straight. "You mean that's the end of him?" he asked hopefully. She shrugged.

"Bad pennies have a way of turning up, but I think he knows you cracked his crown."

"Crown? I'd like to crack his..." She walked on to her room. "Good night, honey," he called after her.

Was he mocking her, or was that a deliberate endearment? She closed her bedroom door and slumped against it. Of course he had good reasons to stay, she thought, reflecting on his explanation, and she had nearly as good a rationale for his leaving. But the reasons why she wouldn't ask him to go were even stronger: he seemed to belong in her home and in her life.

Wade tried not to let his mind dwell on her seductive gait, the luscious curve of her hips and her lovely firm buttocks as she walked away from him. His predicament reminded him of a pool shark caught behind the eight ball. He laughed. This was nothing compared to some of the jams that he'd escaped. He started toward the back of the house to check it and stopped short; in those days he'd risked a lot, sometimes his life, and thought little of it. But with this woman, he risked his heart, something that hadn't been in his plans. And he couldn't make light of it.

He stopped by his lawyer's office Monday morning, collected his mail, and looked at Ellen's familiar handwriting. What next? He read her letter and relaxed. What were they going to do about Christopher? she asked for the first time since she'd sworn to the world that he wouldn't be a competent father because he couldn't provide a stable life for his only child. Now, she was asking his advice. Would he be willing to keep their son a little longer while she got adjusted to being married again, and would he bring the boy to see her?

He didn't want to feel sorry for Ellen, but he couldn't dismiss the thought that Casey, her new husband, didn't want Christopher and that Ellen was buying time. Well, Casey could stop worrying about Christopher Malloy. He spent a few minutes with his lawyer going over his business accounts and conditions for reopening the divorce settlement. He advised the lawyer to ease Ellen's worries without tipping his hand and headed down to New York University, where he'd rented a cubicle in the Law Library. He stashed his sandwich, apple and orange juice in a desk drawer, turned on his smartphone and settled down for serious study. Exams began the week after Christmas.

He needn't have worried about the lawyer leaking his plan to keep Christopher permanently; his son had an agenda of his own, he learned, and wasn't seeking his advice about implementing it. He went over Christopher's lessons with him that evening, and sent the boy off to get his shower.

"Wade, would you please address my letter to Mother and

mail it tomorrow? It's lying on my desk. I don't have any more envelopes and stamps."

"Sure." He picked up the short, clearly written note and read, "Dear Mother, I love you a lot, but I don't love Casey. If it's all right with you, I'll stay with Wade, but I'll come see you all the time and you can come see me, too. Love, Christopher."

Nadine wasn't certain of the wisdom of telling her boss that plans taken from her desk had been found with the manager of the palatial Sky Hotel chain. What if he were in cahoots with the thief? She wished she had discussed it with Wade, but she buttoned up her courage and went to the head office. Norman Perkins had once intimidated her, but not anymore. Five years had done a lot of damage to the once daunting ladies' man. Receding and thinning red hair, puffy jowls and an ever-growing paunch had brought him down to the level of the human race, and she no longer shivered when his olive-green eyes sent her the message that she was as choice a female as he was male.

"Why do you need an office up here on the executive floor?" He dusted his pungent cigar in a sterling-silver ashtray, and she knew his stare was meant to make her ill at ease.

"Because I deserve it," she said with a flash of insight into the man's personality. "What is your biggest interior decorating account at present? Rolling Hills, right? Who got it for you? Me. Right?" She brushed a thick curl away from her face and let her leather-booted left foot dangle from her crossed knee.

"So, what about it?" He puffed strenuously without caring where the smoke went.

"You can have thirty-one-twelve. Decorate it to suit yourself, except please, don't put any pink in there." She could afford to ignore his chauvinist remark, she told herself, wondering whether his ready acquiescence implied guilt.

"You're beaming," Wade said when they met that evening. "I'd say you're happy. Want to share?" She let him open the front passenger door for her because he insisted on it, got in and waited. Waited for what? He didn't keep her guessing, but leaned over and kissed her on the side of her mouth before he started the car. She would have protested if it wouldn't have been such an outright lie. She looked over at him, smiled and saw glittering sparks in his light brown eyes as he smiled in return. Thoughtlessly, she hugged herself, and what she'd communicated to him gave her a sense of unease, when he brought her hand to his mouth and kissed her fingers one by one. As though propelled by an independent force, she moved as close to him as the bucket seats would allow.

"What happened today?" He spoke as though he had the right to know. Maybe he did. She told him about her new office and how she got it, and he praised her presence of mind in not confiding in her boss. He stopped for a red light just before reaching the Major Deegan Expressway, leaned over and, with his hand holding her head still, gave her a full-mouth kiss. She had an impulse to turn into him and hold him, but honking horns interrupted the moment. A bit unsteadily, she leaned away from him, straightened her coat and cleared her throat.

"You aren't mad at me for kissing you, Nadine, so don't talk yourself into it." He patted her knee.

"I'm not angry with you, Wade, but I'm uncomfortable with this relationship. I've told you that." She glimpsed his twitching jaw, a sure sign of his displeasure. "Where did you get so much self-confidence? I get the impression that you think you can do anything you want to."

The twitching of his jaw stopped, and a smile played around his mouth. "That so? Well, I don't seem to be able to do anything about this traffic." Her hand light on his arm wasn't intended to soothe but to nettle.

"Then speed up, and let's fly. Getting airborne ought to be a cinch for you."

In a voice heavy with sarcasm, he warned, "Stop while you're ahead, Nadine."

She tilted her head sideways and watched him from the

corner of her eye. "Could we change the subject? Why Santa Claus has reindeer, for example."

"What's the matter? Scared I'll find a chink in your armor? If you have questions about my competence, let's leave Christopher with Lorna tonight, and by the time you wake up tomorrow morning, you won't have any doubts. Not a single one, honey."

"Why should I believe that?" she needled. "After all, you represented yourself as a chauffeur. The only thing you've said that I can't question is that you're Christopher's father."

"Are you saying you doubt my virility?" he asked so softly that she barely heard him. "What's so sacred about *that?*"

He slowed and pulled into the right lane.

"What are you doing?"

"I'm going to stop over here and give you the chance to tell me to my face that you're *not* provoking me deliberately, that you're not maneuvering me into spending the night with you either in your bed or mine." He stopped the car. "Because that's what you'll get for issuing me that challenge."

"Wade, for goodness' sake. All I said was—"

He interrupted, knocked her seat back to reclining position and leaned over her, his hot gaze piercing and dangerous. Hypnotic.

"What you said in effect was that you didn't believe a night in bed with me could please you. Nadine, if you don't swallow those words, don't even bother to put on your gown tonight." His lips almost brushed hers, and the breath she took was his own. Hot blood pounded in her face when the tip of his tongue touched her bottom lip, and her mouth opened while her arms reached up to him as though of their own will. His groan set her temples to throbbing, and she wanted to curse the seats that separated their bodies when his tongue grazed her mouth with heat such as she'd never before experienced. She stroked his face and squirmed in her seat. A powerful desire streaked through her, scattering her senses, turning her traitorous body into a frenzy of wanting. He raised his head, and the sweetness of his smile shook her to the pit of her soul.

"You needn't worry. No matter how badly I want to, I won't go to your door unless you give me a very clear invitation." He smoothed her hair away from her face, and her right hand grasped his wrist so strongly that it brought a sharp look from him.

"Don't!"

He stared at her.

"What's the matter? What did I do?"

"Nothing. I'm sorry." He straightened up, raised her seat and saw the dampness at the edge of her hair and the tiny beads of moisture on her nose.

"It's all right," he said, when he remembered what he'd done just before she panicked. But it wasn't all right or she wouldn't have frozen on him just when he'd thought, for the first time, that they might take a chance on each other. A real chance.

He eased the Crown Victoria onto the highway and headed for Accord, not sure that he wanted a deep involvement with a woman right then, when his priority was getting custody of his son. But he wasn't sure that he had a choice. His glaze swept over the sweet, and now-troubled, face that seemed to have taken up a permanent place in his mind's eye, to be there for him to see and to relish day and night, no matter where he happened to be. He grimaced and focused his attention on route eighty-seven. She hadn't begun to interfere with his studying yet, but when she did, he'd get a cure. Maybe he'd better get one before he reached that stage.

He knocked on Lorna's door wearing the fixed smile with which he usually greeted the nosy woman, but Christopher opened it, yelled goodbye back to little Greta and dashed toward the car. He corrected the eager youngster, who rushed back and, to Wade's surprise and joy, grasped his father's hand. The child bounded into the backseat, greeted Nadine and reoriented the adults' thoughts.

"Wade, can Granddaddy come here to see me at Christmas? He always used to come see me at Mother's house. Nadine doesn't mind, do you Nadine?"

Wade hadn't thought of his father's annual, week-long Christmas visit with his grandson, a custom that he hadn't shared during his years of work abroad. He'd better make some plans. "Of course, my daddy can visit you at Christmas, though I don't—"

Nadine interrupted him. "We'd be delighted for your grandfather to come for Christmas and stay as long as he wants to, wouldn't we, Wade?" He felt her left elbow nudge his rib cage, and a bit sharply, too, he thought with amusement. But he didn't need prompting; she couldn't know how much her words pleased him and, considering the fragile nature of their relationship, it was just as well that she didn't know.

"Thanks, Nadine." He had to control his voice, because he had a feeling it might quiver. If anybody had told him he was an emotional man, he'd have laughed in their face, but something was happening to him, and Nadine was at the core of it. He assisted her from the car, and she let him do it, her attraction to him blazing blatantly across her face as he rested an arm possessively about her. He looked around. Not a chance; Christopher had glued his gaze to them.

They finished dinner and Nadine went to her office in the basement, while Wade checked Christopher's homework. Nadine taped her drawings for Rolling Hills Village to the wall beside her desk in order to study them better. Being without those plans for over two weeks had cost her valuable time, and she figured she'd have to work every night until midnight in order to make that deadline. She didn't hear Wade enter the room, and she jumped at the sound of his deep voice.

"You sure you want to put curtains on that living room window? Granted they're thin, but I think they detract from that awesome view." She turned slowly and looked up at the man who leaned confidently over her shoulder. She'd already thought of that, but there was a need for privacy even in living rooms. She told him as much.

"Frank Lloyd Wright wouldn't agree. One of his nearly all glass houses had no curtains or shades on the entire first floor. There weren't even any windows, just glass. So come on, be modern." The sound of coins jingling in his pocket told her that he was more than pleased with himself. A slow burn didn't begin to describe her reaction. She was certain that he wouldn't have been able to seduce her right then, not even if he'd stripped down to his birthday suit.

"Anything else?" she breathed, in what she hoped would reach him as heavy sarcasm. It didn't surprise her that he ignored her warning, thrust his hands in the back pockets of his trousers and thought for a while before answering. She'd learned that he took his words seriously.

"Well, I can't see a huge Tabriz carpet on that intricately inlaid living room floor. Why hide all that great work?" Furious as she was with him, his comment had merit and she couldn't help but respond in a professional manner.

"My firm never lays out the money for the research or the furnishings to test these arrangements. We decorators get sponsors, and one of mine is a dealer in Persian carpets, so I've got to use some of his merchandise." She turned around and switched on her computer, effectively closing the subject. Wade was not discouraged.

"Okay. Put a Royal Bukhara on the staircase and in the master bedroom. That ought to hold him. I'd leave the living room floor bare. Of course, I know you decorators don't believe in leaving *anything* uncovered, but this time less is more." She couldn't resist telling him what she thought of his "unschooled" ideas, and he made more than one reference to her pigheadedness. She didn't usually let herself get into arguments about individual judgments, but she was beside herself at his arrogance. Just like a man; he knew it better.

"How do you deign to tell me how to decorate a house?" she spat out in frustration.

"When I'm just your ignorant chauffeur?" he asked in an almost frighteningly quiet tone. She slumped in her chair. It always came back to his being her chauffeur.

"He isn't any chauffeur." They hadn't been aware of Christopher's presence. "Wade's studying for his bar exams, aren't you, Wade? He's studying to be a lawyer." They both turned toward the child at the sharp tone of his voice and became aware of his fury, when they saw the tears that rolled down his young cheeks.

"Wade isn't your chauffeur," he repeated, though she could see that he was begging for confirmation. "He's a lawyer." She tried to breathe normally and to control her reactions, because she didn't want to expose Wade. But she couldn't hide her skepticism.

"Since when?" she asked, softening her voice.

"He told me that's what he's doing so he can stop living in jungles and airplanes, didn't you, Wade?" Nadine knew that her face held a look of disbelief, but she couldn't hide her shock or her ire.

"Yes, I did, son, and that is exactly what I am doing."

She couldn't make herself look at Wade, because she didn't know what he'd see. What her face would show. Right then, she didn't ever want to see him again. How could he have led her on the way he had? She flinched beneath Christopher's hard glare.

"There's no problem, Christopher, so…"

"You always say that," he screamed at her, "but you don't mean it, do you? If he's not your chauffeur, why can't you say so?" To her horror, he ran from the room and upstairs.

Nadine walked into the kitchen earlier than usual, dreading the morning. She'd been right all along in thinking that she'd given Wade his first job as a chauffeur. But that was not the issue. Who was he? So he spent his days studying for a bar exam. So what? After he'd left her the night before, she'd searched her library and verified his claim about Wright's glass house. And after sketching several good possibilities, she'd concluded that a red, Royal Bukhara carpet was just what that huge staircase needed. But how had he known that? She took a carton of eggs from the refrigerator, set out other ingredients for French toast, sighed deeply and sat down. It was Wade's morning to cook. He walked in and stopped when he saw her.

"Can we meet for lunch today, Nadine? I know we have to talk, but we can't do it this morning, and I'd like us to get things settled. I think negative vibes are bad for children, and that's what's flying around here right now."

She sat up straight, started to push her hair away from her face, realized what she'd done and slapped her hand over her ear. She didn't look at Wade, for fear of seeing recognition in his eyes.

"What about you and Christopher?" she said, dropping her hand into her lap with apparent casualness.

"I straightened it out with him last night. I didn't make him happy, but he knows I'm not a liar. He thought this was my place, but he's just learned that it's your house, and that I work for you. To him, a chauffeur is a servant, thanks to Ellen's snobbery. He can't handle it."

"I'm not hungry this morning." Christopher stood in the door ready for school, his belligerence as visible as his face.

"You can't go out without breakfast," they responded in unison. "And I'm going to fix you some French toast," Nadine added. "You always like that."

The boy turned and walked away, and Nadine jumped up to follow him, knocking over her chair as she did so.

"Don't pander to him, Nadine. He's a child. Right now, he's a disrespectful child, and he has to learn not to be rude. The least you should expect from him is a civil greeting, angry or not."

She didn't pause, and found the forlorn little boy huddled in a chair that was so big he seemed lost in it.

"Casey doesn't like me, but maybe I should go back to my mother. Maybe Wade can pass his exams faster, and you won't have to bother with me."

Momentarily stymied, she searched for words of comfort.

"You can't leave with my secret, darling. Besides, this is your home. You have to stay here with me. I don't want you to leave me."

"You don't? What about Wade? Are you mad at him?" And what was the answer to that? She risked putting an arm around him and, when he didn't object, she hugged him to her fiercely.

"Don't worry. He and I will work things out. And Christopher, you must stop using your father's first name—it's disrespectful, especially since he asked you to call him 'dad.'"

"Okay. Gee, Nadine, I have to take my granddaddy's tackle back to the store, 'cause I'm not going to give him that for Christmas. Can I go shopping Saturday?" She wondered why he'd asked her rather than his father and suspected that she and Wade had confused him about his father's status.

"Darling, I can't answer that. You'll have to ask your father. Besides, I'll be working Saturday morning. Now, come on back here and eat your breakfast. We'll have to hurry, because it's getting late." As they walked into the kitchen, Wade placed hot French toast before his son.

"Wow, Wade. I didn't know you could make these," the boy said appreciatively as he savored a mouthful. She wondered how Wade had foreseen the outcome of her little chat with the boy, and couldn't help softening toward the man. He needed her.

Wade stood when Nadine approached the table. It had surprised him when she suggested a restaurant less than a block from her office where they might meet some of her colleagues. He didn't miss the heads that turned as she walked toward him. Stunning. She was some woman! He stepped around to her side of the table and held her chair.

"What's so urgent, Wade, that it couldn't wait until tonight?" He saw that she'd girded herself for battle and told his temper to take a walk.

"Thanks for coming. Let's order first." The waiter brought their menus and greeted her as one well-known to him. Wade watched her eyebrows arch sharply when he gave his order of arugula and fennel salad, roast squab in pine nuts and plum pudding. All right, so it wouldn't tease some palates, but it was what he wanted. He declined wine. Nadine ordered chablis as an accompaniment to her salmon paté, broiled mushrooms and red leaf lettuce salad.

"What's up?" he asked, when he noticed her intense perusal as though seeing him for the first time.

"You've got a rich man's taste buds." She paused. "But why should that surprise me? Everything about you is unusual, including your attempt to appear down on your luck when nothing could have been further from the fact."

"I've never said or done anything to suggest that. You saw it that way because you wanted to. You wouldn't have hired a law school graduate to chauffeur you around, unless he'd just gotten out of school and was wet behind the ears. I needed two things—a steady job and time to study for my bar exams. What was more logical than chauffeuring for a working woman? I'd hoped to be able to sit in the car and study, but you gave me the whole day free, and I study at the NYU Law Library."

"Well, at least I know where you are in case I get sick and want to go home early."

He wrote his phone number on the back of a napkin and handed it to her.

"You've even got a smartphone? Have you got a Lincoln stashed away somewhere?"

"Nadine, I'm doing this so that I can gain custody of my son, something that I was denied because I had to work away from home in order to make a living for myself and my family. At present I'm only entitled to visit him once a week. A judge ruled that I wouldn't provide a stable life for a child and gave my wife sole custody. A man can't bond with his son once every two or three months and have it mean anything. It's now or never for Christopher and me, and if I don't stay in one place for at least a year, I'll still be considered unstable. I decided to learn domestic and family law so that I'll be able to handle my own case, because this is too important for me to entrust to another person. If you want me to leave, of course, I'll go. But I've more reason than that not to leave you." He watched her face for some sign of what she was thinking, though he knew and hated that she wouldn't be able to make an unbiased decision, because her feelings for him would interfere just as his did.

"I don't have any right to pry into your life, Wade. You answered all of my questions when you took the job. If I'm honest, I'll admit that there'd be no question were it not for the fact that we haven't kept personal feelings out of our relationship."

He picked up the fancy tweezers that lay in front of his plate, pulled the bones out of the tiny bird, took a bite and decided that candid honesty was in order. He was tired of pretense.

"That wasn't going to be possible, and I knew it before I agreed to take the job. You and I are the epitome of perfect chemistry." He reached over and covered her hand and, when she let him hold it, he told her, "When we acknowledge that, Nadine, we'll share something wonderful." Her failure to respond would have bothered him had she not turned her palm upward beneath his hand.

"Talk to me, honey."

"It would be best if you went away, but I don't want you to, even though I should fire you for not representing yourself properly. I was furious with you last night, because I felt you made a fool of me." She sighed heavily. "Well, that's water under the bridge. Anyway, Christopher has adjusted to his school, even to the swimming class, and you deserve a chance with him."

"I'd manage, Nadine, but you'd still be vulnerable to robbers and muggers every morning and every evening, and I'd worry about that." He squeezed her hand, hoping to communicate the tenderness that he felt for her. "Can't we admit that we need each other, that life is better now for both of us. That doesn't imply intimacy, though, mind you, I'm definitely not saying I don't want it."

"All right, I'll admit I don't worry about muggers nowadays when I get home. So, let's let it rest."

Wade laughed. She could find numerous ways to avoid saying what he wanted to hear and still not lie.

He spread the side helping of hard sauce thickly over his plum pudding, earning a disapproving mug from his companion. "What's the matter? I like sweet stuff. You ought to know that." From her diffidence, he supposed he'd done an apt job of letting her know what he thought of her. He continued to let his gaze roam over her.

"This hard sauce could take lessons in sweetness from you," he told her, rimming his lips slowly with the tip of his tongue.

"Stop it! You're overdoing this." He meant his slow grin to unsettle her and enjoyed it when she squirmed. "Wade, have you forgotten that this is a public restaurant? Behave yourself. I could…I could…powder you, Wade."

Warm, prickling sensations began to spread throughout his hard, lean body. "Anytime. Be glad to accommodate you." She looked skyward as though appealing to heaven.

"If we had some privacy right now, would you ravish me? If I put myself at your mercy and let you have your way with me, what would you do?"

"I'd box your ears." Her bubbling laughter warmed him throughout, and he wanted to push that hair away from her left eye so that he could see her whole beautiful face and both of her sparkling brown eyes. When her left hand suddenly covered her left ear, he knew that he'd been staring at her, and that he had ruined their precious moment. What the hell was it that made her panic about that hair and that ear? Christopher had stopped questioning him about it, and he suspected that the boy had somehow gotten the facts.

He paid the bill with his credit card, included a tip and gave silent thanks that she'd been sensitive enough not to suggest splitting the bill. He had invited her to lunch, because he wanted to be on his own territory when he tried to settle their differences. He wanted the advantage, and he knew he wouldn't have that at her home in Accord. And paying for their lunch with his gold credit card was part of the strategy. They reached the door as Rodney Ames entered it. The man nodded to Nadine.

"Seems I'm in the wrong profession. Chauffeurs have more fun and, when it comes to bodyguards, I wouldn't even guess."

Wade's arm automatically went around Nadine. He couldn't help it, and he didn't care what Rodney Ames or anyone else thought about it.

"Use a little horse sense, Ames, and stop overstepping your bounds with Nadine Carpenter. I don't like it." He moved closer, and Rodney backed off. "Oh, yes," he continued, "I've been meaning to ask you how you initial your plans? You do use 'RA,' don't you?" The gaping hole that Rodney's mouth had become was all the satisfaction Wade needed. He kept an arm around Nadine until they got back to her office building.

"See you at five." He pondered whether to kiss her, settled for a stroking of his fingers against her cheek and walked off jingling his pocket change and whistling the "Toreador song."

Nadine got to the ladies' room as fast as she could, threw cold water on her face, blotted it with paper and leaned against the wall. Approaching voices and footsteps sent her scrambling into one of the booths, and she locked the door and clung to it for support. Finally, unable to hold them, she let the tears stream down her face. How had she let herself fall in love with a stranger? A complex, problem-saddled enigma of a man who possessed steely nerves, old-fashioned grit, tenderness and a powerful passion that drew her as sweet flowers draw bees. A stranger. And every molecule in her body wanted him. And loved him. And she could think of half a dozen reasons why she shouldn't. He was totally unlike the corporate types, the alpha males whom she had dated since graduate school. He showed his feelings. He hurt and wasn't ashamed to let her see it. And he was a strong, determined man. If she knew him, really knew him, would she still love him? Would she love him that much more?

The door closed and the voices receded. She stepped out and had no sooner begun to freshen up than Dilly, the boss's secretary and the executive floor's gossip courier, walked in.

"Nadee-ine," she sang, "the whole firm is talking about your luncheon date. *Who* was that hunk? Lottie said she'd never seen anything that perfect—smooth dark skin, over six feet, gorgeous brown eyes, flat middle and nice tight behind, and a smile to die for. She swears she's going to thank the Lord for the pleasure of having seen at least one flawless man in her life. And she said he had his arm around you. You lucky girl! The best I can do is Roger Ames tomcatting behind me everywhere I go. But I'm not stupid. I know he wants to get in the boss's good graces. Well, later for him."

The one advantage of Dilly's company was that she did the talking. You weren't even required to answer or even to listen, because she didn't notice. She just talked. Nadine dusted powder on her nose and forehead, brushed her hair and applied a little lipstick and patted Dilly on the shoulder on her way out. She swished past her own, newly acquired secretary, went into her office and closed the door. Immediately, she pushed a button to get her voice mail and leaned back in her chair when she heard his sonorous tone. The first time he'd called her. She wondered why he'd never called her before and whether that meant he cared for her.

"You're wonderful, and I love being with you. See you at five." Nothing else. Not even their names. She could listen to his voice forever. But she had to work, so she punched numbers on the new combination lock she'd put on her desk, took out her plans and started to draw some bedroom chairs that she wanted to have made for her model home. To curve the arms, or angle them; she sketched them both ways, but couldn't decide. *I'll see what Wade thinks,* she told herself, then wondered why that thought had come to her. *Because you know he's clever,* an inner voice said. She argued the wisdom of discussing it with him rather than with one of her professional colleagues. He won.

Her secretary announced Rodney Ames, who entered without her having asked him to and seated himself without an invitation. She didn't correct him, because she wanted him to state his business and leave.

"The whole floor is buzzing about your brazen little caper," he began, and she knew he was seeking balm for the latest wounds that Wade had inflicted on his pride. She leaned back in her chair and eyed him steadily, giving him a warning that he ignored.

"When did you start dating your chauffeur, Nadine? How do you think Norman would take that?" Nadine stopped herself just as she was about to put the pencil in her mouth. Rodney couldn't make her nervous, she reminded herself, because she had his number.

"Rodney, I really don't care about the boss's opinion of my personal life. If you'd like, I'll ask Wade to come up after work and talk with you. And if you run out of conversation, I can always drop in and bring up the little matter of the plans that disappeared from my desk. Now, if you'll excuse me, *I* at least have to work." She imagined that she'd made his leaving awkward, but she didn't look up from her desk to verify it.

Wade buckled Christopher's safety belt, checked the traffic and started back to Accord. The boy had bought writing paper, envelopes and a ballpoint pen. He'd kept his one other purchase a secret, though Wade suspected that it was something for Nadine. Nadine. He cared for her; he no longer questioned that, but what was he going to do about it? He knew nothing of her other than what he'd seen. Her intelligence, warmth, gentle sweetness, compassion, grace and, yes, passion. Wild passion. When he'd been a young turk, that would have been sufficient to tie him to a woman, but he'd been through the battlefield of marriage and the swamp of a bitter divorce; he had to know more.

"Christopher," he began, though he hardly expected a straight answer from the boy while the radio piped out Johnny Hodges' saxophone, "you used to ask me about the way Nadine wears her hair and why she puts her hand over her left ear. What happened? Did you speak to her about it?" When the boy didn't answer, he repeated the question, lowering the volume on the radio as he did so.

"What about it, son?"

"What about it, Wade? It's her hair, and she can wear it any way she wants to." He turned the volume back up and hummed along with the music, raising Wade's suspicions.

"All right. But I know you ask questions until your curiosity's satisfied, so let's admit that you know why she does it and that you don't intend to tell me. You're protective of her. Fine. I accept that. I even like it." Christopher's lack of comment was as much assurance as he needed that the two had talked about it and that a strong bond had developed between them.

The boy pretended to be engrossed in the jazz music. "Christopher, I want you to stop calling me by my first name. I am your father, and it's time you addressed me that way. I'm not giving you up, and I want you to remember that."

"Okay. Do you think we could stop at the farmer's market and get some chestnuts? Nadine said me and her could roast some under the grill this evening." A passing car diverted him.

"She and I, Christopher," Wade corrected.

"Okay. Gee whiz, Wade, would you look at that red corvette? Wow!"

Wade sighed deeply. He wished he knew what it would take or whether it was already too late.

He walked out on the back porch after dinner and watched the season's first snowfall. As a child, it had been his delight to roll in it, hide in it when he could and play games with his imaginary friends, the fairies and sprites that he welcomed from the surrounding woods. He gazed out at the silver-tipped pines that sparkled in the brilliant moonlight.

So beautiful that it threatened to spark a tide of melancholia. No wonder he had so readily become attached to these surroundings; they were in many ways similar to his paternal home in northern Michigan. He had to share the night's beauty, and he needed to share it with his son. He stepped back to the door and called him.

"Christopher, throw on your coat and come down here for a minute." He smiled at the sound of his son barrelling down the stairs, noise that warmed his heart; things weren't perfect with them, but they were together.

"What is it?" He watched as a look of wonder spread over the child's face. "Wow! Those clouds look like little people running around up there. Gee whiz, Wade, it's awesome!" He grasped his son's hand, his sense of oneness with him tearing at his heart. The child had seen exactly what he'd wanted him to see—the mystery of the night as he had known it when he was a boy. He couldn't resist the urge to hug his son close to him, and they stood that way for a long time. Then he knelt to Christopher's level, held his shoulders firmly and, in a voice so husky that he barely recognized it as his own, he told him, "I love you, son. I always have, and I will forever." He shook Christopher's shoulders gently. "Forever. Do you here me? *Forever!*"

Christopher's stare nearly unnerved him. In spite of the night's chill, perspiration beaded his forehead. He didn't know what reaction he'd hoped to get from his son, but none could have hurt more than the silence. With a light hug and a pat on the bottom, he admonished him. "Go back in and get into bed." Christopher lingered until Wade patted him again.

"Go on up, son. Good night." The boy turned quickly, grazed his father's cheek with the barest of kisses and ran inside. It was as though a shadow had vanished from his heart and a weight from his mind. He rubbed the spot idly and smiled ruefully. Wonder how long a man could get away with washing only one side of his face? His son had kissed him, the first kiss he'd ever had from his only child.

* * *

Nadine paced the floor of her basement office, the confines of which loomed like a prison, instead of the place where she had once happily practiced her craft. She didn't want to work, couldn't work; she wanted to go upstairs and find Wade, but that would be too easy. And she might regret it. She tried to come to terms with the fact that she loved Wade Malloy. She didn't try to talk herself out of it, or to diminish the depth and intensity of what she felt. She loved him. It was as simple as that. She turned off her computer, doused the lights and walked slowly up the stairs, all the while talking herself out of searching for Wade and giving herself to him.

"If you're not working tonight, Nadine, could you help me do my science project?" Christopher called down to her. She readily agreed, because third-grade science was definitely better than daydreaming, but she remembered Wade's crusade to win the boy's respect and affection.

"Honey, I'm bushed tonight, but I know your father would enjoy helping you, and he may be better at science than I am. Why don't you ask him?"

"He already went over my geography and my French with me, so I thought you could, you know, help me do my science." She understood then that he wanted attention from her, that he wasn't rejecting his father. She sat beside his desk and asked him to show her his work.

"Nadine, I don't really have to study." He hung his head and looked away from her before continuing in a tentative voice.

"Wade is going to get my leg fixed during the Christmas holidays. Do you think he could get your ear fixed, too? Then you could comb your hair away from your eyes. Could we ask Wade to get your ear fixed, Nadine? Could we, huh?"

"You didn't tell him about it, did you? You promised."

"Scout's honor. He asked, but I didn't answer him. If my leg's gonna be all right, I want your ear to be all right, too." She hugged him and enjoyed the feel of his arms around her, strong for one so young.

"I'll think about it and let you know," she told him, though she admitted to herself that she'd made an idle promise. "Now, hop in bed and go to sleep. It's late." He did, and she pulled the covers around him, paused and brushed his cheek with a kiss. She straightened up, and he smiled. *He's already got a mother,* a niggling voice reminded her.

Wade remained outside, drinking in the soundless night, thinking of Nadine. His first marriage hadn't been a bad one; it just hadn't had the strength to withstand his long and frequent absences on overseas jobs. He'd tried his best, and he supposed that Ellen had, too, but it hadn't been enough to keep them together. He didn't want to reminisce about the past, but if he stayed out there, that's what he'd do. He locked the outer screen door, went in the kitchen and gasped, flabbergasted at the sight of Nadine peering into the refrigerator, every line of her body revealed through a soft, pink silk gown and robe, a picture of feminine grace.

"Did you know I was out on that porch?" His own deep guttural sound warned him to rein in his passion.

Nadine looked up and saw him standing there. Wild and ready and wanting, and with the ravenous look of a man who had known only starvation in his whole life.

"Did you want me to see you looking like this? Did you?" She couldn't move, and she hoped he was out of control, because then she wouldn't have to decide.

"I...I don't know. I didn't think." Tendrils of fear, excitement and anticipation shot through her as he walked slowly toward her, his movements rhythmic, his gaze hypnotic. He stopped, spread his legs and extended his hands, causing blood to roar in her ears and her pulse to race while she stood glued to the floor, fighting her passion. He smiled and reached for her, and she sprang into his arms, grasped his head and wrapped her legs around him as he brought her to him, his kisses ravenous. In all her life, she'd never felt so free. So wild and so wanton. His lips moved over hers and she answered, surrendering to the fire that he built. She parted her lips, asking for more but, as though programmed to do so, he held her from him, his breaths deep and labored.

"Are we going to end this right here, or in your bed? Tell me. You're important to me, Nadine, and I don't want to make a mistake with you. I know you want me, but what are you asking of me right now? Do you want me now? *And can you live with it tomorrow?*"

Answering him wasn't easy. He was fully in control and forcing her to decide.

"I won't deny that I want to be with you and, if you hadn't slowed down, it would have happened. I don't know why you decided that you had to have my complete submission, but I suppose I should thank you for refusing to compromise."

He started to release her, but she held on. If he moved away, she'd have to look him in the eye, and she wasn't ready for that. She marveled at his intuitiveness.

"How do you know that I would have regretted it?" she asked, looking over his shoulder and into vast loneliness, the place where she'd spent most of her adult life. "How did you know?" she repeated. He put her way from him then, though he did it with care.

"Because you haven't accepted me as a man. I'm still your chauffeur. You care for me, and you want me, but you wouldn't mind if that weren't true. You'd just as soon I was someone else." She reached toward him involuntarily, but he didn't reciprocate.

"Wade… You're not just…" She couldn't finish the thought and had to watch helplessly as his face become a mass of bitterness.

"You don't know what I am to you, do you? Or maybe you know, and you don't like it. I am your chauffeur, Nadine. I'm the man you pay to drive you to and from work every day and to protect you here at night. And if you can't acknowledge your feelings for me, your hired chauffeur, where does that leave us? I am not going to quit this job just so you'll feel comfortable making love with me, much as I want it."

She didn't want him to see how vulnerable she was, to know that his words ripped her inside. How could he say that when she loved him with all her heart? She had to grope for composure and turned away to shield herself from his knowing eyes.

"Nadine. Sweetheart. Ah, baby, come here to me. I wouldn't hurt you for anything. Come, honey." They held each other gently until he stirred against her and, with a rueful smile, put her at arm's length.

"I think I've set some kind of record for self-control since I met you, lady." His gaze pierced her. "If it's too much for you, I'll leave."

Idly, she stroked his left biceps, impressed with the strength that its solidness implied.

"I thought we already settled that. What's changed since then?" From the way in which he eyed her, clearly disbelieving, one might have gotten the impression that she lacked some essentials.

"Nadine," he said in a mien that suggested he was having trouble whipping his patience into line, "after the way we went at each other a few minutes ago, do you honestly believe that we aren't going to become lovers? That's what's changed. We suspected it earlier. Now we know." She enjoyed the feel of his strong, gentle fingers as they squeezed her shoulders. "I think you ought to turn in." He smiled the radiant and loving smile that she loved so much, and then his face went rigid.

"If you need help to make it through the night, as the song goes, throw one of your shoes against the ceiling. I won't be asleep." He kissed her hard on the mouth and dashed upstairs. Her gaze followed him as he went; neither would she.

The next morning, Sunday, Nadine parked in front of Lorna's big, nineteenth-century, white frame house with its wraparound porch, metal mailbox beside the front door and oversize American flag that waved from a pole in the corner.

That flag had always peaked Nadine's interest; she'd finally attributed its presence to Lorna's passion for keeping up with the Joneses; both the black Joneses and the white Joneses.

"Thanks for the ride, Nadine. I thought I'd see Wade and Christopher at service with you this morning. And we're still wondering when you're going to bring your…that delicious, honey of a man out to the Saturday night bridge party? 'Course, poor Hugh Cliburn will just die if you do." Nadine reached across Lorna and opened the door, not happy with the turn of Lorna's one-track mind. The woman had attempted to link her with Hugh at their first meeting and seemed to have made getting them together her one mission.

"Lorna, I have never said a word to Hugh Cliburn, nor he to me. Two, I don't play bridge, and three, Wade Malloy isn't mine to take or bring. Now, please drop the talk about Wade and me. It's not helpful."

Lorna's tongue pulled air through her front teeth. "If you say so. But if you believe it, you ain't fooling nobody but yourself. Well, thanks for the ride." Nadine waved at her and drove off.

She changed into jeans, cowl-neck sweater and a heavy woolen sweater jacket, ate an apple and rushed outside for a look at the family of rabbits that she'd glimpsed through the kitchen window. The rabbits disappeared before she got outdoors, so she moseyed down to the creek, leaned against a tree and watched the water swirl and splash in its rush to mate with the Hudson river. Solitude no longer suited her; Christopher and Wade could leave her at any time, yet she couldn't suppress the forlorn feelings that beset her whenever she came home and found them absent. She'd known that they planned to complete their Christmas shopping that afternoon, but she still wasn't prepared for the empty house when she returned from church and couldn't imagine that she ever would be again. Wade. Where were they headed? For a long while, she gazed at her reflection in the rushing stream, wishing that she knew the outcome. He wanted her, but did he care for her?

* * *

She didn't know how long she sat on that log at the edge of the stream. The chill and dampness alerted her to the sparse snowflakes, and she walked to the back door and turned the knob, but met with resistance and realized that she'd locked herself out of her house. She would have taken refuge in the garage but, when she put her car there, she'd followed one of Wade's iron-clad rules never to leave that door unlocked. Hugging herself for warmth, she walked in the rapidly falling snow to her nearest neighbor, two blocks away, but got no response. She walked back past her house to the nearest one on her other side, but fear began to trickle through her: the entire neighborhood knew that when Mr. DeVanzio was at home on a Sunday afternoon, either he, his dog or both could be heard trying to reach high C. Nevertheless, she knocked on his door and satisfied herself that he wasn't there. Deciding against the three-mile trek to the crossroad, she trudged back home in the now heavy snow, shivering with cold and hunger, because she'd eaten only an apple for lunch. She huddled up beside the front door to shield herself as much as possible from the wind and snow and hoped that her prayers would be answered. Wade and Christopher found her there much later soaked and suffering from hypothermia.

"What the…? Nadine, why are you huddled up here? Don't you know…? You're locked out." He unlocked the front door, picked her up and carried her inside.

"Are you okay?" Panic curled his insides when she slumped against him. He looked down at Christopher's anxious, frightened face and tried to assure him that she wasn't in danger.

"She just got too cold, son. Put your things down there and run some warm water in her bathtub while I call the doctor." The boy scurried off to do as he'd been told. Wade pondered whether to undress her. Her clothes were wet, and he had to get her dry and warm, but did he have the right to take her clothes off her? Well, he'd better get her in that tub, so he had to take off her clothes, but he'd leave her bra and panties. He knew that the bath would make her uncomfortable, prickling her as though she lay on needles and pins, but her icy toes alarmed him.

He lifted her from the tub, still barely conscious, draped a bath towel around her and carried her back to bed, his gaze adoring her as she stirred and snuggled closer to his chest. His heart kicked over as her hair fell away from her face and he knew at last why she protected her left ear from human vision. He put her to bed and covered her carefully, then gazed down at her lovely bronze face, fully exposed to him without what he regarded as her "cockeyed" hairstyle. Though rough textured, shriveled and smaller than its mate, in his eyes, it did not detract from her beauty. He started out of her room, remembered that she still wore her wet underwear, reached beneath the cover and eased them from her body while the white satin comforter shielded her from his eyes.

The doctor's brief stay did little to ease his fears, for she still had not fully aroused.

"Wade, don't you want me to sing something to her?" Christopher begged. He'd kept the child out of her room, fearing that her semiconscious state would alarm him.

"Not yet, son. Maybe tomorrow she'll be able to enjoy it."

"Tomorrow? Okay. I won't go to school tomorrow, 'cause I have to stay with Nadine." Wade wondered what kind of stunt the boy was about to pull.

"And you think both of us have to stay?" he asked Christopher. He nearly laughed at the look of incredulity on his son's face.

"You're going to NYU to study for your exams so you can be a lawyer, and I'm going to look after Nadine." How had he lived apart from this wonderful child, this boy whose personality changed daily, who grew more like himself, it seemed, with each breath?

"She has a very high fever, son, and you may not be able to handle that. Let's wait until morning before we decide what to do. I'd better get us a sandwich or something."

When he went back to Nadine's room half an hour later, he noticed that her hair had been brushed over her left eye and looked around for further evidence that she had roused and gotten out of bed. He couldn't find any. Maybe she'd turned over and her hair had dropped down because she'd combed it that way so often. He remembered that he'd have to call her office in the morning. How was she going to complete her Rolling Hills Village plan by the deadline if he didn't help her? And if he did that, he'd have to unmask fully. He gazed out of the window at the thick white winter scene, shaking his head. When she learned it all, she'd probably never speak to him again. It was a chance he had to take.

He put a thermometer under Nadine's arm and waited. One hundred and four. He found a small white basin and filled it with a mixture of alcohol and ice water, sat on the edge of her bed and began to sponge her arms, neck, shoulders and face, pushing her hair away as he did so.

Her groans alerted him, and he leaned closer.

"Wade is so sexy...so..." He listened closely, but she didn't say more. He pulled the covers up around her neck, but she knocked them away. "Christopher, Wade is so nice... Try to call him daddy. Make him happy..."

Wade placed the basin on her night table and leaned over her.

"Why are you worried about Christopher and me?"

"You're a wonderful father, and I want him to love you." She turned over, restless, and he sat down and stroked her bare arm, confident that the fever was dropping and he'd soon have her back.

"You're wonderful, too. And sweet," he told her. She turned over again, and he took her hand. "You ever been in love?" He was invading her privacy now, but he wasn't going to dig for anything that she wouldn't want him to know about.

"Have you?" he whispered. The smile that caressed her face stunned him.

"I'm in love with you now, silly. Nadine Malloy. Does that sound right? That isn't my name." She turned over and pulled her fingers from his suddenly cold hands. He'd had a few surprises in his life, but none so breathtaking as this. And, he wanted it to be true. In her conscious mind, she might not think or feel any of those things, but her words had struck him like a violent blow to his solar plexus.

"What's the matter, Wade? Isn't she any better?" What a time for the child to burst in there?

"She's perspiring, and that means her fever is breaking. So, she's better," he said, watching the boy's furrowed brow, certain now that the child cared deeply for Nadine. Wade saw that she started to throw off the covers.

"Hot... It's so hot... Wade... Where is Wade?" Christopher huddled over her, gazing into her sleeping face. He had to get the boy out of the room, so he sent him to the kitchen for ice water. With Christopher out of the way, he got her gown from a hook on the bathroom door, quickly pulled it over her head and slipped her arms through it. The grown dropped no farther than her waist, but that would suffice. At least if she threw the covers off, she wouldn't expose her bare body to Christopher—or to him, for that matter. When the boy returned, Wade put a bit of the ice water in his palm and brushed it over her forehead. To his surprise, she stilled and a smile bloomed on her face.

"Wade? Christopher?" His pulse accelerated when she abruptly sat up and looked around her. Then she slipped back under the cover and went to sleep.

Suppose she *did* love him. He walked upstairs to his quarters, pensive. If she'd gone that far, she was not going to forgive him. And if she didn't, he was in for some rough times. He changed into casual clothes and went back downstairs. He could barely believe his eyes when he reached her door. She lay on her right side, and Christopher had crawled onto her bed and, kneeling beside her, brushed her hair so that it fell over her left eye and covered her left ear. So that was how it had happened. He ducked back outside the room and tiptoed away. Christopher had done that at least four times during the evening, protecting Nadine, because he knew she didn't want her ear exposed. How had the boy known, and for how long? His chest swelled with pride. The two had a secret, and the boy protected her when she was unable to do that for herself.

"Wade, she's awake." He sprinted up the hall to her room.

"How do you feel, Nadine?"

"How do I…" He reached out to her when she sat up abruptly, fearing that she still lacked full consciousness. She gazed from him to Christopher.

"What happened? Why are you…? Oh, dear." She slipped back under the cover, and he could see that she remembered having been locked out in the cold. It occurred to him, when he sat on the edge of her bed, that she might find that odd or even unacceptable. But they had attained a far greater degree of intimacy over the past six hours than she knew. He told her everything, except what she'd revealed in her delirium and that Christopher had tried to prevent his seeing her ear. She looked down and saw her nightgown, and he knew her next question.

"Did Lorna come over?" He looked her in the eye, and her sudden diffidence was evidence enough that she knew he'd undressed her.

"I didn't violate your privacy, Nadine."

"Then, how on earth did you…" He interrupted the question that she couldn't finish.

"I undressed you in bed with the covers over you."

"Oh!" He couldn't resist the urge to taunt her. "Oh" was all she could say? He'd been in a state of arousal for six hours, and all she could say was "Oh." If his grin was salacious, he didn't care.

"After what I went through to protect your virtue, don't tell me you'd rather I'd given myself the pleasure of a full-frontal view." He winked suggestively.

Christopher reminded them of his presence.

He went over and sat on the other side of Nadine's bed. "I could bring you some more ice water, Nadine." She took his hand and squeezed it.

"Thanks, I'm thirsty." She drank the water and Wade sent Christopher back to the kitchen to put the glass in the dishwasher. The minute the boy was out of sight, he leaned across the bed.

"Kiss me. I'm dying for the taste of you."

"Wade… What happened to make you like this?" He let his finger slide over the silky flesh of her arm, then pulled her to him.

"You scared the living hell out of me. *That's what happened.*"

By midweek, Nadine was out of bed, though confined to the house. She wrapped her heavy robe more tightly around her and sipped the hot lemon tea that Wade constantly forced on her. It might have been good for his mother, she thought sourly, but hers would have livened it up with a shot of rum. Bessie Carpenter had believed in a good hot toddy and a mustard poultice for colds. She could do without the poultice, but a little rum in that tea would do more than warm her. He walked in then with a bowl of tomato soup and two hard rolls.

"Lunch, madam." She blew her tender nose and took the tray.

"Thanks. I feel awful. You should be studying, not hanging around here looking after me." She sniffled and tasted the soup. "This isn't canned soup. Don't tell me you made it." He feigned humility.

"No way. I doctored it up. Nadine," he began, with all the spiritedness of a man facing the gallows, "you aren't going to have your model home ready by January tenth unless I help you. I'll take my bar exams on the twenty-eighth, and I'm ready for them. So let me help you. You doctor wants you to stay home until after Christmas, but if you haven't finished those plans by the end of the week, you're in trouble."

"How can you help me? I have to finish revising those plans…"

He knew that he could put it off no longer; he had to tell her. He hadn't committed a crime, but she'd have every right to believe that he'd been laughing at her all this time.

"I have some skills in this area, I…"

She set the tray of food on the floor and stared at him.

"I was hoping you'd run out of surprises. Now you're going to tell me you're an interior decorator." She supposed that her face had a forbidding look, for she'd never seen him so solemn, nor so lacking in self-possession. He put his hands in his back pockets and paced the floor, and she waited for his next words, knowing that they were going to cost him something, cost both of them something. He stopped pacing and hunkered down in front of her.

"Nadine, I'm an architectural engineer." As though trapped at a formidable precipice, he took a deep breath, let it out and continued, "I'm C. W. Malloy."

"What? You're *who?* You mean to tell me you had the nerve to take a chauffeur's job when all of these unemployed men needed the work? You've been having fun on me, haven't you?" She nearly lost her breath. C. W. Malloy. As a graduate student, she'd used his book on home design. She stared at him, stunned.

"I should have realized it. Christopher. Wade. But I didn't put them together. Who else could have promised Christopher to draw St. Patrick's Cathedral from memory? And origami. Why, that's a natural for you. Well, I don't accept your nice offer."

"You have to, Nadine. Who else is there? I doubt you can lift that big roll, and who's going to arrange the furnishings for you? I'm not after credits, if that's what's worrying you. Let me help."

"Of course you don't want credit for it—the great C. W.

Malloy would deign to decorate a model for a middle-class housing development? Would Prince Charles take his afternoon tea at Howard Johnson's? How old were you when you wrote that textbook on home design?"

"Twenty-six, and you're making too much of this."

She drew the robe more tightly around her, shivering. Why was she suddenly so cold? He stood and attempted to gather her to him, but she extended her right arm full length, palm facing him, fending him off the way NFL ball carriers blocked their would-be tacklers.

"Don't touch me! You've had your fun with me. Pretending to be a chauffeur didn't satisfy you—you had to play with me, had to prove that I'm susceptible to you. You had to toy with my hear…uh, with my emotions. I don't like you, C. W. Malloy, and if it wasn't for Christopher, you'd be leaving here this minute. I can drop garlic and parsley into canned tomato soup as well as you can." *I'm not going to cry,* she admonished herself. *I won't.*

"Go away and leave me alone," she told Wade, struggling to control her quivering lips. She looked up at him, towering over her five feet seven inches, his hard-muscled strength there if she needed it, his sensual charm beguiling her. She backed away and glared at him.

"If you think that all you have to do is open your arms, guess again. I've weathered bigger storms than you."

His eyebrow arched sharply upward. "If you want to be mad at me, okay. But don't cut off your nose just because you're tired of blowing it. I've never lied to you. You didn't ask what I'd done on my previous jobs, and I didn't tell. Be fair, Nadine. You needed a chauffeur, and I needed the job. If I don't help you meet your deadline, you'll forfeit that contract. So, let's put our personal feelings aside and do it."

"I don't want your help." She blew her nose again, and turned her back to him. "I feel so foolish." His strong right arm turned her to face him.

"You're saying that being in my arms, holding me and loving me, giving me what I needed and had never had humiliates you? You're ashamed of having held me and kissed me?" His face, the face that she loved, mirrored his pain and—yes, she had to admit it—his disappointment. "Whenever I've held you, Nadine, your response has been honest, but if you say you're ashamed of it, then I'm glad we didn't go further. Ellen was dissatisfied with our lifestyle, with the long separations, and she was honest about that, but she had no complaints about my behavior as a man. None. And neither do you." She faltered in her attempt to move away from him, and he held her, steadying her.

"I'm all right."

"No you're not. I'm going into Manhattan and will get whatever you need there. Then, let's get to work. By the way, the manager of Sky Hotels reported that Roger was a small potato in a much bigger scam. Seems he was so delighted to be recognized by the big shot engineers and decorators that he fell into a trap and couldn't get out of it. Your firm is now short one decorator." She couldn't help feeling sorry for Roger. He wanted so badly to be recognized as a genius at interior decorating, and now he'd ruined his reputation.

"I can revise the plans myself," she insisted, and sat down, her breathing heavy and her forehead damp with perspiration. He leaned over her, bracing his hands on either side of her chair, and she wondered whether he was imprisoning her or protecting her. His gentle but persuasive tone settled it.

"Honey, you can see that you're too weak to do much. I'm here to care for you. So let me." She wanted to punch him when he grinned and winked seductively. Beguiling her.

"Anyway," he went on, "I'll let you vent your hostility later." She hoped he got the message of her censuring look, but as though he hadn't seen it, he added, "When you're feeling better and we can both enjoy it."

"Don't hold your breath," she replied, reaching up and shaking his shoulders.

Try as she might to sustain her anger, she lost it all and

laughed aloud when he straightened up, furrowed his brow and exclaimed, "I never could figure out why women have to caress you when they're mad at you. Doesn't make a bit of sense to me. I'm going to reheat this soup."

He left for the kitchen, and she trudged back to bed. What choice did she have? If Rolling Hills Village didn't open on January tenth because she'd failed to deliver, she could write *finis* to her career. The governor had agreed to cut the gold ribbon at the front door, and he'd invited television cameramen to record the event. She crawled into bed. What had he done that was so bad? *C. W. Malloy!* She could hardly believe it, but she knew that it was he. And which was worse? To love her enigmatic chauffeur or to love a certified genius? Maybe he hadn't lied, and maybe she'd been so glad to find a man who seemed trustworthy that she hadn't questioned him closely, but he should have leveled with her when he started kissing her, driving her crazy, pulling at the roots of her soul. She turned over and pretended to be asleep.

"Here you are." He helped her to sit up and handed her the warmed soup. "I'm going to run down to Manhattan. What do you need?" She told him, and he wiped the tomato soup from her bottom lip with his handkerchief, leaned over and closed his mouth over hers.

"Things have changed between us, Nadine. Now that you know everything, I can mark my territory. I want you." He smiled, rubbed his lips softly over hers again and added, "I go after what I want." The jingling change and the sound of the Toreador tune zinging through his teeth as he left the house told her that, if a problem existed, it was hers, that he didn't have a care.

But Wade viewed it differently. It had been close; she'd been angry and on the verge of telling him to pack up. She still might do it. But more than Christopher's legal custody and well-being were at stake now, because he wasn't sure he wanted to leave her. Not then. Maybe never. He didn't know when he'd begun to care for her. Wanting her hadn't surprised him; he doubted that any normal man could live around such a woman and not want her. And he did. Sometimes he thought that if he didn't have her, he'd suffocate, but he wasn't a slave to it and he always shook it off; not that it was easy. Caring for her was another matter. When he'd found her huddled out there in the cold, he'd been upset and, later, when her temperature shot up to one hundred and four, he had prayed for the first time since Ellen had gone into labor with Christopher.

He spoke with her secretary, got what he needed from her office and headed back to Accord. On the way home, he had to stop to get Christopher, but he didn't relish meeting Lorna with her insinuations. She never said it, but what that women couldn't do with her eyes and the turn of her head! Biggest churchgoer in town, and he'd bet it never occurred to her to elevate her mind. She had decided that he was a stud, and got her vicarious thrills by attributing who knew what to Nadine and him. He knocked on her door.

"Come in, Wade. Christopher says Nadine's sick and only taking liquids, so if you'll just wait a few minutes, I'll fix some dinner for you all." Appalled, he grabbed the first idea that came to him and went with it.

"I appreciate that, Lorna, but I'll have to get going. I picked up Nadine's medicine and I'd better take it to her." Horror spread over the woman's face.

"She's sick enough for medicine? That's terrible." He could almost see her brain light up. "Can she keep anything in her stomach?"

Wade threw his head back and laughed. He knew he was about to upset her, but he didn't care. "I know you'll be disappointed to hear this, Lorna, but Nadine isn't pregnant and, to my knowledge, she has no reason to be." Her hangdog look warmed his spirit. "Christopher," he called, "get a move on." Christopher walked up to them holding six-year-old Greta's hand.

"Hi, Wade. Can Greta spend the night with me?"

"Can she…" Nonplussed, he looked skyward and silently inquired why kids didn't come with an encyclopedia on child rearing? Seven years old and already moonstruck.

"Christopher, have you forgotten that Nadine has the flu? You don't want to expose Greta to that." That settled the matter; Christopher was protective of the little girl.

He drove up to the house, turned toward the garage and stopped when the figure of a man dashed past the beam of his headlights. He swore. He couldn't leave Christopher and chase the man, and he had to get inside to Nadine. He turned to his son and told him what to do. The boy's speed astonished him. He followed carefully, opened the front door and locked it behind them. In one second, he stood in her sitting room trying to breathe normally, to pretend that he hadn't just been shaken to his core.

"How do you feel?"

"Better. I even ate all of that soup." He didn't care about that, only that she was unharmed. That she sat there smiling at him. Glad to see him. He had to touch her, to let his senses verify what his eyes beheld. He let his hand skim softly over her face, stroking from head to chin, and immediately he regretted doing it, for she jerked away. He pretended not to have noticed, but he swore he'd put an end to that charade. And soon.

He went up to his room, reported the incident to the sheriff and asked that he patrol the area. He still wasn't satisfied, but he couldn't reach the back of the house, because he didn't know where they were nor how many were out there. He busied himself preparing a meal of hamburgers, baked potatos, asparagus and green salad. Cookbooks had their uses, he decided; five consecutive dinners of spaghetti and meat sauce had ruined his taste for it. He ducked back into Nadine's sitting room, formerly the family room, saw that she wasn't there and glanced toward her bedroom. He couldn't believe his eyes. Christopher sat on the side of her bed brushing her hair away from her face.

"It looks better like this, Nadine, and I don't even see your ear. But if you want to, Wade will get it fixed. I know he will if you let me ask him. Please, Nadine. I'm going to the hospital the day after his exams, and you can go to. Can I ask him, Nadine, huh?" What had happened between them? And how had they developed this deep trust, this level of sharing that he hadn't been able to develop with either of them? He went back to the kitchen, but he didn't feel like cooking. And he knew why. The pain around his heart wasn't going to respond to medicine of any kind.

"Feel like going downstairs and working on those plans for a while? I got everything you asked me to bring from your office." She looked down at her hands, and he saw the unsteadiness of her fingers.

"You don't have to draw. Just describe it, and I'll sketch and color for you. I'm good at that, Nadine. Can you trust me with something precious to you just this once?" Her eyes widened as she looked up sharply, and he regretted adding what she could assume was an accusation.

"I don't need help, Wade." Her voice lacked even a modicum of conviction, and he hunkered down before her, searching for the words that would heal her wounded pride and draw her closer to him.

"Maybe you don't need my help, but I need to help you. I need to help you, Nadine." He extended his hand, and she took it. Three hours later, they had finished the top floor of the model home, and she phoned in her orders for fabrics and furnishings.

She faltered as she started to climb the steps that led from the basement to the first floor, but immediately she knew the comfort of his strong arm around her. She didn't have the strength to climb the steep steps, so she didn't protest when he lifted her into his arms, carried her to her room and lay her on her bed. She wondered at the steely determination that glit-

tered in his eyes, so unlike the sweet tenderness with which
he had just laid her in bed.

He leaned forward, and panic gnawed at her when his hands
went to both sides of her face, swept her hair back and caressed
both of her bare ears. Thoughts of her deformed ear and her
fear of its discovery vanished when his mouth covered hers in
an urgent demand for her total surrender. She clutched him for
support as wild tremors raced through her, alarming her and
soothing her, shaking her and steadying her, pitching her into
a cyclone of passion and need. Her parted lips asked for more,
and he gave more in a statement of healing love that rocked
her to the pit of her soul. Her five senses were full of him, and
her body seemed to absorb him—over her, around her, beneath
her and within her. When his sweet mouth moved to her left
ear, kissing, licking, nipping, cherishing and healing, surely
he could hear the wild pounding of her heart.

She brought her gaze to meet his when his finger tipped her
chin, and she reveled in a newfound sense of belonging as he
kissed her with his eyes.

"You're so beautiful, sweetheart. Beautiful all over, head to
foot and ear to ear. And you've no need to be ashamed of that
ear. The skin is a slight shade darker and the flesh is a little
bit rough, but—to my eyes—it's as beautiful as the other one.
Most people wouldn't look close enough to notice a difference.
So stop hiding behind your hair." She wanted to dissolve like
a vampire at sunrise.

"How long have you known?" He dragged a green leather
ottoman up to her chair and sat beside her.

"Known what? You mean about your ear? Ages. I suspected
it early on, then I saw it the day you got sick, and I couldn't
figure out what you were so obsessed about." He stretched out
his long legs and relaxed, leaning against her thigh. "I had a
genuine shock seeing my son sneak into your room when you
were delirious with fever and brush your hair over your ear
so that I wouldn't see it. He must have done that half a dozen

times, and I resented his having a closer relationship with you than with me, but I'm proud that he tried to protect you."

Nadine wondered if she could hide anything from the man. Or if there was anything left to hide. He'd undressed her, bathed her, fed her, made her bed and now, he was the only person alive other than Christopher who'd seen her ear. She felt his lips brush her cheek and realized that he drank her tears. She wanted to ask him if he loved her the way in which she desperately loved him, but her long habit of protecting herself against rejection stymied her. He suddenly wrapped his arms around her, laid his head against her belly and held her. Not speaking. She gazed into his face. Radiant. Peaceful. Quiet. Like the setting sun. She held him to her. He must love her. He *had* to.

The day before Christmas Eve, Nadine put on a brick-red, cowl-neck woolen shift, her favorite style, combed her hair the way in which she always wore it and worried about what Reginald Malloy would think of her. Wade hadn't said much about his father; she knew only that Christopher adored him. Her tension was interrupted by the harsh ring of the telephone, and she answered it, hoping that the call had nothing to do with Reginald's visit.

"Miss Carpenter, this is Sheriff McGranahan. We've got two fellows here that we caught prowling around your place a little while ago, right after Malloy left. Do you want to come down here, or do you want to send Malloy? He's the one who called me." Wade hadn't mentioned that to her, and she wondered what had happened that prompted him to alert the sheriff. She told the man that she preferred to wait until Wade returned. Why hadn't he told her? She went into the dining room to rearrange the flowers for the third time, glanced out of the window and paused. So there *had* been an incident. Sometime, while she'd been ill, Wade had installed floodlights in the back garden. She went to the front of the house to see whether he had put any there and got her first glimpse of Reginald Malloy as he came up the walk with Christopher tugging at his hand and

Wade on his other side. Wade opened the door with his key, and she met them there.

"How are you, Nadine?" Reginald greeted her. "You're exactly what I expected." She took his extended hand and enjoyed the security of his warm and strong handshake.

"I'm glad you could spend Christmas with us, Mr. Malloy. Come on in. It's wonderful to have you here." She knew she was babbling, but the man was off-putting. Whatever she'd expected, it wasn't this. At sixty, Reginald Malloy's face was unlined. He had barely a gray hair and was his son's equal in height and physique. And looks. "Wade, would you please put his things in here," she said, leading them to the guest room that she had been using for her bedroom. Wade's surprised look must have been obvious to his father, for he asked whether he was inconveniencing her.

"I want you to be happy while you're with us, so you're to sleep in this guest room."

"Where're you going to sleep, Nadine?" Christopher asked, his face shrouded in worry.

"Darling, the sofa in my office opens into a full-size bed. I'll be very comfortable." She picked up the man's suitcase and walked toward the room. Wade dashed after her and attempted to take it.

"You don't have to do this." She held on to the bag, her chin up in defiance, and Reginald Malloy laughed a deep hearty laugh.

"I can see that I'm going to enjoy my stay, Nadine." He looked down at Christopher. "Who usually wins?"

"Nadine," the boy announced, proudly. "She always wins, Granddaddy. Wade loses all the time."

Reginald gazed at his grandson and shook his head. "Son, if I'm your granddaddy, Wade is your daddy. I've told you this before—if you can't call him Daddy, it doesn't make any sense to call me Granddaddy." Nadine knew even before she looked at Wade that his pain would be mirrored in his eyes. She hurt for him, but she didn't want Reginald's lecture, which

Christopher certainly needed, to cast a pall over their day. She took Reginald's and Christopher's hands and led them to the family room.

"Sit here while I get us something warm to drink."

Christopher jumped up. "I'll do it, Nadine. Let me help you. Wade said you're still sick."

She kissed his forehead and told him to stay with his grandfather. Alone with Wade in the kitchen, she told him of the sheriff's call.

"What do you think's going on?"

"I don't know," he replied, a bit idly she thought, "but I'd better get down there. Thanks for making my dad welcome. This will be the first Christmas we've spent together since before Ellen and I married. Dad always visited Christopher for the holidays, but I was never able to get home—I had to work." She yielded to her need to touch him and let her fingers stroke his arm.

"Look at me," he urged in a voice that was at once sultry and commanding. She did, and a gasp escaped her as she stared at the blaze of passion that his eyes had become.

"Wade!" His strong arms folded her to him, and his lips found hers in a gentle brush, a tender softness that brought moisture to her eyes. She wanted to hold on to the remnants of her anger at him for keeping his identity a secret, but how could she when he offered what she needed?

"I'd better go. Look after them until I get back." She nodded. He spoke a few words to his father and went out. She stood where he'd left her, thoroughly discombobulated. If he kissed her that way again without telling her what he felt, she'd…she'd… She'd what? *You'd kiss him back,* an inner voice taunted.

Nadine sat with Reginald and Christopher around the fire in her sitting room and ate hot roasted chestnuts.

"Can we save some for Wade? Can we, Nadine?" Christopher begged.

Reginald asked him, "Who did you say?"

Meekly, Christopher replied, "Daddy."

"It didn't kill you to say it, now did it?"

The boy hung his head. "No, sir, but Mother always called him Wade, so—"

Reginald interrupted. "Wade was your mother's husband, so she could call him Wade or whatever she liked, but he's *your* father. She was wrong in not teaching you to call him Dad. You know what's right. Do it."

"Yes, sir."

Reginald turned to Nadine. "I knew from the things Christopher wrote me about you that I'd like you. Tell me about yourself." She did, and he eyed her steadily as though sifting the information, making up his mind. His smile nearly duplicated Wade's, and it unsettled her.

"A man is fortunate to find a woman like you when he's already thirty-five years old. Fortunate indeed." She didn't answer, only smiled. If he'd found her, he hadn't favored her with the information, she noted, but she refrained from saying it. She should get something together for lunch, but she didn't feel up to it. She'd wait for Wade.

Wade returned and told her that the two suspects confessed to having been hired by one of her competitors for the Rolling Hills Village contract to get any plans that she had in her house. They hadn't found a way to get into the house, and they had been instructed not to hurt her. Twice, they had planned to force her to give them up when she arrived home after work, but she had thwarted their goal by driving off. She thought he seemed amused when he said the men complained that hiring him to chauffeur her had thrown a monkey wrench into their plans. Reginald Malloy jerked around and gaped at his son.

"She hired you to do *what?*" Their story elicited a mild exclamation from him. "Well, I'll be. Don't tell *me* that a leopard doesn't change its spots."

Tired after the early flight from northern Michigan, Reginald napped while Wade and Christopher went into the woods to find a tree, and Nadine took the opportunity to wrap her gifts and put them away and to retrieve the tree ornaments from their home in an old-fashioned barrel in which her family had stored them since her childhood. She was glad that she'd done her shopping early, on her lunch hour. What could she give Reginald? She searched through her treasures and found a pearl-handled fishing knife that had belonged to her father and decided that it would make the perfect gift.

Wade and Christopher brought home an eight-foot douglas fir. She tried to imagine Wade's joy in these little daily experiences with his son, but she knew that her perception of it fell far short of its meaning to this man who had turned his life around in order to gain custody of his son and for the sake of the child's love. He looked down at the boy and smiled broadly, and she saw the love in him. How he cherished that boy! A thought occurred to her, and she meant to ask him how and why he had let that situation develop. Surely, with his abilities and his reputation, he could have worked anywhere.

Reginald prepared his special dinner—baked pork chops, rice pilaf and green beans—while Nadine and Wade helped Christopher decorate the tree. The boy's infectious glee filled the house as they hung the ornaments that Nadine had treasured throughout her life. A fire crackled in the stone fireplace, and fresh pine boughs and holly that Wade clipped from Nadine's trees gave the house a festive air. Bayberry-scented potpourri perfumed the hallway, and gold-winged angels heralded the season as their light glowed in the windows. Suddenly, Christopher burst forth with "O, Holy Night," the song he'd sung at his school's Christmas pageant, and Nadine looked at Wade, praying that he would join the boy. But it was Reginald's stirring baritone that sent shivers up her arms as he walked into the room. She squatted on the floor next to the sofa and held her breath, waiting for Wade's wonderful bass baritone. The fire blazed, Christmas tree lights winked and the angels seemed literally to have taken wing. Maybe not, but her world had become unreal. A wonderland. Caught up in the wonder of the moment as Wade joined his father and son, her spirits soared, and she gazed at Wade with a confession of love shining in her eyes. He walked over to her and, without missing a note, sat down beside her and covered her hand with his own. She wanted to lean her head on his shoulder, but she didn't. She had told him, albeit silently, what she felt for him, and the next move was his.

They cleaned the kitchen after dinner, while Reginald read Christmas stories to his grandson. "Grandparents know how to keep children happy," Wade observed.

"They just fall short when it comes to discipline. Christopher is crazy about Dad, always has been, but Dad tolerates things that I won't stand for." To his surprise, she became solemn.

"Wade, I know it's none of my business, but how did you become estranged from Christopher? I mean, your name stands for something even among people who aren't in your field. Couldn't you have gotten a job here, or at least in the States? And how did you let it get completely out of hand like this?"

He put the tray of flatware in the drawer and leaned against a cabinet. He disliked discussing himself with anyone, even when he knew it was necessary, and his reluctance to do so frustrated the people closest to him. Ellen had complained that she could never get inside of him, but he knew that was because they were together too seldom to form the kind of bond that true intimacy requires. From the blunt way in which Nadine had phrased that question, he realized that she, too, had a sense of frustration about him. Where to start?

"Nadine, I had my credentials as an architectural engineer before my twenty-second birthday, but I couldn't get a decent job anywhere. The big corporations weren't hiring young black men, smart or not, and especially not if they lacked experience. African-American companies weren't in need of help—

what they needed were contracts. I wrote a hundred letters, but to no avail. Finally, I got on a radio talk show that had a Houston audience, and a fellow named Magnus Cooper called me. He's part owner of a firm that had building contracts with governments of countries in sub-Saharan Africa and southeast Asia. Two years later, I was head of a division. I designed and built schools, hospitals, office buildings, you name it. When I wrote that textbook on home design, I had just built my first two private homes—as a thank-you—for two Nigerian men who had risked their careers to get me the building materials I needed for my work.

"By this time, I could have gotten a job anywhere, but when Magnus hired me, I signed a contract to stay with him at least until we completed his West African projects. I had to keep my word. If he hadn't taken a chance on me, I'd probably be a chauffeur for real. Ellen didn't like to travel, and she refused to live where she wasn't assured of an unfailing supply of electricity and pure water, and the thought of snakes, mosquitos and ten months of one hundred degree heat cooled her passion for me. I've never faulted her for it. I built us a home in Scarsdale, where she wanted to live, and I got there as often as I could." He looked at the hand that brushed his arm in understanding, and added, "It wasn't enough. She suffered three years of it, two of them after Christopher was born. Her story to the judge convinced him that I wouldn't provide a stable life for my son, and he gave her full custody. As soon as I'd fulfilled my contract with Magnus, I came back here to get my child. But what a legal morass! So I'm satisfying the requirements for stability—" he couldn't help grimacing "—and getting a law degree so I can fight my own battle. I've got my son with me now, and I intend to keep him."

He looked at her hair, still hiding one of the most beautiful brown eyes he'd ever seen. What would it take? Christopher couldn't bring himself to stop calling his father by his first name, and Nadine couldn't believe him when he told her that she was beautiful, ears and all. He supposed it was human nature to feel vulnerability, even the strong. He felt Nadine's hand tighten on his arm.

"I've misjudged you, Wade, and I'm sorry."

"But not so sorry that you've forgiven me for not having leveled with you in the beginning. You're still sore as all hell with me, but if you kissed me right now, you'd give off enough heat to roast a pig. How is that?" He had to suppress a grin at the sight of her quivering lower lip which didn't necessarily forecast tears, he realized, but annoyance, as well. That lip begged for his mouth.

"Did you ever watch a forest fire?" she asked. "Fire makes fire, and a burning tree lights the one nearest to it?"

"And?" In an unusual gesture of familiarity, she reached up, pinched his cheek and let her fingers trail down the side of his face. She must have seen his suddenly rampant desire in his eyes for she stepped away.

"You can get hotter than fire itself," she told him, "so what do you expect from me? I'm a normal woman, and I'm not one bit unhappy about it. Don't want to burn, don't start a fire."

He laughed. They hadn't done much teasing and bantering, and he enjoyed it. "That's your attitude? Well, baby, we can burn together all night, and I'll just be getting started. Trust me." Her surprise showed in her big round eyes and their expression of bewilderment, but she could hold her own, he discovered.

"You're kidding. I've always heard that a fellow blows his own horn when nobody else is willing to do it. 'Course, you're studying to be a lawyer, so that may excuse you. I doubt it, though."

"Are you challenging me?" he asked, eager for an excuse to crush her to him. But she didn't bite.

"Me? Not this time, said the fly to the spider." He noticed that she glanced toward the kitchen door, conscious of possible intrusion.

His deep baritone laugh could be heard all over the house. He didn't know why, but he felt good. Happiness welled up in him, and he wanted to love her, to share himself with her as never before with any woman. But he stopped himself from asking whether she loved him, as she'd confessed in her delirium, because that would give her the right to ask the same of him. And his priority was Christopher. He wouldn't even examine his feelings for her until he knew Christopher was his.

Christopher bounded into the room, his face shining with anticipation. "Can I have the drumstick, Nadine? I always get it when Mother has turkey. Can I, Nadine, huh?" She rested an arm around his shoulder, thinking how much he'd grown since she'd met him.

"Of course you may have it."

"I'm taking us all out to dinner Christmas day, son. You can have it only if it's available," Wade cautioned. The child's protruding lower lip reminded her of a habit she hadn't shed until she'd reached her teenage years.

"We're having dinner right here on Christmas Eve," she told them, adding that her housekeeper would shop and do the cooking.

"I thought she was sick," Wade said.

"She was, and she won't be back to work until the first of the year, but she called and said she'd get Christmas dinner for me. I'm glad, because I'd hate for Reginald to eat Christmas dinner in a restaurant." Christopher tugged at her arm.

"And I can have the drumstick?" She nodded. Tenacious. Like father like son.

At about five-thirty Christmas Eve afternoon, Wade took Christopher to see his mother.

"Christopher, darling. Oh, how you've grown in such a short time." The boy hugged his mother.

"I miss you," he said in words barely audible, as he glanced toward his mother's new husband.

"Oh, honey, I miss you, too. Terribly." Her tear-glistened eyes confirmed the truth of her words. Their warm reunion gave Wade a sense of gratification. Ellen's love for the boy had been his one unfailing source of happiness in his marriage to her. Every child needed a mother's love, and Ellen was a good, loving mother. But one look at Casey was enough. If he hadn't planned to get custody of his son, meeting Casey Richards would have pushed him to it. The man did not like Christopher, nor did the boy like him.

"I'm preparing to seek custody of Christopher," Wade told Ellen. Her genuine alarm was precisely what he'd expected, though one of Christopher's letters should have prepared her.

"Wade, please. I only wanted him to stay with you while I'm…I mean while we're getting adjusted. Then I want him back."

He had to struggle to contain the anger that unfurled within him when Casey pulled her into his arms and soothed, "Darling, it isn't as if he was a girl. Boys need to be with their fathers. You don't want him to grow up to be a patsy, do you?"

"But I thought you said…" Wade left them to their argument, satisfied that he'd have no difficulty gaining custody of his son. He supposed a man had a right to want his own children and not those of a previous husband. But if you loved the woman… He closed his mind to it, walked into the living room and gazed at the beautiful white artificial tree elegantly adorned with white angels and cherubs and shining silver bells. Times had changed. Ellen had always demanded the biggest green douglas fir that he could get into the house. He stayed until he could politely leave and, to his amazement, Christopher was ready to go. He gave his mother her CDs and sweater, and Ellen gave Wade a large parcel for their son. Christopher hugged and kissed her and skipped off without looking back. Wade smiled sadly as he buckled the boy's seat belt. None of himself remained in that house he'd built when he still hoped for his and Ellen's future together. Worse, he was no longer certain that he had ever loved her. They were constantly together in college, and their friends had expected them to marry. Christopher's voice came to him from a distance.

"Wade, how come she married Casey? He's the pits." Wade squelched a laugh. The boy had voiced his thoughts exactly.

"Beats me, son. Love's a funny thing. You can't explain it, you can't create it and you can't regulate it. It just *is*." He glanced down sharply at his son when the boy wiggled closer to him and rested a hand on his knee. He tried not to interpret the gesture as one of love, because if he let himself hope... He put his right arm around the child's shoulder and, if his life had been at stake, he wouldn't have been able to explain why he suddenly began to sing.

"Sing the 'Toreador Song,' Wade." He did, and Christopher joined him in a clear soprano. His mind wasn't on the song, though he sang it joyfully. His thoughts were of getting home to Nadine. He couldn't bear being away from her right then, unable to share with her the powerful emotion that boiled inside of him. Reality struck him with astounding force; he needed her. He had to get to her, to see her and to satisfy himself that he was important to her. Parking in the garage took too much time, so he stopped in front of the house, unbuckled Christopher, and opened the child's door. Why had he done that? The boy could open the door with ease.

As he walked rapidly up the walkway, Christopher caught him and grasped his hand. Wade stopped as though immobilized, touched by the spontaneity of the gesture. He squeezed the boy's hand and walked more slowly. Had his heartbeat run wild and his breathing become short ragged snorts because he'd see her soon? His hand paused above the doorknob; he'd left her little more than two hours earlier. He looked down into the inquiring eyes of his son. Did he see trust and warmth...maybe even... He couldn't let himself *think* the word. Right then, he wasn't sure that his world hadn't begun to spin off of its axis.

"Can't we go in, Wade?" Christopher inquired, a little tentatively, still holding his father's hand.

"Sure, son." They walked into the house, and Christopher ran to find his grandfather, but Wade had a curious feeling of abandonment, bereft because she wasn't here waiting for him. That didn't make sense but, right then, *nothing did.*

"Why are you standing out here?" Had her voice always been soft and husky, and had it always had this soothing effect on him?

"Why?" he repeated. Her smile sent his pulse into a trot. He'd been looking at her for months, but he'd swear she looked new, different. And not because of her dazzling red velvet shift with its rhinestone shoulder straps that matched her spike-heeled shoes. He wouldn't apologize for staring at her; she took his breath away.

She reached for his hand. "Come on. Christopher's getting dressed, and you ought to start. Your dad's ready."

"Oh, yes," he remembered, "Dad wants to go to candlelight service." But he only wanted to close off the world and lose himself in her. He corralled his thoughts, but he didn't intend to let many more hours pass before she was his.

"Where is he?" She told him, and he found his father in the family room, relaxed and well dressed.

"Could we have a word, son?" Reginald asked. Wade nodded and sat down, comfortable as always with his father.

"I've been trying to figure out what's wrong between you and Nadine."

"Well, I'm her chauffeur."

"Forget that nonsense," Reginald said, knocking the air with his hand in a gesture of impatience. "It's unimportant. Ellen is a good woman, but you weren't right for each other. Nadine is your soul mate. She brings you into line without even trying, and the heat between the two of you is so fierce it's almost embarrassing to a third person. Sometimes I feel I ought to leave the room. I like her, Wade. She's real people. Don't let her get away from you." He paused. "The problem is you're both too proud to open up and let your needs show. And you're so unsure of each other. Seems to me anybody could see that you care for each other." Wade didn't dispute that.

"She's been mad with me ever since you've been here."

"You don't say," Reginald drawled in disbelief. "I'd love to see you together when she's pleased with you." Wade glanced at his watch. Nadine was a stickler for punctuality, one of the things he admired about her, and she wouldn't want to arrive late for service. But he needed some answers.

"Dad, how were you sure that Mother was right for you? I think I married young hoping to find what you had. I loved being around you and Mother. Always loving. Always in the same groove. How did you know?"

"Same way you ought to know. She loved me, and I loved her. She didn't need me to rescue her or to take care of her. She just needed *me*. Want doesn't count for much, son. You can satisfy that in a couple of minutes. But need is another matter. Need and deep caring. I always wanted more for your mother than for myself, and I was happy when she was happy. What did Ellen say about Christopher?" Wade stretched out his long legs before the crackling fire, relishing the nearly rhapsodic feeling that washed over him. Sweet contentment. He knew what he wanted, and he'd get it.

"I'll get custody. I'm certain of that. Casey doesn't want Christopher around, and the boy doesn't like him. I don't say Casey is evil, I think he's unsure of himself and doesn't want to be reminded of me. I'll be generous with Ellen, because she's a good mother and she loves our son. If I have to spend every penny I've got, Christopher Malloy stays with me." Wade turned sharply as Christopher bounded into the room, dressed up, whistling the "Toreador Song" and jingling pocket change. He glanced at his father, who nodded in awareness; the boy had copied Wade's habit of jingling change in his right pants pocket.

"Wade, Nadine says everybody's going to leave you here."

"You, too?"

"Yeah…"

"Yes, sir," Reginald corrected.

"Yes, sir. I want to hear the singing."

* * *

Nadine stopped at the kitchen door, not wanting her red velvet dress and jacket to soak up the odor of onions, celery, sage and turkey that permeated the room. "We'll be back about seven-thirty," she told the housekeeper, "so you should be able to leave by ten. Wade or I will drive you home."

"No need for that. I drove myself." Nadine checked the dining room and went to the bottom of the stairs and called Wade.

"Hurry up, slowpoke. We have to be seated in twenty-six minutes." She stood there anxious to see what he'd wear and how he'd look now that he'd taken off his mask. *Down girl,* she warned herself. But she couldn't banish her blissful anticipation, couldn't expel the breath that hung in her throat. She had plans for him. Never again would she let him take her to the brink and leave her there. She loved him. She needed him. And it was time he knew it. She wasn't disappointed. Her lower lip dropped as a small gasp escaped her. Wade Malloy in a tuxedo to celebrate Christmas with her! He loped downstairs and stopped right in front of her. Her reaction to the startling elegance that accentuated his good looks must have been mirrored on her face, because he rubbed the tip of her nose and winked.

"Like what you see?" She opened her mouth to protest his effrontery, remembered her game plan and winked right back.

"Step out of line tonight, mister, and you'll get what you've been asking for." She surprised herself, not to mention Wade, whose eyes widened and eyebrows arched to a point. *Don't back down,* she told herself, shoring up her courage.

"I'll take that as an order, lady," he replied, his dark, husky tones sending shivers through her. She'd have been more sure of herself if he had smiled, but he didn't, and his mesmeric gaze made her feel as though she stood on quicksand. The scent of his cologne mingled with the odor of pine and bayberry, and she had to stifle the desire to caress his freshly shaved cheek, to lose herself in his masculine aura. She shook her head and grasped his hand.

"Let's go. We'll be late."

"But we'll be in plenty of time for what counts," she heard him mutter, and little darts of anticipation shot through her.

Nadine didn't question Wade's decision to drive them to the service in his Thunderbird, rather than her roomier Crown Victoria. She supposed he was telling her that he wasn't her chauffeur that evening, but her escort.

"Warm enough for you?" he asked, taking a woolen throw from the back of his seat and spreading it across her knees. "You're a knockout in that dress, but five feet of your five feet seven inches must be nearly frozen. Come over here." She moved a little closer, and he reached over and pulled her snug against him. "Isn't that better?" She noted the tease in his voice, but she didn't care. She was just where she wanted to be—as close to him as decency would allow, given that the gazes of his father and his son were probably glued to them.

She thought back to the year before when she'd been so lonely that she'd gone to Spain for the Christmas holiday rather than face being alone in her own home. Her fingers itched to touch him, but she told herself to be patient, to gauge his mood, to let him take the lead as he'd hinted he was ready to do. She closed her eyes, suffused with peace and contentment. Christopher's crystal clear "O Holy Night" was soon joined by the voices of his father and grandfather. She opened her eyes and looked at Christmas Eve. Gaily decorated trees adorned the windows of each house and, in many of the front gardens, a well-lit Santa and his reindeer greeted visitors and passersby. The stars overhead shone as brightly as any she'd ever seen, and a lovers' moon raced from behind a cloud to kiss her soul with its unearthly brilliance. She hadn't realized that she'd snuggled even closer to Wade until his fingers grasped hers, though only for a second.

They arrived at the little church with five minutes to spare. Christopher took her hand as they walked up the pavement to the front door, and winged angels with trumpets in hand greeted them as they entered. Hundreds of red poinsettias and unlit white candles adorned the altar and windows of the crowded little edifice, and silver stars dangled above the apse. Immediately, the angels marched to the altar, blowing their trumpets as the audience rose to sing "Hark! The Herald Angels Sing." Chills ploughed through her when Wade took her hand and held it in a firm grip. *I want to be a part of this family,* she thought, *because I've never been so happy in my life.* On the other side of her, Christopher, too, held her hand and earned a reprimand from his grandfather when he jingled his pocket change. Wade smiled. She couldn't imagine why, but it was a smile of joy, and it warmed her heart. The story of Christmas was interspersed with the classic songs of the season and when, finally, they sang "Silent Night," the candles were lit, the lights doused and the little church glowed in breathtaking beauty.

"Hugh, this is the Nadine Carpenter I've been telling you about," Lorna exclaimed, waylaying Nadine as she left the church. Lorna's lower lip dropped when she looked at Wade. "And this is her chauffeur. Nadine is getting to be quite a pillar of our little community, and I know you'll just love getting to know her."

Nadine looked at Wade and laughed. Another inch, and he'd burst. She acknowledged the introduction and added, "Mr. Cliburn, Mr. Malloy is my date this evening." She introduced Reginald, whom she noticed wore a smirk that she'd seen on Wade's face many times.

"I don't suppose you know anything about architectural engineers, but my son is C. W. Malloy, when he isn't chauffeuring Nadine." Nadine enjoyed seeing Hugh's eyes grow bigger; at least he was able to appreciate Wade's status. Reginald might as well have spoken Hindi to Lorna.

"I see you're busy now, but don't you forget," she admonished Nadine. "You come over Saturday night. Hugh's a good bridge player."

"In your dreams, Lorna," Wade told her as he took Nadine's

arm and walked off. She enjoyed Reginald's knowing chuckle. Several people walked away singing carols, and Christopher eyed them longingly.

"Let's go sing, Wade… I mean…" The boy hung his head shyly. "Can we go sing with them? Mother and me used to do that in Scarsdale."

"Mother and I," father and grandfather corrected simultaneously.

"Mother and I," the child repeated idly. Nadine nodded in agreement to Wade's unasked question, and they walked through the little town that blazed with lights, hummed with the tingle of bells and bustled with last-minute shoppers. They gathered more carolers as they went, stopping at homes decorated for the season to sing carols, greeting those who opened their doors. Cold moisture sprinkled her face, and she looked up to see that the moon and stars had disappeared, and snowflakes swirled around them.

"Perfect, isn't it?" he asked, with a new urgency that made her feel as though he wanted them to be as one, at least for the moment. She nodded, wondering about his enigmatic smile. Then he stepped closer, gazing into her eyes as though he had a thousand questions, but she only wanted to answer one.

"Let's go home," he murmured, looking around for Reginald and Christopher. Snow blanketed the car's windshield faster than the wipers could clean it off, and he drove slowly. She looked at his tapered fingers on the steering wheel and saw the strength there, and the power. Her gaze fixed on his strong, square jaw, and she silently promised him: *you don't stand a chance against what I'm planning for you.*

Nadine had decorated the table with red-and-green candles, holly and pine needles, a white linen cloth and napkins. Old-fashioned Christmas carols filled the air, and they stood at their chairs while Reginald said grace. She asked Wade to sit at the head of the table to carve the turkey. *This man is elegance personified when he wants to be,* she thought, watching him dismember the big bird and serve their plates with dispatch.

"Am I getting the drumstick?" Christopher asked. Assured that he was, he focused on his grandfather. "Can you stay until school opens?"

The elder Malloy leaned back in his chair and said, "I don't think so. Three adults can be a big crowd sometimes. Another couple of days, maybe." They finished the meal of oyster stew, roast turkey with sausage and wild rice stuffing, turnips, red cabbage with chestnuts, candied sweet potatoes and lemon meringue pie, the latter because it was Reginald's favorite.

"Time to open gifts," Wade announced, and they sat around the tree, aware of Christopher's sudden tenseness. The boy screamed with delight when his grandfather handed him a little golden retriever that had lived in the bathroom since his arrival. Inline skates from Nadine and a bicycle from his mother seemed to have flabbergasted him, a rarity, since the boy was never without words. He stared in amazement at the state-of-the-art Apple computer, a gift from his father.

"I'm never going to leave my room now. Wow!"

"How will you ride your bicycle or skate?" Reginald asked him.

"Wow" was all the boy seemed able to manage.

Nadine's gift to Wade was a silver ID bracelet on which were inscribed the words *To Wade, with love, Nadine.* With his eyes, he promised her his endless gratitude. Reginald's deep emotion was apparent when he opened her gift, her father's pearl-handled, stainless-steel-blade fishing knife.

"Your father's?" She nodded. "I'll cherish this, Nadine, just as I'll cherish you." He thanked Wade for the gold pocket watch and quipped, "I see you got the hands large enough for me to read when I'm eighty."

"Sure thing," Wade shot back. "Foresight beats hindsight any day." The two laughed, and she supposed that they were enjoying a family secret. They all looked at Wade. What had he given her? He looked at her and wrinkled his nose.

"It's way up there in the top of the tree. I'll get it after a while." She only saw tree ornaments near the top, but he wanted her to wait. She'd wait.

Christopher made a loud ceremony of clearing his throat. "Granddaddy, I'd like to give you my present now." He opened an envelope, removed a card and read. "Dear Granddaddy, I had bought you some tackle, but I took it back to the store 'cause you can buy that yourself. I thought I'd just write you and tell you it's always Christmas when you come to see me, and I'm very happy. I love you, Granddaddy. Merry Christmas. Christopher." He put the card back in the envelope and passed it to Reginald who rose and gripped the boy tightly in his arms.

"I love you, too, son. Merry Christmas."

"Dear Nadine," he read. "If I didn't have a mother, I'd want you to be my mother. Ever since you shared your secret with me, I haven't minded going to swimming class. The kids don't pay any attention to my leg, and they all want me to be on their team, because I'm a fast swimmer. Thanks for my gift. But all I wanted from you for Christmas is for you to pin up your hair. You're so pretty, and my father says you have beautiful eyes, but he can never see but one of them. Pin it up, please. Nobody will notice. I love you. Christopher." Nadine brushed furiously at her tears, unable to say more than thank you. He handed her two unwrapped hair combs.

Christopher walked over to Wade, stood before him and read, "Dear Daddy, I'm sorry I wrote you that stupid letter telling you I didn't want to stay with you. Mother said today that I can stay with you if I want to, and I want to. I told her that I'm not going to call you Wade anymore, 'cause you don't like it and Granddaddy and Nadine say it's not right. Anyway, you're my dad. I'll miss being with Mother, but she said you'd take me to see her anytime I want to go. So I guess it's us guys from now on. I love you, Dad. Merry Christmas. Christopher."

Wade dropped to one knee and embraced his child. "Merry

Christmas to you, too, son. Nothing you could have bought or made could mean as much to me as this letter, these words. You're my heart, Christopher, and I don't want you ever to forget it." The boy hugged him, and Wade ducked his head to hide his raw, seething emotions. He couldn't help looking toward Nadine. He had his son, but he wouldn't be complete unless he had her, as well. He blinked his eyes to make certain that he saw what he thought he saw. With unsteady hands and trembling lips, Nadine pulled her hair back and secured it with the combs Christopher had given her, exposing her face fully. He picked the boy up with one arm and rushed to her.

"You're more beautiful now than I've ever seen you. Lovely." Her luminous eyes showed misgivings, and he stroked her left ear. "No matter what you may think, to me, you're perfect."

Reginald yawned. "Christopher, we've had a long day, and you and I have to get you started on that computer tomorrow morning. So, say good night."

It was now or never. She didn't know what to say to him, how to approach him as he stood before her, the epitome of manhood, every woman's dream. He fastened his unwavering gaze on her, his raw self exposed. If he needed her, why didn't he say so? Desperate, she stood on tiptoe and brushed his mouth softly and quickly with her own. "Thanks for a wonderful family Christmas, Wade." She would have turned to leave had his eyes not become pools of heat. Sensuous heat. Exasperated by his silence and steady stare, and hungry for him, she commanded more sternly than she had intended, "Wade, for heaven's sake, say something!"

"When you were hot with fever and delirious, you told me you loved me. Those words sustained me while I fought for Christopher's love and laid plans to get custody. Did you mean it? Do you love me?" He hadn't told her how he felt, but her words tumbled out of her.

"Love you? Oh, yes, I love you with my whole being. I don't—" In one quick motion, she was cradled in his arms, and her words were lost in his kiss. She thrilled to the feel of his fingers on her bare shoulders and arms as they moved ceaselessly over her. So long. Years seemed to have passed since he'd held her and kissed her. Since she'd known the loving security of his strong arms. She held his head in both hands to increase the pressure of his kiss, but he wouldn't be forced. She gloried in the drugging euphoria that settled over her when he slid his lips from her chin to her collarbone. Her nipples tightened when his tongue roamed every crevice of her mouth, and a strange aching settled in her limbs when his feathered kisses whispered over her left ear and across her face. An odd, inner excitement took possession of her. Then his murmured words of praise for her beauty and courage uncaged her need, and she surrendered to her passion.

"Wade. Oh, Wade. Darling. My darling…" Hot tremors coursed through her as he picked something from the tree, took her hand and strode swiftly down the stairs to her temporary room. At its door, he stopped.

"If I go through the door, Nadine, we'll make love. Do you want that?" She nodded.

"I need to hear the words. You're precious to me, and I'll risk not having you for my own, but I won't chance hurting you." His galvanizing look held a poignant message of deep caring. She opened her arms to him.

"I need you, and I want to be with you." He took her hand, walked in with her and closed the door. She dropped her gaze, unable to look at him.

"What is it, sweetheart? Tell me. I don't want anything to stand between us. I've waited a long time for you, and I want all of you." He put an arm around her and tenderly stroked her face with the tips of his fingers. "What is it love?" She studied the carpet, brushed it with the tip of her right shoe and finally looked up at him.

"You might be disappointed. My total experience at this amounts to one miserable failure when I was eighteen." The strength of his arms was there, holding her, comforting her.

"What happened? Tell me."

"He seemed to lose all interest after he saw my ear. He said that wasn't so, but he cooled off. I haven't risked it since."

"Forget that ever happened. You were both children." His lips brushed that ear and lingered there. "Don't you know that you're beautiful? Lovely? I've never known a woman like you." He changed the mood. "This dress has been driving me nuts all evening. There's nothing to it." He let his right hand find its way into the top of her dress. Hot spirals danced through her body and settled in the core of her passion until, in frustration, she undulated against him.

"Wade. Wade, darling. Please… I…"

"All right, sweetheart, but don't chase it, just let it catch us." He asked if he could unzip her dress, and she nodded. It pooled around her feet, and he sprang to full readiness as only her red spaghetti-string panties, gartered stockings and shoes clothed her. At his gasp, she covered her breasts with her arms, but he removed them and stood feasting his eyes upon her. Her brown aureoles tightened beneath his sultry gaze, and she moved against him in a frenzy of frustration when he brought her to him and loved them with his warm, teasing lips. Impatient now, he tossed the bed covers aside and laid her there while he undressed. She closed her eyes at his nudity, and then opened one of them. He laughed, joined her in bed and, with the skill of a consummate lover, he brought her to fever pitch, caressing her, murmuring words of praise and adoring her until she begged for completion. Slowly and gently, he made them one, loving, teasing and cajoling until she hurtled into ecstasy.

Satisfied that he'd given her something wonderful, that he had loved her exquisitely, Wade surrendered to the awesome surge that shook him from the soles of his feet to the top of his head and knew a completeness that he had never dreamed possible. His heart pumped wildly in his chest and, in that explosive giving of himself, he knew there would never be another woman for him. Her deep short breaths told him that she hadn't surfaced from the consuming power of their lovemaking, and he leaned over her and kissed tears from her eyes.

"Are you all right, sweetheart?" Anxious that he hadn't hurt her, he urged, "Are you?" Her brilliant smile warmed his heart.

"It was wonderful. Oh, Wade, I'm so happy. I can't express how I feel."

"Try," he teased.

"Now, you really are full of yourself."

"I can't help it. I just got something rare and precious from you." He reached down and got the small parcel that he'd laid beside the bed. "I love you so much, Nadine. I don't know the words to tell you how I felt when you said you loved me. Loved me even though you thought I was a penniless chauffeur. I know that you love me for myself alone, as I love you, and I want to spend the rest of my life with you. You, Christopher and as many brothers and sisters as you're willing to give him. Will you marry me?"

"I want to," she answered, snuggling up from her place beneath him.

"What are you grinning about?"

"It's a riot, Wade. I made elaborate plans to seduce you tonight, and it wasn't even necessary." He meant for his stare to signify incredulity. How could she be so naive?

"You wasted your time, honey. I was seduced by the time I walked out of your office the day you hired me. We've got to talk tomorrow, but I want to level about one thing. I'm not anywhere near broke, and after I pass the bar, I'm setting up shop half a block from your office."

"You're giving up engineering for good?"

"We'll see how much of my time the law consumes."

"But you're at the pinnacle of your career. Won't you miss it?"

"No. I'll always have it. I'm in business with Magnus Cooper. Besides, architectural engineer is what I am, not *who* I am. My goal now is to be as good a lawyer as I am engineer. I need you in my life, Nadine. Take a chance on me?"

"I need you, too, Wade, and I've never thought that loving you was a gamble." He slipped his grandmother and mother's engagement ring on her finger.

"If you look on the inside of this ring, love, you'll see the date, XII.24.1912. By some odd coincidence, my father and his father before him got engaged on Christmas Eve. This Christmas Eve is extra special to me, because I'm following in their footsteps, because I have my son and because I have you. Love is the important thing in life, Nadine. And tonight, Christopher taught us all the meaning of Christmas—of all gifts, love is the most precious." He folded her in his embrace and loved her as he would for many Christmases to come.

* * * * *

To the Sparrow: I'll see you in the rapture someday.

Bryant McCray Jr., for being the best listener
and brother a sister could ever have.

Acknowledgments

Thank you to the Atlanta Historical Society
and the Herndon Home, which was the source of
inspiration for this novel. Alonzo Herndon contributed
greatly to African American culture,
and I am humbled by his great achievements.

WHISPER TO ME

Carmen Green

Chapter 1

"Daddy, did you look at my new list to Santa? I texted it to your phone this morning before I left for school."

Slightly perturbed at her father's preoccupation with his tie, seven-year-old Anika Hamilton stopped lolling in the center of his four-poster bed, propped up on her knees next to her twin and fixed him with a penetrating stare.

When he didn't immediately respond, she exchanged an anxious glance with her sister.

"Did you get mine, too?" piped Medina, in a nearly identical voice.

Cedric Hamilton glanced through the tri-paneled wall mirror from his dressing room, his gaze coming to rest on his two favorite women. The resemblance to their mother began and ended with their cinnamon coloring and brown eyes.

They bore the signature genes of the Hamilton ancestors with jet-black hair and dark, half-inch-long lashes.

Dimples like his graced their satiny cheeks, while their intelligent eyes stared back at him with feigned innocence.

He couldn't resist the smile that tugged at the corners of his mouth. Ah, he thought, the gang-up-on-Dad approach.

Familiar with that technique of persuasion, he stalled, adjusting his tilted bow tie. When they began to fidget, he still delayed answering, taking his time to select and slip into polished dress shoes. He glanced slyly at the girls, feeling their unspoken frustration.

Cedric pulled at the sleeves of the starched white tuxedo shirt and crossed thick navy carpet to the armoire outside of the dressing room.

"As a matter of fact," he said, hearing them inhale, "I did receive something." He wiggled his eyebrows mysteriously.

They embraced and giggled and rolled on the bed.

Cedric smiled, wishing he could be so free. But ever since his wife's death, securing their future had been his primary concern. The smile slowly faded from his wide mouth. Things were good now, he constantly had to remind himself. He could breathe without fear they'd end up on the streets where he'd come from.

Contemplating throwing off the stiff white shirt and crooked bow tie, Cedric started for the button at his collar, then stopped. Duty bellowed like a horn on a foggy night.

The benefit auction was his baby. He had to be there.

Resigning himself to his evening's fate, he gave the crooked tie a final pat and pressed the mahogany armoire door. It swung open easily.

Tenderly, he pulled a worn gray velvet box from the drawer. Lenora had given it to him nine years ago. Thinking of his wife, Cedric lifted his eyes heavenward. He knew she was watching over them, protecting the family she'd been snatched away from.

The lid creaked as he tilted it up, and he became aware that the girls' giggles had ceased. They now stood beside him.

"Are those the cuff bw—things Mom gave to you on your wedding day, Daddy?" Medina asked.

Cedric nodded, lifting the black-and-gold studs from the box. In order to keep their mother alive, he'd shared every memory with them. Except the most intimate. Those were safely tucked into a corner in his heart. Lately though, those memories had begun to grow fuzzy, distant.

Inquisitive eyes stared up at him. He finally answered.

"Links. Say it, Medina." Gingerly, he laid them in her palm as she rolled her tongue around in her mouth.

"Bw-bwinks," she stuttered, proud of her effort.

Cedric closed one eye, scratched his head and gave her a nod of encouragement. "Close, and yes, they are the exact ones. Who's going to help me put them on?"

"I will," the girls replied in unison.

Cedric sat on the edge of the raised bed, waiting as they jumped from the handmade footstool to sit beside him. His gaze slid from the stool to the dark mahogany furniture his wife had commissioned for them from her own designs.

It bespoke both their personalities in strength and firmness. Yet the hand-carved designs etched into the drawers and base were unique, complex. Looking at them reminded him of the love they'd shared.

Lately though, loneliness he'd felt only as a child had begun to creep in and steal his rare, private moments of peace. Those haunting childhood memories had ceased once he'd found love the first time. He believed he'd never be alone again.

Cedric stroked his chin, then dragged his hand down the front of his shirt, making sure it was straight. He wondered if he would ever find love a second time around.

Mentally, he pushed the thoughts away. So far no woman had been special enough to fit into his complicated world.

The demands of family and job were first and foremost, and that would never change. It wasn't likely he would find love again.

Cedric sighed, shrugging. Would be nice, though.

"Stay still, Daddy," Anika ordered.

"Sorry."

His gaze traveled over their bent heads, down their long

braided hair. He lifted his shoulders and was fixed with a serious glare from Medina.

"Quit shrugging. I'm aw-most done." He held his breath when Medina's tongue jutted out as she concentrated on fastening the link.

"*Lllll* links," he said, urging her to echo his pronunciation. Instead, Medina smiled adorably at him, dimples denting her cheek.

"You said it perfect. Very good, Daddy."

She bent over his wrist, her fingers intent on their mission, and he felt suitably put in his place. His mother's soft-spoken warning of pushing Medina too hard rang in his head. Difficult as it was for him, he tried to go easy on her. But he'd found out the hard way, life wasn't kind to those with weaknesses.

Anika's little hands pushed the air from his cheeks, making him turn toward her.

"Daddy, do you think Santa can bring all my presents on one sleigh and still fit everybody else's? My list is kind of long." She released his face and rested her hands on his shoulders.

"Wh-what?" Caught off guard, Cedric drew back, unsure he'd heard correctly.

"I think he should have one sleigh just for me," Anika said reasonably.

"Me, too," Medina added.

Anika rolled her eyes in her head. "Okay," she said reluctantly. "He could probably attach a small one to mine and put your stuff on back."

Cedric stared at her, stunned.

"Daddy," Anika went on, "Santa might have to make two trips to the North Pole because he won't be able to carry our things and everybody else's, too."

Anika held two fingers under his nose, forcing his eyes to cross as he looked down at them. "I need two life-size Barbie's, so they can be twins just like us. Two pair of roller blades, three pairs of gold earrings. I saw this carousel when I was in the mall with Grandma and it wasn't that expensive. It had a two, six, zero, zero, dot, zero, zero. Can you get that for me? It's not really a toy, so I don't think Santa will get it."

"Twenty-six hundred dollars," Medina offered as she straightened his cuff, giving his arm a final pat.

"I need..."

"Stop!" His tone commanded silence.

"But..."

"Enough, Anika!" Cedric held up his hands to ward off the completion of a list he feared would go on forever.

Cedric paced in front of them, wondering if these two gift-hungry children were his. He wagged his finger at them.

"Santa is not, I repeat, is not going to drive one sleigh just for your gifts. Have you two forgotten the real meaning of Christmas?" When they shook their heads, a small margin of relief flooded him.

"No, sir. It's Jesus's birthday," Medina said solemnly.

Cedric breathed a sigh of relief, grateful at least one of his reasonable children had returned.

"That's right. It's also the season to give." His voice softened, and he lifted their chins so he could look into their identical brown eyes. "Not just receive."

"Yes, sir," they echoed, resignation weighing down their tone.

A quick glance at his watch indicated the late hour. Hurrying to the dresser, he pocketed his wallet, keys and a few stray coins. "We need to talk, girls. Unfortunately, I have to get going. We'll have to do it tomorrow at breakfast."

"Are you going to make us bw-ueberry pancakes?" Medina clasped her hands together, a pleading look in her eyes.

More blackmail. Cedric did a mental check of pancake ingredients, then nodded. "I'll stop and pick up some blueberries before I come home."

He glanced at Anika. Her chin was thrust upward and her eyes gleamed with determination.

"Daddy, we give away dresses and toys all the time. Isn't that right, Medina? And sometimes you give away money to those kids. I know it's just a couple of dollars, but won't that count for us, too?"

Cedric executed a slow turn toward his eldest child by barely an hour and thought he might see a spoiled debutante in her place. The couple of dollars she referred to was a fifty-thousand-dollar college scholarship he gave every year in his wife's name to a graduating high school senior.

"Anika Michele!" His voice rang with warning. Cedric stopped. Blowing up at her wasn't the answer. Her words went deep, further than she could ever know.

"I said we would talk in the morning. Go tell Grandma Elaine I'm leaving. You, too, Medina."

When the girls quietly closed the door to his room, Cedric shrugged into his single-breasted, athletic-cut tuxedo jacket. One last look in the gold-rimmed, tri-paneled mirror revealed more than he expected.

For the first time in many years, he wasn't pleased with what he saw.

Chapter 2

"Iman, you aren't going to win the painting. Come on, I'm ready to go."

Iman Parrish linked arms with her sister, Aliyah, and dragged her into the crowd that filled the turn-of-the-century home.

"Don't leave yet, okay? I'm going to win." *If you believe, then you can achieve,* Iman told herself repeatedly.

"No, you're not. Have you forgotten this auction is to raise money?" Her sister looked at her with that "duh" expression on her face. "People are here to spend money for a good cause, not bargain. Your bid was so low, I could have bid against you and won."

Iman looked around at the guests. So what if the city's most prominent and wealthy were present? So what if most had enough money to make her bank account look like bread crumbs? So what? Nobody wanted a painting by an unknown child painter but her.

She stared at the painting and was grateful no one lingered near the table. It was perfect. And, she reasoned, it wasn't often she wanted something so bad.

Iman withdrew her arm from Aliyah's. "None of these people want it because the little boy isn't famous. Oh, shoot." Iman grabbed her sister's arm again. "Look at him."

They eyed a tall, dark-complexioned man as he moved close to study the picture of children playing.

From behind, it was obvious his clothes were tailored and expensive. She eased to the left to see him from the side. His generous smile wasn't entirely lost on her. Her belly clenched uncharacteristically.

Everything about him said "I'm rich."

Rich enough to outbid her.

To her dismay he stepped closer for a better look.

Iman's stomach jumped.

She had to stop him from bidding on her painting. Iman circled the table, approaching him head on. His dark eyes gleamed with appreciation. Her stomach plummeted. She'd seen that confident look before in other patrons' eyes.

She'd felt it, too—just before she'd placed her bid.

"He's picking up the pen," she whispered anxiously to her sister for no reason. The noise in the room was at conversational level.

"Told you," Aliyah knowingly replied. She tugged Iman's arm. "Come on. You lost."

Iman stared at the canvas her young friend had painted, longing for it. "I can't give up, Li. I promised Harold if he completed Kwanzaa class, I would buy one of his paintings. I want this one." She turned back to the man with the broad shoulders and long legs and smacked her lips into a determined line.

"He doesn't really want it. What would a good-looking man like that want with a picture of children?"

"Why don't you ask him why he wants it and explain why you have to have it?" Aliyah huffed impatiently.

"No."

"If that doesn't work, cry."

Iman drew in a breath of exasperation at her sister's suggestion.

"Bad joke." Aliyah shrugged, throwing up her hands. "Why don't you go say hi? Make pleasant conversation, use your feminine wiles, and he'll be putty in your hand."

Iman knew her sister was joking now. But she also recognized the devilish twist to Aliyah's brows and cringed. The matchmaker in her was rearing its ugly head.

She couldn't help considering the idea for a moment. The dark gentleman was something. Tall and broad across the shoulders, in a way she'd always found appealing in a man, his black hair cut close to his scalp, and the smoothness of his clean-shaven face made her hand itch to caress it. He studied the painting with one hand in his pocket, the other hanging at his side, an aura of casual intensity surrounding him.

Iman felt the overwhelming sensation of wanting to take her place by his side. She stepped back, shocked.

He had probably come with someone. Probably not looking for company. Probably unavailable.

"Nah," she said, as offhand as possible. "He's not my type."

Aliyah's expression echoed her disbelief, but she kept quiet. Instead, she pushed Iman ahead.

"Let's see if we can sneak a peek at Mr. Handsome's bid. Maybe you can beat it."

People filled the space between them, halting their progress. "Shoot," Iman exhaled in frustration when the lights began to flash.

"May I have everyone's attention?"

Reluctantly, she and Aliyah turned toward the aristocratic voice of the hostess.

"My name is Imogene Osborne, and I am the director here at Stone Manor. I'd like to thank each and every one of you for coming this evening to support the fight for a cure for children afflicted with the AIDS virus.

"We all know there is an answer but we need resources to find it. Benefits like this help bring us one step closer to saving a child's life." Iman applauded while sneaking another look at the table. Her gaze was drawn away from the painting to the man beside it. He acknowledged her with a nod of his head. Iman bared her teeth in a semblance of a smile and returned her attention to Imogene, who had clasped her hands together, gesturing with her index fingers pointed.

"Thank you for being so generous in your bids. It's for a good cause. While final bids are taken and the tallying completed, those of you with red tickets please convene in the west room to begin your tour of the house. Those with black, the east room, and those with green, remain here. Please respect the barriers protecting the rooms, and stay on the brown carpet. You will be notified after the tours are underway if you have won any of our auctioned items. Your tours will begin momentarily. Thank you for your support."

Applause rippled through the crowd and Iman turned back to the table. Her heart pounded. The collecting attendant picked up the book.

"Wait!" Pushing past a large woman in a red sequined dress and over the long wing-tipped shoe of her companion, Iman stumbled before she stood between the man and the attendant. A measure of satisfaction curled through her when Mr. Handsome, who'd been leaving the table turned and frowned. "Wait." She held up her hand to stop the attendant. "I want to place another bid."

"I'm sorry, ma'am. The bidding is closed." The attendant's sorrowful smile only made her want to plead. He moved to the next table leaving her to stare at his back. Aliyah walked up beside her.

"Did you catch him?"

"Yes. He said the bidding was closed."

Iman turned back to the man. "I was trying to catch the attendant," she offered, unable to hide her disappointment.

"I noticed." He stuck out his hand and she looked at long, strong fingers. "Cedric Hamilton. And you are?"

Her sister nudged her arm.

"Iman Parrish. Please excuse my manners," she said, grasping his hand. His warm touch made her shiver to the tips of her glittery shoes. She looked up and was captivated by caramel-brown eyes, but she couldn't hold back her wistful tone. "I really wanted that painting."

His name rang a bell of familiarity and Iman searched his face until she realized how she knew him. Cedric Hamilton was on the board of directors of Stone Manor. He was one of the main reasons why she was there.

An elbow shoved into her side made her look at her sister. "Sorry. This is my older sister, Aliyah Easterbrook. Cedric Hamilton."

"Do you have to tell everyone I'm your older sister?"

Iman ignored the testiness in Aliyah's voice. The handsome Cedric was having a strange effect on her. He extracted his hand from hers to take her sister's. Their shake was brief.

"Nice to meet you," she heard her sister say. "Hope to see you again. Good night."

Iman snapped out of the spell. "Wait, Li, where are you going?"

"Jerome will be back from Jacksonville tonight, so I thought I would slip into something more revealing and be home waiting."

Iman frowned at her sister's brazen announcement and gave her a disapproving look. "Li." Her face heated in embarrassment and she knew her nose was beginning to glow a faint red.

Cedric's laugh tickled her spine. "He's a very lucky man. I hope to see you again, too." When Iman turned a stunned expression to him, both he and Aliyah burst out laughing.

"Not like that." He touched Iman's arm, leaving a warm spot before sliding his hand in his pocket. "I meant socially… with her husband."

"I knew what you meant." Aliyah winked, encouraging Iman toward Cedric with a nod of her head.

Iman waited for her sister to stop grinning like a fool. "Aliyah, I'm not ready to go yet. Why don't you wait for me? You drove, remember?"

"Yes, I remember. Catch a cab, all right? I'm ready to go home. Good luck with the painting." She kissed Iman's cheek, then turned to Cedric and shook his hand.

"Good night, Cedric. Call me tomorrow, Iman."

Iman watched Aliyah's cream dress swish around her legs as she walked into the crowd that was headed toward the west room. Aliyah raised her hand to wave and Iman did, too, wishing her sister had stayed. At least with Aliyah there, she would have an opportunity to control her roiling emotions. The intensity of her physical attraction to Cedric startled her.

Iman turned back to him and looked up. The blend of shadows and firelight cast from behind him gave him a familiar yet larger-than-life presence.

"She's quite a lady. Is she always like that?"

In the warm light from the fireplace, his smooth, dark skin looked as delectable as Godiva chocolate. She fought the overwhelming urge to press her lips softly along the side of his face. Iman didn't know she had a thing for sideburns until she noticed Cedric's.

His questioning gaze broke her reverie.

"Always. Nothing Aliyah says surprises me anymore," she answered quickly, hoping her Rudolph nose wouldn't betray her. "Should you be getting back to your date?"

"I am my date this evening."

"Oh," Iman said. *Yes!* she thought. "And by day?" Talk about brazen. Aliyah must be rubbing off on her.

He regarded her with a long, penetrating stare. "I don't usually date myself. I'm single."

"Really?" she asked, watching the movements of his lips, wondering how they would feel touching her skin.

He nodded.

"How—" their gazes caught and held "—how nice."

"I think so."

Iman pivoted on her high heels trying to get her bearings. She wasn't quite sure how to handle the explosion of desire that burst within her. She focused on the guests who entered the room using them as an easy distraction.

The lights dimmed. Unable to stop herself, Iman looked at Cedric. Something flickered to life within the dark brown depths of his eyes. It reached into her and warmed her making the backs of her thighs tingle and her knees wobbly under her gray-and-white evening dress.

He moved close and his jacket scraped her fingers. Intimacy was more than she'd bargained for.

His husky voice whispered close to her cheek. "Have you toured Stone Manor before?"

"No, I haven't had the pleasure yet." Iman inhaled his cologne, the faint bouquet of wine on his breath and felt light-headed. She wanted to rest her cheek on his shoulder.

But her shoes were smart. They stayed rooted in place. His hand touched the small of her back and veered them away from the crowd to a door marked Private.

"Let me give you the grand tour. I'm an excellent guide." Iman found it difficult to say no. She nodded.

He opened the door allowing her to step through first. The hallway was long, narrow and dark. Iman turned back in time to see Cedric fumble with something in his hands.

Apprehension snaked through her and she berated her hasty decision to follow him. Board of directors or not, she didn't know him. She took a step back.

"I think I should go back."

Cedric took her hand and placed a long object in it. He pushed a button. Light spilled to the floor. Iman stared down. A flashlight. Luckily the darkness shielded her telltale nose and her guilty thoughts.

He pointed to the end of the hallway. "This is where the tour should actually begin. At the front door. Who ever heard of starting something in the middle?" His large hand closed around hers as he led her into the darkness, the round white circle their only guide. "There's nothing to be afraid of," he said softly. "I'll hold your hand the whole way."

As he led her from room to room, Iman listened intently to the history of the house and its occupants. She was most impressed with Cedric's knowledge of the antique European furnishings and the unique sculpturing carved into the foundation of each room by black craftsmen. He knew every detail, even down to the year the silk damask wallpaper was hung in the dining room.

"Every room has a balcony but this one was designed to overlook downtown Atlanta." His fingers threaded through hers, his voice soft. "Isn't it beautiful?"

"Spectacular." Lights twinkled in the darkness and from this far away, the city noise eluded them, allowing them to witness its quiet splendor undisturbed. Iman loved the powerful feeling that she and Cedric were on a private island. "It's so secluded. So private."

"Like an island made for two." He looked down at her. "I feel that each time I come here."

It pleased her that his thoughts ran along the same line as hers. The mood shifted as they drew closer against a cool wind. Involuntarily, she shivered as much from the cold as from the budding emotions that sprang within her tonight.

"How long did the son live here after his father and stepmother's death?"

"Another forty years. Mitchell owned several businesses, and followed in his father's footsteps in philanthropy. He's one of my role models."

"How so?"

Cedric walked to the other side of the wooden balcony. His shoulders were stiff and he jabbed his hands in his pocket. He seemed troubled as he gazed into the cloudless sky.

"I want to teach my children those kinds of values. Mitchell learned from his father to never let adversity stop his dreams.

His father was a slave, then opened a barber business in Atlanta and became a very wealthy man." His voice was awed. "Can you believe that?"

"It amazes me what people can overcome when they set their minds on a goal." Iman walked toward him.

"My girls are my pride and joy, but they're the most spoiled little people I've ever had the pleasure of meeting. I think their goal is to own the local toy store at seven years of age."

"Seven?" She shook her head, surprise making her eyebrows raise. "A precocious age. They must be a handful raising them alone."

"I'm fortunate to have both sets of grandparents to help whenever I need it. They help in the spoiling, too, though. The girls love it."

This time Iman smiled. "Girls are made for spoiling. Don't be too hard on them."

He shook his head, his forehead creasing with thought. "No, they're worse than spoiled, and tonight for the first time, I feel the way I'm raising them may be a mistake." He finally looked at her. "Do you have children?"

"Not yet. One day."

Another breeze blew, this time making them step back with its chilling force. Iman shivered again.

"I wasn't thinking. Come back inside. You must be freezing." Guiding her by her elbow, he led her through the door and unfastened his jacket. "Put this on until you warm up."

"Thank you." She wrapped the coal-black jacket around her shoulders, his body heat warming her. "I really should be going soon."

"What about the painting?" This time his eyes danced when he smiled.

Iman rolled her eyes. "You're trying to be funny, aren't you?" Cedric led the way back to the main area of the manor, a huge grin on his face. He left the flashlight in its original spot. "I'm sure my five-hundred-dollar bid was slammed the moment you picked up the pen. Take care of it. A good friend of mine painted it."

Iman reluctantly slid out of his coat, handing it back to him. Their scents mingled enticingly, and the loss of its weight made her feel fragile.

He failed at looking wounded. "You make me feel guilty for wanting the painting." Iman knew he was joking. He didn't look guilty. He looked edible.

The centers of his eyes were dark pools and Iman felt herself absorbed by the black depths. She wanted to caress the masculine lines on his face, feel the sandy texture of his jaw against her palm, rest her head on his strong, broad shoulder. Instead, she had to look up several inches from her above-average height to focus on his slightly crooked bow tie, Cedric's only outward imperfection.

Then their gazes locked. The house was now quiet, having been vacated by the other guests. Waiters quietly cleaned around them.

"I don't mean to make you feel bad. It's for a good cause." Iman stopped Cedric's fingers from drawing lazy circles on her arm. "Maybe if you win, you'll let me see it sometime. Right now, I need to get a taxi. It was an unexpected pleasure to meet you, Mr. Hamilton."

Iman squeezed his hand and hurried away, afraid if she stayed any longer, she would embarrass herself by stepping into an embrace he would break. She retrieved her cape, spoke to Imogene for a moment then looked over her shoulder before she called a cab.

No Cedric.

It was probably just as well. This Cinderella feeling had to be a warning. He probably was too good to be true.

Chapter 3

The outside of Stone Manor provided its namesake. Stacked stone walls installed in the early 1920s bordered the ground level of the house. Erosion made it necessary to relandscape the property, but the magnificent house had survived the years well. There remained the old Southern style that made the house an unofficial historical monument in downtown Atlanta.

Iman descended the stairs into the parking lot and checked for her cab. A car rolled to a stop in front of her.

"May I play a humble second to a yellow cab?"

Iman shifted on cold toes, bent down and stared at Cedric in the silver luxury car. The last car in the driveway pulled around them and Imogene Osborne waved good-night. There were no yellow cabs in sight. Heat wafted from the open window beckoning her. She wanted to get in, but held back.

"I should probably wait."

"I don't want to leave you out here. It's your choice."

A brisk breeze swept up her cape, the imitation fur collar doing nothing to protect her neck and head from the assaulting wind. She decided quickly. "If you insist."

Iman pulled the door handle and as elegantly as her stiff legs would allow, slid in. "I live near Piedmont Park. Were you really going to leave?"

His dimpled smile warmed her in places that hadn't felt heat in a long time. He turned the steering wheel and soon they were traveling down Martin Luther King Drive. "I saw your cab leave a long time ago while you were talking to Imogene. I was pretty sure I could convince you."

Iman nodded, remembering their brief chat. She fastened her seat belt and settled back in the luxurious leather.

"You didn't forget your purse, did you?"

Iman couldn't resist teasing. "Imogene told me you won my picture, now you want my money?"

"I wasn't asking because I want your money," he chuckled. "You're very funny. It's been a while since I've found anything to laugh about." He pumped the brakes as they turned the corner. Iman enjoyed the rumble of his laughter, and his eyes twinkled when he smiled.

"I didn't really think you were asking me for money."

"I'm glad to hear that. I asked out of habit. My girls are seven, and if we leave the house without their purses…" His brows furrowed in a pained expression. "There's hell to pay."

"You know all that tissue kept in those purses is very important," she teased. "What are their names?"

"Anika and Medina. Quite a combination."

"First grade, right?"

He regarded her from the corner of his eye. "Lucky guess."

Iman shook her head. "Experience. I worked with a group of seven-year-olds last summer in a reading program. I have a way with them."

He laughed. "You do, do you? My girls can change any person's mind about kids with their antics." He laughed to himself. "They're my life."

Iman studied him for a moment as they drove in silence. He seemed to have erected a barrier around himself with his pronouncement. A single father raising his daughters alone was something she didn't see very often, but if he handled them with the same smooth control he used to maneuver the car, they were probably just spoiled little daddy's girls.

She thought of the close relationship she'd had with her own father until his death several years ago. Being a daddy's girl was very special.

"I think they've spoiled you. You wear fatherhood well."

He blinked several times, surprised. "Thank you." Iman knew she'd caught him off guard with the compliment, but parents were rarely patted on the back for a job well done.

As the car slowed then stopped at the red light, Iman noticed women hovering over sidewalk grates for warmth.

White smoke fogged them, obscuring their faces, but it was obvious they would spend the cold November night on the street. Cedric leaned over to watch as a short person slipped out of a box. It horrified Iman to discover it was a young girl.

Iman couldn't drag her eyes away from the sight of the two homeless people, until she heard Cedric's voice in the phone. He gave the women's location and description and instructed the person to make sure they had a warm bed for the night if they wanted it.

She released a pent-up breath, and allowed the relief of Cedric's actions to wash over her. How she viewed him grew disproportionately to his average male size.

A hero, she thought, his chivalrous attitude touching her more than she thought possible. They pulled away from a green light and the image of an old and young woman fitting themselves into the box were left behind.

"What a life," Cedric murmured.

"Because of you, at least they won't freeze." Iman turned to look out the back window as the women grew smaller the farther away they drove. Eventually they disappeared, but the memory would forever be embedded in her mind.

She was a little taken aback at the harshness of his voice when he spoke. "There's nothing like being cold and not being able to do a damn thing about it."

The seat belt pulled across her chest and Iman adjusted it to a more comfortable position.

"Ever been cold?" His voice held more challenge than curiosity.

Controlled pain tightened the skin around his mouth. She sensed an underlying current of anger. It had something to do with the women they'd just seen. Iman reached out to comfort him. She answered cautiously, unsure of where it would lead. "I've been plenty cold. I grew up in Buffalo, New York."

He grimaced and patted her hand, as if to dismiss her response. "You were lucky. That was voluntary."

Iman remained quiet for a tense moment then asked, "Do you want to talk about it?"

"No." Cedric shut her out. She resisted the urge to try to soothe his troubles away. Iman withdrew her hand and watched the lights of cars passing on the other side of the street.

"I need to stop at the store before I take you home. Do you mind?"

"That's fine," she whispered.

Cedric turned the steering wheel and they entered the near deserted interstate. Fewer cars passed the farther they drove. The store had to be an out of the way place because there wasn't much open at this late hour in this direction, she thought.

Iman trusted the instincts that told her she was in good hands. Cedric Hamilton was known and well respected in the community. Besides, Imogene had spoken so highly of him tonight, the discussion had piqued her interest.

Iman settled back against the seat and let the smooth motion of the car calm her questions.

Finally, Cedric glanced at her, then returned his gaze to the road ahead of them. His voice was more relaxed when he spoke.

"How do you think the auction went tonight? We planned it with the hopes of raising money for AIDS research, but we also wanted to bring the needs of Stone Manor to the public's attention."

"Considering I lost my painting, I'm sure somebody," she exaggerated, "left happy."

"You can come see that painting anytime your heart desires." His fingers linked with hers and squeezed lightly. Tiny jets of sensation shot through her arm.

"Anyway, I thought it was a huge success. I was honored to meet the governor and the mayor. Even the police chief showed up. Imogene and the board really pulled out the stops on this. I know you're on the board of directors. How close is Stone Manor to being accepted as a historical site?"

His eyes narrowed thoughtfully. "The chairman of the historical society was there as well as several of the members. The board hopes to know something soon."

"Do you think tonight's event raised enough interest?" Iman asked. Stone Manor was too important to Atlanta history to be destroyed for lack of funds.

"Definitely." His voice rang with confidence. Cedric disengaged his hand from hers. As he wrestled with his tie, Iman watched. He looked immensely pleased with himself when he tossed it over his shoulder onto the backseat.

"Better?"

"Much." He grinned. "You want to—"

"No, thanks. I think I'll keep all my pieces on."

Their silence lengthened and Iman's thoughts gravitated back to the man beside her.

Cedric's work to save Stone Manor had brought him to her attention many months ago. Widely respected as a shrewd and powerful businessman, his fundraising abilities had saved the old home from the wrecker's ball.

Iman had been informed by chatty Imogene Osborne over lunch two weeks before that Cedric sat on the board of directors of several prestigious companies. She'd also reported that while Cedric Hamilton was a successful businessman, his personal life was a bit of mystery.

At the time, Iman had listened with polite indifference. Now, she had a strong need to know. She cast a sidelong gaze at her riding partner and enjoyed what she saw. His warm eyes and gorgeous lashes made her think of relaxing in a smooth Caribbean pool. His reassuring touch and easy manner also didn't jive with Imogene's veiled assessment.

There was nothing mysterious about the way she felt about Cedric. Her attraction was bold. And though she hadn't known him long, his work had been one of the reasons she'd accepted the offer to teach a class about Kwanzaa at the manor. Something clicked in her mind. Iman turned to look at him.

"I really admire the work you did last year to open Robinson Community Center. I'd heard about the private investors not coming through with the necessary funds. Aliyah and I wouldn't be teaching there now if you hadn't stepped in and raised the money."

He smiled appreciatively. "You were a natural choice because of your teaching experience." His voice was velvet soft. "Of course, had I known what I know now, there wouldn't have been any competition."

"And what do you know? I hope my qualifications set me above the other candidates."

He leaned toward her. In the faint light from the dashboard she saw the outline of his face and the firm set of his jaw. "There's no question about that. We had many offers to teach, but once Imogene reported to the board that she'd taken your class and how it changed her life, you were in." Iman felt relieved and proud.

While Imogene was chatty and a bit of a gossip, she and many of the board members had worked hard this past month to pass along the principles of Kwanzaa at Robinson Community Center.

Kwanzaa was meant to bring families and communities together to celebrate the "fruits" of their labor and to set new goals and make plans for the next year. Cedric had been an instrumental part of that successful team of people who made it all come together. She wondered if he knew what a great effect his deeds had had.

"There are a few more reasons," he said.

Her stomach fluttered when his lips curled in a seductive smile. Somehow she didn't think her master's degree had been what tipped the scales.

"What are they?"

"We have the same taste in art, you're beautiful, single and have a nose that glows. You were a shoo-in."

Iman touched the tip of her nose. Heat rushed to her cheeks. Soon she would look just like Rudolph.

She laughed. "So you've rounded out your résumé with comedian. I think somebody should keep his day job."

He hooted, laughing. "I think somebody should be nice to me, especially if said individual wants to see that painting ever again."

"I'm crushed you'd hold that over my head."

"I have to keep some leverage, don't I?"

"Tell me about your work at Dix."

"I'll tell you only on the condition that you tell me about Kwanzaa first. The other reason we decided to utilize Stone Manor's facilities for the classes was because of the overwhelming interest in the celebration. Refresh my memory. It sounds like something my daughters need."

Iman always enjoyed sharing the story of Kwanzaa's beginning.

"Dr. Maulana Karenga first celebrated the holiday in 1966. His intention was to give African-American people an opportunity to learn about their history and customs. Many of us fall into the commercialism trap that surrounds Christmas. We spend money we don't have and buy things we don't really need. Kwanzaa isn't like that."

"How is it different?" He frowned. "It's on the tail end of Christmas."

"It's based on the concept of a harvest festival that was

traditionally practiced throughout Africa. It brings communities, friends and family together to celebrate the 'fruits' of their labor and to give thanks to the Creator for their blessings. As a collective group, you evaluate your achievements and set goals for the year ahead."

He considered this a moment. "I've heard there are rules you follow during that week."

Iman shook her head. "Not rules. Principles, and it's not just that week. It's a lifelong commitment. We start on the twenty-sixth with Umoja. It means unity. Kujichagulia, self-determination. Ujima, collective work and responsibility. Ujamaa, cooperative economics. Nia, purpose. Kuumba, creativity, and Imani means faith. When you have all those factors working in harmony in your life, you're physically, morally and spiritually able to harvest success."

"It seems as if those principles are practiced by people everyday, anyway."

"They are to certain degrees. Kwanzaa is about incorporating all those principles into one celebration and governing your life by it."

"Do you have a favorite part of the celebration?"

Without hesitation she answered. "Kutoa majina."

"What's koo-too-a?"

Iman enunciated the words. "Koo-Tee-ah ma-JEEN-ah. It's the calling and remembering of ancestors and heroes. I always remember what a fighter my father was. He was a fireman. My dad was a hardworking, but gentle man. He was my hero." Cedric took her hand seeming to sense her vulnerability.

Iman blinked back the moisture that gathered in the corner of her eyes. It had been a long time since she'd felt emotional about her father passing. She held on to Cedric's hand and tried to catch a glimpse of the highway sign as they headed off the exit. The car wound up and around, seeming to go in an endless spiral. Dense bare branches tangled on the side of the road, visible only in brief glances. She glanced at the dash clock, surprised to discover they'd been riding over two hours.

Iman looked out the window at the restaurant that stood at the top of the mountain.

"Pardon my French, but where in the blazes are we?"

Cedric answered solemnly. "Lookout Mountain, Tennessee."

Chapter 4

"Do you do this often?" Iman asked after returning from the ladies' room, taking the seat beside him. A fresh application of red lipstick coated her lips, and he drew his gaze away from them to meet hers.

Cedric felt himself relax for the first time since they'd entered the restaurant. Her teasing smile lightened the load on his mind. "I promise." He held up his hand in a Boy Scout's honor salute. "I've never done this before. You're the first woman I've ever brought to Tennessee for a date."

"I'm thrilled at the honor." Her voice grew husky and her eyes shimmered seductively.

Over entrees of fried chicken, loaded potato skins and fried cheese sticks, Cedric took the opportunity to study Iman. Short, carefully styled curls accented her smooth nut-brown complexion. The dark warmth of her eyes was addicting, making him feel calm, at ease. Cedric resisted snuggling against the delicate curve of her slender neck and inhaling deeply of her. He just wanted to relax and enjoy her company.

She munched heartily on the chicken leg, oblivious to his visual examination. She finished and laid the bone on the extra plate. After she wiped her mouth with the cloth napkin she looked at him.

"You're not worried about your arteries, are you?"

Cedric waved his hand in a sometimes expression. "I like fried chicken. I know what doctors say about cholesterol. But the best chicken in Tennessee is served—" he poked the table with his finger "—right here."

"You didn't have to bring me to Tennessee to get fried chicken. My kitchen would have done nicely."

"Seriously?" His expression bordered on disbelief. "Don't tease me, Iman. I don't get good fried chicken everywhere, so you'd better be prepared for a visit if you're serious."

"I am. Call first," she teased. "I don't do 'to go' orders."

"What's your number?" He was pleased when she rattled off the numbers and started in on her meal again.

She didn't eat much fried food, Cedric assessed. Her figure was too nice and shapely in all the right places. He was relieved she hadn't slapped him for damn near kidnapping her and bringing her to Tennessee.

Hideaway Mountain Restaurant was one of his favorite places and without consciously thinking about it, he'd wanted to share one of his private places with her.

His gaze glided over her figure-hugging gray dress. She was quite beautiful. *Would she like my kids?*

Where had that thought come from? Cedric hurried to retrieve his clattering fork. The waiter rushed to replace it and scooted quietly away.

"Is something wrong with my dress?"

"Not at all," he said appreciatively. "I like your dress just fine." He scrambled for a graceful way out. "It's just that I would think you would be dressed more traditionally. More." He hesitated, not wanting to offend her.

She gave him a knowing look. "More African?"

"Well, yes. I suppose that's what I mean. I have to confess, I don't know much about the traditions." She wiped her mouth on her napkin again. Cedric couldn't explain his sense of regret at the gesture.

"I do dress traditionally on occasion. But that has nothing to do with Kwanzaa directly. I dress in traditional African clothes because I feel good in them. I think they accentuate the inner beauty of the person wearing them." She laid her fork on the table and looked him over in a way that set his pulse racing double-time.

"In fact, this evening I imagined you wearing the traditional clothing." She eyed him from head to toe. "You looked quite handsome."

"Were you checking me out?"

Iman looked away, controlling a grin that revealed even white teeth. Her long earrings hit against her jaw. "No, I wasn't."

"You're lying," he said and shoved a forkful of spicy rice in his mouth to hide a teasing smile.

"Not."

"I can tell, Iman."

"Who are you, Santa? You can tell whether I've been naughty or nice?"

Cedric groaned, crossing his index fingers in front of her. "Bad word. Tonight my daughter Anika asked me if Santa is going to make two trips to the North Pole because the first sleigh full of presents will be hers. She texted me an updated list this morning. She's sure she's getting that many."

"Is she?"

Her serious tone caught his attention. Cedric sat back in his chair. He rarely spoke of his girls. His mother and stepfather and Lenora's parents called him overprotective, but he didn't care. The girls were so important to him, in the past, he'd refused to share them.

Iman covered his hand. "Don't get quiet on me. I'm just asking if she has any reason to believe she's getting less than she thinks." Cedric looked down at her hand. It was soft and supporting in a way that if he weren't careful would have him spilling his guts.

He answered honestly. "No, she doesn't."

Iman resumed eating. "So, what are you going to do about it?"

"What?"

"Her theory that Santa will return to the North Pole after stopping at your place. Millions of children around the world will be disappointed if Santa gets too tired and doesn't get to deliver their presents."

Cedric felt a bubble of laughter build in his chest. He grinned sheepishly, leaned his head back and groaned. "That's crazy, isn't it? What am I going to do?"

"Can her mom talk to her?"

"Only to her spirit. My wife is dead."

"I'm sorry." Her gaze dropped to her plate. Cedric wiped his mouth and sipped his imported beer. "It happened during their birth. She began to hemorrhage, and the doctor couldn't stop it. She died two hours after Medina was born."

"I'm sorry," she said. An odd expression crossed her face. He wondered if she felt sorry for them. Cedric hurried to quell any such thoughts.

"Thank you. We've overcome it."

She smiled tenderly and his heart expanded. Cedric glanced at his watch, the late hour making him wish for once he could add more hours to the day. He signaled for the check and paid the bill. Iman said nothing when he left a large tip, but Cedric noticed her eyes widen.

They hurried against the chill to the car and with relief got inside. Its comfort enveloped them as they drove back toward Atlanta. "Where do you live again?" he asked.

Her smoky laughter tickled his ears and he couldn't help reciprocating with his own chuckle.

"Near Piedmont Park. I'll direct you once we get close."

He nodded. "This may sound like a silly question, but do you believe in Santa at all?"

"No," Iman said quietly. "I believe in Christmas. I celebrate the religious aspects of the holiday rather than the commercial." She grew thoughtful. "But if I had children, Santa would visit our home. Aliyah and I used to have so much fun watching the snow fall in Buffalo hoping we would catch a glimpse of ol' Saint Nick. It was a wonderful time in our lives. My children deserve that thrill."

Cedric remained quiet. He'd never had a tree. Santa never visited the leaking, one-room apartment he'd shared with his mother. He hadn't had a reason to believe. Not as a child. Only through his girls he was able to recapture those lost moments.

"Now that I've talked your ear off about what I do, tell me about your plans for the future at Dix."

Cedric launched into a discussion on his dreams of finding medicines that would aid in the irradication of diseases like sickle cell anemia, diabetes and AIDS. He was surprised at how easy Iman was to talk to, but soon they were admiring the twinkling lights that draped bare branches throughout her neighborhood. Cedric stopped in the driveway she indicated. He left the engine running, not wanting her to go inside. He realized the evening had been the best adult fun he'd had in a long time.

Over the gray fur collar of her cape, she turned to look at him. His chest tightened.

"Iman, I—

"Take my card." They spoke in unison.

"I don't—"

"Oh. You don't want it?" She fidgeted with the card, then dropped it. It fluttered to the floor.

"No—" Cedric shook his head. He bent to retrieve it, but she stopped him.

"I understand. I just thought…well…" Her brows furrowed and when she met his gaze, Cedric saw a flash of determination.

Iman held up her hands. "Cedric, I hardly ever give advice on raising children. But I've worked with kids and I know that

Kwanzaa teaches them responsibility, they learn to love and care for things, and they also learn how to earn them. Let me help you," she said softly.

He sank into her gaze. "Yes—"

Cedric stroked her bottom lip with his thumb. To his delight it quivered and she lightly caught it between her teeth, before letting go. Maybe he could let her know how much he wanted to see her again with his touch since his voice was failing him. His hand dropped to his side.

"I try to make class fun for them." She dampened her lips and went on. "You said yes, didn't you?" she whispered.

The shaking sigh of her whisper drove him wild inside. "I said yes."

Iman opened the door, the lights brightening the dark interior. "I'm sorry. You have to stop me sometimes. I can go on and on."

"Really," he said, a smile tugging at his mouth as he leaned closer. "I hadn't noticed."

Cedric lay in bed, head resting against his palms. He had been this way for over an hour since dropping Iman at home and picking up the blueberries for breakfast. Yet sleep hadn't come. The last few moments in the car with Iman replayed in his mind.

For an instant, he had been a tongue-tied kid again, and had blown his opportunity to ask her for another date.

Quickly, he flipped on the bedside light and hurried into his dressing room. Inside his tuxedo jacket pocket, Cedric found what he sought. Taking her business card back to bed with him, he crawled under the covers and stared at it.

Iman Y. Parrish. The scripted lettering looked whimsical and made him think of what a good sense of humor she had. Though easily embarrassed, she was charming.

At the bottom of the card were both her home and work numbers. He stared at them until they were etched in his memory. So there was hope for his last-minute loss of speech capabilities. At least he could call her.

When he'd leaned close before she'd gotten out of the car, instinct told him she was going to let him kiss her good-night.

Only her lips never touched his.

Cedric resisted kicking himself. Some kind of businessman he'd turned out to be. His job involved controlled predictions, near perfect assessments and precision. There was no margin for error. But those learned techniques had eluded him this evening.

In the darkness of the car, Iman had lifted his hand, maneuvered it over and around hers several times, then let it go. She was out of the car and into the house before he could react.

He hadn't caught on until it was too late. He hadn't even walked her to the door. Now, of course, he knew what she'd been doing.

She'd given him a soul shake.

"Can I pour the blueberries in now?"

Plastic high heels clomped against the floor as Anika headed toward them holding the cup of blueberries over her head. Cedric reached behind Medina to steady Anika's arm as she slid between them.

"Pour them in," he instructed, then let her arm go. He glanced toward her feet. "Must you wear those now?"

Keeping a watchful eye on Medina, who held the hand mixer precariously over the mixing bowl, he took hold of Anika's arm again and helped her to the chair. "Medina," his voice raised with warning.

"Yes?" they both answered.

"Be careful."

Cedric took one look around the kitchen and made a mental note to get an extra special Christmas gift for his housekeeper, Joan. How she did it every day, he would never know. From top to bottom, the kitchen was a mess. He dreaded cleaning it.

Medina took his moment of reflection to raise the mixer. Pancake batter spewed everywhere.

"Stop!" he barked.

The order came too late. Startled by his voice, Medina lost her balance and slipped backward. The mixer flew across the counter spitting batter as it twirled.

Cedric bit back a curse, grabbed the handle and pulled. "Sit down. Right now!"

The cord snapped from the wall and the kitchen fell into a stony silence. Cedric held the counter for support, counting to ten, then back to zero. The girls stared at him with worried expressions. Medina's chin quivered and her mouthed bowed.

"I'm sorry," he started, hoping to head off the inevitable. "I didn't mean to yell."

Cedric cringed when Medina let a loud wail rip, anyway.

"You screamed at me!" Sliding on heels that matched her sisters, Medina stomped to the kitchen door. He wondered for an instant if she would storm out, something he absolutely forbade.

"May I be excused?" she asked tearfully.

Cedric decided they both needed a moment to cool down. "Yes, go ahead."

Anika crossed her arms over her chest in a way that reminded him of himself when he was lecturing them.

"You should say you're sorry."

Cedric bit his tongue as he listened to his seven-year-old offer him advice. He looked at her inquisitively. Why was everything always Dad's fault? He braced his sticky hands on the counter. "I already apologized, Anika. But your sister is stubborn. She'll be back."

"You always say stubborn is good. Is it bad now?"

The sticky mixture on his hands made him want to eat his words. "No. It's just that you have to listen to learn. You girls have only been here for seven years. You don't know everything. I've been here thirty-two years, and I don't know everything."

Wisdom-filled eyes stared at him. "You know a lot, Daddy. Otherwise you couldn't have passed to the tenth grade." Anika patted him on the back and then stuck her finger in the mix. She licked it off while he wiped at the drying goo on the counter.

"Thank you, sweetie. That makes me feel better." He rubbed her back in return. "Do me a favor and go get your sister, please."

Cedric cooked as many pancakes as batter would allow while alone in the kitchen. When they returned, they wore their fuzzy bear slippers and had brushed their hair. The gesture was meant to appease him and it did. He hugged them both and waited while they quietly got their place mats and set the table.

"Daddy? It's okay if you lose your temper and ye-yeww, and make me cry sometimes."

Cedric had a fleeting flash of the future when the girls would have boyfriends and eventually husbands. He didn't want them to think any type of verbal abuse was all right. Silently, he damned his behavior.

Thick maple syrup oozed down the pancakes and onto the plate before he turned the bottle upright. He brought the plates to the table and sat down.

"Medina, it's not okay to yell and make you cry. I'm sorry."

"I forgive you, Daddy." Cedric felt worse when her forgiving gaze rested on him. Children were so innocent. So pure. She actually felt sorry for him for yelling at her.

There had been a lot of yelling when he was a child, but nothing was worse than the silence that remained once his father had left for good. He pushed that memory from his mind. It didn't matter now. No one could turn back the hands of time.

They said grace and began eating.

Iman's declaration of having a way with children flew into his mind. He immediately remembered his decision about

Kwanzaa. Cedric decided to broach the subject while they were eating.

"Girls, I thought it would be fun for us to learn about a celebration called Kwanzaa. It's Kiswahili, meaning 'first fruits.'"

"Why?" Anika asked between bites.

Cedric smoothed more thick syrup over his pancakes before he answered. "Because it teaches you about African-American culture and traditions." Iman's voice seemed to come from the air as it reminded him of the rich celebration he'd never explored.

"There are seven principles of the—" Cedric searched his mind for the word Iman had used last night "—Nguzo Saba. I can't explain it all, but I think we should give it a try."

Both girls shrugged, looking unconvinced.

"Where are we going to learn it? Television?" Anika's voice was hopeful.

Cedric cringed. That was his weakness, especially old black-and-white movies. He shook his head to her question. "I met someone, a woman named Ms. Parrish." Cedric enjoyed the way her name tripped off his tongue. "She teaches the class. She's a very nice lady."

The girls started snickering. "Daddy, you have this goofy wook on your face. Is she your girw-friend?"

Caught off guard at the question, he stuffed his mouth full of pancakes. His jaws worked and he tried to stop smiling. "She's not my girlfriend. She's just a very nice lady. So, what do you think?"

The girls consulted each other and Medina nodded, while Anika regarded him suspiciously.

"We still get our presents from Santa?"

"Yes. One has nothing to do with the other. But I'm going to warn you, Santa doesn't take kindly to greedy children. And I know for a fact that any act of selfishness will not be rewarded. I haven't mailed your lists yet, but I think if you cut them down to four items, Santa will be pleased."

Dumbfounded, they stared openmouthed at him. He chewed thoughtfully then wiped his mouth. "Maybe three items."

"No, four!" they practically sang. "May I be excused?"

Before he could properly answer, they dashed from the kitchen leaving a puff of flour in their wake.

Cedric smiled and withdrew Iman's card from his pocket. Suddenly kitchen duty didn't seem so bad, after all.

Chapter 5

"What did you do again?"

Iman sipped from an ancient teacup as Aliyah paced in front of her. Shaking her head, she lowered the cup and bent low over her old Singer sewing machine, completing the edging on the mkeke mat. The phone rang and her gaze snapped to it. She held her breath, hoping, but not wanting to get her hopes up. They deflated when Aliyah lowered the receiver and continued her tirade.

"Why couldn't you just ask him to take you out again, Iman? Have I taught you nothing about dating men?"

"I gave him my card. Well, almost," she muttered, remembering her fumbled attempt. "Anyway, that's how it's done these days. You've been out of the dating scene too long," Iman informed her sister knowingly. "People give each other cards and hope the other will call."

"Did he give you his?"

Iman bent her head over the machine, her foot leveling the presser foot. Fabric spilled from the back of the machine. "No."

"See. He was probably wondering what planet you were from," Aliyah scoffed. "He was probably wondering if you had dated anyone over eighteen recently. Only kids play games like that. Back in our day—"

"The man asked the woman out," Iman finished for her. She defended herself. "He must not have wanted me to have it because he didn't offer it."

"Well, after you gave him the soul shake, can you blame him?" Aliyah pounded her chest and gave her the Black Power fist. Iman burst out laughing.

"You're a fool. Don't we have another order you can prepare while you advise me on the finer points of dating? For which I might add you have no experience since you've been married this entire decade."

Aliyah gave her a sisterly kiss on the cheek and mussed her already destroyed hairdo.

"I just hoped you would get married before the next century begins."

"You're soo funny."

"Tell me really, was he nice?"

"He didn't scratch his butt once." Iman straightened at her sister's warning glance. She didn't want to tell Aliyah she hadn't slept a wink all night. *Correction,* she reminded herself. *All morning.* And it was broad daylight before she'd even closed her eyes. Once she had, every gesture and facial expression, every shrug and even the timber of his laughter replayed itself over and over in her mind.

"He was more than nice. Li, I've never met a more attentive man. He really listened. Usually, I yawn and sigh in that order when I'm out on a date because I'm bored to death listening to my date drone on and on about himself. Cedric wasn't like that. He asked about me and listened to my answers. Honey Child, I could get used to that." She shook herself from the cloud. "He's got to have faults. Nobody is that good and still single."

"It's possible. I hope he calls, Sugar Baby." They slipped easily back into the names they'd made up for each other so many years ago.

Iman lifted the mkeke mat from the machine and held it

carefully flat. The cardboard box lying on another worktable was half full of items needed to have a Kwanzaa feast.

"Aliyah, make yourself useful and give me the kinara. I already have the candles packaged, but I'm missing some things." Her sister brought the wooden candle holder that would hold three red, one black and three green candles.

"Let's go down the checklist." Aliyah glanced at the contents in the box. They positioned themselves assembly line style. "Do you have the Mazao fruits and vegetables, and the mkeke mat?"

"Got it," Iman nodded affirmatively.

"Zawadi gifts?'

Iman hurried to the shelves lining the back of the room and retrieved the forgotten examples of gifts. "Got it."

"Condoms?"

"What!"

"You should always be prepared," her sister said with a leering smile. "I'll drop some off this afternoon."

"I can handle my personal business, Aliyah. What's next on the list?"

"The phone," Aliyah said to the ringing interruption.

"Got it," Iman answered, relieved to change the subject. "Hello?"

"Iman Y. Parrish, please."

"This is—" She shivered in anticipation. She knew immediately who it was. After all, once she'd fallen asleep this morning, all she'd heard was his voice.

"This is Cedric Hamilton."

"Hi." Iman fanned herself with one of the "Addie" books her company suggested as a Zawadi gift. It had suddenly gotten hot in the office.

"What does the *Y* stand for?"

"Mmm?"

"The *Y* in your name."

"Yvette."

"Very nice." His voice deepened, and she swooned for Ali-yah, who left the room with a huge grin on her face. "Does anyone ever call you that?"

"No. My sister calls me… Never mind."

"What?" he coaxed.

"I'm not telling," Iman vowed. Hearing *Sugar Baby* off his lips seemed too intimate. It was a natural defense, she assured herself. They'd only known each other for such a short time. But that didn't explain why her attraction felt absolutely right.

"Don't tell me," his voice echoed in her ear. "I like uncovering secrets." The challenge came through the phone lines, leaving her ear heated and tingly.

"Well," she teased to ease her discomfort. "This is one you'll never hear from me."

He laughed and the hope that she would be able to complete any more work flew out the window. There were orders to fill, but Iman knew she wouldn't be able to focus. His laugh and the sound of his voice through the receiver would dominate her thoughts.

"I called to apologize," he said.

Disappointment ebbed through her veins, slowing her thundering heart. "You forgot to tell me you're engaged to be married, right?"

"No, that's not it."

"You're a wanted man and the police are at your door?"

He chuckled. "No, to both parts."

Her heart rate returned to its former drum roll pace.

"Well, then, what?"

"I meant to walk you to your door last night, but I was stunned by your—"

"Handshake," she finished for him. "It surprises people sometimes."

He cut off her nervous chattering. "I enjoyed your company and I want to see you again. Do you have plans for later today?"

Excitement rushed through her. "No. I don't have any specific plans. What did you have in mind?"

He chuckled deep in his throat. Iman's lower body warmed in response. She sat straight up in her chair.

"I thought we'd go skating. Dress casual and bring a change of clothes for dinner."

"Sounds like an adventure. I'll be ready. Cedric?"

"Yes?"

Iman blurted before she lost her nerve, "Thanks for calling. I'll see you later."

"Cedric, got a minute?"

"Sure, Ronald," Cedric said, while depositing the receiver into the cradle. He waved his vice president into his office. "Come on in. What's up?"

Ronald sat in the chair across from Cedric's before he answered.

"A representative from an organization called Retired Seniors of Georgia, or RSG, is requesting to see you. I've talked with the gentleman on several occasions, but I don't think what I've said is satisfactory anymore."

"What does he want?"

"He wants Dix to lower the prices on twelve medications that are predominantly used by the elderly. Here's the list."

Cedric's eyebrows quirked as he stared at the neatly typed medications. He whistled low. "Does he want the shirts off our backs, too?"

Ronald shrugged. "Eventually we're going to have to see him. He's threatening to picket if he doesn't get a meeting. He's here right now."

Cedric stood and buttoned his jacket. "Ask him in. Might as well deal with this now." Ronald rose from the chair and walked to the door. "Any kinks I should know about in the Blythe deal?"

"No, sir. Business as usual." Cedric nodded and the man left.

Patiently Cedric waited for Jack McClure, president of RSG, to stop speaking. The elderly man was soft-spoken, but had the eyes of an eagle. He seemed to sense whenever Cedric wanted to interrupt and would neatly thwart his objection with a pre-planned counterargument.

After fifteen more minutes of careful listening, Cedric tried to inconspicuously smooth frustration from his face. This was going on too long. "Mr. McClure," he cut in, "I understand your concerns, but from a business standpoint, I can't simply cut prices."

"Why? The cereal companies did it. You can do it."

"Yes, sir," Cedric said admiring the man's quickness. "But they're conglomerates. The levels in this company are far smaller, the profit margins are also. Really there is no comparison. I'm afraid Dix can't do what you're asking. Perhaps we can devise another program where seniors can go for blood pressure or diabetes checkups once a month."

The elderly man's smooth face broke into a smile.

"Appeasing will only get us so far without the proper medications. But, we'll take it. And a decrease in the drug prices, too." Jack extended his hand. He spoke before Cedric could object. "We may have lost round one, but, Mr. Hamilton, old folks are like pesky relatives. Everybody knows one, got one or gonna be one. We'll meet again."

Cedric shook the man's hand and saw him out.

Iman massaged her rear and watched with jealous envy as Cedric roller-skated with great ease toward her. It seemed as though she'd spent more time on her bottom than on her skates.

"I used to be good at this," she grumbled when he dug in his stopper and halted by her side.

"You told me." Cedric's patience was exhausting as he helped her up for the fifth time. "The next skate is couples only. That should stop you from running over those bothersome kids again."

"That's not funny." Yet, Iman couldn't help laughing. She swallowed a groan when she straightened from the hardwood floor and held on to Cedric's waist. Relieved to be standing, she let him guide her. He bracketed his arms around her on the carpeted waist-high wall, while watching the skating monitor clear children from the floor.

Her body moved before her brain could send out the stop order. She lifted her hand to his jaw, turned his face to her and kissed his lips.

For a suspended moment, Iman thought she'd made a mistake. "Oh, shoot," she murmured against Cedric's mouth.

The air was squeezed from her lungs. His arms tightened around her waist until her skates left the floor.

Her hesitation evaporated with his words. "Don't move. This is right." His lips covered hers gently, persuading them to accept him. Iman opened without hesitation, enjoying the silky feel of his tongue as it lit fires within her depths.

Suddenly she was floating, the strength of his chest never separating from hers. Iman wound her arms around his neck and broke the kiss, but not the bond that forged itself between them as they skated around the rink.

Skating had been a dream compared to horseback riding, Iman thought as she slid off the back of the powerful animal and walked as if it were still between her legs. Her aching bones were why it took Cedric nearly two weeks of daily dates and smooth talking to convince her to give riding a try.

The stable hand led the huge brown mare away to be rubbed down in the barn.

Iman sighed, glad to see the horse go.

She groaned uncomfortably. Her body was paying for every ounce of pleasure she derived this afternoon.

She glanced back at Cedric, who was dismounting. Fluid grace, she thought with a tinge of jealousy. She had all but fallen off the back of her horse.

Cedric stood beside his black mare offering it carrots and worshipful pats. His face was unmarred by strain as he played with the animal. He looked at home on the ranch. Iman rather liked it, too. She dragged her hands over her wind-blown face and shivered. They'd started early that morning, but now the temperature had begun to drop.

"Cedric, I'm freezing."

He left the horse in the care of another stable hand and squeezed her shoulder, dropping his hand to her waist.

"You're always cold," he said gently.

Iman let her hand rest on his and enjoyed the leisurely stroll back to the house and the secure feeling his solid chest provided. The unexpected invitation to spend the weekend with his family gave her a special feeling deep inside.

Iman gazed up at him and reveled in the wave of tenderness that washed over her. That Cinderella, swept-off-her-feet feeling claimed her again. Iman walked on more slowly. She had to admit Cedric got points for originality. She swung her arm around his back and hooked it into his belt loop.

He tightened his arm around her waist and looked down at her, warmth radiating from his eyes. "Sore?" he asked.

"Nah." Iman tried to cover her wince of pain with a smile. "These muscles are in great shape." They stopped and he looked down at her abnormally wide stance, and laughed.

"I can tell."

They resumed walking.

The girls and Elaine, Cedric's mother, greeted them at the porch. Anika jumped in front of Iman causing her to step back. Her body protested furiously.

"Miss Iman, did you like the horses?"

Iman tried to smile, but her face hurt from the cold air. Initially, she had trouble telling the girls apart, but she'd learned that Medina had a slight lisp, and the more she got to know them, it became easier to tell them apart.

She answered Anika's question. "Love them." Iman reached for the porch railing and groaned.

"Help her, girls," Elaine said, taking pity on her.

Iman smiled her thanks at Cedric's mom and accepted the girls' shoulders to rest her arms on.

"Elaine, you're a wonderful woman." Iman dragged herself through the screened porch door and into the large Afrocentric-decorated great room. She immediately plopped down on one of the overstuffed sofas and laid her head back.

"Son, you had a call from Ronald Eubanks. He said there's going to be a huff on the news. Something about a deal you made going through. He said turn it on at five o'clock. Channel eleven."

Iman lifted her head and turned to Cedric who stood just inside the door. He looked so handsome in his cowboy attire. Faded denim pants hugged his body in all the right places. The red flannel shirt, covering a black turtleneck, was drawn taut across his broad shoulders and flat stomach. As sore as her arms were, Iman lifted them to reach for Cedric, but under strenuous protest, lowered them.

She prided herself for not acting on her wicked thoughts. He'd been the perfect gentleman, holding her hand, kissing her cheek, even draping his arms around her waist occasionally. Their relationship was progressing but there were times she saw a raw hunger in him. It matched hers. She wondered how long it would be before they acted on it.

Their days and nights had been filled with family fun. Cedric never conducted business when they were together.

Now, stress lines marked his forehead. Iman silently cursed Ronald Eubanks for bothering him. Cedric glanced at his watch then at her. He strode into the room.

"Why don't you soak in a hot bath with some Epsom salts? After that, I promise you some private time."

Distractedly, he glanced at the desk he kept in a corner of the great room. "I need to find out what's going on."

"Sounds fine to me."

He offered her a hand up, and to her embarrassment, her bones cracked. The girls giggled.

"Be nice," he scolded them lovingly. Cedric walked her to the stairs and swatted her bottom gently before he walked off hand-in-hand with the girls.

Iman climbed into the hot water and soothing bath salts and sunk into the luxurious heat. Her rear still tingled where Cedric had playfully touched her.

She soaked until the water cooled then toweled herself, her muscles no longer protesting so stringently. Cedric was a patient man. He had allowed their relationship to grow steadily, and now it seemed he was placing it in her hands.

She stared at her reflection in the mirror and the comfortable navy sweat suit she'd just put on. Iman looked into her own eyes and knew she was ready. She wanted the relationship to move to another level.

What that was, though, was unclear.

The clock chimed five times and she walked on stiff legs back to the great room. She sat across from Cedric who had also showered and changed.

The newscaster's voice captured their attention. Iman gasped sharply when a none-too-flattering picture of Cedric flashed across the screen. It was made to resemble a mug shot.

"Another corporate hit man has struck. Cedric Hamilton of Dix Pharmaceuticals is a living Scrooge in the eyes of many Blythe Pharmaceutical employees. One hundred people got their pink slips today as they entered the building for work. Mr. Hamilton was reported to be vacationing with his family at his company's Helen, Georgia, ranch and was unavailable for comment."

Iman felt terrible for Cedric as they watched the newscaster interview an ex-employee. The woman called him insensitive, boorish and claimed his heart was dead.

Iman barely heard the rest of the report as the girls' bickering interrupted the announcer's words.

Cedric's mother asked, "Did you do the right thing, son?"

"I did what I had to do. It's business, Mom."

"I know, honey," she said loyally. "Come on," she said to the twins. "Let's go fix dinner."

Iman tried to forget the grimness of the announcer's voice, but couldn't. It permeated the air, thick as smoke, leaving her to wonder about the man she wanted to get to know better. Cedric worked hard, she told herself. Certainly he had a good reason to let so many people go—particularly right before the holidays.

Silence surrounded them. Cedric swiped his head with his hands and brought them down over his face. Tension radiated from him. "It's business."

The curt word bored into her as did his gaze, seeming to beg her to understand. He stretched out his hand to help her up. "Come on," he said roughly. "We're leaving. I need to be alone with you."

Iman waited while he held her coat. She shrugged into her short wool coat and winced only once as she wrapped his scarf around her neck.

"Shouldn't we tell your mother where we're going?"

Cedric gently took Iman's hand. Sounds of his mother and daughters discussing dinner filtered into the room.

"We'll be back," he called. He couldn't know how his words made her tingle.

In the fall, Helen, Georgia, was a place vibrant with color and blooms. Now, it was asleep, preparing for the spring buds to restore it to its eclectic luster.

The bare brown branches seemed to float by as they drove unhurried through the quiet town, neither sharing their thoughts.

Cedric turned on the radio of the ranch's pickup truck, flipped around the dial then turned it off again.

"Corporate hit man! Ridiculous," he muttered. "They didn't

bother to mention that one hundred other employees still have their jobs."

"Why right before Christmas? Surely you can understand how the employees must feel." When he continued to scowl, Iman spoke in a measured, careful tone. "Would it have hurt the company to wait until after the new year?"

Cedric turned off the main highway onto a dirt path. It stretched endlessly ahead. Iman slid her arms out of her coat and stored it behind the seat.

"Is it ever a good time to lose your job?" He drummed his thumbs against the steering wheel as the car continued to roll over the hard, bumpy road. "Should I have let those parents buy gifts they couldn't afford? I guess you think it would have been better to do it after the new year, after everyone had gone into debt buying things they don't need."

He came to a stop in the clearing and Cedric eased the gearshift into Park, letting the truck idle. He turned to look at her and his eyes sparkled with smoldering anger.

"Would it have been better to keep everybody on and in six months when I couldn't meet payroll, lay everybody off?"

Iman shook her head wanting to ease his frustration. This wasn't how she'd hoped to spend their first moments alone.

"No. You have to do what's best for everyone. I realize I work far from the corporate world, but I'm guessing that the timing could have been handled differently."

Iman stroked his stubbled cheek to soften the directness of her words. When he closed his eyes, she bathed him with her touch. She drew her index finger lightly over his forehead, down his nose and around to his cheek.

He looked so tired.

Cedric's chest filled then sank as he exhaled. "I tried to keep the people who would best help both companies. We offered early retirement, and severance pay. Those that stayed, took a risk." He finally looked at her. "There wasn't much more we could do."

"Don't think about it now," she whispered. "Where is that happy man who rode his horse today like a champion?"

He captured her hand in his. "You're so beautiful."

Iman felt the familiar flush rush through her cheeks. Cedric leaned over to kiss her nose. His arms were around her. His mouth settled roughly against hers demanding a response. Iman's banked desire unleashed and met his fevered passion, but she yelped in surprise when Cedric brought her to him.

"Seat belt," she muttered. His fingers grappled with the release, freeing her. He pulled her until she straddled his lap.

Iman groaned as much from the ache of her sore muscles as she did from the pleasure of feeling the thick bulge of desire curving from Cedric's pants and pressing into her. He drank of her mouth, the trail of kisses on her neck burning silent promises into her flesh.

Iman sighed against his lips when he gently kneaded her thighs. He lessened the pressure to a caress.

"Still sore from skating?"

"And horseback riding," she breathed heavily.

He whispered in her ear, "Lean on me." Moving his hands up her thighs, he trailed a path to her back. Iman rested her cheek on his shoulder, her lips a breath away from his neck.

She closed her eyes, languishing in his touch.

His callused hands massaged the sore tissues, eliciting a contented moan from her. His fingers slid down her sides, then around her back to the waist of the sweatpants. He took hold of her bottom, kneading it into complacency. It felt so good.

Cedric then dragged the sweatshirt over her head. He unfastened her bra and it fell away, making her gasp at the exposure. Their gazes met briefly, before he decided which of the twin peaks to taste first. Iman arched toward Cedric's mouth when his eager tongue lapped at the right. He came up for air to nuzzle at her chin. "You're beautiful, and you taste good."

Iman chanced a look at Cedric's tongue when he went back

to stroking her erect nipple. "Mmm" was all she could manage, when he claimed the other one.

Masterfully, he tasted her until she dissolved into a helpless, quivering mass on his lap. His mouth sapped her energy. All she could do was let him fulfill her desire.

She fumbled with the buckle of his belt trying to loosen the metal clasp.

Cedric held her and leaned forward to give her easier access as she slid the leather from the loops then dropped it to the floor. His flannel shirt was tucked inside his jeans, and Iman struggled to free it while he drove her crazy with his mouth.

She finally got the shirt half up his chest.

She sought the button at the waist of his jeans, then hesitated, her fingers tangling in his dark hair.

I'm going to do this in a truck?

Cedric blew on her nipple and it hardened into a tight nub. She sighed. *Possibly.*

"Don't stop now," he urged seductively.

His gaze sought hers in the darkness and he pressed his erection into her softness. His hand stroked her once through the fabric and a shudder rippled through her. He passed his fingers over her desire again and her head fell back as she shook with anticipation.

"Having second thoughts?" he asked, but continued the rhythmic pattern. Her head dropped to his chest. She couldn't think straight under the tender assault.

"Yes." His thumb pressed the space where her opening was and she shook some more. "No, sweet mercy. No, I'm not." He stroked her there again. Iman caught his face between her hands and offered him her breast.

He obliged, much to her delight.

"It's up to you, Iman," he murmured, his mouth full.

Iman doubted that as his lips closed over her breast again and he shook his hand. Arrows of heat and desire tore through her. She couldn't deny him.

"I want you now," she said weakly.

Iman urgently helped him peel her sweatpants from her body. She tugged at his jeans, but her hands shook, so she let him work the zipper and drag the jeans over his hips. Their lips met again as he guided her above him.

The phone in the truck rang. Iman jumped at the intruding sound. Holding her close, Cedric reached around her and picked it up.

"Hamilton here." Iman felt him change immediately. He patted her rear. She stayed still.

His voice demanded an answer. "Was any equipment damaged?" His gaze flicked to her and he murmured out the corner of his mouth, "It's business."

Iman leaned to the right when he more firmly patted her side. Reality dawned on her. He wanted her off his lap!

"Did they arrest anybody?"

Iman kept anger under control as she raised herself and moved off his lap. He never looked at her, while he pulled his pants over his bottom and carefully tucked himself in.

Iman drew on her clothes, anger blocking her pain.

"Johnson from research was there, too? Not surprised." He added, a grim tone to his voice. "I'll be back in the morning. No." He hesitated, looking at her for the first time. "I'm into something tonight. See you in the morning."

You're into something all right. Iman crossed her arms over her chest and sat as far against the passenger door as possible.

She waited until he hung up. "Everything that woman said about you is true. You're insensitive and boorish." Iman looked down at his waist, then up at him. As sweetly as she could manage she said, "You need me to zip those for you?"

Chapter 6

Two weeks of Kwanzaa class made a believer out of him. Anika and Medina had changed. They no longer talked only of Christmas lists and toys. Now their animated discussions were about all the new friends they'd made and Zawadi gifts.

Anika had even surprised him by asking if she could have five dollars from her savings account to buy books for Medina.

But what touched him deeper was the close relationship they'd developed with Iman.

Cedric's gaze swung to her as she kneeled in front of the class, rehearsing dance movements with the dancers who would perform in a week at the Karamu.

He inhaled deeply, remembering.

So many wasted days had passed since their night in the truck. Cedric tried hard to forget his abhorrent behavior.

Iman had refused all of his apologetic overtures. Every gift he'd sent had been returned. She'd only kept one thing. A card he'd finally written late last Friday night, while sitting alone at home.

It had been the first time he realized that he didn't have to be alone because there was somebody special in his life. Someone he enjoyed and who, for some reason, liked him.

Those feelings were what had carried him to his desk and

what had spilled onto the paper. Cedric grew warm thinking about his heartfelt apology. He hoped Iman would give them another chance.

Slightly off-key singing drew his attention back to the children and Iman. The children sang the first principles harmoniously, but the second was a tongue twister. Several of them mumbled, and Iman nodded encouragingly, singing louder.

"Umoja, unity. Kujichagulia, self-determination." They survived the five remaining principles, then Iman applauded them for their effort.

He waited until after the final call of "Habari gani! Umoja!" before making his way toward the throng surrounding Iman. His girls pulled Iman toward him.

"Daddy," Anika said, "Miss Iman said she would come over to our house and work on our speeches with us, didn't you, Miss Iman?"

Cedric faced Iman. He wanted to apologize and make her understand how sorry he was. He wanted to pull her into his arms. To touch her intimately the same way the soft African material hugged her body, and to relive their near-union. To make the end of their evening together something beautiful, as beautiful as Iman deserved.

She held the girls' hands and looked away from him to Medina.

"Yes, sweetheart. I said I would help you. We can do it at my house, or stay here, I suppose."

He touched her. Her gaze snapped up. "You can come to our house tomorrow."

Aliyah approached, halting Iman's response.

"Iman, Ada is asking for you." She pointed to the other side of the room. "I'll keep Cedric and the girls company while you see what she wants."

Cedric felt Iman's impatience. She dropped the girls' hands. "We've got to talk," she said decisively to him.

"I'll wait here for you."

She nodded as she started away.

Aliyah stepped beside him to give his girls room to run around. "Long time no see."

Medina tagged Anika, who then turned to chase her. He didn't bother to stop them. They could have somersaulted over his head and he wouldn't have said a word. Iman was coming to his house tomorrow. Thoughts of her telling him to get out of her life forever plagued him. He pushed them away. It was too sobering.

He turned to Aliyah. "How have you been, Aliyah?"

"I'm always fine, Cedric." Her feline grin made him shake his head. Her humor was infectious.

The weight on his shoulder lessened.

"So, when are you going to ask Iman out again?"

His eyebrows shot up. Had Iman told her about their weekend? He grew slightly uncomfortable. "We're handling it," he said, avoiding a direct answer. Something occurred to him. "What's her nickname?"

"Sugar Baby. Why?"

It was his turn to smile. "Just wanted to know."

Aliyah's thirteen- and fifteen-year-old daughters fussed over Anika and Medina, giving him time to watch Iman and the older woman named Ada.

His gaze was riveted to her as Iman hugged the older woman. Iman broke the embrace when the woman's body began to rack with a hacking cough. There wasn't much to her slight frame but a colorful head wrap. But the frailties of her bony hands and wrists was obvious.

Cedric stepped forward to offer assistance as Iman held her gently around the waist, a look of concern on her face. But the coughing spell ended and another woman assisted Ada into her coat. The threadbare wool, thinned with age, wasn't much protection from the cold winter air.

Cedric was taken aback when Iman unwrapped the scarf

that covered her own head and draped the woman's neck. Her generosity humbled him.

It was too cold to be without a hat or scarf, yet Iman gave without regard for herself. Her actions reflected how deep her beliefs lay. Iman had a way about her that attracted people.

Cedric was surprised at the strength of his attraction.

It was far more serious than he realized as he watched her from beneath hooded lids. He thought of her all the time, could describe her in his sleep, how she smelled and tasted. Everybody loved her. *I could love her, too.*

The idea startled and provoked him.

His heart thundered against his ribs. *Not me,* he decided over his body's raging response. *Too soon.*

Iman returned with her bags of books and her purse in hand and silently gave them to him. They stood before each other in a face-off.

"Daddy? Daddy?" Anika tugged on his hand to get his attention. "Can we go outside with Miss Aliyah?"

"Please?" She and Medina begged in unison. Cedric glanced from Aliyah to his girls, then to Iman. He needed to talk to Iman alone.

"I think I'm outnumbered. Behave," he said more sternly than he'd planned. Anxiety always made his voice harsh when he didn't really mean it to be. He softened it. "Behave, girls." They ignored the warning and ran toward the door.

"Wait. Anika, Medina," Iman called, snatching their coats off a nearby chair and shaking them. "Coats, hats, scarves and gloves." She kneeled down waving them back. "I can't have my best speech readers sick, can I?" She bundled the girls up and tied their hoods tight.

When they resembled something out of an arctic clothing catalog, she patted their heads and let them go. They waddled off, barely able to move.

Cedric waited as she attended to each child who came within her reach, repeating the task until every child was bundled up.

He felt oddly out of place as it was he who usually tended to his girls. Yet a big part of him enjoyed watching her take care of the children.

Finally, they were alone in the room.

"You've been avoiding me," he stated without preamble.

"I know I have. I needed time."

Greedily he drank in the sight of her. Cedric shifted the bags in his hands to a chair.

"I've been trying to apologize for two weeks. It was my fault." When she didn't disagree, he smiled. "Why wouldn't you let me apologize face-to-face? Why did you return all my gifts?"

She looked up at him. "Because they weren't from your heart. Your card told me how you really felt." She rubbed her neck. "I forgave you days ago."

His brows knit in confusion. "Then why didn't you call me?"

"Because." She turned, but his hand on her arm stopped her. Her nose started to glow. "I had some things to sort out." The tip reddened. "I've been thinking about you." She looked at him, then away. "And me."

Her voice dropped, just above a whisper. "Sometimes you look so tired, I think you're going to tumble off these horrible metal chairs. But you still come to class, girls in tow." The flush spread to her cheeks. "I know it's hard, but you do it, anyway. You're a devoted father." Her hand stroked her neck where the red had begun to travel like hot lava.

Cedric yearned to bury his face in the heat.

"I wasn't sure how to tell you…"

His insides clenched nervously. "Tell me?"

Iman fidgeted with her hands, her lips trembled. He reached out his finger to stop them.

"I don't know why I feel this way. When you're business, you're all business." He grimaced. "But I know that's only a part of who you really are. You were a sweetheart to those homeless ladies." She pointed to his chest. "I know there's a heart in there. So here goes."

Cedric got lost in the beauty of her gaze. He desperately wanted to tell her everything was going to be all right.

A nervous smile parted her lips.

His heart thundered when her voice dropped to a whisper. He strained to hear. "A part of me is falling in love with you."

Cedric pulled Iman to him, and pressed his lips to her matted curls. He wanted to share his warmth with her, to let her feel the beat of his heart. It felt as if someone swiped at the world and set it spinning on its axis. Her words set his whole body afire. Everything was going to be all right.

Cedric lifted her chin saying, "I think we should celebrate that good news." He lowered his head, their breath mingling. Her lips parted in expectation...

"Uh-hmm, Mr. Hamilton?" the janitor interrupted.

"This better be good." Cedric's voice rang with irritation.

"I'm locking up, sir. Should I give you another few minutes?" Cedric took one last look at Iman's wonderful mouth and swore under his breath. He wanted to taste her so bad he could feel desire to the marrow of his bones.

Her breath quickened when he inched her closer to him. Because of her revelation, his heart hadn't stopped singing.

"It's getting kind of late. And Mrs. Winston will want me home soon..." The janitor's voice trailed off.

Cedric spoke loudly, while still maintaining eye contact with Iman. "No, we're coming now, Mr. Winston."

Iman backed out of his grasp and got her coat.

"I'll be at the door waiting," the older man called.

Cedric didn't hear him. He was too intent on Iman. He stopped just behind her. "Thank you for telling me."

She nodded and buttoned her coat. Black curls stopped at the collar of her bare neck. He unwrapped his long gray scarf from his neck and covered hers with it.

"I hoped you would join me tonight for a special date," he

said, drawing her back against his chest. He felt a deep sigh leave her body.

She turned and a light burned in the soft depths of her eyes. "Where did you have in mind?"

"The mall," he said casually.

Surprise made her mouth O. "The mall? And Aliyah thought you were too mature for me. I think we're about equal." Her teasing lessened the tension that bubbled between them.

"I have to pick out some things for the girls, and I need a woman's opinion." He added in an offhand manner, "No one can say you're not opinionated."

Iman pretended to pinch him. "I hope you're not implying that I'm not a woman."

"You're all the woman I need. How about it?" They walked out the door and checked on the girls. Aliyah stood watching over the brood.

"What about the girls?"

"My mother and stepfather would love to watch them. How's seven o'clock?"

Medina raced by, bumping Iman as she went. Her apology was lost as Iman struggled to regain her balance. Their breath mingled into mist as Cedric firmly gripped her waist, steadying her.

"Thanks." She stepped away. "Okay. Seven is good."

Anika tugged on his coat, looking up. "Daddy, it's cold. Can we go home now?"

He tore his gaze from Iman's to look at his daughter. "Yes, baby. Go tell your sister it's time to leave." Medina appeared at that moment and took her father's other hand.

"Goodbye, Anika. Goodbye, Medina. Harambee." The girls looked at Iman quizzically. "It's a Swahili greeting," she told them. "It means, let's work together."

Cedric waited until she was safely in her car. A slow grin,

like the slow heat rippling through him, curled his lips. He read her lips as she drove slowly past them.

"I'll see you later."

Chapter 7

Iman glanced through the rows of clothes at Neiman Marcus and cringed at the prices.

"Great! They'll like these." Cedric picked up two dresses and checked the tags. "Do you see two size eights? Only in different colors?"

The fluffy dresses made Iman think of a bed of whipped cream. Not right for two active seven-year-olds.

"Cedric." She looped her arm through his and steered him away from the billowing ruffles. "Don't you think the girls would like something more, how do I say this," she considered out loud. "More playful?"

He stared at her. For a moment she thought he was angry. Then his face fell. "They hate when I shop for them. I like ruffles and fluffy stuff. It reminds me of when they were babies. But since they're big first-graders they don't like my style." He sounded hurt. "They beg my fifty-two-year-old mother to shop for them."

Iman held in her smile at his crestfallen look. He obviously took this issue to heart. She steered him toward a place she knew was a hit with Aliyah's girls.

Music pumped as they entered the store and Cedric visibly cringed at the attire on the mannequins inside the window.

"Come on, Dad," she said, hoping to lessen his reluctance. "Don't take yourself so seriously. Let's look for one outfit each. If they don't like them, you can bring them back."

"Kids don't like this stuff." He flicked distastefully over the tight jeans and hooded shirts. "It's all too big."

"Kids do like this stuff," Iman countered. Her eyes drifted to the denim that covered his muscular thighs and bottom. He looked good in a suit and polished shoes, and great in a pair of jeans and shirt. Cedric needed to loosen up. He was definitely too upper-crust.

"Just look at one outfit," she said convincingly. "You asked for my help, remember?" That seemed to straighten him up a bit as his lips pursed into a smirk.

Telling him her true feelings hadn't been so bad, Iman reflected, trying to keep things positive. Although he hadn't responded the way she'd hoped. The fact that he didn't share her feelings stung, but the words were out. Too late to take them back.

"May I help you?" A young woman who looked about twelve bounced to Cedric's side. Iman held his arm so he wouldn't flee the store.

"No, thanks, ma'am," Iman said around a giggle. "We're just looking."

"Okay. Let me know if you need anything." Happily she skipped away. Cedric stared at her with a disbelieving look on his face.

"Doesn't Georgia have child labor laws?"

"She's old enough. My, my, for such a young dapper dude, you sure have old fogy taste."

"Oh. Is that right?"

Iman offered token resistance but let herself be guided to him. When she was close enough, he slid his hand under her coat, and tickled.

Iman jumped, laughing. "Stop. People are looking. Cedric!"

Giggling, she grabbed for the rack and in the process knocked clothes all over the floor.

"Now look what you made me do." She glanced around guiltily, enjoying herself immensely. Cedric's expression remained innocent. "I'll get you for this," she whispered.

"Is there a problem over here?" the young clerk demanded.

"I'll take each of those in a size eight, please," Cedric said casually, before moving away. Iman stared in amazement as the young woman's frown turned into a smile.

"Just a minute—" Iman peered at the girl's name tag "—Sissy." She followed to Cedric. "There's at least ten dresses down there. Are you sure?"

"Definitely."

He pointed to the clothes. "I want all of those." Iman tried to hide her shock. He took her hand leading her toward a rack of expensive jackets. "Come help me pick out two of these."

Two stores and an hour and a half later, Iman sat under a mountain of packages, barely able to move. She stared blankly across the mall at a television that telecast a follow-up report on corporate hit men. Cedric's picture filled a corner of the forty-two-inch screen. His photograph flashed away. The newscaster began talking about the phone company president.

Each time she'd seen a report on company closings, Iman visualized she and Cedric locked in an intimate embrace in the truck. But the dream would be shattered when he would say, "It's business." Iman wondered if he could survive without business. The answer in her heart left her cold.

"Hello, Iman? Are you asleep with your eyes open?"

Her stomach felt weak. "Mmm? What did you say? I was drifting."

"Do you like these?" He held up some earrings carved in the shape of the Black Madonna. Iman took them in her hand and was surprised at how heavy the beautiful pieces were. She raised them high and her eyes widened at the price tag.

Carefully she chose her words. "They're beautiful. But for

two little girls, you might, perhaps, maybe you could go with something less…"

"They're too big, right?" His thumb caressed the earrings. "I thought so, too."

He turned to the salesman. "I'll take these and two pair of the smaller ones identical to these." This time her mouth gaped. The final bill was staggering.

"Are we ready?" Iman asked once the order had been packaged.

"Just about. I need to make one more stop." They walked to the valet parking attendant who took the packages and stored them away. Cedric took her hand and steered her back inside the mall. "I thought we could get something to eat, then make the last stop. Did you have any other plans?"

Her stomach growled in response. "Not really. I'm so hungry a box of rocks sounds appetizing." She fell into step beside him.

"Why didn't you say something before? We could have eaten hours ago." He stopped and turned fully to her. "Just tell me what you need and it's yours."

"I didn't want to end up at the top of Lookout Mountain again."

He laughed and pressed his lips to the back of her fingers, chills chasing her doubts away.

The dimmed restaurant was crowded with other late-night shoppers but was festively decorated. Red-and-white stockings adorned the waitresses' heads, and holiday streamers hung from the ceilings. Holly-laced tablecloths covered the tables while red candles provided romantic light.

Quickly they were shown to a semicircle booth, and a waiter appeared to take their coats. Before they could slide in, the waitress stopped them.

"Now that you're comfortable, you know what to do."

For the first time, they both noticed the mistletoe arched over the entrance. Neither moved.

"The only people who get away without kissing are sisters and brothers. Are you two related?"

Iman's eyes were fixed to Cedric's lips. She shook her head almost imperceptibly.

"Then do it. I'll bring complimentary glasses of champagne in the meantime. I'll know if you don't kiss her," the waitress said to Cedric. "The bartender will make everybody boo you." She left them alone.

Images of hot fervent kisses filled her head. Involuntarily, she licked her lips.

"Shall we?"

Iman nodded. Cedric stepped forward and their lips met awkwardly. Her nose and his meshed together, then slid up, then down, until the fit became perfect.

Absolutely, blissfully, perfect.

His mouth tenderly touched hers, giving just enough satisfaction for the moment, but leaving sensual promises in its wake. He smiled against her lips before he broke away, leaving her body crying for more.

The bell clanged and people applauded, enjoying their embarrassment.

"That was unreal," Iman muttered as she slid inside the booth. He sat beside her and surprised her by placing another proprietary kiss on her cheek.

The champagne arrived and they took a moment to order.

Iman sipped from her glass and hoped her feelings were from hunger. No matter his blind side about business, being in his arms made her want to commit herself forever. Iman felt as if she had just dived off a very high cliff into darkness. She focused when he repeated the question.

"Is Ada related to you?"

"Not really. We've kind of adopted each other. She's been a member of the Kwanzaa Association for a long time. Every fall Ada heads up a fundraiser so members of the association can teach Kwanzaa classes at local schools and community centers.

"Recently, she's had a bad cough. The medicine her doctor prescribed is sixty-seven dollars a bottle! She just can't afford it. I called the pharmacist today, and they suggested I call around to get a better price, then they would match it. Can you believe that?" Iman shook her head, disgusted. "Bartering medicine prices. What are these drug companies thinking of?"

"The bottom line." He grimaced. "We have to stay in business."

"I wasn't making an indictment against your company," Iman said quickly. "I just can't help feeling the elderly are taken advantage of, when it becomes their job as the patient to find the best price."

He shrugged off her apology. "Unfortunately, competition in this field is fierce. You can have a drug that works well, but the company down the street has a generic brand. Every company has to fight to stay one step ahead. That's why they make you call around for pricing. Nobody is willing to lower their price and lose profits. I tried to explain this very thing to Jack McClure, president of Retired Seniors of Georgia recently. What he's asking is impossible."

"What does he want?"

"Dix to do the unthinkable. Lower the prices of twelve medications." He shook his head. "Can't be done. No amount of petitions or pickets can change the current situation. It's business."

"Well, business sucks," Iman said distastefully.

Cedric laughed. "That's one way of putting it. Look at it this way. Nobody is sitting around with a room full of dusty dollars. Every drug company reinvests the money in new drugs to find new cures. We're still trying to help people. Despite—" he gave her a candid look "—situations like Ada's."

"I don't think she'll be able to do the farewell for Kuumba. She suggested we find an eloquent, dynamic speaker who will wow the crowd. She suggested you."

"No." Cedric shook his head adamantly.

Iman went on as if he hadn't spoken. "I thought of asking

one of the brothers, but when Ada brought up your name, I agreed you're the perfect choice." She eyed him speculatively. Cedric began to suspect he was a specimen under a microscope, being studied by a mad scientist.

"I'll think about it," he said, warming slightly. "Ada reminds me a lot of my own mother." Cedric stopped short, a black abyss gaping open before he could finish the sentence. He faced the dark hole, contemplating what lay on the other side. The urge to share his tragedies and triumphs with Iman was overpowering.

He waited for the feeling to pass as the waiter placed their food on the table and sprinkled grated cheese over his spaghetti.

Only it didn't go away. The closer Iman sat to him, the more her wonderfully female scent snaked into his senses, the more he wanted to bare himself before her and confess all his secrets.

"In what way?" The hollow musical strands of her voice reached inside him and unlocked his private room.

"My mother was sickly. Jobs weren't sympathetic to her illnesses, so just as soon as she got a job she'd lose it for absenteeism. It wasn't easy for us, but we made it."

"How did you live? That must have been very hard."

"Let's just say I have a working knowledge of how to fold a box just right to block the wind."

"The two women on the street..." she whispered.

Her expression was sad, stunned. She barely managed to utter her words. "I'm so sorry."

Cedric couldn't seem to stop himself once he got started. "Not long after that I got a job, and ever since I earned my first paycheck, I never looked back." He closed his hand and realized he'd linked it with hers. "It felt like gold bouillon."

She studied him. Her voice rose barely above a whisper. "You know that's not going to happen to you ever again, right?"

He breathed easier, drawn to the trust radiating from her dark eyes.

"Logically," he managed around an uncharacteristic croak. "But you never forget."

She slid close and placed her hand beneath his arm urging him toward her. Heat spread through him when his arm grazed her breast.

Her lips touched his ear. She whispered, "The girls are safe. It's never going to happen to them."

Involuntarily, he jerked, his body shaking once before he regained control of himself. She had found his biggest fear and confronted it.

Iman brightened an otherwise bleak place with her unqualified trust in him. Cedric grasped hold of her belief and let it rage through his blood. He tried to relax, but his stomach did violent somersaults. Her hands hadn't left his arm. He finally gazed into her eyes.

"How did you know?"

"Honey, you bought the girls ten dresses today." Her gaze softened on his. "Have they worn all the others in their closets?"

"No, but—" Cedric started to respond but she cut him off.

"It's natural to want to protect them, and you have. From what I can see, they're very well cared for. It's time to stop worrying, Cedric."

"I don't worry."

"Ah, well." She nodded. "But you can go too far in certain instances. If you want to improve their value system, let them follow their daddy's example." She patted his hand and gentled it into a caress. Love filled her eyes. "You turned out just fine. They will, too."

She let him go, and resumed eating.

The enveloping darkness that once surrounded him faded, leaving him glowing in her wisdom. He twirled his fork in his hand for a moment.

Iman was a very smart lady.

Cedric's thoughts turned to the upcoming Christmas holiday. He couldn't imagine a day without her. The past weeks proved that.

"Iman, do you have any plans for Christmas?"

"Christmas afternoon I always spend with Aliyah. My famous holiday goose is a hit despite what Aliyah says." She smiled at him. "Why?"

"I want you to spend some time with me and the girls. I want you to share Christmas with us."

Her eyes shined. "I would love to. 'Course, I'm hoping for a white Christmas."

"Why?" Cedric asked incredulous at the thought of not being able to go to work if snow fell.

"I guess my fondest holiday memory is the winter of seventy-seven. We were snowed in for days. I don't know how much fun it was for my mother and father, but Aliyah and I had a ball."

"Sounds like Anika and Medina," he said dryly. "They enjoy fanning the smoke detector when I burn something in the kitchen."

She shot him a wry look. "Kids are supposed to have fun. During that snowstorm, we must have played Chutes and Ladders, Monopoly and Candy Land at least fifty times each."

The memories made her giggle. Cedric loved the light in her eyes. He wished he could have been there.

"The fourth day of the storm, my dad ran from the room yelling at the top of his lungs that he would fling himself in front of a snow plow before he played another board game. My mom suggested he tell us stories."

Her tone grew wistful. "Once he started, there was no stopping him. He told us all about his grandmother and grandfather. Then somehow we got on the subject of Kwanzaa. It wasn't as well-known as it is now. But from those tales, I felt a connection."

"Tell me some," Cedric encouraged. He rested his head against the high back of the booth and folded his arms. Her voice was soft and melodious as she recounted the tale of a young African warrior who was brought across the ocean to America.

Some of the fables were funny, others were serious, but he was sure of one thing. Iman was indeed the best storyteller he'd ever heard. Her voice truly entranced him.

"You should tell stories all the time," he said when she finished. "You're very good at it. Was this fable passed down from your father's grandparents?"

Iman nodded, her eyes still glowing, but she had grown sad. "Yes. I miss my father's interpretation, but I've added my own twists and style. To keep them alive, I tell my nieces and someday, when I have children, I'll tell them. I plan to tell a few at this year's celebration."

The waiter brought the check. Iman slipped into her coat, bypassing the mistletoe.

Cedric couldn't put into words how he looked forward to their good-night kiss. He paid the bill and they started walking. "How are the plans for the celebration shaping up?"

Iman draped her head and neck with his long, gray cashmere scarf. He'd always considered the scarf efficient, useful. Now it was pretty because it protected the silky curls on Iman's head. Cedric shook his head in wonder.

"It's going to be the best celebration yet. A New York dance troupe has confirmed. We also have local dance groups performing, a drum selection, a karate demonstration. The children have planned some surprises."

"That's what Medina was talking about?"

"Yep. Oh, and our farewell speaker is going to dazzle us with his eloquence."

Cedric handed the valet attendant his ticket and glanced wryly at Iman. "Don't count on it."

She whispered, "You're going to be great." The valet stopped the car in front of them.

He raised his eyebrows inquisitively. "Why do you do that?"

Her lids lowered and a shy smile danced around her mouth. "What?"

He whispered, "Whisper?"

"Because then you can hear me."

Cedric stopped. She was right. She had his undivided attention.

It took twenty minutes for the men to decide how to pack the car with all the bags. Iman watched, careful not to offer advice as they loaded the trunk. Cedric's jacket hung open as he wrestled with a bag full of ornaments. Memories of being in his arms floated back to her as she paced the sidewalk to stay warm.

No wonder he was successful, she mused. He focused to a fault on whatever he was doing at the time.

"We'll be done in a minute," he said over his shoulder, just before he unloaded the car and started over.

Iman shook her head.

She focused on his hands as he piled in one bag at a time. Those hands were always gentle with the girls, quick to clap or praise them with fatherly love whenever they were near him.

Cedric turned a box sideways and cupped his hands to his mouth to heat them before grabbing another bag.

Those same hands carefully draped her in gray cashmere when she was freezing outside Stone Manor earlier that night. And, she blushed, had strummed her intimately and made her keen with pleasure.

She followed the hands to the face of the man she had fallen in love with. It was more than a part of her that loved him, as she'd told him. Somehow, her heart had grown committed to him, somewhere over the past few weeks.

Iman felt strangely light.

Cedric's bottom stuck out of the car. He uncurled to his full height and looked at the bags at his feet, then at her.

"We've almost got it. Not too cold are you?"

"I'm okay, do you need any help?"

"No." He glanced at the valet, who looked annoyed. "We can handle it."

Iman waited fifteen more minutes then couldn't take another cold breeze attacking her ankles. "I'll hold those two on my lap," she offered when Cedric started to unload the car again.

"I'm glad you offered. That guy looked like he wanted my blood." Cedric started the car and heat bathed her cold feet.

Iman half turned in her seat and looked at the full backseat and then at Cedric, who drove carefully away from the store and onto the highway.

"Where are you going to hide all this stuff?"

"I hadn't thought of that. The girls are at my mother's but they know every hiding place in my house. They go through there like gift-sniffing dogs."

"I did the same thing. We had a crawl space in our house and my parents hid our gifts there until I left for college."

"I can drop them by my office, then Monday, while they're at school, I'll sneak the gifts into the house. Of course that doesn't help about wrapping them. But I can do that the night before."

Iman smirked. "You smart guys know how to complicate things."

"What? I thought that was a very well-thought-out plan. Okay, smarty," he challenged. "You come up with something better."

"You can bring them to my house and wrap them there. Then when Christmas Eve arrives, pick them up. The girls can search the Hamilton home to their little hearts' content, they won't find a thing. I'll even help wrap. Easy, huh?" Iman fought to hide her grin of satisfaction.

"I was going to suggest that as plan B," Cedric said, pasting on his best poker face.

"Yeah, sure you were."

"Really. It was on the tip of my tongue."

"Uh-huh. Sore loser." Iman savored the thrill of victory.

He started a slow grin. "I was just going to say that."
"Your nose is growing, Pinocchio."
They bantered lightly all the way to Iman's driveway.

Chapter 8

Iman showed Cedric to the second floor bedroom where he stored the gifts. A worktable cluttered with Kente fabric and materials for mkeke mats covered one wall, while books spilled from shelves opposite it. The floor space was wide open until bags and boxes, colored wrapping paper and clothes filled the hardwood. They backed out of the room, gawking.

"That's insane." Cedric appeared stunned. His usual cool, eluded him. "I can't believe we did this much shopping in one day."

Iman led him downstairs to the kitchen where she had coffee brewing. "That was you," she threw over her shoulder, her delicate fingers gliding over the black glazed countertops. "I'm an innocent shopping bystander."

He spooned one sugar into his cup and sat at the glass-topped table for four in the cozy kitchen.

Cedric's presence in her home made Iman nervous. She straightened the pictures of her nieces that hung on the wall by the sink and wiped the stainless counter with her hand. She wiped her hand on her jeans.

"Are you nervous about me being here?" Cedric asked quietly.

Iman washed and dried her hands, stalling. Finally she answered, "It's silly, but I am. I shouldn't be," she rushed on, her voice higher. "I mean, we just made up, I told you how I felt…" Iman stopped abruptly and covered her face with her hands. "I'm making a complete fool of myself."

"No you're not. I cornered the market on that the night in the truck."

Iman sat beside him. "I missed you," he said.

She looked at him. The words were plainly spoken, but had the impact of a one-two punch.

"I missed you, too."

He tugged her into his lap and she went willingly.

"I want to make love to you. No phones, no interruptions, no truck." He nipped at her earlobe.

The promise in his voice turned her insides to mush. A yearning beyond conscious emotion seized her.

Iman brushed the soft curls that swirled on her head with her hand, her gaze on the floor. The checkerboard pattern of the tile blurred under her penetrating gaze.

She'd forgiven Cedric, but she hadn't forgotten how hurt she'd been.

"We should take it slow." Iman had difficulty talking, with her ear in his mouth. His lips released her. "Cedric, this feels too much like we're teenagers. Like we're being careless. It feels too right," she whispered hoarsely.

She looked into his eyes, and found understanding. "I never used to believe in love at first sight. I never thought I would tell a man I loved him before he told me." She rushed on. "I'm not trying to pressure you."

"You're not," he reassured. "We'll take it slow." He gathered her closer to him, as sexual awareness swirled between them. His hand moved possessively up her side and around her back. His voice was uncharacteristically ragged.

"I'll wait until I can't stand it anymore. Until the sound of your voice makes me so hard I'll just about explode at my desk at work. Then I'll come looking for you, Iman."

"I'm in trouble," she murmured once she looked into his eyes.

"You sure are." He kissed her tenderly.

Cedric was a patient, deliberate man. He wouldn't have to wait too long, the way she felt.

Iman was first to break away. "I can come over tomorrow about four-thirty to help Medina. If you need some help with your speech, I'd be glad to give you some books."

"I'll take all the help I can get. I'd better get going before I break my promise to wait."

Rising from his lap was difficult. Iman wanted to stay locked in his embrace, letting desire take them where logic had no place.

But she'd made the rules. Cedric steadied her on her feet. Iman retrieved his coat from over the arm of the chair. "I had a good time."

He pulled a new scarf from his coat pocket, brushing her breast as he looped it around her neck drawing her near.

"I had a good time, too."

His lips descended on hers for a fiery reminder. Their good-bye kiss lasted another five minutes.

"I...I meant shopping."

A flush colored her cheeks when she came up for air.

"I didn't." Cedric's arms draped possessively around her back and they stayed close enjoying the feel of the other. She rested her head against his chest listening to the quickened beat of his heart. It matched her own.

He tilted up her chin. "Good night, Iman Yvette Parrish. My Sugar Baby." He kissed her brilliant nose and walked out the door. Iman walked on watery legs back to the sofa and collapsed.

Chapter 9

"Say it again, Medina. Take your time. Start here." Cedric handed her the paper and waited for her to start. He drew a frustrated hand over his hair as he listened to Medina recite her speech for the tenth time in two hours.

"Kwanzaa is a time to draw people into your homes and ask them to ce-webrate—" she cringed but kept reading "—with you. Fami-wy and friends— Daddy, I can't do it."

Cedric folded his hands in his lap and exhaled. "Stop saying you can't." He rubbed his temples, his nerves frayed. "You have to try harder. Practice the *ll* sound. Don't start crying. Why are you crying?"

"I'm tired and thirsty," she said rebelliously.

"You can get a drink, but we have to go over this again."

"I don't want to," she wailed, tears dripping off her chin. "Miss Iman's nice to me when she helps me. You're yeww-ing again and you promised to stop." She let the paper slip from her hands. "I don't want to do this anymore."

His patience snapped. "Well, too bad. You made a commitment and you have to keep it. Iman's been coming over here all week to help you and in a few days, she's going to need you to do this speech. You're not backing out!"

Cedric heard the doorbell, but ignored it. He paced his study and watched his daughter.

"Daddy, it's too hard. I don't want to do it anymore. I quit."

"You can't quit!"

"Hello."

Cedric hadn't realized he'd raised his voice until he heard Iman's low familiar tone from the door. He cleared his throat and glowered at Medina, who raised her chin stubbornly.

"Medina, can I talk to your daddy alone for a minute?"

The little girl nodded, then took off like a shot.

"You're coming back," he yelled from the door. Medina's bedroom door banged shut.

"I swear, Iman, why don't kids come with a manual? They give them to you and then don't tell you how to raise them." He stalked past her. "She says she's not going to do her speech." Cedric collapsed into the high-back leather chair behind his desk.

Iman entered the room and laid three bags beside the sofa on the floor. "Why do you always have so much stuff?" he asked with irritation.

"These are books I thought might help you with your speech on Kuumba. Don't attack me because you're being unreasonable about Medina."

He scoffed. "Unreasonable? She has to learn the same way everybody else does that if she makes a commitment to something, she has to keep it." He shook his head and waved his hand carelessly. "I won't have any of this fickle maybe I will, maybe I won't."

"I thought she was happy with her speech. Why did she change her mind?" Iman loosened the sash on her coat and sat down.

He glowered at her. "Because she has a speech impediment. She can't pronounce some of her letters correctly and she's shy about it. Practice," he announced. "She needs to practice."

"Cedric, I'm not going to tell you how to raise your children," she said softly.

"Sure you are," he cut in sarcastically.

Iman ignored him and continued. "But it seems to me that another way to handle someone like this is with positive suggestions. Give her positive encouragement. Tell her things like, you can do it, I believe in you, you did great." Her warm smile captivated him. She was whispering again.

Cedric felt himself falling.

"Iman," he warned.

"I believe in you, you're going to be great." She grinned sweetly. How he loved her mouth. Cedric shook his head.

"How come you think you know me so well?" Her smile widened victoriously. Cedric was hopelessly lost.

"I know you want Medina to believe in herself. That's why you work so hard to help her. But you get frustrated when she doesn't try as hard as you think she should."

He shrugged, agreeing. "I try not to be so intense with her."

"I know, I heard you. The housekeeper let me in. I listened awhile before I came in here. I know you want the best for her." Her voice was soft. "Try to take it easy on her. She's just seven."

"How come you know so much about children? You don't have any." Hurt and anger played across her face and he stopped short. "Sorry, that was unfair."

"I may not have children, but I've worked with them for years. And as you've said, they don't come with a manual. Any fool could do it."

His lips quirked. "I guess I deserved that. But if I have to give my speech, so does she, damn it." Cedric sighed raggedly. "What are you laughing at?"

Red looked so good on Iman. She slipped the wool coat from her shoulders and threw it on the couch. A brilliant red silk shirt was tucked into nicely fitting jeans with a complementing vest hanging open in the front. Long earrings dangled from her ears and she wore a thin gold chain around her neck.

"She's doing it, damn it," she mimicked his deep voice. "Cedric, do you think your terrorist tactics helped? Positive thinking gets positive results."

He shook his head, mimicking her silently, and waved off her assessment. Cedric could see where this was going and he didn't like it one bit. Somehow he knew he was going to be wrong. He dragged his gaze away from her matte red lips and stared out the side window.

"I'm not the one who's wrong here. I agree my tactics may need some work." He scowled. "Medina made a commitment and she's going to keep it." He needed to change the subject. His body ached for Iman. "Come here."

Iman stayed where she was. She arched an eyebrow at him. "Ask nicely."

"Come here, damn it," he said, smiling. He was winning. He could feel it.

"Come here, damn it, please," Iman tossed back.

Cedric pushed his chair from his desk and planted both feet firmly on the floor. "Come here, damn it, please, Iman, and take care of your man."

Iman took her time closing and locking the door to his study before she came to him. She placed her knee between his legs on the chair and rested her hands on his shoulders. "That's much, much better."

She tasted exactly as he remembered, only better, Cedric thought fuzzily. He slid his tongue over her lower lip, then sucked on the fullness. Her mouth eased open in invitation and her breath rushed out. He sampled the velvet warmth, losing himself to her flavor.

"The girls," she murmured, when his hands stole beneath her vest and found the buttons of her shirt. He wrestled the silk shirt from the waist of her pants bunching it beneath her breasts. The vest fell to the floor.

Cedric dropped his head and sucked on her indented belly button. Iman gasped and writhed when he licked up her rib cage. Her fresh scent deepened into a powerful aphrodisiac as her temperature rose.

"Daddy? Can we come in?"

They both jumped off the chair. Iman fumbled with her blouse, shoving it hastily into her jeans, bumping into the desk as she headed for the couch.

"Just a minute," Cedric called. "Iman," he whispered, waving her back. He tucked the flap of her shirt into the front of her pants, helped her into her vest then grasped her face between his hands. He kissed her soundly. "I just wanted to make sure this wasn't a dream or a conspiracy against me for wanting you so much." His bulging pants relayed his desire.

"It's for real," she agreed, pressing herself lightly into him. "Open the door before they think we're up to something." Cedric got to the door and grabbed the handle but didn't open it. "I'm definitely up for something." Her nose brightened and a moment of silence hung between them.

"I…" The words stuck to his tongue, and Cedric didn't force them. He just couldn't say what lay in his heart. Iman smoothed her hair and looked questioningly at him. "Cedric, do I look okay?" She fussed with her shirt and vest, then smoothed her jeans. She was gorgeous.

"You look fine."

He flipped the latch and turned the handle on the door.

The girls burst in and headed straight for Iman. Both spoke at once. "Hi, Miss Iman."

"Hi, Anika, hi, Medina." Iman inclined her head in their direction. "Let's leave your daddy to his work and go practice our speeches." They crowded out the door, leaving him alone.

Cedric stood in the doorway helplessly aroused with no outlet readily available. He watched Iman disappear around the corner with the girls and resigned himself to work. If only he could manage to concentrate.

He worked on his speech for Kuumba and leafed through the

books Iman had in her bags. He quickly completed the thinner books, saving the thicker ones for later.

The sound of giggling filtered into his office through the half-closed door.

He laid his pen down, and contemplated joining them. The legal pad he'd been writing on held only a partially completed speech. With Kuumba only days away, there was little time to waste.

Cedric shook his head and tried to concentrate.

But the sound of Iman playing with the girls and their joyous laughter was too distracting. It didn't help his body recover, either. He still wanted her.

Cedric picked up the warbling phone on his way to the kitchen. "Hello?"

"Cedric, it's Mother. Are you lifting weights? You sound out of breath."

Cedric refused to look past his waist again. It wouldn't do any good. "Something like that," he said dryly. "What's up, Mom? Everything okay?"

"Of course it is," his sprightly mother replied. She claimed good health now, but he still worried about her.

"I'm just asking. How's Richard?"

"Richard's gone hunting with his son. Don't know what you could kill in the middle of winter, but I said go. I called because I want my grand-bunnies to come over and spend the weekend with me. If you don't mind."

"Yes! Mom, you saved my life." Cedric responded before he could think twice. The pulse in his lower region thundered in anticipation. Relief was just around the corner.

His mother laughed. "You must have plans. Got a hot date with Iman?"

"I plan to make one. Thanks, Mom," he said before hanging up.

Cedric passed the picture he'd bought at the auction. The

one Iman loved so much. It depicted children playing, their carefree spirit leaping off the canvas.

The first night he'd seen it, it had touched a lonely space inside him. He'd wished he could have been one of those children. Then he'd met Iman and he hadn't been lonely since.

The picture belonged to her. She'd seen it for what it was and she'd found something in him. It was her spirit that held the strings of his heart.

Cedric picked up the painting and headed for the basement, where he wrapped it carefully, then stored it in the trunk of his car. He'd surprise her with it later.

He headed up the stairs to the girls' room. The door was ajar and he peeked through. Iman lay on her stomach on the floor, with Anika on her right and Medina on her left.

"My dad is very smart. He graduated to the tenth grade," Anika said importantly.

Iman shook her head. "He went to college, didn't he?"

Cedric held his breath. For some reason, uneasiness crept through him.

"No. He went to work. He has extra skin on his hands 'cause he had to work so hard." Medina crinkled her nose. "Sometimes he peels it."

"Then we put lotion on it," they said together.

"Your daddy is a very good man." Iman's husky voice made his heart swell. "We'd better get back to work. Medina, I don't want you to worry about your *l*s. You did perfect, tonight. Absolutely, positively perfect."

"For rea-wl?" Hope surged in Medina's voice. She looked at Iman as if she'd hung the moon.

"For real," Iman reassured.

Cedric's heart swelled more than he thought it could.

"Anika," Iman went on. "Nobody told me you could sing. I think I have another job for you." Both girls giggled.

"Don't ask Daddy to sing. He sounds just like a rhinoceros." Anika giggled.

Cedric started to push the door open.

"Miss Iman, are you married?" He stopped and waited.

"Not yet."

"Are you going to marry our daddy?" Median asked.

Iman sat back on her knees away from the girls. They followed her up and sat beside her with their legs crossed. She seemed to be studying the cranberry-colored carpet intently. Cedric held his breath.

"He hasn't asked me."

"If he did, would you?"

She laughed. "You two sure are inquisitive." She stood and reached for their hands, pulling them up. "Let's just say that if he brings it up one day, I'd think about it. How do you feel about that?"

"Good," they responded unanimously.

"Really? Why?"

Cedric pressed his head against the door while they considered her question. It occurred to him they might be unhappy. His chest tightened, not knowing. Finally Anika spoke.

"Everybody in our class has a mother. We just want to have one, too. Daddy needs a wife so he doesn't have to be by himself all the time."

"I see," Iman said. "Well, I'm sure things will work out for him."

Cedric knocked on the door. He wiped mist from his eyes before he walked in. "How's everything going?"

"Fine," they all responded. Cedric looked at Iman. She stared at the floor for a long time before meeting his gaze briefly.

"Grandma wants you to come spend the weekend with her." Cedric pretended to shake from the girls' squeals of happiness. "Since that's a yes, we'd better get some things together. But you have to practice your speeches while you're there." He walked to the mirrored wall closet and slid the panel open.

"Daddy, can Miss Iman help us?"

"Well…"

"I don't mind," she said, coming to stand beside him.

Cedric touched her arm. "I'll be waiting downstairs." He walked from the room, closing the door behind him.

Chapter 10

Iman stared at Cedric's long legs, which were stretched out in front of him. She'd come to know his favorite reading position as he crowded the corner of the couch with his lean frame, giving the book on his lap his undivided attention.

They had come to her house after dropping off the girls and he had assumed that position an hour ago, working fervently on his speech.

Troubling thoughts assailed her. He was in her house, her life, but he hadn't said a word about her confession of love. What if he didn't feel the same way? Had she made a complete and utter fool of herself? Iman silently berated herself.

She tried to imagine herself without Cedric and the girls, but couldn't. Their reason for seeing each other so often would soon be gone.

What would happen to them?

Iman lowered the book from her lap and strolled to the window unobtrusively so as not to disturb him. The clear, cold, starlit sky held no fireworks, no exploding bombs, no blazes of light that scorched *Love* in neon lights in the stars.

But they were bright. Luminous as if she'd never seen them before. Some formed a smile, while others danced.

Iman shook herself. Who'd ever heard of dancing stars?

"The stars are beautiful tonight," she remarked. Surely, if he looked, he would see what she saw.

Absently he glanced over his shoulders and nodded. "Mmm."

Discontent swirled through her.

Iman settled back in the armchair to watch the man she couldn't imagine being without and wondered why he didn't see the same damn dancing stars she did.

Earlier in his study, she'd thought he might say he loved her. Instead, he opened the door for the girls and the opportunity vanished.

He loved her, she could feel it. But would he ever say it?

"I'm going upstairs to wrap presents," she announced, hoping he would stop her. Her hopes were dashed when he only nodded.

Iman took the wooden steps slowly. She gathered wrapping paper, clothes, boxes and bows and dragged them to her room where she got comfortable on her queen-size bed.

Methodically she cut, wrapped and taped. Bows and ornaments in brilliant reds, greens, blues and purples lay strewn on the bed and she peeled the backs off several, matching the perfect bow to each color paper.

Iman tossed the others in a growing pile of discarded wrapping paper which covered the top corner of her bed. A flash of guilt coursed through her at her wastefulness.

Her thoughts wandered to the woman on the television screen from Cedric's company. Iman knew it wouldn't help, but she folded several of the larger pieces to use later.

"Need anything?"

The door to her room was wide-open and Cedric leaned one shoulder against the frame. Although his stance was casual, tension radiated from him. It made desire coil inside her like a hot spring.

His smoldering gaze caressed her bare leg that dangled over

the side of the bed. Slowly it moved up and over the colorful wrap that gathered at her thighs.

She watched his tongue caress his lower lip.

Iman began to perspire.

His gaze lingered at her breasts, then locked with hers letting her know it wasn't Christmas presents he was talking about. Her concerns slipped away under the heat of his gaze. "I need you."

He stared into the room. Iman slid both legs off the bed, her knees slightly apart.

She closed her eyes when his strong fingers tunneled through her hair, forcing her head back.

The long zipper on the back of her shirt made a cutting noise in the silence, broken only by the sounds of their heavy breathing. The silk pooled around her waist.

His hands guided her up and the kente print top dropped around her ankles. Strong fingers slid under the straps of her bra and peeled them down her arms. His forehead touched hers and his mouth was slightly open.

Their lips met and the tip of his tongue tantalized her.

Iman reached around and unhooked the back of her bra. It dropped between them, deep brown nipples peeking over the lavender lace.

"You want me?" she asked seductively against his mouth. His thigh nudged hers and his hand slid boldly up between her legs. Her panties were no match for his probing fingers.

Iman cried out, raising on her toes, wanting more.

He held her still and sampled her wetness. With the slowness of a predator stalking its prey, his fingers drew a moist path through her dark patch of hair, stopping long enough to make her left breast ache, then mercifully ending at her lips.

Cedric tilted her chin up and stroked her other breast lazily. "Do you want me?"

Iman nodded yes, mute.

He suckled, and licked the rest of the clothes from her skin. It was maddening, his loving was so good.

"I don't want to be naked by myself." Iman reached for Cedric, but he stepped out of her arms. She couldn't control her shivers of anticipation as he performed a slow striptease for her. Iman crawled to the center of her bed and waited.

This was what she'd dreamed about. Yearned for. Desired so much. Him. With her. Inside her. Taking her places she hadn't been in a long, long time. Iman silently thanked Aliyah's forethought as she handed him the little foil packet. Her heartbeat quickened when Cedric kissed her his thanks. She didn't know what she would do if they had to stop.

Wrapping paper protested under her back as he lay her down and loved her with such tenderness her eyes dripped tears from the splendid ecstasy.

Afterward he stroked her until the tears subsided and the pleasure began again. This time when the back of her thighs met the front of his, it was with an intensity surpassed only by their coupling of moments ago.

Iman lay on top of Cedric, her arms resting on his broad shoulders, her head against his chest. He held her still as he peeled another Christmas bow from her bottom.

"Ouch, what was that?"

"Christmas bows. Be still." She jerked when he disengaged the last bow from her skin.

"No," he groaned. "Don't be still. I like when you do that." His large hands rotated her hips against him.

"I tingle," she murmured.

"Is that all?" He slowed the movements and looked down at their bodies pressed together.

Iman grabbed the bow from the scattered covers. "I meant my rear tingles from where you pulled this darn thing."

He took it from her hands and pressed it on the tip of her breast. Iman slapped playfully at Cedric's arms when he swiftly flipped her onto her back and loomed over her.

"Hey, how are you going to make sure that doesn't hurt when you take it off?" He lowered his head. "Oh, good, yes," she said and sighed a moment later when he used his tongue to remove it.

Chapter 11

Cedric reclined against the wooden headboard and watched Iman sleep. She was beautiful in all her naked glory. Her skin was a soft brown, even in coloring from her head to her feet. Except her nipples. The tips were as dark in hue as his skin. And tasted better than any delicacy he'd ever sampled.

He'd had a chance to taste every inch of her over the past three hours. His body stirred at the memories of their passion. She loved him. She loved him.

The next move was his. But what did Iman want out of life? Did she want to be a wife, an instant mother?

Those thoughts plagued him as he silently slid out of the bed and into his jeans. Her house was Southern, comfortable in a way he'd experienced only later in his life. It hadn't been until he was grown and on his way to wealth that he'd been invited into nice homes.

Life was strange. Iman seemed happy with her life in a way few people were. She loved what she did.

He couldn't say the same thing. A long time ago, Dix had been a golden opportunity, a means to an end.

It didn't hold the same meaning anymore. The takeover of Blythe Pharmaceuticals bothered him more than he cared to admit. He couldn't get the faces of the people out of his head.

Company morale remained low and for the first time, his personal life was good. He wanted everybody to be as happy as he. Damn it.

Cedric hurried to the car and got Iman's painting from the trunk. At least he could do one thing right. He hung it in the spot she'd indicated the first time he'd come to her house and then went to the refrigerator. Something in his life had to change.

He provided a stable home and had secured a solid future for Anika and Medina. Not bad for a man with a tenth-grade education. So what was missing? Would having someone to come home to cure his restlessness?

"Are you trying to cool off America with that door open?"

Cedric closed the refrigerator door and leaned against it. "Just thinking." A long, white lace robe sheathed Iman. The darkest parts of her were still visible. He could feel himself growing and tightening beneath his half-closed jeans. His gaze raked her. "Is that thing supposed to do something?"

She struck a pose, then slid her hand down from her waist to her thigh where she parted the thin material.

"It's supposed to titillate, tantalize and tease the mind, body and spirit." She walked forward slowly. "Is it working?"

He kissed her nose. "I'm completely under your spell."

Iman raised on her toes and kissed his mouth. "I know it's the middle of the night, but I want something to eat. Are you hungry?"

"Only for you."

Iman opened the silverware drawer, pulled out a spatula and swatted at him with it. "Back. I was talking about frying some chicken."

"Chicken is good, too. What do you want me to do?"

She handed him some potatoes. "Peel."

Iman had the chicken in the frying pan in no time.

Cedric dropped peeled and cubed potatoes into a pot of

water on the stove, while Iman pulled two beers from the refrigerator and set them on the table.

When everything was bubbling appropriately, they sat at the kitchen table with their drinks.

Iman studied Cedric. He seemed so relaxed with his naked chest and bare feet.

The discussion with the girls that afternoon gave her a better understanding of him. She now realized he was so intense because of the immense responsibility he'd had from a young age. The knowledge that he'd only been educated to the tenth grade stunned her. His recent problems with the two companies merging came to the forefront of her mind.

"Have things settled down with your new employees?"

He shrugged. "Some are resentful their friends got let go. Others are grateful they still have jobs. Others are worried I'll fire them next month. Overall, it's been a cautious undertaking." Iman sensed something more, something he wasn't saying.

"Would you do it again?"

"Yes." He looked into her eyes. "It's not personal. It's business."

Iman shivered at his tone. "I know. But you must understand how they feel."

"What am I supposed to do? If it weren't my company it would be somebody else. I didn't let forty thousand people go like one of the Bell companies. I didn't pull something like that. It was one hundred people. Let's drop the subject."

He got up and stalked to the stove. The grease popped as he turned the chicken, then he slipped the metal cover over the snapping oil. It sizzled, then settled back into its regular bubbling level.

Too restless to sit, he leaned his shoulder against the refrigerator and crossed his arms.

"When did you discover teaching was right for you?"

Iman watched him closely. Cedric didn't like talking about

himself. Whenever he was uncomfortable, he changed the subject. He'd done it before. She decided not to call him on it and answered.

"I've known since I was a six years old. What about you? Will you always run Dix?" Iman felt driven to know the "It's business" part of Cedric. For an inexplicable reason, it mattered.

He put the cooked chicken on plates and dished out the potato salad. "I don't know." His answer shocked her. They began eating. His potato salad tasted delicious.

"Have you ever considered doing something else?" she asked.

"No. I never have." Iman looked up from her plate at him. There was a finality to his voice that made her sad. He was bound to something she got the impression he didn't like. Iman felt sorry for people who didn't like their jobs. She loved hers so much.

The overwhelming urge to cuddle with Cedric filled her. Silently, she eased onto his lap and wrapped her arms around him.

It took a long time before she felt his arms move. Then his body curved and molded to hers. Their strength, bonding.

"Let's go back to bed," he murmured against her hair.

"I'll race you." The seductiveness of his touch made her anxious to repeat their earlier pleasure and to forget the world.

Cedric swept her up into his arms. "We both win, we have all night."

"Ada, it's Iman. Where are you?"

Slightly out of breath from climbing three flights of stairs to Ada's apartment, Iman dropped her key on the table close to the door and stepped back.

Ada's apartment always overwhelmed her when she first entered. Having called the same place home for over fifteen years, Ada had long ago filled every corner to decorate out.

Now everything went up. Iman always had the sneaking feeling that something was going to fall off the wall and land on her head.

She heard Ada's answering cough and hurried to the bedroom. Her frail body was dwarfed beneath a mountain of ancient hand-stitched quilts. The vaporizer hummed a steady cloud of steam, while crumpled tissues littered the floor.

"Iman," she wheezed. "Chile, what you doing here? We don't have much time before Umoja. You got everythin' taken care of?"

Iman took off her coat and dropped it at the foot of Ada's bed. Despite the woman's weakened state, the room was tidy. Iman threw the stray tissues in the can. She touched Ada's forehead, sucking her teeth at the dampness.

"Everything's fine. I came looking for you. I called you yesterday but nobody answered."

"I had a doctor's appointment at two o'clock. He gave me a new medicine, but I took the last of it last night."

"Why didn't you call me? I would have taken you." Iman caressed Ada's hand while she talked. She couldn't bear to think of her in the cold winter air by herself. Ada gave her hand a strong squeeze.

"I knew you were at the manor decorating and practicing for the Karamu. That doctor must be crazy to think I'm going to spend sixty-seven dollars for a bottle of medicine.

"Don't worry about me, chile. I mixed up something myself."

Medicine bottles, a cup with dark goo in it and a half-melted candle cluttered the bedside table. Iman wrinkled her nose when she picked up the foul-smelling cup and took a whiff of the concoction.

"Honey, what is this?"

She drew her nose back sharply from the pungent odor.

"It was good enough for you crumb snatchers," Ada said

sharply. She coughed long and hard. "Only thing is, I didn't have enough eye of newt to finish it."

Iman laughed softly. That was Ada's way of putting her in her place. She was proud of her Haitian heritage and scoffed at conventional methods of healing. Only, the medicine she needed today was very conventional and very expensive.

Iman made her some tea and held her head so she could sip it. "Do you have any more sample bottles of medicine from the doctor?"

"No. He only gave me one."

Ada raised up on her elbows when Iman stood.

"Don't go rousting the pharmacist, Iman. They told me how you showed up last month trying to get that other medicine for me at a discount. They're giving me the best they can. It's my own fault I'm like this."

Iman held her through another coughing fit. "No, it's not. It's the drug companies' fault for overpricing these medicines. And I intend to do something about it."

Ada's eyes followed her movements. "Chile, I smoked cigarettes for fifty-five years. These old lungs belong only to me. I made them this way."

Iman straightened Ada's covers, raising her chin stubbornly. "You would be well if you could afford the medicine."

Iman gently patted Ada's shoulder. She followed the phone cord to Ada's rotary phone.

"I'm calling Aliyah to come sit with you while I go pay our friendly pharmacist a visit. The last time I was there, he said the drug company was right here in Atlanta. I'll need this." Iman grabbed the bottle from the table and shoved it in her coat pocket. She braced the phone under her chin twirling the dial. "Don't you worry, I'll take care of everything."

"Oh, goodness," Ada groaned. "Have mercy on them."

Chapter 12

Iman stalked into the lobby of the Dix Pharmaceutical Company, Inc. Before she left, Ada had almost passed out from the coughing fit that shook her frail body. But like always, she refused to go to the hospital.

Iman was desperate and she knew of only one person who could help her. The ride up to the fourth floor of the washed-stone structure gave her a chance to formulate her scattered thoughts. She squared her shoulders and stood tall. She would present her argument in a logical, reasonable way, and he would see reason.

The doors breezed open. Iman stepped into the lobby and walked the few steps to the receptionist desk.

"Cedric Hamilton, please."

The tiny receptionist flicked down the mouthpiece of her headphone and looked at her.

"Do you have an appointment?"

"No, but he'll see me."

The woman gave her a polite smile. "Mr. Hamilton is a very busy man. He operates on an appointment basis only."

Iman impatiently nodded her head. "He'll see me. I'm his—" She stopped. They hadn't defined their relationship with labels. She'd said she loved him, he'd said thank you.

"His girlfriend," Iman managed.

"Just a minute, ma'am." The woman hurried away and slipped into a room down the hall. Iman clenched and opened her fists. She reassured herself that things would be fine.

The door opened and Cedric stepped out. He approached her in long strides. Immense relief flooded her once her hands were within his.

"What's the matter?" His concern made her weak. Everything was going to be all right.

"It's Ada." He wrapped his arm around her shoulder.

"Did she…die?"

She hurried to reassure him. "No, she isn't dead."

"Then what is it?"

Iman looked into the eyes of the man she loved. In his arms she had found pleasure beyond her wildest dreams. Now she felt support. She knew why she loved him. Words spilled from her mouth.

"Ada needs our help. Cedric, your company manufactures the medicine her doctor prescribed to make her better. You have to lower the price so she can afford it." Iman retrieved the bottle from her coat pocket and pressed it into his hands.

The pencil the receptionist had been writing with snapped.

Cedric took her by the hand. "Come into my office." He guided her down the hall and closed the door behind them. The expensively decorated office was a blur as Iman turned to face him.

"Cedric, did you hear me? Ada needs your help."

"I can't do what you're asking."

"Why?" She searched his features for a clue.

Cedric pushed himself away from the door and walked around his desk.

"Iman, drug prices can't arbitrarily be lowered. That's not how business is done. There are two hundred people that work for this company. Those people have families that depend on them. They count on me to make sure they get paychecks. If we're not profitable, then people lose jobs."

A steel trap seemed to be closing over her. Iman fought for air. "Cedric, this is Ada we're talking about. She's not some nameless, faceless person from RSG. She's my friend." Her voice quivered, but she continued to meet his level gaze. "Be reasonable." The words were more personal than she intended. Iman waited, hoping he would transform before her eyes.

His expression remained one of pained tolerance. "I'm being reasonable, and it seems as though I'm the only one who's doing so. What you're asking is ludicrous."

Fire rushed through her. Her voice came raggedly in impotent anger. "I know the medicine from that little bottle doesn't cost sixty-seven dollars to make. For goodness' sake, senior citizens are the predominant market for this drug." She flung her arm out. "Most of them are on fixed incomes. How are they supposed to afford it?"

He settled behind his desk in the high-back leather chair, unfazed by her outburst. Iman's hope began to unravel.

"Most of the people who use this medicine have some kind of insurance or another. There's only a small number that actually pay market price."

She braced her hands on his desk. "Then what do the Ada's of the world do?"

His steepled fingers flew open. "It's not for everybody. Iman, this is business—"

Iman held up her hand. She resisted screaming at Cedric's tolerant look. "If you say that to me one more time, I swear, I'll scream."

Her throat constricted, but she forced herself to go on. "You know, that's your problem. You're so wound up in business you can't see your own face. Cedric, you've forgotten what poverty is like because you're hiding behind expensive suits and useless dresses for the girls." His eyebrows shot up, but he remained silent. Iman went on.

"You've reached a comfort zone that many don't ever see. You're too rich." Iman shuddered distastefully.

His voice was as sharp as jagged glass. "I worked my butt off to get where I am today, and I won't just give it away on a whim. I give back to this community the way I know how. I do care. Lowering the price of a medication is not the answer. Why can't Ada get on one of the social programs?"

"She's afraid she'll be deported. She's not a United States citizen." Iman's eyes watered. She made her final plea. "Cedric, please. I've never asked you for anything before. For Ada." *For me,* she said silently.

"Lowering the price of the medication isn't the answer." His voice rang with finality.

Iman firmly placed her purse strap on her shoulder.

"My bottle, please." She extended her hand, she couldn't look at him.

"What are you going to do?"

"I'm going to take care of Ada myself."

"You mean buy the medicine yourself."

She looked at him. "Yes."

Miles separated them.

All Cedric cared about was his precious bottom line. She should have known. It was business. Shame washed over her. The last time he'd said that to her should have served as enough of a warning.

Iman focused on the reddish-brown bottle in his hands and waited for him to give it to her. She wanted to leave before her tears started to flow.

Cedric placed the bottle on the desk between them. Iman slowly took it and dropped it into her purse. She walked to the door.

"Are you going over there now?"

She nodded. Breezy indifference failed her. Her voice wavered. "I'll be busy over the next few days."

"Let me come with you."

"No. I don't need—" Iman struggled with the words that pushed at her throat. "You've done enough."

"Will w-we—" he stammered. "Will I see you later?"

"No." She met his bewildered gaze. She deliberately whispered, "Goodbye."

Iman disappeared through the door.

Chapter 13

"**M**r. Hamilton, may I have a word with you, please?"

Cedric looked up from the computer screen surprised to find he wasn't alone. Most of the skeleton staff of employees had already left for the day. Considering it was the day before Christmas Eve.

Debra Gray, his receptionist, waited expectantly in the doorway. "What is it, Debra? I thought everyone was gone."

"I was leaving about an hour ago, but a delivery arrived. It's waiting for you in the conference room."

He rose from the desk, annoyed. "If it's a normal delivery, why didn't it go through receiving? I don't have to sign for every little package that comes into this office."

Cedric followed the silent woman to the conference room, further aggravated that she didn't defend her actions.

Ever since his showdown with Iman earlier that day, he'd been spoiling for a fight. He stepped through the door into darkness.

"What in the hell's going on here?" The overhead lights flickered and illuminated the room.

Cedric's jaw went slack. At least one hundred brightly wrapped Christmas packages spilled from the table onto the chairs. When that space ran out, the gifts covered the floor of the conference room.

All of Anika and Medina's Christmas gifts from Iman's house were wrapped and ready to be delivered.

Debra stood silently behind him. He finally spoke.

"When did she come back?"

"She left about five minutes ago. She said not to disturb you. You were busy..." The rest of the sentence died on her lips.

"She said I was busy doing what?"

"Fleecing the elderly."

Cedric pushed a gift to the floor and sat in a conference room chair. A bow and ornament stuck to his pant leg, and he pulled it off.

The brilliant purple glass ball distorted his facial expression. His head was wide, making the grim set to his mouth seem monstrous.

Probably how I looked to Iman and Jack McClure when I said no.

"Thank you, Debra."

The door closed quietly.

He caressed the thin glass. It was perfect in shape, pleasing to the eye. That was the main reason he'd chosen it. Cedric looked around the room.

Everything mirrored the same controlled perfection. Books stood upright as if monitored by a military general. His office, always impeccably neat and orderly. The staff at Dix, efficient and highly qualified. And it was all his.

On the surface, everything looked great. He'd even tried to have perfect children. Guilt over his behavior toward Medina assaulted him. Indeed, he had used tyrannical tactics to make her into the person he wanted her to be.

But the finely woven fabric of his suit couldn't hide his true identity. That poor, cold child from his past still lived inside.

Once a skinny kid, he'd been fattened, polished by strangers. People who stood to gain nothing personally. But they loved him enough to instill in him the values of hard work and achievement which later fostered his success. Those were the values he wanted to pass to his children.

Cedric rose from the chair and packed the gifts in his car.

Back in the office, the printer surged to life after he hit the command and signed off the computer. He stared at the numbers that declared Dix's hefty profits on all twelve medications, Ada's being one of them.

Cedric lowered himself into his chair. What had he become? Too rich, as Iman claimed? So far above others he no longer cared for their suffering?

A man of too much ability and means, but lacking the one thing money couldn't buy.

Where was his heart?

I can do this, echoed in his head. The pronouncement shook him to the core where his deepest fears lay. His past replayed through his mind like photos from a single-framed camera. Highlights of the worst times flashed. Bitter cold, nonstop hunger pains that eventually ebbed into full flatness. Hopelessness. Fear. He shut his eyes, immersing himself in all he used to despair.

Then there was Lenora. Michael Dix. His beautiful children. His mother on her wedding day. Iman.

Iman. His love, his life.

I can do this. Cedric looked in the Rolodex and punched buttons on the phone. "Jack, Cedric Hamilton, sorry to bother you at home. I've decided to lower the prices on the medications on your list."

Cedric smiled when the man's buoyant laughter echoed through the phone.

"A Monday morning meeting sounds good. Good night, Jack."

Cedric grabbed his coat and drove slowly, making decisions that would change his life forever. He prayed Iman would want to share the future with him.

* * *

Cedric checked the doors as he locked up the house for the night. The girls were asleep, his house still twinkled with white lights and the Christmas goose was a few pounds lighter than when it had arrived with his mother and stepfather hours ago.

But Cedric was alone.

Iman hadn't wanted to see him. She'd declined to spend Christmas with him. She'd taken time to call and speak to the girls, wishing them a happy day, but when he'd gotten the phone when they were done, he'd met a dial tone.

Today, unlike less than a week ago, there was no giggling. No anticipation growing inside him like the last time she'd been there.

He was alone, and he hated it. Convincing her to share her life with him might not happen. Cedric shook off the depressing thoughts as he stacked the unopened presents under the tree. The girls had been so ungrateful. They'd only wanted two things, and when they found them, refused to open any more.

He shook his head.

"Daddy?" Cedric stood from his crouched position. He approached Anika and placed his hand on her forehead.

"Hey, there. You feeling okay?"

"I feel good. Medina went back to sleep so I came to talk to you about our plan." He sat down on the couch and drew her onto his lap. "What kind of great plan could pull you from your bed in the middle of the night?"

She pointed to the tree. "We want to give our Christmas presents away."

Cedric drew back, stunned. Realization surged through his veins. When he found his voice it was emotion-filled. He stroked her long braid. "Why?"

"Because we got a lot. More than other kids." Her solemn gaze met his. "We won't do it if you're going to get mad."

Cedric shook his head recognizing how they'd all changed. His voice filled with pride. "I'm very proud of you and your sister for making such a grown-up decision." He scooted her off his lap and held her hand as he guided her to the stairs. "You know, your old man could take some lessons from you girls. You're very smart." He tucked her in and kissed her forehead.

"You're very smart, too. I love you, Daddy." Anika snuggled next to her Addie doll and drifted off, unaware of the love glistening in her father's eyes.

Chapter 14

Kuumba was upon them.

Cedric ran his hand nervously over his head and knocked off his kofi. Hastily he put it back on and dropped his hand to his side. He rolled his head on his shoulders and shrugged to loosen himself.

"Daddy, you're going to be great. Re-wax." Medina squeezed his hand, her eyes dancing merrily. Cedric knew he was acting uncharacteristically nervous, but tonight was important.

"I'm okay, sweetie." He kneeled down, a rush of paternal love filling him. Medina was a smart girl. And he told her so.

"Medina, I'm very proud of you. It doesn't matter how you do today, I just want you to know that I love you and…" Cedric stopped when her name was called to join her class.

"I love you, Medina."

She kissed his cheek in an exuberant rush and hugged him with a quickness that almost had him on his bottom. She walked away then turned and said, "I love you, too, Daddy."

Cedric barely controlled the tears that sprang to his eyes. She'd said it. The perfect *l*.

He turned his attention to the capacity crowd that filled the basement of Stone Manor. Just over a month ago, he'd come to the magnificent house alone, and incomplete.

Through his studies of Kwanzaa, he'd learned more about himself and the course his life would continue on.

Yet, there was one part missing.

Iman.

He'd spotted her earlier with Ada, who looked healthier and happier from taking her medication properly. He'd visited her several times during the week and had been pleasantly surprised by her snappy humor and straightforward opinion on his and Iman's relationship. He held on to her confidence that everything would work out. Several members of RSG were present also which made him feel even better about his decision.

Cedric turned his attention to the program. Impromptu dancers from the audience dazzled the crowd during the drum-playing segment much to everyone's delight.

Then a libation was poured to deceased ancestors. Cedric wished he could hold Iman's hand. He knew she was thinking of her father.

Then all the children congregated in front of the stage for the lighting of the candles. Medina and Anika read their speeches and everyone applauded loudly giving the youngsters a standing ovation for their effort.

Iman hugged each child, exclaiming how proud she was of them. She told stories, just as she'd promised, captivating the crowd with her voice. She was a hit.

Cedric gave the New York dance troupe and karate demonstration only half his attention. His focus was on Iman and their future together as a family.

"Lift Every Voice and Sing" started, and the crowd rose and sang, then a local dance group concluded the evening with uplifting African dances.

Cedric took a deep breath. He'd researched Kuumba and labored over his speech for days. It was perfect. He was ready. Finally, it was time.

He walked onstage and shoved the speech in his pocket. The applause died down and he called, "Habari Gani!"

The crowd echoed its response.

Cedric stood before the audience in full African attire looking very kingly in gold, the color of prosperity and royalty.

"Tonight my charge was to be eloquent and moving. But I stand before you humble in my responsibility." He gazed out over the crowd and found Iman.

"When I was first asked to present the farewell, I said no. I thought, what do I have to say that's good enough to take our families into the next year? Then a little voice said to me, 'You're going to be great. I believe in you.' The funny thing is, the other day, I began to believe it, too."

Cedric's voice reached inside her and stopped Iman's pacing. "I'll tell you what I've learned through Kwanzaa."

He folded his hands on the podium and looked out over the crowd. "Opening yourself up and stepping outside your comfort zone are the scariest things a person can do, because outside represents the unknown. It's where fear hides, doubt reigns.

"I used to believe that until recently. Someone I love challenged me to do my collective work and responsibility toward my fellow man. At the time, I didn't know what she meant."

Several people nodded. Others shook their heads. Iman stared, amazed. She couldn't believe Cedric was telling everybody their story.

He continued. "I felt I had served my purpose, done what I was supposed to do. Given all I could give." He shook his head. "I didn't know how much more needed to be done until I was faced with losing something…someone special." He looked into the audience and seemed to address each of them personally.

"Don't be like me and put worldly goods before things that really matter like imagination, trust and, most of all, faith and love. My challenge to you is to utilize your talents, knowledge and beliefs to help improve the lives of those around you. The rewards will come back to you one hundred times over."

Through blurred eyes, Iman watched Cedric straighten and catch himself being eloquent and moving. He'd relaxed as he'd spoken and moved away from the microphone, his confidence captivating the capacity crowd.

He stood behind the podium again.

"Most important of all, listen to the voice that whispers. It's probably telling you something you can't afford to miss. Thank you."

People applauded around her. Cedric left the podium and headed to the back of the stage. Iman tried to reach him, but it was time for the feast.

She didn't see him again until the entire festival was over and only a few stragglers' remained. Elaine had long since taken Anika and Medina home with her, leaving them free to talk undisturbed.

Cedric stacked the last of the chairs, while Mr. Winston and other brothers completed the cleanup.

"You two go ahead and leave, we've got the rest," Mr. Winston said.

Iman hesitantly dragged on her coat. She wrapped Cedric's scarf around her head and waited while he pulled his coat on. She turned to face him. "Thank you for the picture. I didn't get to say it before. You didn't have to."

He stood beside her, staring intently into her soul. He reached for her bags, speaking softly. "It was your Zawadi gift from me."

They walked down the long hallway that led outside.

"Want to take a ride?" he asked.

Anticipation surged within her. Her mouth quirked. "Sure."

This time she paid attention when they entered interstate seventy-five heading to Tennessee.

"I have a lot to say to you." Cedric drummed his thumbs on the steering wheel nervously. "Iman, I'm sorry about Ada. I know how important she is to you and I never wanted to hurt you or her. It's just that, well, when you asked me to lower the price of the medicine, I took it as a personal attack. I know how irrational that sounds, but I couldn't get past the thought that my family would suffer the way I had."

He looked at her briefly before returning his attention to the road. His voice was soft. "Dix has been my life for a long time. I got my start there, and it's provided a stable future for my family. A part of me didn't want to disturb what's gotten me where I am today."

Iman broke in. "I was being unreasonable. I had no right to challenge your livelihood. It's just that I don't want to lose Ada. And I took my fear out on you."

"You didn't, you opened my eyes. I love you for that. I realized lowering the prices isn't going to hurt anyone. In fact, so many people will benefit, maybe other pharmaceutical companies will do the same. Even if they don't, I know I did the right thing. However, there is a question about our future."

Cedric guided the car to the side of the road and stopped. He turned toward her.

"What about it?"

He took her hands in his. "I love you. And I hope you still love me enough to give us a chance. I want us to start a life together."

"I want that, too. Do you really love me?" she whispered.

He gathered her in his arms, and touched her softly with his lips. Happy butterflies danced in Iman's stomach.

"Very much. I want a future with you," he whispered, "forever," then nibbled her ear and neck.

"Forever?" she asked breathlessly. "As in today and the rest of our lives? As your…"

"As my wife. Do you have a problem with that?" His deep voice rumbled close to her ear.

"Not at all." Her heart soared. His kisses were tender as they moved against her lips, marking his territory, leaving unspoken promises.

Iman responded with all the love inside her. She caressed

his face with her fingertips. "How much farther to Lookout Mountain, Tennessee?"

"Thirty minutes. Why?" Cedric took her hand, love radiating from him.

"Because I can't wait for us to start our future where we began our lives together."

* * * * *

THE FIRST NOËL

Felicia Mason

Prologue

Angry flames licked up the bedroom walls, the heat so hot it singed her skin. Kia stared at the fire consuming the curtains. She'd saved money from babysitting jobs and got them on sale at Sears. Now they were burning up. Everything was burning up.

Mesmerized, Kia watched the fire dance from panel to panel. It jumped to the broad beam that supported the roof.

"Kia! Kia! Where are you? Where's the baby?" Her sister's voice came from a distance, but it was enough to spur Kia into action.

Joshua! She snatched the crying toddler from his makeshift playpen. Protecting his head with her hand, Kia dashed toward the door. A panel of wood crashed down, burning embers cascaded around her.

Kia screamed.

Joshua's frightened tears turned into a wail.

She stomped at a piece of smoldering wood near her feet. Clutching the child to her, she tried to quiet him so she could think.

"Shh, precious. It's okay it's okay. Auntie's here. Auntie's here."

Kia glanced around. There had to be a way out. The only other option was the dormer window, but it was tiny and they were on the third floor. Even if she managed to get herself and Joshua to the window, she couldn't jump. It was too far.

"Kia!"

"Up here. We're in the attic."

"Mommy!" Joshua cried. The child pulled toward his mother's voice.

Kia clutched him closer. "Stay with Auntie, precious. We'll get out of here. I promise."

Trapped in the attic room, Kia watched the flames close in.

Off in the distance, Kia could hear the fire engines. Help was coming. But it was coming too late.

Chapter 1

Seven years later

"Come on, Josh. You're gonna be late!"

The eight-year-old dragged into the foyer, his coat trailing behind him on the floor. "Do we have to?"

"Yes. We do. Where are your mittens?"

"It's not that cold out. Besides, mittens are for kids."

Kia Simmons cocked her neck at her nephew. "And you, I suppose, aren't a kid?"

Joshua shrugged. "You know what I mean."

Kia tried not to smile. Joshua had been excited about First Baptist Church's Christmas pageant, until he found out he was a shoe-in for the role of Joseph. Joseph had to be nice to Mary. Kia knew that Joshua's crush on Shelby Knight, the little girl portraying Mary, would leave her little man tongue-tied and flustered.

It was time for that talk with him, probably past time. But Kia hadn't figured out how to broach the topic.

Without thinking, she brushed her hand over his fade haircut and caressed Joshua's cheek. He was growing up so fast.

"Ma, not the hair, okay?"

Kia laughed. "Come on, Mr. *GQ*. I'm going to warm up the

car. Zip your coat and put your gloves on. Don't forget your hat, either."

By the time Kia pulled her Camry into the church's parking lot, snow was falling. "I hope the roads won't be too bad when we get out of here."

"There's Mike, Ma. Can I go ahead?"

"All right, just don't forget…"

"To zip up my coat. I know. I know."

In a blur of bulky winter clothing, Josh was out of the car and crunching through the snow to see his Sunday school friend.

Kia smiled. Before she knew it, he'd be headed to college. Maybe she could convince him to go to Pitt or Duquesne, schools nearby.

A moment later she laughed. "First, you've got to get the boy out of elementary school."

Bundling up, Kia pocketed her keys and reached into the backseat for the book she'd read while the children practiced. She made sure Josh got his dose of religion. Kia had long ago abandoned her own spiritual upbringing. Her job now was to make sure Josh was exposed to the basics. He could make up his own mind about church and faith when he got older.

For tonight, Kia's plan was to find a seat somewhere in the back of the church's multipurpose room and start the murder mystery novel she'd been itching to read.

Once inside, she shrugged out of her wraps and made a beeline to the back of the room where tables and chairs had been pushed out of the way.

"Oh, Sister Simmons. So glad to see you. I saw Joshua a few moments ago. Brother Tyler will get all the kids rounded up in a couple of minutes. Come give us a hand."

Kia bit her lip and quickly looked for an out. Mavis Washington was the sort who'd put you to work if you weren't careful. Kia had been dodging the woman's efforts to get her into the young adult missionary group for more than a year. Without telling the busybody outright that she didn't do the church thing, Kia could only hope for a disappearing act.

"I'll be right back, Sister Washington," Kia said. "I'm going to run to the ladies' room."

With haste, she got out of the woman's line of sight. Kia had absolutely no intention of spending the evening in the restroom. Maybe she could find an unlocked, and out-of-the-way, Sunday school classroom.

Ducking down the hall that led to the classrooms, Kia heard the Sunday school superintendent ringing a bell. That, she knew, was the children's signal to gather around. Brother Tyler ran a tight ship. Josh and all the other children knew that, so she didn't worry about his welfare while at the church. First Baptist was about the only place where Kia didn't fret over Joshua's safety and well-being.

Kia tried the door at the first classroom. Locked.

She frowned and went across the hall to the next. The doorknob turned. Kia felt against the wall for a light switch. When light flooded the room, Kia saw walls decorated with bold posters of Bible heroes. A big picture of a manger scene was taped to the whiteboard. The riot of colors all over the place reminded her of a classroom at the school where she worked as a teacher's aide. All of the red-and-blue chairs at the round tables were Lilliputian size. The primary-grade children obviously met in this room.

"That won't do."

Turning off the light, Kia closed the door and headed to the next classroom. Just as she was about to turn the handle, she heard the children's voices ringing out as they sang "Silent Night."

"No fair hiding."

Kia started. She looked up, then up some more. He was the size of a lumberjack—not that she'd ever actually seen a lumberjack. His plaid shirt looked like soft flannel. The jeans and workbooks added to the effect. Everything about this man was just plain big. Not fat, but solid, dependable. Like a rock.

"You scared me."

"Sorry about that," he said, but he looked more amused than sorry.

Kia had never seen him around First Baptist and assumed he was a new member.

"If you're trying to find a place to hide from Sister Washington, a few other parents are in the room two doors down."

Kia immediately took offense.

"What makes you think I'm hiding? I'm not. I was just..."

He grinned. "Yes?"

She gave up and laughed. "Okay, so I was looking for a quiet place to read."

He glanced at the book in her hand. "Hmm, that looks like interesting church reading."

The twinge of guilt Kia had already been feeling about taking a novel into church intensified. But a murder mystery was a better option than her first choice, a hot romance. Surely God wouldn't mind if she spent an hour or so reading a mystery in his house.

"Well, it's either this or, uh, never mind..." Kia's voice trailed off as a tantalizing image of this man as the hero in her own personal romance came to mind.

She shook her head. If she wasn't careful, the Lord was gonna send a lightning bolt straight to her head.

"I'm Franklin Williams," he introduced himself as he stuck out a hand in greeting.

Kia swallowed and tried to get her errant thoughts out of the gutter. "Hi. I'm Kia Simmons. You must be new here."

"I was just thinking that about you."

Her smile widened. "You were? I mean, no. I'm not new. I just don't attend the morning services. Usually just Sunday school."

"Well," he said, "Looks like I need to start coming to Sunday school."

Franklin smiled. So did Kia.

Suddenly, she couldn't think of anything else to say.

When he bent down to pick up a toolbox, that's when she noticed his hands. They were large and well shaped.

"Nice to meet you, Kia Simmons. Maybe I'll be seeing you around sometime."

Kia's flirtatious smile held lots of promise. "Maybe so."

Hefting his toolbox in one hand, Franklin slipped a hammer through a loop in his jeans. "Time to get to work," he said.

Kia enjoyed his backside view as he headed toward the multipurpose room. She wanted to claim that the warm fluttering feeling in her stomach was simply the heat warming the large church building, but she knew that couldn't be the case.

Her sister had always said you could find a good man at church. For the first time in Lord only knew how long, Kia found herself interested in a man.

"Maybe Kim was right, after all."

Franklin listened to the instructions on how the pageant director wanted the set built. Unfortunately, his mind kept straying to the woman he'd just met in the hall. All the adults working with the children were in here. That would mean she was one of the parents. But which child was hers?

While he knew many of the kids, he didn't know them all. He glanced over Sister Redfield's head trying to figure out which cute little girl or active little boy was Kia Simmon's child.

"Will that work out all right?"

"Beg pardon. What was that again, Sister Redfield?"

The woman patted his arm. "I'm being a worrywart again, aren't I? After all these years, you know how to build the set."

"Yes, ma'am. I do. Just show me where you want it."

Franklin let the pageant's stage director lead him to the spot where the manger scene would be. With half an ear, he listened to the things she wanted done differently this year.

When he smiled, Sister Redfield took that as encouragement to launch into an even more detailed description of her ideas about this year's set. It had been a long time since he'd flirted with a woman. Kia Simmons looked so guilty standing in that doorway he couldn't help rib her about it. She had a pretty smile and her skin looked as soft as her hands had been.

While Sister Redfield chattered on, Franklin wondered if there was a Mr. Simmons in Kia Simmons's life.

Chapter 2

Peeking over the edge of a door decorated with tinsel and angels, Kia spied the likely hideout room. She knocked on the open door before entering.

"Hi. Is this the waiting room?" she asked.

A man and a woman chuckled. "Yeah," the older man said. "If you're waiting until Sister Mavis forgets she wanted you to do something."

"This would be the place, then. Hi, Shirley," Kia greeted her friend as she walked in. "I was just looking for a quiet place to read," she added as she held the novel up, confirming her intent.

"Come on in. I'm here grading papers. The last bunch before Christmas break. Glory hallelujah!"

"You know you miss those kids when they're gone," the man said.

"Uh-huh. Well, right now, they're working my last nerve. I told them Friday if they didn't straighten up and fly right, there'd be no Christmas party."

"And they believed you?" the man said.

"Sure. They think I have an in with Santa Claus," Shirley said. "Kia, have you met Willie Smith? He has the twins."

The man stood up and Shirley completed the introductions while the two shook hands. After a few moments of small talk;

Kia settled into a chair at the conference room–style table. Willie leaned back in his seat and propped his legs up on a second chair to resume his nap. Shirley went back to her papers, and Kia opened her book.

The story started with a bang, and under any other circumstance would have kept her riveted. But after reading the fifth page three times, Kia gave up the pretense. Her thoughts kept straying to the man she'd met in the hallway. Franklin Williams.

It was a strong name for a sturdy man. Kia had to admit, she'd always been partial to husky men. She liked them solid, like a wall of protection.

"Hmmph. Who are you kidding?" she thought. "It's been so long that you don't even know what your preference is anymore."

Her last serious relationship had been… Kia frowned. How long had it been? She calculated for a moment. Not since before the fire.

Has that much time really passed?

For the answer, all she had to do was think about Joshua.

Kia sighed. She probably wasn't even Franklin's type. And although he had flirted a bit, he was probably married. Some church men were like that, just naturally friendly.

Forcing her thoughts away from a path leading nowhere, Kia again turned her attention to her novel. A few minutes later, she marked her place with a dollar bill and told Shirley she'd be back.

Kia made her way to the ladies' restroom. She pushed the door open and smiled. The comfortably feminine lounge area always amused her. A faintly sweet scent came from baskets of potpourri. With its soft lighting, pink floral sofa and easy chairs, the room seemed far more inviting than the sanctuary. It looked more like a parlor than a restroom.

"I wonder how many people hide out in here on Sunday mornings?" she mused as she made her way to the stalls.

Kia had barely secured the door on her end stall when she heard people burst into the lounge area.

"Girl, I tell you, that brother is fine."

"Let me see that lipstick. I need to touch up these lips. Make 'em more kissable. You think he'll ask me out?"

"He better not. He's going to ask me out."

Kia smiled. She couldn't help being party to the conversation. Girl talk was the same all over the place. She was going to have a time on her hands shielding Joshua from fast girls like the ones in the lounge.

"Hmmph, you have a man. What you need with another one?" said the one with the husky voice.

Kia waited for the answer.

"Hey, the more the merrier, I always say."

"You heard Pastor Jamison preaching about greed."

A sudden clatter let Kia know that one of the girls had either dumped her purse or her makeup bag.

"That's right." The girl's next words were a bit muffled. Kia strained to hear. A moment later, a kissing sound came from the lounge area.

Lipstick, Kia surmised to herself.

"And you heard him talking about the lust of the flesh."

The two women chuckled in a knowing way. Kia suddenly wondered if they were a bit older than she'd originally estimated.

"Let me smell your perfume," the husky-voiced one said.

"This is Shalimar. But I'm wearing Chanel No. 5."

"I think I'm going to trap him with a bit of cleavage."

"Girl, you better quit. You in a church, not a club. My hair look okay?"

"It's the bomb, girl."

The two giggled together.

Kia could only assume that they primped in front of the mirror.

"You gotta go?"

"Nope."

"Me, either. Let's go make ourselves seen."

Kia heard some rustling and then a snap. A few moments later, she heard nothing but silence. The two had obviously gathered their cosmetics and departed.

Kia left the stall, washed her hands and touched up her own lipstick. The lingering scent of Chanel floated through the lounge. She envied the freedom of the two young women. If teenagers, they were probably sixteen or seventeen, years younger than Kia's mature twenty-five. Not that she'd change anything about her life—except maybe she'd add a little male companionship. Kia realized and recognized that she'd had responsibility thrust on her at an early age. Consequently, she'd missed out on a lot of the frivolity of youth. That was a fact of life.

Besides, she thought, *how could you really miss something you've never had?* Her thoughts quickly turned to Franklin Williams, the man she'd met in the hallway.

"Now, he is one fine brother," she said, mimicking the girls she'd overheard.

Back in the hideout classroom, Kia settled in a chair and reached for her book.

The door flew open. "Oh, there you all are," Mavis enthused. "I've been looking all over the place for you."

Willie Smith groaned. "That's why we were in here," he said under his breath. Shirley hit him with the pen she was using to grade papers.

"Sister Simmons and Sister Thompkins, Brother Tyler needs your help with the children in the fellowship hall. You schoolteachers know how to get them in order."

"Well, I'm not really a teacher," Kia protested under her breath.

Glancing at Kia with a guilty smirk, Shirley gathered up her papers.

"And Willie Smith!" Mavis said, clapping her hands in front

of her ample bosom. "Why, I didn't know you were here until Brother Williams told me. I thought you'd dropped off the children and left. Brother Williams was just asking if you'd come help him unload supplies from his truck. Oh, it's such a blessing to have so many parents interested in our young people's pageant every year."

With that, Mavis sailed out the door, confident her charges would follow.

"We'd be more interested if we had someone a little less enthusiastic," Shirley said, clasping her hands together in imitation of Mavis.

"Next time I'm staying in my car," Willie muttered.

"It's cold outside, Willie," Shirley pointed out.

"Better cold than at the mercy of Mavis."

"It can't be that bad," Kia said.

"You ever see a tornado close-up?" Willie rumbled.

"No. Just on television and in the movies."

"Hollywood comes out here and follows Mavis for a week to see what real destruction is all about."

The two women laughed. "Shame on you, Brother Willie," Shirley said.

He grunted. "It's the truth and you know it."

Laughter and conversations bubbled in every corner of the multipurpose room. More than once, an adult voice could be heard over the hubbub, saying, "Listen, children," or "Shh."

A woman Kia didn't recognize worked with the youngest children, the four- and five-year-olds, in one area. The six-year-olds were making so much noise in their corner that Kia couldn't tell if they were loud because they were supposed to be learning carols or if they were just being regular six-year-olds.

She searched the long room for Joshua. It didn't take long to find him. He sat quietly in a small circle of children, seemingly oblivious to the squeals, play and conversation all around. The little girl sitting next to him looked just as uncomfortable. Kia had to smile. She waved at him, then chuckled at his grimace.

Shirley joined her, looking out over the organized chaos of the pageant's first rehearsal.

"Is it always like this?" Kia asked.

Shirley laughed. "Every year. Remember, though, this is just the first night. In a week, you'll see things coming together. By the nineteenth, the night of the pageant, you won't believe how it all just flows. Mavis can be bossy, but she knows how to put on a show. Where's Josh?"

"Over there," Kia said, pointing him out.

"You've done a good job with him, Kia. You should be proud."

"He's a good kid," she said. "I'm proud of him."

Shirley was one of the few people at First Baptist to whom Kia felt really close. That was because their friendship had developed at work. Shirley knew how much Kia doted on Joshua.

"Have you met Franklin Williams?" Shirley casually asked.

Too casual in Kia's estimation. She eyed her friend. "Yes, a little while ago."

Shirley glanced at her and smiled. "He's a master woodworker. Cute, isn't he?"

Kia hesitated, not willing just yet to take the bait.

"If you like big teddy bears," she eventually mumbled.

"Um-hmm," Shirley said with a knowing smirk. "Just so you know, he donates his time and talent to the church whenever something is needed. And he always builds the sets for our plays and pageants."

"That's nice," Kia said.

Shirley cleared her throat and leaned in a bit toward Kia. "He loves kids. He's single, too. I think you two would look great together."

"Shirley, I've told you before, you don't need to go around trying to fix me up with your friends. I'm fine."

"Yeah, fine like Sleeping Beauty. You need a handsome prince to come kiss you awake."

With that bit of advice hanging, Shirley motioned Kia in Franklin's direction, then sauntered away.

Kia just shook her head.

Looking around to find the best place to use her limited pageant skills, Kia's gaze found Franklin's. He smiled, and she took that as an invitation to join him.

"Hello again," he said when she arrived next to his temporary sawhorse.

"You ratted on us."

"Just looking out for my own interests," Franklin said.

"What does that mean?"

Before he could answer, Mavis Washington swooped in with a clipboard and orders.

"Sister Simmons, right over here, please. If you'll direct the children to their spots. Everything is marked on the floor. Here's the guide. I'll be with the teenagers in classroom number eight."

With no opportunity to object, Kia found herself hustled away and suddenly surrounded by little people asking questions. Above their heads, she caught Franklin looking in her direction. She shrugged her shoulders. When he smiled at her, Kia felt a distinct fluttering somewhere in the region of her heart.

"First my stomach, now my chest," she surmised to herself. "Maybe it's the flu."

The rest of the rehearsal time flew by quickly. Before long, the Sunday school superintendent rang his bell announcing dismissal. Within five minutes, the multipurpose room was full.

"Where in the world did all of these people come from?" Kia asked.

"All over the complex," a deep voice answered.

Kia turned and saw Franklin. Her heart did a surprising little somersault. Definitely not the flu, she decided.

"The young adult choir had rehearsal tonight and all of the teenagers were down the hall getting their parts for the Christmas program."

She'd noticed the teenagers, a diverse group of young people, and wondered which two were the ones from the restroom. "I thought there were a lot of cars in the parking lot," she said. "How long have you been a member here?"

"All my life."

Brother Tyler's closing remarks cut short the rest of Kia and Franklin's conversation. They joined the others, who were forming a snaking circle around the room.

"I want to thank you all for coming out tonight, and especially the parents who are helping," Brother Tyler said. "We couldn't do this without your support. All the children should have their parts now. I'd like to ask the parents to make sure they rehearse during the week."

Joshua ran up to Kia's side. "Here's my stuff, Mom."

She took the papers and nodded, motioning with a finger to her lips for him to be quiet.

"As you leave," Brother Tyler continued, "please be sure to pick up a copy of the schedule. We'll have rehearsals here at the church Wednesday and Friday and then again Monday, Wednesday and Friday next week. The children will be fitted for their costumes this Friday. The ladies from the women's sewing circle will be here to get everybody's measurements. Now, does anybody have any questions?"

Mavis Washington stepped forward with her clipboard. "Don't forget the Friday-night fellowship, Brother Tyler."

"What's that?" Kia whispered to Franklin.

"A church get-together. We haven't had them in years, but Sister Mavis thought this would be a nice time to start them up again. It's BYOD."

"BYOD?" Kia asked.

But before Franklin could lean down and answer her, Brother Tyler was talking again.

"That's right, I almost forgot. This Friday, after the pageant rehearsal, we'll be having a fellowship service. For those of you who don't remember those, we sing and play games."

"And eat!" someone hollered out.

The adults in the room chuckled, and a discussion started about Sister Emmalyne's rolls and Sister Brisbane's sweet potato pie.

Brother Tyler rang his bell again, this time to quiet the grown-ups. After a moment, the conversations ceased. "Everybody, bring a dish to share and we'll all have a nice time in the Lord. Any other questions?" he asked.

When no one had any, he asked the people to join hands for closing prayer.

Kia noticed Josh trying to decide if he should move or just take little Shelby Knight's hand. The decision was made for him as the circle closed. He glanced up at Kia, then took Shelby's hand to his left and his mother's hand to his right. Kia smiled as she bowed her head.

A second later, her right hand was enveloped in a warm, large but gentle grip. Kia's eyes flew open and she glanced right. Franklin's smile was almost shy as he bowed his head when Brother Tyler started praying.

Kia prayed, too. But her prayer was that she not faint in the next five minutes. Their hands fit together like they were made for each other. She could feel the calluses on his hands and she wondered what her own felt like to him. She hadn't had a manicure in ages.

By the time she relaxed, Brother Tyler was saying "Amen." Kia hadn't heard a word of the prayer.

Franklin squeezed her hand before letting go. Kia wanted to believe it meant something. But when she looked up at him, his steady gaze and honest eyes didn't hold any hidden communication, at least not any she could detect.

"It was a pleasure meeting you, Sister Simmons."

"You, too," she said. "And call me Kia. Sister Simmons sounds so old."

"Can I start the car?" Joshua asked.

"No, young man, you can't. Did you speak?"

"Hi," Joshua said to Franklin.

"Hello, my name's Williams. Franklin Williams," he said as he stuck out a hand to the boy.

Joshua looked at the big man, then shook his hand, man to man. "My name is Joshua Simmons and this is my mom."

"Pleased to meet you, Joshua. And you, too, Mom," he added to Kia. "What role are you playing in the pageant?"

"Joseph," Joshua mumbled with a marked lack of enthusiasm. "I have to be Mary's husband."

"That's a very important role," Franklin said.

"It is?"

"Sure. Joseph was Jesus's earthly father."

Joshua considered that for a moment. "Yeah, I guess so. But I have to," he paused and glanced at Kia.

She hesitated for a moment, then took the cue. As much as she wanted to fulfill every need in his life, she knew Joshua lacked male role models. A man who, according to Shirley, donated his time to help the church and loved kids couldn't be all that bad. Could he?

Kia decided to trust her instincts. "I'm going to get my coat and a copy of the rehearsal schedule. Then I'll warm up the car. Don't forget…"

"To zip up my coat," Joshua finished.

"That's right," she said. "Nice meeting you, Mr. Williams."

With another look at the child she'd raised as her son, Kia left the two. She felt something close to a pang of jealousy when Joshua immediately turned back to Franklin and started talking. From the corner of her eye, she saw Shirley approach.

"You don't have to worry about him with Franklin," Shirley said.

"What makes you think I was worrying?" Kia said as she slipped on her coat.

Shirley raised an eyebrow at her, and Kia sighed.

"He just took to the man in a matter of seconds and I was dismissed so they could discuss men stuff."

"And what's so wrong with that?" Shirley asked. "Josh has a good head on his shoulders. And there are some things a man just can't talk to his mother about."

Kia tugged a bright-blue cap on her head, then put on matching gloves. "First of all, Josh is eight years old. That's hardly a man. And second…"

Shirley placed a hand on Kia's arm. "And second, you have to let him grow up. Would you rather he look up to some street-corner thug or drug dealer?"

"No," Kia mumbled.

Taking a deep breath, she quelled the retort that begged to slip off her tongue. She provided everything that Joshua needed. Josh was her responsibility. She couldn't let anything happen to him. Kimberly would never forgive her if anything happened to the boy. But Shirley was right, and she knew it.

"Let it go, Kia," Shirley said. "You can't protect him from all the monsters in the world. You can, however, make sure he has a solid foundation and knows right from wrong. You're doing that, but you have to give him some wings to fly, too."

Kia swallowed back the unexpected tears that threatened to flow. "Thanks for being my friend."

"Anytime, kiddo."

The two women hugged, then Shirley shooed Kia out the door.

"What did you two talk about?" Kia asked Josh as she maneuvered the Camry along the street. Plenty of salt had been put down, but the snow continued to fall pretty heavily. Slick spots were hidden from view.

"Guy stuff," Josh answered. "Mr. Franklin said only the best and most mature eight-year-olds get to play Joseph in the play."

Kia glanced at Josh for a moment before turning her attention back to the snowy road.

"Then you should feel honored," she said.

Josh nodded and looked out his window.

"Hey, Ma. If it keeps snowing like this, we might not have school tomorrow."

"Don't count on it. This is Pennsylvania, remember? Snow doesn't slow things down."

"Mr. Franklin said he's looking forward to the Friday Fellowship. I am, too."

"That a fact?"

"Can we bring something special?"

Kia wasn't sure what Josh had in mind as special, but payday was another week away. Whatever they took to the dinner, it would have to be in the kitchen already.

As Josh chattered on, Kia wondered what she could make that might please Franklin Williams.

Chapter 3

Wednesday night, Kia had an appointment. With a reminder to be on good behavior and a promise to pick him up promptly at eight o'clock, she dropped Josh off at the church.

He was unusually quiet at home that evening. Every one of her attempts to get him to talk fell flat.

She watched him lay out his clothes for school. He paid such care to each choice and piece that Kia knew something was up.

"Special day tomorrow?"

"Huh?" Josh turned, obviously surprised to see her at his door.

Kia entered the bedroom and leaned on his dresser.

"You look like you're preparing for something special," she said, taking a look at the pants and shirt he considered.

A pile of apparently already discarded options was on the floor. Kia scooped them up and headed to Josh's closet to hang them up.

"Try this," she said, tossing him a vest. "Combined with the shirt you have there, she should be really impressed."

"Mooomm."

Kia replaced the last shirt on a hanger, then sat on Josh's twin bed. "Yes?" she innocently said.

"I'm not dressing up for a girl."

Wisely, Kia didn't say anything as she watched him stare at the clothes on his bed.

"I'm just thinking about my image, you know," he said.

"Your image?"

"Yeah. How I project."

Apparently satisfied with the vest and the outfit, Josh moved the clothes off the bed and draped them over his desk chair. He checked his book bag, then snapped the flaps together.

"Hey, Mom?"

"Yes, precious?" Kia waited for his usual protest to the "baby" endearment. When it didn't come, she smiled.

"What does it mean to sacrifice?"

Kia's eyes opened a bit. She knew she could give him lots of examples, including sacrifices she'd made along the way. But she had a feeling Josh was talking about something else.

"Why do you ask?"

Meandering from the desk to his dresser, Josh opened the second drawer and pulled out underwear and a T-shirt. After tossing them in a chair shaped like a basketball backboard and hoop, he faced Kia.

"Tonight, Mr. Tyler was telling us about why we celebrate Christmas. He said baby Jesus grew up and sacrificed a lot for us."

Hardly a theologian, Kia nodded. She could only hope her less than stellar and awfully dusty knowledge about this sort of thing wouldn't let her down. She'd stopped believing in miracles and whatnot a long time ago.

"So that got me to thinking," Josh continued. "If he sacrificed his life and I'm playing his earthly father in the pageant, shouldn't I make a sacrifice, too?"

Kia nodded. "That sounds like a good idea. What did you have in mind? Maybe giving up a couple of toys or games and giving them to needy kids?"

His mouth dropped open and his eyes grew wide.

Kia chuckled. "I guess that's not what you had in mind, huh?"

"Uh, no. I was thinking I could just sacrifice and, you know, act like Shelby's okay to be around. Know what I mean?"

Biting back her smile, Kia nodded. So that's what the clothes…and the secret conversation with Franklin Williams were all about.

"Tell you what," she said. "Since you and Shelby are playing important roles, why don't you think about getting a Christmas present for her."

Josh's face lit up. "Really? I can?"

Kia nodded.

"How much do I get to spend?"

"That's up to you. How much do you want to sacrifice of your own money to buy something for her?"

"My money?" Josh asked.

"Sure. You get an allowance. Surely you'll be able to buy Shelby a present from that money." When he didn't look too excited about making that big a sacrifice, Kia offered another suggestion. "You're quite the artist. Why don't you make something for her?"

Josh's frown amused Kia, but she did her best to hide the smile she knew her little man wouldn't appreciate. She got up and headed toward the door.

"Mom, it takes money to please a woman."

Kia paused at the doorway. "Who told you that?" That was the last thing she needed him to grow up thinking. Sure, money made a difference, but it didn't make a person.

Josh shrugged.

Kia tried again but couldn't get an answer out of him. "Is that what your friends at school say?"

He just shrugged again.

"It doesn't take money to show your love, Josh."

"Yeah, I know. But it helps."

She couldn't disagree with him on that point. For a moment, she wondered if Josh knew or suspected just how precarious their financial situation was. On the next payday, Kia had to pay the rent, the car insurance, buy enough food to get through the end of the month and eke out something to pay on the bike she had on layaway for Joshua. She definitely knew the meaning of sacrifice.

Right now, it didn't at all look as if the ends were going to meet.

"Well, I'm sure you'll think of something," she said, then wondered if she said it to convince herself rather than her young charge. "Christmas is still two weeks away. Lights out in thirty minutes. I'll be back to tuck you in."

Long after Josh lay in bed softly snoring, Kia stared at the ceiling from her own bed. She'd been flying blind raising her nephew. Kimberly hadn't left an instruction manual on how to care for her son.

"Raise him the way we were raised, little sister," Kim had said. "Make sure he loves God, respects his elders and grows up a gentleman."

Kia remembered the words as if they were spoken just yesterday. She wiped the sudden tears from her eyes and turned over on her stomach, a plump pillow braced under her arms.

She stared in the darkness toward the photograph that had been taken right before Kim died.

"I'm trying to do right by him, and by you, big sister," she whispered. "Sometimes I just don't think I have it in me."

As usual, no answer came to her soft-spoken worries. In the beginning, shortly after she'd convinced the Social Services people that she could take care of a toddler even though she was only a few months shy of eighteen, Kia relied on Kimberly's voice to guide her. It always seemed to come when she found herself uncertain about what to do or say.

But the guidance stopped coming more than a year ago. At first, frightened, Kia panicked. Then she realized that she'd been relying on all the wisdom her sister had imparted during their years together. For all intents and purposes, Kim was the only mother Kia had ever had. The two sisters always looked out for each other, Kim leading the way.

"A boy is different, though," Kia said, her voice now muffled by the pillow. "Sons are to be cherished, molded into strong black warriors."

Laying her head on the pillow, Kia closed her eyes and tried to imagine what her sister would do with an eight-year-old. She waited, and waited. Nothing came, though. Not the answers she sought, not even sleep, which would have been a sweet escape from the worries she harbored.

Several hours later, a restless sleep did come. The thought, however, that stayed with Kia as she tossed and turned through the night was that while she knew nothing about properly training a warrior, Franklin Williams would.

Friday arrived quickly. Kia decided that trying to impress anyone, including a tall, dark carpenter, probably wasn't one of her better ideas. She ended up making a chicken potpie, one of Josh's favorite meals, as well as a hearty offering for the church's Friday fellowship on a blustery winter day.

Several vehicles arrived at the same time in the First Baptist parking lot. Greetings were shouted out as heavily bundled people scurried to the warmth of the fellowship hall.

"Whoo-wee, I tell you, I'm not used to these Pennsylvania winters," a woman said.

"Ruth Childers, you've lived here all your life," someone answered.

"That don't mean I'm used to or even like wintertime," Sister Childers said on a laugh as she deposited her big pot on a table, then shook out of her coat, gloves, scarf and hat. "Let me wash my hands and get my apron, then we'll see what we have here. Emmalyne dropped off 'bout six dozen rolls earlier today, so I know we got some bread."

As Ruth Childers and a few women hurried to open up the kitchen, several men made quick work of setting up tables and chairs for the potluck dinner. They left plenty of room for the young people to practice. As fast as a table was put right, two teams of women came through rolling out white table coverings and situating pinecones as centerpieces.

After hanging up his coat and Kia's, Josh ran off with his friends. At loose ends, Kia stood in the middle of the floor looking and feeling out of place. Everyone seemed to have a job to do. Taking note of what everyone was wearing, Kia gave a silent sigh of relief. At least she'd dressed properly and appropriately, or "decent and in order" as she'd heard someone say years ago. At the last minute, she'd changed out of the jeans she'd planned to wear and opted for a pair of corduroy slacks and a cream sweater. No one except some of the younger children wore jeans.

Josh, of course, looked as though he'd just left a photo shoot for *GQ Jr.* Kia smiled. At least with his new crush, she didn't have to fight with him about taking baths or wearing clean underwear.

"What book are you reading tonight?"

Kia turned and found Franklin Williams standing right there. The sudden and now-familiar warmth infused her, and she felt a smile fill her face.

"I thought I'd do a little work tonight," she said.

"Well, that's the least you could do given that shameful behavior Monday night."

His smile let Kia know that the teasing came with good spirits.

"This fellowship is BYOD you told me. So, where's your dish, Mr. Williams?"

He leaned down, close to her ear. Kia got a subtle hint of an aftershave or cologne that made her suddenly want him even closer.

"Call me Frank," he said. "And I make a mean spoon bread."

"I'm impressed."

Franklin grinned. "I'm a single man, Sister Simmons. And I like to eat."

Kia took a breath. She may not have had a lot of practice in the dating arena, but that sure sounded like an opening. Dare she flirt?

Yes.

She opened her mouth to say something saucy like "I'll remember that."

"Hi, Brother Williams."

The words Kia had been about to utter died on her lips as she watched a very buxom woman sidle up to Franklin. A moment later the woman's heavily applied perfume reached Kia's nose, and apparently Franklin's, too.

He turned away a moment before letting loose a big sneeze.

"Bless you," Kia automatically said.

"Excuse me."

"Oh, that's all right," the young woman said. "Are you coming down with the flu? It's going around, you know."

"Uh, no," Franklin said while waving the air in front of him. He tried to stifle another sneeze. "Charmaine, what in the world are you wearing?"

The girl looked at her clothes. "Just some leggings. You like them?"

Kia had had enough. Franklin obviously had a prior relationship with her.

"Excuse me," she said as a general farewell to both of them.

"Kia, hold up." He reached out and grabbed Kia's hand before she could escape. "I'm talking about that bottle of cologne you dumped on before you came in here."

Charmaine pouted.

Kia paused.

A closer look at the girl indicated she wasn't as old as her voluptuous figure indicated.

"You always treat me like a baby."

"That's because you're fifteen. Did you speak to Ms. Simmons?"

Charmaine rolled her eyes and stuck a hand out to Kia. "Hi."

Uncertain, Kia glanced between Franklin and the girl. "Hello. I'm Kia Simmons."

"Charmaine's my name. Is Joshua your son?"

"Yes. Well, I mean… You know him?"

"He's a cutie. My little sister likes him."

Right then and there Kia decided maybe she needed to monitor Josh's activities in church, as well. If the little sister was as fresh as this one, Josh would be in way over his head—sort of like the way she felt with Franklin.

"Aren't you supposed to be in choir rehearsal or something?" Franklin asked.

"I can take a hint," the teen replied as her gaze dipped to the hand Franklin held in his. The girl sized up Kia, then sent a sly smirk Kia's way.

With another not quite innocent look at Franklin, Charmaine sauntered away.

Even though she had ten years on the girl, Kia felt as if her own body belonged to a teenager. She knew she didn't have the classic looks of a Halle Berry or a Tyra Banks, and that was just fine. But when standing next to a teenager built like this one, Kia felt pretty certain she looked more like a flat-chested Olive Oyl.

"I'd better go," she said as she tugged on the hand Franklin still held in his.

"Will you have dinner with me tonight? I'd be happy to share my meal with you."

Kia glanced at their joined hands. Franklin didn't seem in any hurry to let her go. Truth be told, Kia liked the feeling of being enveloped in his arms, particularly since holding his hand was about as far as anything would go between them.

"We're, uh, we're eating here. At the church I mean."

"I know. Sit with me."

His smile made Kia forget what it was she'd been thinking. *Breathe, girl.*

Kia took a breath. "I, uh… Joshua…"

"Is welcome, too."

"Oh." The small word sounded more like a whispered sigh.

"Is that yes?"

Kia managed a nod. Franklin squeezed her hand.

"It's a date, then."

A moment later, he was gone. Kia stood there in a daze, wondering what had just happened.

"You work it, girl. I saw you and Franklin Williams earlier. He's just your type."

"I don't have a type, Shirley. I've never even had a…" Kia fell silent and glanced around to see if anyone had overheard her near confession. But too many conversations were taking place all around them for anyone to be concerned with theirs.

"Um-hmm. And that's the problem. I keep telling you, you're going to wake up one day and Josh is going to be gone and you'll be sitting around wondering what happened to your life."

"My life is just perfect, thank you very much."

Kia spied Josh with a group of boys and girls and waved for him to join her. His immediate frown let her know that eating dinner with her wasn't what he'd planned.

"He'll be fine," Shirley said. "You're the one who needs some socialization skills."

"I have a son to raise. I don't have time to socialize."

Shirley shook her head. "We'll just see about that."

Josh ran up just as Shirley got up and took off. "Yes, ma'am?"

"It's time for dinner. That deacon's going to pray."

"That's the pastor, Mom. His name is Reverend Jamison."

Kia took another look at the man who was calling for everyone's attention. "Oh, well, whatever."

"Can I eat with Mike and Grady? Please?"

"Well…" Kia began.

"We'll be right over there," he said pointing to a table that had been claimed by two boys and three girls. Kia noted that little Shelby Wright sat among them.

"Okay," she reluctantly agreed. "Just make sure…"

Josh was across the fellowship hall before she could change her mind or finish her sentence.

"…to eat some vegetables."

Moments later, the room fell silent while the pastor blessed the meal. Then, table by table, the church members went through the buffet lines filled with the casseroles and other dishes brought by each family.

"Is this seat taken?"

Kia looked up. "Yes. I think you reserved a spot here."

Franklin smiled as he pulled out the chair next to Kia.

"I could eat a horse," he said. "I had a busy day and missed lunch."

"Sorry, no horsemeat allowed in my kitchen. But it looks like you'll have plenty to choose from," she said with a nod toward the buffet tables.

"So, what did you bring to share?"

"Come on folks, don't dawdle. If Reverend Jamison gets up there before you do, there won't be anything left."

The people at the table next to Kia and Franklin's laughed as the church's husky youth minister put an arm around the shoulder of the senior pastor.

"Now, you all know, I've been trying to cut back," the reverend said. "You gotta tell the missus to stop cooking like she does."

Franklin held Kia's chair as she rose. "You'll like everyone here. We're just one big family," he said.

"Frank, how's the set coming along?" the gray-haired Reverend Jamison asked.

"I made a lot of progress tonight. We'll pick up the hay in

time for next Wednesday's practice. No need tracking all that in here too early."

The two tables of church members made their way to the buffet line. Kia looked around to check on Josh. He and his friends were busy talking while they waited to be called up.

"I see you have some help this year," Reverend Jamison told Franklin. "I don't think we've met," the minister said to Kia.

Franklin made the introductions. "Reverend Avery Jamison, this is Sister Kia Simmons. Her son is portraying Joseph in the pageant this year. And Reverend Thomas here is our youth minister. He leads the children's church services."

After the how-do-you-do's, the youth minister excused himself, and Reverend Jamison made no secret of sizing up the couple. He nodded. "It's about time, Franklin."

"Now, Pastor," Franklin said.

Kia watched the exchange with interest. Time for what? she wondered. Then she got a hint and felt heat rush up her cheeks.

"Oh, Reverend Jamison!" Mavis Washington hustled over and put an arm through the pastor's. "We need your help in the office."

"Duty calls," Reverend Jamison said.

"You want me to make you a plate, Pastor?" asked one of the kitchen women monitoring the food supply.

"Yes, thank you kindly, Sister Smith. And, uh, make sure I get a double helping of that ham and some of Sister Emma-lyne's rolls."

"What about that pressure of yours, Pastor?" someone in the line called out.

The minister chuckled. "I tell you, you all are worse on me than the missus."

"Pastor, this really is important," Mavis Washington interjected a moment before she hustled him off to her emergency.

When Kia and Franklin finally made it to the serving dishes, Franklin looked around. "All right, which one?"

Smiling, Kia pointed out the deep dish potpie she'd brought. Franklin took a double helping.

"You're not going to save any for anyone else?"

He glanced at her as he moved on to a green bean casserole. "I like to savor the good stuff."

Not at all able to think of an appropriate comeback, Kia dipped a serving spoon into what may have been potato salad.

Back at their seats, Kia stared at her plate trying to figure out where all the food came from. She'd apparently taken a little of this and a bit of that; which would have been fine if she could have identified half of it. That looked like mashed sweet potatoes. Kia stuck her fork in.

"I was washing the sawdust off my hands and clothes and missed grace," Franklin said. "Would you say it with me?"

"Oh, uh, sure." She lowered the fork to her plate and bowed her head.

Franklin took her hand in his, and her eyes popped open.

"Father God, thank You for the food we're about to eat. Bless the hands that prepared it for the nourishment of our bodies. And thank You, Lord, for the beginning of a new friendship. Amen."

With that, he dug in like a man who hadn't eaten in days. Kia sat there. Was she the new friend?

After taking a long gulp from his glass of fruit punch and wiping his mouth with a paper napkin, Franklin turned toward her. "So, tell me about yourself."

Chapter 4

"You took the question I was about to ask you," she said. "What do you want to know?"

"Everything."

Kia chuckled. "Well, that won't take long. I've lived here with Joshua about two years. I'm a teacher's assistant at Tubman Elementary. And Josh is playing Joseph in the Christmas pageant."

Lifting her fork to her mouth, Kia used eating as an excuse for not revealing more. "What about you?" she asked.

"Now, wait a minute. You left out all the important stuff."

"Like what?" she mumbled between bites.

"Like where you learned to throw down on some chicken potpie." He lifted her free hand. "You sure you're not married?"

Smiling now, she nodded. "I think I'd be the first to know. And thank you. That's one of Joshua's favorites, so I figured I couldn't go wrong."

They both looked toward the table where the children were arriving with their plates. Josh put his plate down, leaned toward Shelby and said something. A moment later, he straightened and headed back to the buffet line.

"What's he doing?"

Franklin smiled. "My guess is, trying to please the little lady."

Kia leaned up to get a better view, then started to rise. "Maybe I should…"

Franklin stayed her with a hand over hers. "He's okay. He just went to get extra napkins. See?"

A little embarrassed, Kia sat down again and picked at her food. "I guess you think I'm smothering him."

With a gentle finger, he lifted her chin. Kia's breathing stopped. She met his gaze with wide eyes.

"I'm not thinking anything like that."

Right then, Kia knew she wanted him to kiss her. She savored that thought for a moment, then tuned in to what he was saying.

"From what I've seen of Joshua, I already know you're a terrific mom. He's a good kid, well behaved. It's easy to tell which ones have some home training and which ones run wild."

She blinked and smiled a tiny smile.

"Take Charmaine, for instance," he said. "That girl has been grown since she was ten. Her mother works doubles in Pittsburgh. That forty-minute commute each way really eats up into the time she's able to be at home with her kids. There's an older brother, but he's in jail, and the little one, well, at least a responsible neighbor looks out for her."

"But she comes to church," Kia pointed out.

Franklin pointed around the crowded fellowship hall. "That's because the boys are here."

"So are the men," Kia said, thinking about the way the girl had eyed Franklin.

"Yeah, well, she's also a first-class flirt. But most of them are at that age. I bet you were, too."

She shook her head and carefully studied the food on her plate. "No, not really."

The admission came out sounding almost resentful, something that surprised Kia. She'd been tried and tested, but she could honestly say she'd never resented anything about her life. Until maybe right this moment. She regretted not having more experience at flirting.

Suddenly uneasy with the direction of her thoughts, Kia frantically tried to think of something to ask him. Her mind, however, refused to cooperate. So she focused on her food.

"Kia, what's wrong?" Franklin asked before taking another forkful of potpie.

Wondering if her uncertainty showed that easily, Kia asked, "What makes you think something's wrong?"

He shrugged. "You just seem suddenly quiet. I didn't mean to make you uncomfortable."

She shook her head, pasted a smile on her face, and cut a small piece of ham. "You didn't. I'm fine. Tell me about you."

Franklin studied her, then let the moment pass.

"My life's an open book. What would you like to know?"

"Everything," she said, repeating his earlier request of her.

Franklin smiled and then told her about learning to whittle at his grandfather's knee. "My first big woodworking project was a bookcase for my bedroom."

"How'd it turn out?"

He chuckled. "A mess. I was barely ten, but learned quickly. These days I concentrate on furniture and smaller items, things that can be shown or sold in galleries."

"I'd like to see some of it," Kia said, hoping she wasn't being too forward.

"It's a date, then," Franklin said.

A date? Kia stared at him, mouth open and eyes wide. "You want to go on a date. With me?"

Franklin lifted her hand and pressed a quick kiss to it. "I'd love to. Thanks for asking."

He winked at her, then grinned. After taking a deep drink from his punch glass, Franklin excused himself for a moment.

Before Kia had time to recover from the surprise kiss, he was up and gone.

Kia sat there stunned. What had just happened? Did they suddenly have a date planned?

Shirley plopped into the seat across from Kia. "So, how's it going? You two seem to have hit if off. He's perfect for you, you know."

With eyes still a bit unfocused, Kia looked at her friend. "I think I need a babysitter."

"Excellent!" Shirley's outburst drew a couple of curious glances.

"Shh," Kia pleaded.

Shirley waved a hand. "Don't worry about these folks. I'm so glad this is working out. He's a strong man, and not just physically, either. He's strong in the Lord."

Kia sighed. "Then why is he interested in me?"

That, Kia realized, was what had her so confused. Franklin was a church man. She, on the other hand, could find Genesis, the Book of Psalms and Revelations in the Bible. Other than remembering the Lord's Prayer, that was the extent of her religiousness.

She couldn't even claim to be the most attractive woman in the church. She didn't know how to flirt or really communicate with adults. Her entire work and home life revolved around children.

"Maybe he sees what I see in you," Shirley said.

"What's that?"

"Potential. And what's this about needing a babysitter?"

Kia's smile, tentative, hopeful and happy, told the story. "It seems I have a date."

Franklin watched the boy, not at all surprised that Joshua followed him into the men's room. He'd seen the young man watching him from across the fellowship hall.

"What's going on, buddy?"

Joshua shrugged as he leaned against a white porcelain sink. Franklin paused at a urinal and did his business, all the while looking at Josh through the mirror. He patiently waited for the boy to voice his concerns.

When Josh didn't make a move, Franklin mused aloud. "Sometimes," he said, "a man needs to have a heart-to-heart talk with another man. Someone who's been there and maybe could share some ideas. Somebody to bounce things off, you know?"

Joshua nodded, but didn't say anything. Franklin zipped his pants and went to the sink next to Josh to wash his hands. He took his time at it, sensing Josh seemed to have a weighty matter on his mind.

When Franklin reached for a paper towel, Josh finally spoke up. "Brother Williams, I, uh, need to talk to you about something."

"Shoot," Franklin said as he tossed the balled-up paper towel in a trash bin. "What's up?"

Joshua looked at his feet, then, taking a deep breath, he stood up straight and tall and looked up at Franklin.

"I saw you talking to my mom and I want you to know it's all right with me. You have to be nice to her, though, if you take her out. And no kissing on the first date."

To keep from smiling, Franklin bit the inside of his mouth. Then he folded his arms and stared down at the boy. "What makes you think I'm interested in your mom that way?"

Mimicking the older man, Josh folded his own arms. "I saw the way you were looking at her."

Franklin nodded and pursed his lips. "Sort of like the way you were looking at Shelby Knight?"

Josh lost some of his bravado at that. But to Franklin's delight, the boy rallied quickly.

"It's different with grown-ups."

"I see." Franklin considered things for a moment, then decided to negotiate. "No kissing on the first date, huh?"

"That's right. Kissing leads to babies. And we don't have room in our apartment for a baby. There's just enough room for me and Mom. She's not really my mom, though. She's my aunt. My real mom died a long time ago."

That was news to Franklin. He concealed his surprise by asking another question. "Is holding hands okay?"

Joshua thought about it for a moment, then nodded his consent.

"Any other rules?" Franklin asked.

"You have to treat her nice. Mom doesn't know about going out. She always stays home with me."

Another bit of intelligence Franklin found particularly useful. That meant there was no other man in Kia's life.

"And you have to buy her a Christmas present," Josh added.

Franklin did laugh at that. "Did you have something particular in mind?"

Joshua shook his head no. "I'm going to do something nice for Shelby. I don't know what, though," he said with a frown. "I don't have a lot of money."

"Hmm, maybe I can help you with that."

"I'm not allowed to take money from strangers."

"Oh, so now I'm a stranger?" Franklin asked, while giving Josh bonus points for being a levelheaded kid.

The boy shook his head. "You know what I mean."

"Actually, I do. And I wasn't considering giving or loaning you any money. I had something else in mind."

"What?"

"I can teach you how to make something for Shelby. It'll be extra special because the gift came from your hands and your heart."

Josh pondered that for a moment or two, then his face lit up. "That's a sacrifice, isn't it?"

"Well, it could be. You'll have to sacrifice some time that you might otherwise spend with your friends to make your gift."

"Shelby has a lot of that girl stuff that she puts in her hair.

And she has a lot of purses, too. Could I make something for that?"

Franklin nodded. "You could make a jewelry or keepsake box, or maybe something similar to a keyholder that her ribbons and purses could hang from."

Franklin watched as Joshua considered the possibilities. When a smile lit the boy's soft brown face, Franklin gave a sigh of relief. He hadn't truly realized just how much he'd been hoping for a connection with Joshua. But he also knew he had a responsibility to every young male in the church.

Apparently satisfied with the conversation, Josh headed to a urinal, then washed his own hands.

"One more thing, Joshua."

The boy glanced back at the man as he set up his paper towel for a free throw.

"He shoots," Franklin said, following the toss. Josh's balled-up tissue landed squarely in the trash bin. "And he scores."

"What's the other thing?"

"No kissing Shelby. It's a little early for that. You have to respect our women and girls. That means being courteous and treating them the way you'd want your mother or your sister to be treated."

Josh shuffled his feet. "Well, a couple of the guys were talking about how they, you know, how they get girls to do things."

This isn't exactly where Franklin thought the conversation was headed, but there was no going back now. It was better for a young man to get the facts than to get that raggedy street knowledge that led to so many problems.

Franklin stooped down so he was at eye level with Joshua. "What your friends and acquaintances do has nothing to do with how you act," he said, pointing to the boy's chest. "You have to listen to your head, not the other parts of your body. Sometimes it's difficult, but walking in the way of the Lord isn't always easy."

"What's God got to do with it?"

"Everything," Franklin said as he stood up. "The Lord sees you even in the places you think no one's watching. He's there to forgive you when you mess up, to guide you when you need direction, to give you support when you think you're all alone. You know, Joshua, it takes a man of courage to walk the path no one else walks."

As the two headed to the door, Josh looked up. "I have courage."

"I know you do. Now let's get back to the fellowship hall before we miss all the desserts."

Later that night, Franklin wondered if he'd overstepped the bounds. He was, after all, essentially just another man at the church. He didn't have any claims to Joshua Simmons or any of the other children.

In his workshop, he cut the wood he'd need to make the garden planters for one of his customers. The pieces would go on the couple's backyard deck as soon as spring arrived.

"Another five months from now," Franklin muttered.

Western Pennsylvania's winters lasted a while, but Franklin could work on the projects he didn't have to think about while his mind wandered.

He'd made a date with Kia Simmons for Saturday night. Franklin grinned. He couldn't wait. He also knew he needed to tell her about Josh.

In her own bedroom, Kia paced the floor. Josh had fallen asleep long ago, but as the clock ticked later and later, Kia found sleep elusive. Shirley had agreed to watch Joshua.

"That was the easy part," she said of finding a babysitter. "The hard part is the going out."

What would they talk about? What would they do? Not only did she have no idea, she didn't have the first clue as to what to wear.

At twenty-five, Kia had never been on a date. It wasn't

that she hadn't been asked. Her focus had always been Josh. The "almost boyfriend" she'd had in high school moved away right before things got serious between them. Then Kimberly died and left her a toddler to raise. There had been no time for dates, no money, either. It had taken all these years to get where she was today.

Kia walked to her closet and surveyed her wardrobe. An hour later, she still hadn't decided what to wear. But she was too tired to stare or care anymore. When she finally fell into an exhausted sleep, she dreamed of strong hands creating a masterpiece. When the wood turned and bronzed light cast upon it, Kia saw a family in the carved image: a woman who looked a lot like Kia, a child who could have been Joshua's twin and a man. Try as she might, Kia couldn't get a clear image of the man's face; it wouldn't come in focus. She strained to see the father's features, but they slipped from her view like mist on a foggy night. In her sleep Kia kicked off the covers on her bed, not realizing she called Franklin's name aloud.

Chapter 5

"I have a confession to make," Kia said.

"Sounds interesting," Franklin replied. "Tell me more."

They strolled along Pittsburgh's Fifth Avenue looking in decorated store windows. The weather forecasters predicted snow accumulation over the weekend. Franklin could have been a catalog model the way everything fit him, from the corduroy slacks to the Cosby-esque sweater.

She, on the other hand, fretted most of the day Saturday over what she should wear. In the end, Shirley pulled several coordinating pieces from Kia's closet and handed them to her. Kia was glad she'd dressed warmly.

"I almost didn't come tonight."

As a light snow began to fall around them, Franklin waited for the explanation. Kia stopped walking and stared at winter sprites frolicking in a snow wonderland scene. The animated decorations in the window brought a smile to her face.

"I was afraid."

"Afraid of what?"

Kia glanced up at him. He looked so at home in this environment, as if he knew exactly what to say and do on a first date.

"Having a good time."

Franklin's chuckle came from deep within. The sound of

it brought a smile to Kia's face. She liked hearing him laugh. They'd done a lot of that first over dinner and then through a new Christmas comedy at the movie theater.

"Well, if that's the case, I hope you've been miserable all night."

It was Kia's turn to smile. "You know I haven't. This has been perfect. Thank you."

For a moment, they simply stared at each other, oblivious of the snow falling and the people moving around them. Then, Franklin reached for her gloved hands. "No. Thank you, Kia Simmons."

Her smile blossomed. Kia slipped her arm through Franklin's and they resumed their window-gazing.

"Oh, look," Kia said, pointing to a window decorated with a choir of golden angels. "Isn't that beautiful?"

"Yes," Franklin answered. "You're very beautiful."

Kia turned and opened her mouth to respond, but something in his eyes stayed her words. She watched as he leaned forward. Her eyes drifted closed and she leaned into him, waiting for the kiss she knew was coming.

The only thing she felt, though, was snow falling. She opened her eyes and stared into Franklin's.

"What?"

He slipped a glove off and caressed her cheek. "A man's word is his bond. And I'm a man of my word."

Confused, Kia shook her head. "And?"

"And I promised Joshua no kissing on the first date."

Kia's mouth fell open. A second later, she snapped it shut and stood erect.

"What does Joshua have to do with this?"

But she already knew the answer. Josh had everything to do with every aspect of her life. She'd put her life and her dreams on hold because she was all he had. She shouldn't have even stayed out this late.

"Never mind," she told Franklin before he could answer. "I shouldn't have expected… Uh, never mind."

Kia felt her face flame, and she looked away, embarrassed, ashamed. She shouldn't have expected to get intimate with him. But she'd wanted that kiss, had anticipated it more than anything else since the moment outside her apartment when Franklin leaned toward her to unlock the passenger door of his pickup.

When she tried to walk away, Franklin called her name.

In two steps he covered the short distance that separated them. "Kia, I've enjoyed your company tonight, enjoyed it immensely. I'd like to see you again."

"I don't think that's a good idea."

"Because of your son?"

She shook her head. "Because of me."

"I see."

They fell into step as they headed toward the garage where Franklin had parked the truck. When Franklin opened the door for her, Kia climbed in and reached for her seat belt, but he paused her hand.

"You can't run away forever, Kia."

"You have no right to lecture me. You don't even know me."

"Exactly," he said. "I want to get to know you. But if you shut me out, I can't."

"I need to get home to Joshua."

"He's fine and you know it. Shirley Thompkins is a school teacher and one of your friends. He's probably having the time of his life."

"Are you saying I spend too much time with him?"

"No, I'm not," Franklin answered as he shut her door. A moment later, he sat next to her. "What I'm saying is, you are a young, beautiful woman. I know you love Joshua. He loves you, too. That's why we had a little talk."

Kia turned toward him, concern etched on her brow. "About what?"

"Man stuff."

"Stop it. Just stop it. First Josh shuts me out saying he had to talk to you man-to-man, now you're sitting there telling me the same thing. I've done the best I could. I couldn't go to college and raise him so I got the best job I could find with a high school diploma. I had to learn how to be a mom and an adult and a cook and everything else. I'm his mother and his father."

Franklin sat quietly through the storm. When tears started falling midtirade, he handed her a handkerchief.

"Thank you," Kia muttered. She removed her gloves and blew her nose and stared out the window at the station wagon parked next to them.

"You want to tell me what's wrong?" Franklin said softly.

Kia sniffled and shook her head.

Franklin put the key in the ignition and turned on both the heat and the radio, which was tuned to a Christian station playing gospel. He didn't make any effort to touch Kia or to exit the garage.

"I'm sorry," Kia eventually said. "This has been a terrific evening and I messed it up."

"You didn't mess anything up."

"Yeah, I did," she insisted. "Do you know what else I was afraid of about tonight?"

"What's that?"

"That I'd end up pushing you away." Kia sighed. "I think I just succeeded."

Franklin scooted a little closer to her. "No, you didn't. It'll take much more than that to push me away. I'm made of pretty sturdy stuff."

"Like a big redwood tree or a towering oak, huh? I've needed some stability in my own life."

"Tell me how you came to have Josh."

Kia sighed again and looked out her window.

"Tomorrow is the anniversary," she said.

When she didn't seem inclined to say anything, Franklin asked the obvious follow-up. "Anniversary of what?"

"Since the fire. I was ten when my parents were killed in a car crash. My sister Kimberly was twenty-two and had just graduated from college. I was a midlife surprise baby," she added with a small, sad smile. "Kim raised me. Then she died trying to save me and Josh."

"What happened?"

"Our house caught fire. There was some faulty wiring that had been smoldering inside the walls. By the time I woke up, flames were all over the room. Josh and I were trapped up in the attic."

"And your sister?"

"She came through the fire trying to get to us. The burns… She died two days later. I promised her I'd keep Josh safe, that I'd take care of him and make her proud."

Franklin nodded, understanding finally dawning on him. "So you dedicated your life to Josh." It wasn't a question.

Kia sniffled and stared out the window.

"Do you have any children?" she asked.

"No. I've always wanted them, but I've never been married. Children are gifts from God. Whenever possible, they need guidance from two parents."

"That's not always possible," Kia said. "Sometimes people are thrust into situations they can't control."

"I know. You seem to have made the best out of a situation that was thrust on you."

"You're right," she said after a moment. "About what you said earlier. There are some things I just can't teach or show Josh the way a man could. Kimberly asked me to make sure he got some religion, that's why I take him to First Baptist. He seems to enjoy it. And he gets to interact with male role models."

"What about you? I don't recall ever seeing you attend services."

Kia frowned. "That's because I don't. My parents were real big on church and God and that whole thing, but I stopped believing in God when He stopped believing in me. He took my mother and my father. Then my sister. God took everyone I've ever loved. I'm not going to let anything happen to Josh."

For a moment, Franklin didn't say anything.

"Everything happens for a reason, Kia. The Scripture tells us there's a time and a season for everything."

"Well, it's been dump-on-Kia season for a long, long time. I don't particularly care for it."

She glanced at him, saw the hurt in his eyes and felt contrite.

"It's nothing against people who do the church thing, it's just not for me."

"Then why do you take Joshua to Sunday school? Why do you hang around the church when the children practice for the Christmas pageant?"

Kia didn't have an answer for that, at least not one that she wanted to share with Franklin. Of late, she'd been wondering why her life felt so empty, so void of life. Josh always came home raving about his Sunday school class and he bugged her about letting him join the youth fellowship program. Kia hadn't agreed to that, but she had been reading his Sunday school materials.

Slowly, the lessons she'd been taught as a child came back, stories about miracles like Moses parting the Red Sea and Daniel in the lion's den. She'd even surprised herself when she realized she remembered a few Bible verses. But reciting a Bible verse or the Lord's Prayer didn't mean much, especially not to someone like Franklin. Shirley had called him "strong in the Lord."

Looking at Franklin, she finally answered him.

"I don't know," she said with a shrug. "It seems like what I'm supposed to do.

"A long time ago I believed in miracles. I was baptized as a child. But then I grew up and realized that the miracles were just stories, and being baptized is…" She shrugged again, not at all willing to voice the doubt that would sound like blasphemy.

"I see," Franklin said.

He pulled his seat belt on and Kia did likewise. When he reached for and squeezed her hand, Kia didn't resist.

"Sometimes, Kia, the Lord whispers to you and leads you to the people He wants you to know and places He wants you to be."

"Is that why I met you?"

Franklin raised her hand to his mouth and kissed the back of her hand. "I don't know, but I'm starting to hope so. Let's pray about it."

The next morning, Kia woke up early. She made breakfast for Josh and tried to forget what day it was. By the time Josh ran into the kitchen, Kia had made up her mind.

"Wow. That's a nice dress," Josh said. "Where are you going?"

Kia put three pancakes on his plate and pulled a tub of margarine from the refrigerator. "We are going to Sunday school and then church."

"Really?"

"Really." She ran a hand over his hair.

Josh cringed and ducked. "Ma, not the hair. It took me a long time to brush these waves in."

Kia laughed, the sound refreshing even to her own ears.

On the drive to First Baptist, they sang Christmas carols along with the CD Kia popped into the player; Kia's voice was slightly off-key, but nonetheless exuberant. She saw Josh to his classroom and then went in search of an adult Sunday school class.

Not at all like she remembered them being, Kia found herself enjoying the fellowship and the discussion the twenty-something group was having about traditional gospel music versus hip-hop gospel.

Kia's innocent question, "What's hip-hop gospel?" led to another round of spirited debate followed by someone hopping onto the piano stool and playing "Amazing Grace." Kia sang along, the words to the old hymn of the church coming to her as if she sang the song every Sunday.

"That's old school," the piano player said. "Here's the way we sing it now." With that, the man launched into a rowdy version of the hymn that, with a tambourine added and complicated-looking and -sounding clapping from the rest of the people in the class, sounded to Kia's ears more like dance club music than something that was supposed to be sung in a church.

Before she was ready for the class to end, the leader asked everyone to gather around for closing. With head bowed and eyes closed, Kia waited for someone to pray like the pastor did. But instead, the class leader asked each person to say something he or she was thankful for.

Kia's eyes flew open. By the time the person next to her spoke, Kia knew what she would say.

"Thank You, Lord, for getting my grandmother home from the hospital," the young woman to Kia's right said.

Then it was Kia's turn.

"I'm thankful for finding my way here this morning," she said. "And I'm thankful for new friendships and the people God puts in our lives."

Kia looked for Franklin before she and Joshua slipped into a pew for the eleven o'clock service. The sanctuary at First Baptist filled quickly. The congregation sang the morning hymn and a deacon prayed. When the worship leader stood at the pulpit to give observations, Kia figured she wouldn't see Franklin at all.

The worship leader said a special offering for the homeless would follow the morning announcements and the welcome of visitors.

"How long does this last?" Joshua whispered.

Kia shrugged and opened her bulletin.

"This is the day that the Lord has made. And we're glad you're here with us this morning."

Kia looked up. A smile split her face.

"Look, Mom. It's Mr. Franklin."

"Shh."

"Would all visitors please stand," Franklin said.

Kia looked around and then toward Franklin. He nodded and she rose, along with about twenty other people scattered throughout the sanctuary.

"It gives me special pleasure to welcome you to First Baptist Church this morning. Let's give our visitors a warm welcome."

All of a sudden, Kia and Josh were surrounded by smiling faces and handshakes of welcome. A quick glance around showed that all the other visitors were being greeted in the same fashion.

Relaxing, Kia smiled, then took her seat when Franklin finished the welcome. A moment later, he slipped into the space left next to her on the aisle. She moved to make room for him. Joshua grinned.

The rest of the service passed in a blur for Kia. She felt slightly guilty that the only thing she remembered was the feel of Franklin's leg pressed against hers on the crowded pew. Then, when the minister called for altar prayer, Franklin looked at her before standing.

"Come on, Josh," she said.

Together, the three made their way with others to the front of the church. Franklin stood in the middle with Kia to his right and Joshua to his left. When they bowed their heads for the altar prayer, Franklin entwined his fingers with Kia's.

She smiled. And this time, she had no problem thinking of something to be thankful about.

Fifteen minutes later, they stood outside the church. It was cold but clear and sunny.

"Hungry?" Franklin asked.

"I am," Joshua piped up.

"Josh, please."

"How about I treat the two of you to lunch?" Franklin suggested.

"Cool, man. Let's go."

Kia scowled at Josh. "That's really not necessary," she told Franklin.

"I know it's not necessary. I want to."

The simple words carried a double meaning to Kia. She looked at Franklin. In his overcoat and hat, he himself looked like a preacher.

"Please, Mom."

One look at Joshua and Kia's mind was made up. "We'll follow you so we don't have to come back for the car."

Chapter 6

They were seated in a booth in the no-smoking section at Eat 'N' Park, Franklin and Kia next to each other and Joshua across the booth's wide table.

"I want spaghetti with extra meatballs," Josh announced loud enough for people three tables away to hear.

"Joshua, what has gotten into you?"

Josh shrugged and grinned broadly at Kia and Franklin. Kia could only wonder what was going through the boy's head. He'd seemed in an entirely good mood all day.

Before she had the opportunity to analyze his behavior anymore, their waitress arrived. Introducing herself as Cindi, she filled their water glasses.

"We all went to church together today," Josh told the waitress.

The woman smiled. "I'm sure you and your mom and dad had a nice time. I have to work Sundays so I usually go to Friday night mass."

"We're not…" Kia started to protest.

"What's mass?" Josh asked.

Franklin took Kia's hand in his and gave it a small reassuring squeeze. "It's okay, honey," he told her. "Mass is the religious service for people who are Catholic, Josh. There are lots of different faiths and religions in the world."

"Do you celebrate Christmas?" Josh asked the waitress.

"Sure do."

"I'm playing Joseph in our church's Christmas pageant," he said, the pride echoing in his voice.

"Well, that's a very important role, you know."

Josh fairly beamed. "I know. He told me, too."

All of a sudden, Kia's mouth dropped. Had Franklin called her "honey"?

She glanced between her nephew and Franklin, then up at the friendly waitress. They were all in cahoots, she decided, with the single mission of embarrassing her.

She tried to tug her hand free from Franklin's. But he held on, and a moment later, Kia felt his thumb gently caressing the back of her hand. Whether the action was deliberate or unconscious Kia didn't know. What she did know was that the soothing caress stirred something in her, something she hadn't realized she didn't have until just now. Peace.

With more than a touch of wonder in her eyes, Kia shifted in her seat to study Franklin. After all this time, had the right man finally come into her life? Or was she just on a spiritual high after the rousing church service?

"Mom?"

"Kia?"

She blinked and noticed three sets of curious eyes gazing at her.

"What can I get you for lunch, ma'am?"

Embarrassed at both the direction of her thoughts and the fact she'd been caught woolgathering, Kia pointed to the first thing on the menu.

The waitress leaned forward, taking a look at Kia's selection.

"That's our early-bird breakfast special. It's only available Monday through Friday. The buffet is really good today."

Kia nodded.

"I'll be right back with your drinks."

"Can I go get my salad now?"

"May I," Kia automatically corrected.

"May I?" Josh asked again.

"Just get what you plan to eat. And save room for your spaghetti."

Seconds later, Kia and Franklin sat alone, close together in the restaurant booth.

"Penny for your thoughts."

Kia smiled as she glanced at their still-joined hands. "What about the inflation factor? Thoughts don't come cheap these days."

Franklin simply stared into her eyes.

"What?" she asked, suddenly nervous.

"This is our second date. So I'm allowed to kiss you."

Kia scooted away from him, snatching her hand from his in the process. "I, uh, I don't think that's a good idea."

Clasping her hands together, Kia licked suddenly dry lips and glanced around at everything except Franklin.

"I didn't mean right this moment," Franklin said.

"Oh."

He smiled. "You sound disappointed."

Kia sighed. "You make me confused."

"What's there to be confused about? I'm attracted to you."

"Is that allowed?" she asked.

The edges of his mouth quirked up. "It better be."

Then, in one smooth movement, he exited the booth. "Salad bar?"

Kia stared up at him. The dark blue suit was conservative but well made. He looked just as comfortable in church clothes as he looked in his lumberjack outfit of jeans and plaid shirts.

Being honest with her errant thoughts, Kia silently conceded that the man was sexy no matter what he happened to be wearing. She, however, was another story. She'd been worse than Josh dressing for little Shelby Wright. In the end, she'd chosen a black sheath with a strand of faux pearls. Black was always a safe bet.

He held out his hand to her and Kia brought her thoughts back to the present.

Franklin wanted to kiss her?

Chapter 7

The three lingered over lunch talking about Christmases past. Franklin regaled them with stories about previous pageants at First Baptist, the time they used live animals and the night during the dress rehearsal when a candle set the entire manger scene on fire.

Kia gasped, and Joshua's eyes widened in fear.

"What's wrong?" Franklin asked, concerned about both of their responses. "What did I say?"

Kia reached for her glass of ice water and took a sip. After a few shaky moments, she managed to tell him. "Fire is, well, it's something we don't like to talk about," she said by way of explanation.

Franklin studied Kia's face for a moment. When she wouldn't meet his gaze, he turned toward Joshua hoping the boy might shed a little light on whatever had upset Kia. But the boy sat there, twisting a paper napkin and blinking back what looked like tears.

"Hey, guys. I'm sorry," Franklin apologized as he reached a hand out toward Josh and the other to Kia.

She sniffed. "It's okay. It's been a long time. You'd think we'd have traveled a little further on the emotional road."

Franklin gave Kia a knowing look as he recalled Kia's story about how her sister died in the fire.

"We don't like fire because that's how my mom died," Joshua eventually said, not knowing that Kia had already shared their story with Franklin. "I don't really remember her, but I remember the fire."

Kia's mouth trembled a bit. Franklin wondered if it was because Josh admitted he didn't remember his mother. Franklin squeezed her hand, comforting her in the best way he could given their surroundings and the circumstances.

Kia then paused and glanced at Josh. She then told Franklin about seeing Kim covered in flames as she frantically tried to reach her son and sister. She told him about Kim's injuries and her funeral. She also told him about the days and weeks after the fire, about how difficult it had been to convince people who didn't have faith in her that she could, indeed, raise her nephew.

"It's been just the two of us ever since."

When Kia finished, silence fell over the table for a moment, each person lost in quiet reflection.

"Thank you," Franklin whispered to Kia.

Kia nodded.

"I have a picture of my other mom in my room," Josh said. "I'll show it to you when we get home."

Home. Franklin liked the sound of that. And he liked the idea of keeping them safe from harm. As he paid their lunch bill and they bundled up to face the cold outside, Franklin wondered what it might take to make this special woman his wife and Joshua his son.

He saw Josh and Kia safely into her Camry, made sure they had seat belts on then admonished Kia to drive safely.

"Mom, can we go look at the lights? It's almost dark."

Kia glanced at Josh, then at Franklin, who stood outside next to her door. "Every year we drive through neighborhoods to see all the Christmas displays," she told Franklin.

"It's lots of fun," Josh added. "And best of all, it's free."

At Kia's blush, Franklin smiled. "I have an idea," he said. "I'll follow you two home, then we can all go in one vehicle. How's that?"

Kia glanced at Josh, who was all grins. "Sounds like a plan," she told Franklin.

About twenty minutes later, Franklin pulled his truck next to the curb behind Kia's car. Before he turned off the engine, Josh was at the passenger door.

Seeing that the decision about who would drive had been made, Kia closed and locked the doors on her car, then made her way through the slush on the street to stand near Josh.

"I want to sit by the window," he announced.

By that time, Franklin had the door open for him and overheard Josh's request. Franklin's eyes met Kia's. Before he could shield it, a dawn of something intense flashed in his eyes.

Kia's heart pounded as she stared at him. If they rode three abreast in the cab and Josh got the window, that meant she'd be next to...

Franklin smiled, and Kia got the distinct impression that he knew exactly what she'd been thinking, and liked the idea of them sitting thigh to thigh.

"Hold on," Franklin said. "I'll come help you up."

Moments later, the three sat in the roomy cab of Franklin's big Ford pickup.

"I've never been in a truck before," Josh said. "This is cool. We get a great view."

Kia clasped her hands over her purse and sat primly between the two males. She tried not to touch Franklin while at the same time giving Josh enough room to wiggle around as he was prone to do while looking at Christmas-light displays.

"Comfortable?" Franklin asked.

"Yes, thank you."

Kia knew she sounded like a prudish schoolgirl, but she couldn't help it, especially not when all she could think about was cuddling close to Franklin. He started the engine, put his left signal on and pulled into the street.

"Where to, Josh?"

"Let's start over by the school. They always have lots of lights there."

"Tubman or Bethune?" Franklin asked.

"Both!"

Franklin and Kia chuckled at the boy's enthusiasm.

"Josh, if you'll open the glove compartment, there's a Christmas CD we can play. It's gospel, but I think you'll like it."

With gospel versions of Christmas music playing in the background, they drove up and down neighborhood streets "oohing" and "ahhing" at the expressions of Christmas spirit.

"Goodness, I'd hate to see their electric bills," Kia observed at a house that had every inch of brick structure and snow-covered lawn strewn with reindeer, Santas, elves, snowflakes and a miniature train village circling the whole of it.

"Wow!"

Franklin glanced over at Josh. "I know where there's an even awesomer display."

"Where?" Josh asked.

"I'll just head in that direction. I think you'll see it."

In a few minutes, Josh yelled and pointed out the front window. Every house on two streets was decked out in holiday splendor. Franklin dimmed the lights to parking ones and joined the line of vehicles slowly and orderly parading through.

They pointed, smiled and laughed at the various holiday scenes played out in elaborate designs and tableaux.

More than an hour later, Franklin drove them home.

"That was really cool," Josh said for the third or fourth time as they entered the apartment. "Thanks, Mr. Franklin. Today was really cool."

"I enjoyed it, too, Josh. Thanks for the company."

Josh shrugged out of his coat, scarf and gloves, hung them on a rack and ran toward the bathroom.

"Would you like to come in for some coffee or cocoa?" Kia invited as she tugged off her gloves.

Franklin held the storm door open and shook his head. "I'd better not."

A bit of the joy Kia had been feeling faded. Her disappointment must have shown on her face. Franklin removed his own gloves and took her hands in his.

"I'd better not," he said again, "because temptation can be a terrible thing."

"What do you mean?"

Franklin pulled the door a bit as they stood facing each other. Then, staring into her eyes, he lowered his head. He paused a breath away from her lips, giving her plenty of time to retreat. But that was the last thing Kia had in mind. She lifted a hand to his face and drew him closer.

The kiss they shared spoke more of passion than innocence. Kia had been anticipating this kiss all day, ever since Franklin's comment at the restaurant. When his lips covered hers, she realized that all of her life she'd waited for this moment and this man.

Kia thrilled at the sensations coursing through her. She'd never felt like this before—as if she walked on clouds with a chorus of angels rhapsodizing all around. Franklin deepened the embrace and Kia moaned. His kiss grew urgent and exploratory as he traced the contours of her mouth. She shivered as an intense sweetness built inside her.

"Kia," he said against her lips. "I need to go."

"Okay," she murmured as she pulled him closer.

He rained small kisses along her temple, her jaw, then closed his mouth over hers again.

A moment later, Franklin wrenched himself away from her. "Good night, Kia."

Her pleading eyes and her kiss-swollen mouth begged him to stay. Franklin shook his head. "I… We…we shouldn't."

Kia didn't say anything. She didn't have the words. She

brought a hand to her lips and gently touched them. Then, leaning forward, she pressed her fingers to his mouth.

A sound that could have been a groan or a moan escaped from him. Kia's smile was shy as she slipped inside the apartment.

Long after she'd closed and locked her door, Franklin stood in the cold night taking deep breaths of the bracing winter air.

"Lord, give me strength," he prayed, the short entreaty all that he could manage given the physical circumstances he struggled with.

Chapter 8

And that's the way it went. Over the next two weeks, Kia and Franklin saw each other at church, during pageant rehearsals and at the eleven o'clock service Sunday morning. A couple of afternoons during the week, Kia dropped Josh off at Franklin's shop so he could work on his Christmas present for Shelby.

Josh wouldn't let her see what he was making, though. "It's a surprise," he'd say.

Kia let those moments go, even though they hurt a bit. Josh had never had secrets. When she asked the eight-year-old what he and Franklin talked about while they did their woodwork, Josh would shrug and say, "Nothing special."

Glad that he had someone to talk to and that he was learning the benefits of sacrificing his time, Kia tried not to feel like something of a third wheel. It was hard, though, particularly when Josh and Franklin seemed to have developed a close bond in a few short weeks. Kia didn't want to admit it to herself, but in her heart of hearts, she knew that Franklin was just the influence Josh needed in his life.

"And what about your life?" she asked herself.

Not willing to consider the answer to that question, Kia completed her shopping. She'd borrowed a little money from Shirley to get Josh's bike out of layaway.

The three of them had Sunday dinner together again, and with Shirley babysitting Josh, Franklin and Kia went on a date or two. Sometimes the three of them played Monopoly or Clue until it was time for Josh to go to bed. Then Kia and Franklin would sit in her living room watching a movie or quietly talking.

That's where they were Friday night when Kia gathered her courage to ask the question she'd been wondering about for a few days.

"Franklin, remember the night when we saw the neighborhood lights?"

He nodded as he crossed his leg and tucked her into the groove between his arm and chest. "That's a night I'll remember for a long, long time. Our first kiss."

She smiled. "I'll remember it, too," she said. "But I was, uh, wondering about something."

"What's that?"

Kia grimaced, not quite sure how to bring up something like this. She leaned forward, reaching for the remote control. Then, shaking her head as she clicked the television set on, she told him never mind. "It's not that important."

But it was important.

She really wanted to know why he hadn't made any other moves toward intimacy of some kind since that night. They sat together in church and held hands sometimes, but that was as far as it went. Ever since that steamy kiss at her door, when Franklin kissed her good-night it was a chaste kiss on the cheek. She wanted more of what they shared that special night, or at least the reassurance that she hadn't suddenly developed bad breath or something.

Franklin sat up. "Kia, if there's something you're worried about, it is important. What's up?"

She bit her lower lip, then opened her mouth and chickened out.

Just because she found him attractive didn't mean the feeling was mutual. She enjoyed looking at him, being with him. But maybe to Franklin she was just a way to pass the time leading to the holidays.

Instead of getting into territory she didn't know how to navigate, she decided to ask a different question, one that had been bothering her just as much as the kissing issue. This, too, was a difficult line of thought, but it was easier to deal with than her personal wish for another kiss.

"Well," she ventured, "you and Josh have been spending a lot of time together lately."

Franklin nodded. "He's a good kid."

"He's seemed withdrawn lately," she said. "Even a bit moody. And that's not at all like Josh."

"Well, he's a little worried about the pageant. It's just two days away and he's gotten a sense of how important his role is."

Kia frowned. "He's worried about it? He hasn't said anything to me."

"He knows all his lines. He's ready. They're going to be great. You'll see."

Franklin reached for the *TV Guide* on the coffee table. "Anything decent on tonight?"

Concealing her sigh, Kia reached for the half-filled bowl of popcorn they'd been munching from earlier. Franklin clicked the television on and went straight to the Christian station. A televangelist preached from a pulpit framed with lush green plants. Kia looked at the TV preacher, then looked at Franklin. Maybe that was it, she thought. Maybe his religion kept him from doing anything more than being a perfect gentleman on their dates and get-togethers.

"Why haven't you kissed me the way you did that night?"

The question came out of nowhere. Kia couldn't believe she'd actually just blurted it out like that.

"And lusts of the flesh shall be the deciding factor that separates the sinner from the…" the TV preacher boomed.

Kia looked mortified. Franklin muted the sound.

"What was that?" he asked.

Kia hopped up. "Nothing," she said as she grabbed the popcorn bowl and headed, in a rush, toward the kitchen. She didn't realize that Franklin had followed her until she turned and bumped into him.

"Kia? Did you ask me why I haven't kissed you?"

She lowered her head and stared at the floor for a moment. Then, gathering her courage yet again, she faced him. "Franklin, I don't know anything about flirting and dating and that sort of thing. I've never had the opportunity to date. I have a responsibility to Josh, and that's always come first in my life. I was beginning to think that maybe we, you and I, were, well…" Her voice trailed off.

Franklin reached a hand out and cupped her chin. The mere touch of his hand sent a warming shiver through Kia. Her skin tingled and she suddenly wondered if she'd waded into too-deep waters.

"Do you feel that?" he asked.

"What?" The question was a breathless sigh.

"The electricity between us. It's intense. Do you feel it?"

She nodded and leaned forward when his hands skimmed her arms, sliding down to her hands. Their hands entwined and the driving need she felt surprised her, made her wonder what was missing. Involuntarily, she leaned into him. Her eyes widened when she felt the evidence of his attraction to her.

"If you must know the truth," Franklin said, "it's that I don't trust myself around you."

"What does that mean?"

"It means whenever I'm near you, I want to do things that are, well, that Christians shouldn't do." He stepped back a bit, putting a few inches of distance between their bodies.

"Oh," Kia said, the word sounding like both a question and a disappointment. "Christians aren't allowed to kiss?"

Franklin chuckled, then pulled her close for a quick hug.

"It's not the kissing that's the problem, Kia. It's what it can lead to."

For a moment, they stood together, their bodies as close as they could be while fully dressed. Kia writhed against him and Franklin groaned. Then slowly, reluctantly, he pulled away from her. They were both breathing deeply.

"Oh, my," Kia said. This time her "oh" signaled a dawn of understanding. She took a breath, trying to calm her racing heart and other parts. "So, I don't have like BO or something?"

Franklin burst into laughter, a deep, hearty laugh that made Kia smile.

"Hardly."

"Well, that makes me feel better," she said. "I thought maybe you'd, you know, changed your mind about even wanting to…"

He took her hands in his and kissed them. "I haven't changed my mind about anything. As a matter of fact, I'm more sure than ever that what we have is special, one of a kind. But we have to wait."

As Franklin gathered his coat, Kia wondered just what they had to wait for.

Saturday, the night before the pageant, Joshua asked to be excused from the dinner table. Concerned, Kia leaned forward.

"You feel all right, honey?"

Josh frowned and tossed his napkin onto his plate. "I'm not a baby, Mom. Stop acting like I am."

With that he scraped his chair back and ran from the room.

Openmouthed, Kia stared at the empty chair, then looked up at Franklin. "What in the world…?"

A moment later, Josh's bedroom door slammed. Kia rose to go check on him.

"Leave him be," Franklin said.

Startled, Kia turned toward Franklin, a quizzical look on her face. "I beg your pardon?"

For just a moment, his voice sounded like the commanding one she remembered, though vaguely, of her father's. He'd been a sergeant in the army and ran his household like a platoon of troops.

"He'll be okay. Have a seat," Franklin said, indicating her chair. "Finish your meal."

"Franklin, what he just did and said was rude, not to mention uncalled for. I swear, I don't know what's gotten into him lately. He's been acting odd all week. With Christmas coming, you'd think he'd be on his best behavior."

"He's a boy, Kia. He has things on his mind."

Uncertain, Kia glanced from Franklin to the hall where Josh had retreated. She stood as if poised for flight, obviously torn between wanting to check on Josh and trying not to overreact to every little thing.

"And what do you know about children? You don't have any."

A shadow crossed his face, and Kia instantly regretted the words. She reached toward him. "I'm sorry, Franklin. I didn't mean that the way it came out."

He nodded, then wiped his mouth with his own napkin. "I'll go talk to him."

One hand rose to Kia's hip. "What makes you think you should talk to him? He's my responsibility."

Franklin got up and went to Kia's side. "You use the word *responsibility* as if it's a chain around your ankle. Eventually, Kia, you've got to cut the shackles off. It's not an easy process, but the ankle can't grow and develop properly if it's constantly restricted."

"What are you saying? Are you trying to tell me you think I treat Joshua like a slave?"

"No, Kia," Franklin said. He traced a large finger along the now-trembling edge of her mouth. "You're a terrific mother to him. But sometimes there are things that a boy growing into a young man just can't talk to his mother about."

With that, Franklin turned his back on Kia and headed down the hall to Joshua's room.

Kia heard the rap as Franklin knocked on the bedroom door, announced himself then asked if he could come in. When Franklin turned the knob and entered, Kia's heart lurched.

"He doesn't need me anymore." The whispered words an anguish she never thought she'd ever face.

Staring blankly, she sank into the chair at the table. First Franklin, now Joshua shutting her out. She'd been rejected by both of them. She was all Joshua needed. At some level she'd always known that he would eventually grow up, that he'd find his own place and way in the world. But that wasn't supposed to come until he was eighteen or twenty-one.

"Not at eight. He's still a little boy."

She'd loved him, nurtured him and guided him all these years, years without Franklin Williams's help. Now, all of a sudden, she'd been declared unnecessary. Kia knew she was overreacting, but she couldn't help it.

First one translucent tear fell. Then another, and another.

She swiped at her eyes, a valiant attempt to stem the flow before it became a rushing broken dam. Blinking several times, Kia looked around the table. Joshua hadn't eaten much. He'd mostly played with his food, smashing and twirling it around to look as if he'd actually been eating.

Maybe he was sick!

The thought rushed through her head and her breath caught.

A moment later, she sat back. His appetite had been just fine earlier in the day. Kia sniffled. With another glance toward the bedroom where the man and boy closeted themselves, Kia stood up and cleared the table. With the stiff motions of an android following orders, she put the leftovers away, washed the dishes, left them in the strainer to dry, then looked around the otherwise immaculate kitchen.

A glance at the clock on the stove told her they'd been in there for more than half an hour now. Kia wiped her already-dry hands on a cotton kitchen towel, then tiptoed down the hall. She felt like a thief in her own home, but quelled the guilty thoughts as she leaned an ear close to Joshua's door.

For the first time, the relative thinness of the walls didn't serve any good purpose. A murmur of voices told her they still talked. Unfortunately, Kia couldn't make out a single word.

Giving in to the pain of being found unwanted, sort of like a defective toy or last year's video game, she bit her lower lip. In all the years she and Josh had been together, Kia never imagined that he'd reject her counsel or throw back her concern for him. They'd had their share of disputes, but he'd never acted out like he had tonight.

With a heavy heart, Kia straightened, stared at the door for a long tense moment, then turned and slowly walked to her own bedroom.

"You owe your mother an apology," Franklin told Joshua.

"I know."

"And you've probably hurt her feelings."

Joshua sighed. "Why do women have to be so concerned about feelings? Who cares about that stuff?"

Franklin wanted to smile but he knew Josh wouldn't appreciate it. "They care. That means we need to care, too. Do you have Shelby's gift wrapped?"

Joshua nodded, then went to his dresser. Pulling open the bottom drawer, he reached all the way to the back and retrieved the package.

"Do you really think she's going to like it?"

Franklin knew that Josh's nerves were stretched thin. The boy feared he might be rejected by Shelby. But Franklin had seen the way Shelby reacted around Joshua.

"She'll love it," he said. "You took the time to make this for her. It's a piece she'll have for lots of years. It shows her you care."

Joshua didn't look at all convinced.

* * *

The pageant went off without a hitch. Not only did Joshua remember and project all of his lines, he helped two of the younger kids with lines they'd forgotten.

Kia and Franklin were known to be something of an item at the church. With the exception of an evil look shot her way by the flirty teenager Charmaine, everyone seemed happy for them. They sat together during the fellowship service after the pageant. Presents were exchanged.

With interest Kia watched Joshua present his Christmas gift to Shelby. The little girl, who'd changed from her Mary costume into a pretty red velvet dress, smiled shyly, kissed Joshua on the cheek and handed him a gaily wrapped package. They stood there smiling and blushing at each other.

Kia smiled. Her little boy was, indeed, growing up.

Kia had racked her brain trying to figure out what to get or make for Franklin. She eventually settled on a bottle of cologne and a scarf she managed to knit in her few spare hours.

The rest of the week leading to Christmas was spent in the usual way. Kia baked cookies, and with Franklin's help, they put up the tree.

On Friday night, Christmas Eve, Franklin called and said he had a surprise if Kia and Josh wanted to go for a late drive.

"Can we look at the Christmas lights again?" Josh asked as Kia handed the keys to her car to Franklin.

"Where are we going?" she asked.

"You'll know when you see it," Franklin said mysteriously. After driving for miles, at least forty, Franklin took a parkway exit.

From his position at the window, Joshua pointed into the distant sky. "Look at that star, Mom! It's huge."

The glow from a star off in the distance got her attention, too.

Franklin smiled. "In biblical times, the shepherds and the

three wise men followed a star to the place where baby Jesus lay."

"In the manger, like for the pageant," Josh said.

"Exactly."

"Is there a manger up there?" the boy asked. Kia, too, looked to Franklin for an answer.

All Franklin would do was smile. "You'll see."

As they got closer, the traffic grew heavier. Franklin found a spot at the far end of the huge lot and pulled the car into a parking space. "We'll walk the rest of the way."

Kia didn't comment when, while walking three abreast, Franklin slipped his gloved hand into hers. As they approached the church, the star above seemed to shine even brighter. Lots of people gathered around the live manger scene being played out on the church lawn.

Josh's eyes widened and he broke free of Kia as he scrambled closer. "They're real animals!"

A sheep bleated as if confirming Josh's observation. He turned back and grinned at Kia and Franklin, then crept closer.

The life-size manger scene was being portrayed by people dressed as Mary, Joseph, wise men, shepherds and inn guests. Bales of hay in a horseshoe shape around the crèche scene served as seats for onlookers who'd arrived early. Several sheep, a dog or two and even a cow completed the barnlike scene. A baby cried, and the woman leaned into the wooden manger to lift him out.

The crowd "oohed" as if they were watching the actual baby Jesus being comforted by his mother, Mary.

Kia kept an eye on Joshua as he pressed closer to the front to see. A moment later, she felt an arm around her shoulder. When she glanced up, Franklin smiled down at her. It seemed the most natural thing in the world for her to put an arm around his waist and lean her head into his chest.

When the infant quieted, the woman portraying Mary gently placed him back in the manger with a small bottle, and a man in long robes stepped forward. He opened a large black Bible and began to read.

"'And she brought forth her firstborn son, and wrapped him in swaddling clothes, and laid him in a manger; because there was no room for them in the inn. And there were in the same country shepherds abiding in the field, keeping watch over their flock by night.'"

The minister continued reading the famous passage from the second chapter of Luke. When he concluded, saying, "Glory to God in the highest, and on earth peace, good will toward men," a choir of white-and-gold robed men, women and children sang the hymn "Away in a Manger."

Then, another man in a shepherd's outfit asked everyone to bow their heads for prayer. At the conclusion, he told the crowd to join the choir in singing "Silent Night." That solemn hymn was followed by "Hark! The Herald Angels Sing" as all of the onlookers gathered a bit closer. When that song ended, the choirmaster motioned for two people, a man and a woman, from the choir to come forward. He lifted his hands for quiet, and then, in a rich contralto, the woman began to sing.

"'The first Noël, the angels did say, was to certain poor shepherds in fields where they lay.'"

Her voice rang out over the entranced audience. Kia didn't realize that she and Franklin were so close until they began to sway with the music.

"This is beautiful," she whispered to him. Franklin's answering smile made Kia settle even closer. Everything seemed right in the world.

As the male soloist, a tenor, began to sing the second verse of the beloved Christmas carol, Kia glanced up at the star that shone above the church.

Right then and there, she opened her heart to the Lord, thanking Him for leading her back to His grace. She thanked God for Joshua and for bringing Franklin into her life.

In that moment, she also realized that what seemed to be

developing with Franklin was right and meant to be. Glancing up at him, Kia smiled, then looked at the bright star again.

"Thank you," she whispered.

As the two soloists alternated singing the remaining verses of the carol, Kia realized that this—being together with family and with friends while sharing the real meaning of the holiday—was what made Christmas a time of joy.

For so long, she'd associated the Christmas season with shopping, cooking and grieving the loss of her sister. But the spirit of Christmas, the spirit of Noël, was more, so much more than presents and baked goods. When Kia smiled, her smile radiated as much light and joy as the star shining above.

Franklin leaned down toward her. Kia closed her eyes and let the moment happen.

When his lips touched hers, her lashes flew up for a moment, then drifted closed. The kiss was everything a kiss should be: tender, gentle, exploratory and oh, so sweet. Before it became more, they broke apart. Kia smiled at Franklin and he slipped his arm around her again.

The outdoor congregation sang another Christmas carol together, then the choirmaster began singing "Joy to the World." The smiles all around as people sang from their hearts sent a spirit of joy through the cold night. After the song, the crowd slowly dispersed as greetings of "Have a Merry Christmas" were exchanged.

Franklin waited until most of the people cleared the area, then he led Kia and Josh to one of the now-abandoned haystacks. Kia took a seat and gazed first at the crèche then up toward the bright star.

"Thank You," she whispered again. "And happy birthday."

"Josh," Franklin said.

The boy grinned up at him and nodded.

Kia's smile was indulgent as she looked at the two people who meant the most in the world to her. "What are you two up to now?"

Franklin sat next to Kia and faced her. Josh stood just over his shoulder.

"Christmas is tomorrow, but I want to give this gift to you right now. It's a two-parter."

Kia glanced from Franklin to Josh. "A two-parter? What does that mean?"

"It means you get to open this part now, but you have to wait until tomorrow morning to open the other part," Franklin said.

"It's under the tree," Josh explained.

"Okay," Kia said. "What is it?"

"Close your eyes and unbutton your coat."

Kia's look, dubious at best, told him she had no intention of freezing to death.

"It'll just be for a moment," Franklin promised.

With another look in Josh's direction, Kia unwrapped her scarf and unbuttoned her coat. From a pocket somewhere in his coat, Franklin pulled out a flat brown box flecked with gold swirls and handed it to Kia.

"Merry Christmas," he said.

"It's maple burl," Josh said. "I picked out the wood and helped make it."

Kia traced her fingers over the smooth hard wood. "It's beautiful, guys. Thank you."

"Open it," Franklin said.

With yet another look at this man she'd fallen in love with in just a short time, Kia lifted the top from the box.

"Oh!"

Franklin lifted the diamond star necklace from its secure place in the box.

"Do you like it, Mom?"

"It's beautiful," Kia whispered.

Franklin lifted the delicate gold chain and dangled the star in front of Kia for a moment before he placed the necklace around her neck.

"You guys are terrific. This is a wonderful surprise," Kia said. "Thank you."

She glanced up at the large star in the sky, then smiled at Franklin.

"Merry Christmas to you both."

Epilogue

Kia promised Joshua that she wouldn't open her gift from Franklin until he arrived for breakfast at ten o'clock Saturday. Kia made French toast, bacon and eggs, and fresh-squeezed orange juice from the oranges she'd gotten at school.

When they finally got to open the presents, the guys made Kia go last. Dying of anticipation, Kia waited her turn, then opened the long bag from Josh. He'd made a hood-based organizer for her to hang her handbags or scarves.

Franklin's gift, in a huge box, intrigued her most. Kia ripped the paper off only to find a small box inside. And so it went, box after box of gaily wrapped, but empty boxes...until...

The small velvet box could only mean one thing. Kia smiled, already knowing exactly what her answer to the question would be if the little box in her hand held what she thought it did.

"I love you, Kia Simmons. Will you marry me and allow me to be father to Josh, husband and lover to you?"

Franklin opened the box and presented it to Kia. The diamond ring matched the necklace at her throat.

"It's beautiful," she said, leaning forward to kiss Franklin.

"Mom, you have to answer the question first," Josh said.

"What question?" Kia asked, genuinely confused for just a moment.

"Marry me?" Franklin said.

"I want him to be my dad," Josh said.

"Well, I guess that settles it, then," Kia said, smiling as Franklin slipped the ring on her finger. "And I want to walk by your side all the days of my life."

Josh grinned.

This time when Kia and Franklin kissed, it was a joining of two hearts who'd found each other for Christmas and for always.

* * * * *

REQUEST YOUR FREE BOOKS!

2 FREE NOVELS
PLUS 2 FREE GIFTS!

KIMANI
ROMANCE™

Love's ultimate destination!